HIDE AND SEEK

JENNIFER HAYDEN

JENNIFER HAYDEN

ISBN: 1460995651
ISBN-13: 978-1460995655

HIDE AND SEEK

2

PROLOGUE

Seattle, Washington

He stared down the hall as she carefully swung her purse over her shoulder and jingled her keys in her fingers—long, slender fingers. She fumbled through her purse and pulled out a cell phone, lifted it to her ear. She smiled at whoever was on the other end of the line. Then she laughed. He stepped back deeper into the shadows, his dark eyes carefully watching her. She was perfect in every way. Long blonde hair, beautiful blue eyes that were so light they were almost white. Her skin was flawless. She was tall. He guessed her height to be nearly six feet. He usually preferred women more on the petite side. But she was absolutely exquisite.

Sweat beaded on his forehead. He knew he should be careful. The woman only had to turn her head and she would likely see him, even though he was partially hidden by a long row of blue lockers. He waited earnestly for her to finish her

3

conversation. When she had disconnected her phone, she shoved the key into the door in front of her and gave it a quick twist. Then she pocketed her keys and headed straight toward him. She walked past without so much as a glance his way. He stared at the nice sway of her behind as she walked out the front doors and into the night, unaware that he was going to be right behind her.

With careful footsteps, he followed her, making sure to stop the shutting door from making even a creak. She was heading for the faculty parking lot, her black high heels clicking against the pavement with a clatter. *Click, click, click.* He blinked, keeping a cautious amount of distance between them. He knew she drove a white Ford Explorer. The vehicle was a newer model with black tinted windows. Her plate number was 544HFD. There was a small dent in the rear fender and one of her side signals was burned out. She kept her bags on the seat next to her, and always buckled in carefully before backing up. She took Ventura to Fourth Street and then Camden Drive the rest of the way to her white, two-story home, which was about a mile and a half from the school. She parked in her garage, shut the door down before exiting the car, and then went straight through the house and up the stairs to change her clothes. He'd learned this over time of course. Yes, she was a creature of habit. That would make this night that much easier.

As she reached her vehicle, she balanced some books on her hip and clicked the keypad to unlock her doors. A beep sounded and then she opened the door. He looked around, checking his surroundings thoroughly. It was late enough that the place was pretty much deserted. She didn't even glance backward, had no chance of seeing him as he approached her carefully. When he was just behind her, he caught a whiff of her perfume. It was sweet and smelled of flowers.

Blinking, he watched as she started to turn her head, obviously sensing someone behind her. When she saw him, she jumped, clearly startled.

"Good Lord, you scared me half to death. What are you doing out here? I thought everyone was gone."

"I'm having some car trouble. I was wondering if I might talk you into giving me a ride. I don't live far—just a mile or so."

She frowned as though she wanted to protest, and then checked her watch. "I have plans tonight. I don't have time to go far out of my way."

"I promise it's not far. Like I said, around a mile."

She was thinking things over and he knew he was in. She wasn't the type to leave someone stranded alone in the parking lot at night.

"I suppose it's not that big of a deal. Just let me call and let my boyfriend know I'll be late."

Now it was his turn to frown. He had seen her boyfriend before. He was tall, brawny and somewhat abusive. For the life of him, he didn't understand what she saw in the sonofabitch. Oh well, after tonight the bastard wouldn't matter anyway. "Sure thing," he said easily, smiling. She made the quick call and scowled when she apparently got voicemail. She swore under her breath and hung up. Then she unlocked the passenger door and allowed him to climb in. It was all so easy. So unbelievably easy. He buckled in, shut the door and waited until she climbed inside too. Then, with as much force as he could muster, he reached across the seat and slammed his fist into her face, immediately knocking her out cold.

ONE

Baylie Sutter cursed as she struggled to balance a large pile of paperwork, her lunch sack, her purse and her cell phone in her overflowing arms. She managed to click the lock button on her key ring and sighed in relief when everything didn't fall to the ground around her.

Henry Jackson High School loomed up before her, its brick walls lined with green ivy and numerous types of fungus that did the science department proud. The twenty-year-old building looked worse than it should for its age. It had been through numerous earthquakes, rainstorms and God only knew how many other natural disasters. Seattle, Washington had its share of wrath from Mother Nature, that was for sure.

For the past year, Baylie had taught tenth grade History. It wasn't her choice to teach the subject. Her passion was English. She loved anything to do with literature. Unfortunately, there had been no openings for that subject at Jackson High, or anywhere else in the district. So here she was, teaching something she really didn't have much interest in, on a daily basis. At this point, she was just happy that she had a job. She'd moved to the city of Seattle eleven months earlier, unsure whether she wanted to teach anymore or not. After all, she'd had a rough go at the last school she'd taught at. That could be chalked up to Kevin and his irrational behavior, which had eventually forced her to resign.

Thinking of Kevin Bledsoe made her blood run cold. He managed to pop up into her mind at the most inopportune times. She'd only dated the guy for six months, and in that time he'd managed to completely destroy her credibility as an authoritative figure in the mid-sized community of Chapman, Montana, where she'd lived peacefully for two years. She'd loved the picturesque little town. When she'd met Kevin, the nice man who ran the local newspaper, they'd had a lot in common. They had both loved writing. They had loved Emily Dickinson and all types of poetry. They had loved leisurely strolls in the park. He had seemed like the perfect guy—until he'd started getting a little too overzealous. He'd asked her to marry him and though she'd cared for him, something had been holding her back. She still didn't know what exactly, but somehow she knew he wasn't the man for her long term. She'd told him so and attempted to break things off with him. This was easier said than done. He'd begun sending gifts, as well as following her, calling her at weird hours of the night and sabotaging things for her at the junior high school where she'd taught. Eventually he had literally snapped and all hell had broken loose. At that point, she'd had no choice but to resign. And she'd been forced to find another place to live—another job. She'd been forced to start her life over.

Sighing, she quickened her steps toward the school building. She'd made mistakes throughout her life. She'd been a kid in the system. She couldn't remember all the foster homes she'd been in as a child. Over and over again she'd moved, from place to place. She understood the plight of the child who just couldn't belong, no matter how hard they tried to fit in. That was why she'd gone on to become a teacher.

"Here, let me help you," a voice said, stepping up beside Baylie and reaching for the pile of paperwork in her left arm. "Why don't you just make two trips?"

Baylie recognized the voice of Susan Hanover, another teacher in the History department at Jackson.

Blonde with dark eyes and a to die for body, Susan was extremely popular among both staff and students at Jackson High. She was tall and slim, with a sense of style that made Baylie re-check her own appearance daily before coming to school. Susan had an air about her that reeked of self-confidence. Baylie only wished she had half the confidence Susan had.

"Did you hear the latest news?"

Baylie readjusted her load, now that it was significantly lighter. "What news? I just got here."

"It's about Giselle Lindsay," Susan went on, holding the front door to the building open so Baylie could enter before her.

Baylie grimaced. Giselle Lindsay was not her favorite person. Over the past year, she had tangled with the head of the History department on more than one occasion. Giselle was one of those women who had to have control of everything around her, people included. Over and over again, she'd let Baylie know she was watching her like a hawk. Baylie hated to be watched like a hawk.

"She's missing," Susan went on, following Baylie's footsteps toward her classroom.

Baylie faltered, surprised. "What do you mean *missing?*"

"I mean she stayed late Friday night and no one has seen her since. Rob called me this morning and asked me if I'd seen her."

Baylie frowned. Robert Barnes was a math teacher at Jackson. He and Baylie and Susan, along with a couple of other teachers, including Giselle, had regular margarita nights at a local Mexican restaurant.

10

"Apparently her rat bastard boyfriend finally reported her missing yesterday." Susan paused when they reached Baylie's classroom. She waited while Baylie unlocked the door. Both women entered the room and deposited their loads on Baylie's desk.

"Are you joking?" Baylie asked, almost feeling like this had to be a joke. "Because it's too early on a Monday morning for jokes. Especially after all the paper grading I had to do this weekend at home. I don't feel like I had a day off at all."

"I'm not kidding, Bay."

Baylie frowned again. "I don't believe it."

"She's missing. Rob said Harris called him at home and said the police are going to be here today asking questions. From what I've heard we're all going to have to talk to them."

Great. Just what she needed. Baylie cursed. "She's probably visiting relatives or something. Maybe hanging with a friend."

"This is Giselle we're talking about," Susan said, folding her arms across her ample chest. "She's not exactly overflowing with friends at this point. In fact, I'd hedge a bet that we're pretty much the only friends she has."

Baylie couldn't argue with that. "So what do they think happened to her?"

"I don't know. I only know that her boyfriend reported her missing and the police are looking into the matter." Susan rolled her eyes. "Knowing Giselle she'll turn up with bells on. She loves attention. This would be just the kind of thing to get her some."

Baylie was thoughtful. Susan was right. Giselle liked to have people talking about her. She'd had numerous rumored flings with different teachers around the building over the past year since Baylie had started work there. And she did nothing to quash the rumor mill. Still, Baylie had a niggling fear that maybe Giselle was in trouble.

"Wouldn't surprise me if Peter finally did her in. I'm telling the police so when I talk to them," Susan said, referring to Peter O'Donnell, Giselle's less than kind-hearted boyfriend. It was no secret that he liked to knock Giselle around. For whatever reason, Giselle stayed and took his abuse.

"Maybe she finally got sick of Peter and took off," Baylie said, speaking her thoughts aloud.

Susan shrugged. "Maybe. I doubt it though. She's more theatrical than that. I don't think she would just disappear."

Baylie didn't answer. The sound of the bell ringing snapped her out of her trance. "Let me know if you hear anything more."

Susan nodded and left the room.

For the rest of the morning, Baylie concentrated on her history classes. They were preparing for a test in the next two weeks and they had a lot of ground to cover. Hours went by in a blur and it was quickly lunchtime. Baylie took her sack lunch and went into the teacher's lounge—her usual routine.

Susan and Rob were there already, busily chatting. When they saw Baylie, they both scooted over and made room for her. She sat down and dug into her lunch bag.

"Have they called you yet?"

Baylie un-wrapped her turkey sandwich before she looked at Robert Barnes.

In his early thirties, Rob was a decent looking guy with blond hair and blue eyes. He was a little on the short side, definitely several inches under six feet. If Baylie were being honest, she had to admit that on occasion Rob suffered from short man's complex. He had asked her out on numerous occasions and she had turned him down every time. He just wasn't her type.

"Has who called me?" she asked, taking a bite out of her sandwich.

"The police."

Baylie frowned in mid-chew. "You mean about Giselle?"

"I had to leave my third period," Susan said, sucking on a straw of milk. "Rob got called out of fourth."

"No one has called me," Baylie said, swallowing her food. She couldn't help but feel anxious as she thought of the police questioning her. After her

13

debacle with Kevin back in Chapman, she had less than a little faith in cops.

"They were asking about our margarita nights," Rob said, taking a sip of cola. "And they wanted to know when I saw Giselle last." He frowned. "I told them we hadn't had a night out in weeks because of the semester change and the fact that we were all too busy. They kept asking more and more questions."

Baylie knew Rob was sensationalizing things a bit. He was known for his dramatics, much the same way as Giselle was. "If she's missing, they *should* ask questions," she responded. "What do you expect them to do?"

Rob shrugged his shoulders. "I'm starting to worry that something has really happened to Giselle. I mean at first this morning I thought she was pulling a fast one to lose Peter. Now I think that maybe the bastard hurt her finally. I mean bad."

"Did you tell the police that?" Baylie asked.

"I mentioned the abuse. But they said it's pretty much hearsay. No one has pictures to prove anything," Rob answered.

"Everyone saw the bruises," Susan said, leaning back in her chair. "We'll all attest to that."

"So what did the cops say?" Baylie asked, her curiosity getting the better of her.

"They said they have no leads at this point and they're not giving out any information," Rob answered. "I'm sure they'll be in to see you this afternoon. There are two detectives on the case."

"Hotties," Susan said, winking. "Tall, dark and brooding, just the way I like them. Well one of them was, anyway. The other one was stuffy rather than brooding."

Baylie ignored Susan's description of the police. "I hope they've got Peter in custody."

"They haven't arrested anyone yet," Rob informed her.

Baylie felt a pang of pity for Giselle and her situation. She may not like the woman much but she was still human. "I should get back to my classroom." She stood up and tossed her garbage into a large bin. On her way back to her classroom she received her daily dose of sexual harassment.

Hobart "Jeepers" McClain was not her favorite student. In fact, she loathed the kid. He was seventeen and angry at the world. His parents were rich beyond belief and let him do whatever he wanted. No matter what kind of trouble he got into, they always got him out of it. That included each and every time he sexually harassed a teacher.

"Nice legs, Ms. Sutter. Care to give me a closer look after school?"

The sneering came out loud enough for her to hear, as well as anyone else who was within several feet of her. She stiffened and turned toward the boy. He was leaning against a row of lockers, his usual cronies at his side.

Hobart McClain was a nice enough looking boy, if one could look beyond his foul personality. Most people couldn't. He had dark hair—a little on the longer side—and brown eyes. His build was average for a seventeen-year-old boy. Baylie guessed his height to be around six feet. He was lanky at this point in his life, but most likely would fill out in the next few years. That is if he stayed alive that long. Jeepers was known for his addiction to trouble. It was likely that that kind of trouble would eventually lead to his demise.

"I'm going to pretend I didn't hear you say that, Hobart," she said, with a smile she knew did not reach her eyes. No one ever called Jeepers by his given name. Of course she couldn't blame the kid for hating it. It wasn't the hippest name of the new millennium, but his family came from old money. It was the cross he would have to bear. Apparently, he didn't share her humor because his smile faded and he straightened.

"Shouldn't you be on your way to class?" she prodded, her gaze moving from Jeepers to his two friends.

Tank Riley and Jonah Kramer snickered from beside Jeepers.

"Just waiting to check out your goods, Ms. Sutter. We could go in the bathroom right now and

16

I'll give you something to scream about," Jeepers said, sneering again.

Baylie wanted to slap the kid. He was the most obnoxious teenager she had ever encountered. Since the first day she had arrived at Jackson, he and his toadies had been giving her a hard time. She didn't fear him exactly. He was a trust fund kid with more bark than bite, but that didn't mean he didn't annoy her to no end.

"I think she's turned on, Jeeps," Tank said, taking a step toward Baylie.

Tank Riley did not get the nickname Tank for no reason. He was a huge, though rather dense boy, who never thought before he spoke. He had a military short haircut on his head and was missing one of his front teeth. Needless to say, this boy was not only unpopular with the teachers, but also with girls.

"Leave her alone," Jonah said, tossing an elbow at Tank, in spite of the fact that his friend outweighed him by a hundred pounds at least. Jonah was the quietest of the three boys. He was an inch or two shorter than Jeepers, with dark hair and decent enough looking blue eyes. He generally kept out of trouble and had fairly good grades. She wasn't sure why he had chosen to hang out with a creep like Jeepers. But then teenage boys were a mystery to her. Who knew why they did anything?

"I'm going to give you all one last chance to go to your classes," Baylie said, her patience thinning. The truth was, she knew what would happen if she chose to formally reprimand Jeepers—lots of paperwork and very little consequence. Not as long as his money bags father was on the city council.

Jeepers grinned and reached for Baylie's curling blonde hair. His hand was abruptly cut off by a larger, stronger hand that seemed to come out of nowhere and manacle his wrist. Baylie watched as Jeepers reddened from the neck up. His eyes narrowed and he frowned menacingly.

"I suggest you apologize to your teacher," a quiet voice said from behind her. She turned her head. Her eyes roamed up a long, muscular arm, attached to a set of shoulders that were wide and well built. When her eyes climbed higher, she saw dark hair—almost black, a nicely chiseled jaw—cleanly shaven, a perfectly shaped nose and a pair of deep, blue eyes, surrounded by the most exquisite male face she'd ever seen. The face was not smiling.

"Who the fuck are you?" Jeepers asked, though his voice was lowered somewhat. "This your boyfriend, Ms. Sutter?"

Tank snickered in response to his friend's ballsy jibing.

"I'm going to be your worst nightmare if you don't apologize," the man said. It was then that he lifted the tail on his sport coat and Baylie saw a golden badge glittering from its attachment to the

18

belt at his waist. A large caliber handgun was in a shoulder holster, resting not far from the badge. He was a cop. Baylie watched as his long fingers tightened their hold on Jeepers, who had the decency to wince.

"I ain't done anything to her," the boy said, though he didn't sound very self-assured anymore. "Honest. We were just kidding around."

"You're not very funny," the cop said, glaring from one boy to the next. "Now apologize."

Jeepers looked as though he wanted to argue, but thought the better of it. He continued frowning as he glanced at Baylie. "Sorry."

The cop squeezed harder on the boy's wrist. "Like you *mean* it."

Jeepers swore. "I'm sorry, Ms. Sutter. *Really sorry.* It won't happen again."

Baylie would have smiled had she not been so stunned. She had never seen anyone handle Jeepers McClain that way. Not even Principal Harris.

She didn't realize that the cop was waiting for her to say something until she looked up and saw that he was watching her carefully, as if to ask whether she was satisfied with the apology. "It's fine," she said, trying to ignore the response she had to those earth shattering blue eyes of his. No doubt, this was one of the *hotties* that Susan had been referring to.

The cop roughly shoved Jeepers free. "Beat it, kid."

Jeepers continued frowning. He gave Baylie a dirty look for good measure, then turned and headed down the hallway, his friends on his heels.

Baylie let out the breath she hadn't even realized she'd been holding in. Turning, she looked up at the cop again. He really was stunning. Definitely *hottie* material. She forced a smile for his benefit, suddenly slightly self-conscious. It was times like this when she wished she had the confidence that Susan seemed to ooze at all times. "Thanks," she said quietly.

His lips thinned into a frown as he watched Jeepers disappear around the corner. "I get the feeling that's not the first altercation you've had with Prince Charming."

She followed his gaze and shrugged. "I'm used to him. But thanks, all the same."

"You should report him. Kid's trouble waiting to happen."

"I have reported him. He comes from money." She didn't say anything more.

He swore and nodded his head. "Councilman McClain's kid. I've seen him around the station before. Little bastard."

Baylie didn't argue. "Well, thanks all the same. I need to get to my classroom." She made a move to step around the man. He blocked her way.

"Baylie Sutter?"

She wasn't surprised he knew her name. Cops had a way of knowing everything about everyone. She slowly nodded her head.

"You're on my list. I need to speak with you. Is now a bad time?"

It actually wasn't. It was her planning period. Still, she didn't want to spend her planning hour with a cop, answering questions about something she knew nothing about. "I don't know Giselle Lindsay that well," she said, before she could stop herself.

He raised a brow, folding his arms over his broad chest.

Way to look at ease, she chastised herself. "What I meant to say is that I don't think I can help you much. That's why you're here, right?" She wished she could shove something in her mouth to shut it. Silence ensued and she felt a little like squirming. Why did police officers always make her so damned nervous? It wasn't as though she had anything to hide.

"Is that right? Because I was told you and a few friends regularly have drinks with Ms. Lindsay. That not true?"

Now it was her turn to frown. "It's true that we meet at a restaurant with a group of people. In other words, *not alone*."

"Uh huh. And you don't think that makes you an acquaintance of hers?"

She supposed it did. Damn it. She cursed Giselle. "Well, yes, but—"

"Can we talk somewhere a little more private?" he interrupted, indicating her classroom down the hall. Great, he had already staked her out. Knowing she couldn't really avoid the questioning, she nodded.

Moments later they were seated in her classroom, she behind her desk, he in a chair next to it.

"I'm Detective Dylan Stone, by the way. Seattle PD." He did not offer her his hand and she didn't know why but she was relieved. He did flash his badge at her. She glanced at it absently. She'd already heard who he was. There was no point in scrutinizing him.

"Baylie Sutter. But you know that already."

For the first time he smiled, displaying a nice, even row of perfect, white teeth. "I do," he agreed, flipping open a black notebook and taking a pen from his breast pocket. "So tell me when the last time was that you saw Ms. Lindsay?"

Baylie thought that over. "Friday," she decided aloud. "We do teach in the same school."

"After school? Before, during?" he prodded.

"All of the above," she said, shrugging. "She's the head of my department."

"History, right?"

"That's right."

"Did you leave before she did Friday night?"

"I left around four. I'm not sure when she left."

22

He made a few notes and she wanted to squirm again. She glanced at the clock and willed time to pass quickly.

"What's your normal margarita night?"

She narrowed her eyes. "Excuse me?"

He didn't even blink. "You've admitted you and Ms. Lindsay attend a regular drink night with friends. What night does that usually take place on?"

"Tuesdays," she answered, without preamble.

"Every Tuesday? Never changes to Fridays or Saturdays?"

"We've only gone on Tuesdays. We haven't even done that in a while. End of the semester. We've all been busy."

"I see. So you're positive you didn't go out for drinks Friday or Saturday night then?"

Annoyed, she frowned. "Of course I'm positive. I had papers to grade this weekend. Even if the others had been going out, I wouldn't have been able to make it."

"So they could have gone out without you knowing it?"

"Well I'm not their keeper," she snapped. "What are you getting at?"

"Are you familiar with Giselle Lindsay's boyfriend?"

Finally, a question she had anticipated. "Yes, I know of Peter." Something in her voice changed and she knew it. She cleared her throat, trying to mask it, but he was too smart for that and caught on.

"So you don't like him."

Brilliant deduction, she thought. "I suppose not. No."

"Care to tell me why?"

"Because he hit her. I'm sure I'm not the first person to tell you that, am I?"

He ignored her question and asked another one of his own. "You saw bruises yourself?"

"On occasion."

"How many occasions?"

She thought that over. "I don't know. Several, I guess. She never told me things outright. I told you before we aren't close."

"And you don't like her," he figured out aloud.

She knew he was goading her. She forced her voice to remain even. "I've been working here a little under a year, Detective. Giselle is my department head. We don't always agree on how things around here should be run."

He studied her for several moments. "So you had words with her on occasion."

She managed to keep her expression impassive. "Most people occasionally have words with their co-workers."

"True enough," he said, leaning back in his chair. "Did you ever actually see Peter O'Donnell lay a hand on Ms. Lindsay in a threatening manner?"

24

She thought that over. She hadn't. "Giselle went out with us as a group. Peter came along once in a blue moon. I know him only on a very casual basis. He never hit her in front of me."

Apparently satisfied with that, he nodded.

"Do you think he hurt her?" she found herself asking, even though she doubted the cop would give her an answer. Cops were notorious for asking questions, not answering them. He didn't surprise her.

"We have no proof of that. What we know is that she didn't come home Friday." He dug into his pocket and pulled out a business card. Sliding it across her desk, his blue eyes locked with hers. "I'm going to need you to call me if you think of anything that may help us locate her."

"Do you think she could have gone to visit relatives or something?" she found herself asking.

"Do you?" he countered, staring at her intently again. Damn, she hated cops.

"I don't know. She's never talked about her family with me. That's why I was asking you."

He stared at her a moment longer, then stood so abruptly she jumped. "I may have more questions for you, Ms. Sutter. Just fair warning."

She stood up too, not liking the tone to his voice. He wasn't accusatory exactly, just smug. It was unnerving. "I've told you everything I know."

"Uh huh. Well if you think of anything else, give me a call. Or look me up. It's likely that we'll be in and out of the school for the next day or two."

She forced herself to nod and watched as he strode toward the classroom door. A moment later, he disappeared into the hallway.

TWO

Dylan Stone watched as his partner looked over his notes. Alex Sinclair and Dylan had worked together for three years now, as part of the Seattle Police Department's Missing Persons Division. Alex was two years older than Dylan's thirty-four years. He had two kids, a wife named Penny and a dog named Rover. He had a total storybook home life. Sometimes Dylan found himself envying that. *Sometimes.* Most of the time he was happy as a clam with his no strings attached bachelor life. It allowed him to live in his man-cave house on Queen Ann, without the bother of a honey-do list or a PTA meeting. He had no one nagging him about the Sunday football games he loved to watch. And he had no one crying tears when he forgot her birthday. He'd played that game. For two short years, just out of his twenties, he'd lived with a woman. Mandy had been great at first. They'd had a great time together. But life as the significant other of a cop was not easy and soon she'd split for greener pastures. He'd been very careful about getting too involved with a woman on a serious basis since then. He was all about having fun and keeping it easy.

"What do you think of Giselle Lindsay's co-workers?" Alex asked, interrupting Dylan's thoughts.

Dylan shrugged. "Typical. She's not real popular with the women. Maybe too popular with the men."

"That's my take too. Principal's an ass-kiss so it's going to be hard to tell anything from him."

"The majority of the staff think she's a bitch and keep their distance," Dylan pointed out. "All but the ones on that list. They have their little drink night. Even those friends keep her at an arm's length, if they can be believed."

"You don't believe them?"

Actually he did. The staff at Jackson High School had all been fairly open with him. They had been more than forthcoming with any information they could provide, especially regarding Peter O'Donnell, who was definitely looking more and more like a viable suspect in Giselle Lindsay's disappearance. The fact that he had waited two days to even report her missing was suspicious enough. But on top of that, he had a violent reputation. He was an abuser and he was an abuser that hadn't hidden his abusing. This would not bode well for him. All the same, Dylan had no proof that anything violent had even happened to Giselle Lindsay. No body, no evidence of a crime.

"She may be hiding on purpose," Alex suggested, propping his feet up on Dylan's desk.

Dylan thought that over. He supposed that was possible. Several of her coworkers had attested to the fact that O'Donnell hit her. It was definitely in the cards that she could have split on purpose to get away from him. "My instincts are telling me no," he finally admitted, yanking at his tie. He hated ties. They drove him nuts.

"Mine too."

"I want to run checks on her co-workers. All of them."

Alex nodded in agreement. "We can switch it up. Re-question them again. The ones who spent any time with her anyway. Maybe someone will change their story."

"Maybe." He'd already thought about that. He had gotten a strange vibe off of one of the math teachers at the high school. Robert Barnes was his name. The guy had been somewhat evasive. The principal had also been less than helpful, and almost appeared as though he had something to hide. Dylan got the idea that he was quite possibly involved with the missing teacher on a more personal level, but the married man had not admitted as much. Then there was the cute, little history teacher. That one had been jumpier than a polecat. She had definitely distrusted him on sight. That usually indicated a prior run-in with the law. He was going to look into that one ASAP.

"The principal rubbed me wrong," Alex said thoughtfully. "You think maybe he had a thing with her?"

"It's a definite possibility. I'm getting a strange vibe off of him."

"You and me both," Alex agreed.

"The boyfriend's a prick. He's still number one on my list."

Dylan couldn't argue. Peter O'Donnell was the most likely suspect at this point. Again, without a body or even a vehicle or some shred of evidence insinuating a violent act had occurred, they really had no crime. All they could do was keep looking for Giselle Lindsay.

Baylie sipped her cup of tea, her eyes scanning the front window of her small, two bedroom rambler. The front yard wasn't large. It had enough room for a small flowerbed and a decent sized elm tree. There was a cute, white picket fence that separated the sidewalk from the grass. It certainly wouldn't keep out unwanted perpetrators but it added a little ambiance to the place. She had fallen in love with the little house the moment she'd seen it. For now, she was renting. In time, she would think about buying. Provided things all went well for her here.

Now with Giselle disappearing, things were taking an interesting turn. It seemed that no matter where Baylie went, cops ended up in her life. Even as a kid, it had been that way. She had been six the first time she'd been placed in foster care. She couldn't even remember those days anymore. Her first couple of foster homes were blurs to her. She only knew that her parents had died and she'd had no other living relatives. That had left her a ward of the state.

One of her neighbors drove up and turned into the driveway next door. Jerry Fannon and his wife Carolyn were friendly enough. They were an older couple who had hit retirement age a few years back. He spent the day working on cars in his garage and she spent her days gardening. Baylie didn't know them well, but they exchanged pleasantries, which was more than she could say for the last few homes she'd had.

She waved as Mr. Fannon noticed her in the window. He waved back before heading into his house. Baylie liked her neighborhood. For the first time in a long time, she was comfortable.

Hearing her phone ring, she glanced at the portable handset. *Private Name* popped up on the caller ID. Wasn't that always the case? What good did caller ID do you if everyone just blocked their number anyway?

Sighing, she set her tea down and answered the call. She received silence in return.

"Hello?" she repeated, irritated.

"Hello, Baylie."

The sound of his voice shouldn't have sent shivers up her spine. It was smooth and dark — like rich chocolate. In addition, it literally sent her heart into a tailspin. Her hand jerked, spilling her tea all over the table in front of her.

"I know you're going to hang up on me. Just wait a minute. I just want to say my piece."

Baylie was frozen. She hadn't heard Kevin Bledsoe's voice in over a year. Not since he had taken off, in a mad run from the police.

"You have to listen to me, Bay. I need you to listen to me."

Baylie's fingers clenched the phone tighter. *Hang up*, she told herself repeatedly. But she couldn't.

"It's taken me a long time to find you. I can't talk long. I need for us to meet."

As if the cat finally let go of her tongue, she spoke. "No."

"Baylie, you need to listen to me. You have to know I didn't do what they're saying I did. I know I made some mistakes with you, but I would never do..." His voice broke off. "I need you to meet me. We can't talk over the phone."

"I'm not talking to you at all, Kevin. Don't call me again." Baylie disconnected the phone and jumped up from her chair, ignoring the spilled tea.

She ran over to her front door and checked her locks quickly. He'd found her. Kevin knew where she lived. He had her phone number. He was going to come after her again.

Taking several deep breaths, she reached for the curtains and pulled the polyester material shut with a swish. Then she made the rounds of her house, checking all doors, windows and locks. After that, she sat down on the couch in her living room and struggled for some control. She could call the police. Kevin was wanted. The Montana State Police had him on their most wanted list.

Feeling herself starting to shake, she ran a hand through her hair. She didn't want to think about the fact that Kevin had found her — that he knew where she lived — that he likely knew where she worked.

An ugly thought filled her head and she tamped down on it. It was coincidence. There was no way that Giselle's disappearance had anything to do with Kevin. No way.

Her phone rang again and she stared at it from across the room, desperate for the ringing to stop. This time her machine picked up.

"You can ignore me if you want. But sooner or later you need to talk to me. If you want this all to stop, you need to talk to me, Baylie. I'll try you again. And if you know what's good for you, you'll answer." Click, the line went dead.

33

At the same time, there was a knock on her front door. Baylie nearly jumped into the ceiling. She could see the outline of what looked like a man through the curtain in the front door. The outline was too small to be Kevin's. She felt slight relief but still remained silent.

A knock sounded again, this time more urgent. Baylie heard some scuffling and then a familiar voice. "Baylie, it's me. Susan. And Rob. Open up, will you?"

Baylie jumped up, not sure whether she was thankful for the intrusion of her friends or not. She lifted the curtain back and looked through the window. Sure enough, Rob and Susan stood on the front porch. Baylie reached over and unlocked the door, carefully opening it and allowing them inside.

"Thank God, you're home. We need to talk to you."

"It's a little late, don't you think?" she asked, looking beyond Susan and into the empty front yard. Paranoia had completely taken her over at this point and she was half-afraid Kevin was going to jump out from behind the tree in her front yard. Thankfully he didn't. The yard remained still.

"What are you doing?" Rob wanted to know. He frowned at her. "Shut the door, will you? It's freezing."

Baylie shut the door. Then she turned to them. "What's going on?"

"Rob needs your advice," Susan said pointedly.

The idea that Rob would need her advice on anything was surprising. He was typically a know it all of all trades. "About what?" she asked cautiously.

"He was sleeping with Giselle," Susan blurted out, before Rob could speak.

Baylie narrowed her eyes. The more she thought about things, the less surprised she became. After all, rumor had it that Giselle had slept with Principal Harris and numerous other people around town.

"I know, he's a pig. I already told him so," Susan said, folding her arms over her chest. "The idea that he kept asking both you and I out on dates when he was screwing Giselle is disgusting."

Rob rubbed his face tiredly, then let out a sigh. "Susan, that's not the issue here. I'm more concerned with how much trouble I'm in for not telling the police."

"You didn't tell them?" Baylie asked incredulously.

"Of course I didn't."

"Why not?" Baylie asked, her eyes narrowed. Suddenly Rob didn't look as harmless as he had a few moments ago.

"Because I didn't think it was necessary, that's why. It won't shed any light on her disappearance," Rob said, pacing the room nervously. "It doesn't matter. She's slept with a lot of men."

35

"It doesn't matter what she's done with other men, Robert," Susan said. "The cops have a way of finding things out like this. And if you hide it, you look guilty."

"She's right," Baylie said, still eyeing Rob curiously. Could it be possible that he had done something to Giselle? Kevin's phone call replayed itself inside her head and she shuddered involuntarily.

"You have to tell the cops, Rob. There's no way around it," Susan snapped, annoyed. "I really can't believe you were stupid enough not to tell them in the first place."

"Did Harris tell them *he's* sleeping with her?" Rob demanded standing up, now clearly upset. "Because he is, or at least he was. And so is the Neanderthal that owns the Pool Cue downtown. He almost wiped up the floor with my face the other night when Giselle and I went in there together for a drink. And let's not forget O'Donnell. Hell, she lives with that bastard."

Clearly Giselle was a slut, Baylie decided. However, she still didn't know what to think of Rob. "You should tell the police everything and let them do their jobs."

"What if I become a suspect?" Rob asked warily.

"A suspect in what?" Susan asked. "There's been no crime committed. Giselle is just missing at this point. She could turn up tomorrow, alive and well."

Baylie couldn't argue with that. "She's right. If there is no crime scene, there is no crime. You should come clean now or the truth will come out on its own." She knew how that worked from personal experience.

Rob let out a muddled groan. "I wish I'd never met Giselle. I knew she was bad luck. We got too drunk one night and one thing led to another. I've slept with her three times. That's it."

"It doesn't matter," Baylie said, noticing that Susan was spending an awful lot of time glaring at Rob. For someone who had supposedly turned all of his requests for a date down, she was looking mighty upset that he had been sleeping with Giselle.

"O'Donnell did this. I know he did. If I admit to sleeping with her —"

"It will give them even more reason to look closer at O'Donnell," Susan said, then looked at Baylie. "Don't you think so?"

"I suppose," Baylie said absently. She was still preoccupied with her worries about Kevin. Forcing herself, she looked at Rob. "More motive on his part," she added.

"Or motive on mine," Rob said, distressed.

"I'm not going to baby you through this, Robert. You are the one who slept with her. You get yourself out of this mess."

"Am I missing something here?" Baylie finally asked.

"You mean the fact that he's sleeping with me too?" Susan snapped irritably.

Baylie looked at Rob, disgusted. "I don't know who's worse, you or Giselle."

Rob ignored that. "So what do I do?"

"Go to the police. Tell them the truth," Baylie said simply.

"And when they ask me why I didn't tell them this information before?" Rob asked matter-of-factly.

"Tell them you're stupid," Susan said sulkily.

"Listen, Susan, you and I aren't exactly exclusive either. You've been dating other guys. You told me so yourself."

"I'm not *sleeping* with other guys."

Baylie listened to their exchange for a few more minutes. It was a mystery to her that she could have gone for drinks with these two every Tuesday night for nearly a year and not noticed they were more than friends. Of course she was rather self-absorbed. "Okay," she finally said, growing impatient with their arguing. "Enough fighting. Go to the police, Rob. It's the right thing to do. The important thing here is finding Giselle."

Rob took several deep breaths before he finally seemed to screw his head back on and think straight. Then he slowly nodded. "Okay. You're right, you're right." He looked over at Susan. "I don't suppose you'll come with me."

"Hell no," Susan said, glaring at him. "I've had too much already. Man up and face the cops yourself."

"Maybe you should go with him," Baylie suggested, not because she felt sorry for Rob, but because she was a little worried that he might possibly change his mind about confessing his affair.

Susan just frowned for a long moment. Apparently, she came to the conclusion that Baylie was right. "I'll go. But I'm pissed. Let the record show that."

"The record's clear," Rob said on a sigh. "The record needs to be shown that Harris screwed her too. Who's going to tell the cops about that?"

"He's married," Susan said, softening a little. "I'm sure his wife won't like this little indiscretion to become public."

"Probably not," Baylie agreed. "But if the news comes from anyone other than Harris or Giselle herself it's just hearsay. For now there's nothing you can do about that."

Rob cursed.

"Let's go," Susan said, still glowering.

Baylie walked them to the door. Again, her eyes scanned the front yard carefully. Not so much as a leaf moved. She shivered. It was almost too quiet.

"Are you okay? You're acting kind of jumpy," Susan said, her frown more pronounced.

"I'm fine. It's been a long day, that's all."

Susan looked as though she wanted to argue but Rob was halfway down the driveway so she shrugged her shoulders and turned to follow him.

Baylie shut the door and locked it quickly. Then she stood there, her mind reeling. Wrapping her arms around her middle, she leaned back against the door. Why did Kevin have to come back now? He'd gotten away. Why show his face again? It just didn't make sense.

The phone began to ring again and she shivered as she listened to it chime. Damn him! Walking over to the table, she picked it up and checked the caller ID. *Private Number* again.

"Stop calling me!" she snapped into the phone.

"Just listen to me!" Kevin said, desperation clear in his voice. "I know you're alone. I need you to hear me out."

His words made her skin crawl. He was here. He was watching her. "I'm not alone, Kevin." The words were meaningless and she knew that. He could see her. He was out there watching her again. The nightmare was starting over.

"Baylie, listen to me. I didn't kill those girls. I didn't kill anyone. You have to believe me."

"Where is Giselle?"

"Listen to me!" he said, raising his voice. "Someone else is doing this. Someone connected to you."

"Is she dead, Kevin? God, did you kill her?" Panic ate at her insides, making her feel nauseous. "Where is she?"

"I don't know who you're talking about!" He screamed back at her, now sounding out of breath. "If you don't listen to me, you'll be next, Baylie. He's after you! Don't you see that? You're the key here."

She shook her head, disconnecting the call. Then she backed up and stared around the empty living room, her heart pounding a mile a minute. He was out there and he was watching. He was coming for her. She was next. Tossing the phone down, she hurried through the house and into her bedroom. She checked the windows again. They were all locked.

Hearing the phone ring again, she wanted to scream. He wasn't going to give up. He wasn't going to stop this until he finally got what he wanted. *Her*.

Panic ate at her again and she listened as her machine picked up. She expected to hear his voice again. Instead she heard scratching and then a muffled female gasp. A moment of deadly silence ensued before she heard what sounded like a moan and then screaming. Her brow broke out in a sweat. Suddenly the screaming stopped. She heard a thud and then a voice came on the line. *"Don't worry, Nikki. I'm coming for you next."*

41

JENNIFER HAYDEN

THREE

Baylie sat huddled in a blanket on her couch,
watching as two police detectives confiscated her
answering machine tape. She'd half-expected Dylan
Stone to show up when she'd placed a call to 911,
and he had. But she also had a new detective to
deal with. He had identified himself as Detective
Scott Sherman. He had steamrolled into her house
and literally taken over the premises. She disliked
the man on sight. As abrupt as Stone had been, he'd
had a bit of a human side to him. This man did not.
He was large and intimidating. She supposed some
of the intimidation came from the fact that he was as
bald as Mr. Clean. He also frowned a lot—in fact
constantly. He had only softened minimally when
she had started shaking like a leaf. That's when
Stone had rustled up a blanket and set it over her
shoulders.

"We're going to need to take this with us,"
Sherman said, indicating her answering machine
tape.

42

"I figured as much," she managed to mutter. She wished he would just go away. He was making her anxiety worse.

"I'm going to need to ask you some questions," he went on, reaching into his pocket for something.

"I've got this."

When Baylie looked up, she realized Stone was back in the room. He'd spent the majority of the evening in the bedroom near the answering machine, where they had played the messages so many times it had made her head hurt.

"I've got it covered," Sherman said, pulling out a black book.

Baylie grimaced. She knew what the little black notebook meant. She wasn't sure she could take more brow beating.

"This is my case, Sherman. Go chase a parked car."

Sherman frowned. "What's your problem, Stone? You were busy. I got here first."

Stone frowned back and Baylie could see the two men were obviously going to take part in a pissing contest. "I'm here now," was all Stone said.

Sherman looked as though he wanted to protest but instead he shrugged. "Whatever, dude. Do your thing then."

Stone waited until Sherman had backed away. Then he walked over and sat down on the edge of Baylie's coffee table. He stared at her for a long moment, his eyes not quite as cold as Sherman's had been, yet clearly filled with distrust. "You shouldn't have lied to me."

"I didn't lie to you." She hadn't. Not really. She just hadn't told him about Kevin—which had been a mistake obviously. He had clearly found out the truth on his own. He was a cop. Her entire life was at his fingertips. She should have known better than to keep quiet about her past.

"Listen, Ms. Sutter. You've got a couple of choices here. You can talk to me—come clean right now in your own words about what you think is going on here. Or, you can wait until I read your file, which my partner has on his desk as we speak. It will take me a little while to get through the paperwork but I can go that route if you want. And then I'll be back—and I won't be as nice to you. I don't like irritating legwork."

"I didn't lie to you," she said again. She knew how lame she sounded, but she couldn't help it.

"Omitting pertinent information isn't any better than lying. Now who is this guy?"

"I don't know," she said quietly. His frown grew more pronounced and she shivered again. The truth was, she didn't know. The man who'd left the last message on the machine had not sounded like Kevin. Of course that didn't mean he hadn't disguised his voice.

44

"Ms. Sutter, you're wasting my time here. A woman may possibly have died tonight. Do you understand that?"

She winced, the sound of those horrific screams replaying themselves inside her head. "I understand that," she said, forcing herself to take a deep breath.

"You had better start at the beginning. Why is this man calling you?"

"Because I used to date him," she said wearily. "Three years ago. I lived in Chapman, Montana. He asked me to marry him and when I broke things off, he was unhappy."

He raised a brow. "You mean he didn't take no for an answer."

"He stalked me," she finally admitted. "And then two girls from the school I taught at turned up dead. Not long after, two more women were murdered. It took the police awhile but eventually they tied the murders back to me, and eventually to Kevin."

"Kevin Bledsoe," he said, confirming her hunch that he had at least gotten the highlights from her file.

"That's right."

"Go on."

She shrugged her shoulders. "He was brought in for questioning. They released him. There was really no hardcore evidence until they realized he had had a relationship with one of the murdered women. By then, he had gone on the run."

Stone straightened. "And you haven't heard a word from him until tonight."

"No."

He stared at her until she wanted to squirm. Then he let out a sigh. "You told the first officer on the scene that he called you multiple times tonight. What did he say when he called the first time?"

She struggled to remember exactly what Kevin had said to her. The truth was, she was so rattled she couldn't think straight.

"Take your time and think," he said, his voice softening a little.

"He wanted me to meet with him. I was so stunned to hear his voice that I just hung up. Then he called back again and left a message."

"And you didn't call the police?"

She wished she had. "No. I didn't."

"Why? He is a wanted man. Didn't you think it was a good idea to call the police once he'd contacted you—especially in light of your colleague's disappearance and his past history?"

"I didn't get the chance to call the police. Company showed up at the door right after he called. I got sidetracked."

He gave her a look that told her he thought she was lying and she shifted uncomfortably.

"He caught me off guard, Detective. I haven't talked to him in over a year. I had hoped to never talk to him again."

She could see he was still skeptical but he let it drop. "So who came to your door?"

"Some friends of mine. We talked for a few minutes and they left."

"What friends?" he asked.

She knew there was no getting around it. "Susan Hanover and Rob Barnes."

His brow rose, as she knew it would, but he didn't comment. "How long did they stay?"

"I don't know. Maybe twenty minutes."

"Short visit," he commented wryly.

"They had somewhere to go," she snapped back, annoyed that she was in this position again. It had been the same way three years earlier when Kevin had dragged her into this mess before. She just couldn't get away from it.

"So what happened next?"

Her head was beginning to pound and she rubbed at her temples. "He called again," she finally said, sighing. "This time I was so angry that I answered. I told him to stop calling me, but he wasn't listening, he was talking. He kept saying I needed to listen to him. He kept saying he was innocent and that someone was after me." She looked up and met Stone's gaze. "He told me that I was next."

"And then hung up?"

"*I* hung up," she said, frustrated. "I asked him if he had Giselle and he acted like he didn't know what I was talking about. After that, I didn't want to hear anymore. I disconnected."

"So then he called back again, and this time you didn't answer?"

"I didn't want to talk to him."

"But again, you didn't pick up the phone to call the police." It wasn't a question. His voice was angry and full of disbelief. "Not until after he called back a fourth time and left the final message we retrieved from your machine."

"I was scared, Detective. I went into my bedroom to check the windows. I wanted to be sure the doors were locked." She glared at him. "I wasn't thinking completely clearly."

"Not until after he called back and quite possibly killed someone, while your answering machine recorded the assault. Then you were thinking clearly enough to call for help?"

The air was ripped from her lungs and she struggled for breath. God, he was right. Very likely, she'd stood by while some poor woman was being killed. Possibly Giselle.

"I'm sorry. That wasn't fair. Are you all right? Do you need some water?"

She shook her head slowly. Guilt ate at her. "It didn't sound like him," she finally said.

He narrowed his eyes. "What do you mean it didn't sound like him?"

"The last voice on the answering machine. It was different."

"It was a whisper, Ms. Sutter. How could you really tell?"

She knew he was doubting just about every word she said and she couldn't blame him. "I'm pretty familiar with Kevin's voice, even after all this time. I just can't be certain it was him the last time."

"We'll have someone look into that. The tape is poor quality though. It won't likely give us anything definitive." He rested his arms on his knees. "So who's Nikki?"

Baylie had nearly forgotten about the name uttered on the machine. *Nikki.* Who was Nikki? She had no idea. "I don't know."

"A victim's name? A nickname for you, maybe? An acquaintance?"

"I said I don't know," she said, folding her hands in front of her as they started to shake. "I don't know anyone named Nikki."

"He thinks you do. He wouldn't have said what he said if he didn't."

She supposed he had a point. Still, she didn't know who Nikki was. "I can't tell you what I don't know."

He looked as though he wanted to argue but he didn't. Instead he stood up, his hands shoved into the pockets of his black slacks. "I will read through your file, Ms. Sutter. At that point I may be able to make heads or tails of some of this."

"You mean because I'm leaving things out," she figured out, her expression drawn. God, cops were all the same. It didn't matter whether you were in Chapman, Montana or Seattle, Washington.

He didn't dignify her comment with an answer. Instead, he changed subjects. "You live alone. Is there anyone you can stay with for the time being?"

Startled, she tensed. She'd heard these words before from the police. Her home was no longer safe. They couldn't provide her with twenty-four hour police protection. She should find someone to stay with until they managed to track Kevin down. Only they never managed to do that. So she'd run. She'd run here. Now she would have to run again.

Sensing her turmoil, Stone sat down on the table again. "Don't get that look in your eyes."

She glared at him. "You don't know me. Don't presume you do."

"I know a runner when I see one. It would serve you well to stick around and help us catch this guy, Baylie. Running hasn't served you well in the past."

"He's after me," she said quietly and watched as his expression softened.

"Maybe."

"How can you say, maybe? You have tape-recorded proof. I can't wait here like a sitting duck!" She stood up and he stood too. Before she realized what he was going to do, he reached out his hands and grasped her shoulders.

"We don't intend to have you sit here and wait for him to come for you. On the other hand, running will just put off the inevitable. At least we know he's on to you here. We can keep an eye on you."

She'd heard that one before too.

"You have my word, Baylie. I can keep you safe if you let me."

Something in those deep, blue eyes of his seemed to eat right into her soul. "Why should I trust you?" She didn't know why she asked the question. He was a cop with a cop face. He could probably snow her into believing anything, just like the others had.

"Because you don't have a choice. Running forever isn't the answer. People will keep dying."

She wanted to argue with him but she knew he was right. "Giselle may be dead already. That might have been her on the machine."

He had the decency to wince. "You can't think about that now. What's done is done. It's possible that Giselle Lindsay's disappearance and your situation are completely unrelated. All the same, I'll have a car out in front of your house for the time being," he offered. "And one at the school. It won't look suspicious to anyone, given the fact that Ms. Lindsay is still missing. As for you, the reality that you need to be extra careful goes without saying.

We'll tap your phone. If we can get a location on this guy, it's a great start."

Everything he said sounded hunky dory. The problem was, she just couldn't let herself trust him. And she wanted to. That was the surprising part of the whole thing. "I lost my job before. You'll see that when you read my file. I was forced to resign. My career won't take another hit like that and survive. Not when the public gets hold of my past."

His expression remained impassive. "If you stay here and help us, I'll do what I can to help you. I already told you that you have my word. The Chapman Police should have done the same thing."

"Well, they didn't. They helped the school give me my walking papers."

"This isn't Chapman," was all he said. He dug into his jacket pocket. He pulled his business card and a pen out. After scrawling something on the back of it, he offered it to her. "Clearly you lost the card I gave you. Here's another. My cell and my home numbers are on there. If you need me, call."

She reluctantly took the card, a little surprised that he was opening himself up to her this way.

"It's possible that she isn't dead, Baylie. This may have all been a set up for you—something to get you thinking so that you'd do something stupid like meet with Bledsoe. Without a body, there is no murder. Remember that." He looked down as his cell phone vibrated. "I have to take this. Keep that number handy. I'll be in touch."

She watched as he walked out her front door. The minute he was gone, her anxiety returned full force. She was alone again—a sitting duck. Peering outside, she watched as a lone police cruiser pulled to a stop in front of her house. Its lights turned off. The officer inside looked her way and gave her a small wave. She acknowledged it, then let the curtain fall closed. Backing up, she sat down on her couch and stared into space. This was obviously going to be a very long night.

FOUR

Dylan read through the file on Baylie Sutter for the third time. It was nearly two in the morning and he was hunkered over his desk staring at a pile of paperwork a mile high. He'd had nothing but two donuts and some coffee in the last twelve hours and he was pretty sure he stunk to high heaven. The life of a cop. It was more than trying sometimes.

"So what do you think?" Alex's weary voice asked from where he sat across from Dylan, his feet propped on the desk. He'd already spent a good portion of the evening looking the Sutter file over.

"I don't know yet," Dylan said, leaning back and rubbing his hands over his eyes. Then he let out a deep breath. "Everything she told me checks out."

Alex didn't argue. "So?"

"She got a raw deal last time."

"What's your point?"

"My point is that if she runs again, we'll lose this guy. He's attached to her for some reason." That

54

was where things got sticky for him. He'd looked over Kevin Bledsoe's file. The guy had had a run-in or two with police over his behavior with a prior girlfriend. Charges were dropped. Then he had apparently hooked up with Baylie Sutter. Just as she'd said, he'd eventually begun stalking her. She'd filed numerous reports and obtained a restraining order. And then the murder charges had come to be—four women, all with ties to Baylie Sutter. Two were students of hers. They had been fourteen-year-old girls, barely into their high school years. The other two victims were older—in their thirties. One had been a secretary at the school Baylie was teaching at. The other had been her neighbor. All four victims had died in similar ways. Strangulation with one weapon or another—a rope, a scarf. Bare hands on one victim. There had been no sign of sexual assault, which was odd. Typically, these types of crimes tended to be sexually motivated, especially when tied to an ex-lover. So what was this guy's motivation?

Dylan looked at the picture of Kevin Bledsoe a second time. He was a decent enough looking guy. Dark complexion. Light brown hair. His mug shots weren't complimentary but there was a snapshot of him that had been personally provided that gave a better view.

"He looks like a Ken doll."

Dylan just grunted in response to that. Sure, the guy was somewhat of a pretty boy. More and more, it seemed that sickos were getting prettier and prettier. "She doesn't think he was the one who called the last time."

"I couldn't tell from the tape. What's your take?"

"I don't know. The last message is a whisper. It's too quiet to tell. We sure as hell can't say it absolutely isn't Bledsoe."

"Do you think he'll come after Sutter?"

"Maybe. I'm not convinced this is the guy responsible for Giselle Lindsay's disappearance. We still have O'Donnell to look at. He's been violent with her in the past. Maybe he got a little too violent and killed her."

Alex thought that over. "He swears he didn't. He admits to hitting her in the past but he says for the last few weeks he's kept his distance from her. She was apparently threatening to report him and he didn't want to get in trouble. That's why he says he didn't report her missing for two days. He thought maybe she'd decided to stay somewhere else for a while. When she didn't answer his calls or show up for her clothes, he got concerned."

"Nice of him," Dylan snapped. "And you believe him?"

"I actually do," Alex replied. "He's admitted to hitting her. He's been honest about their tumultuous relationship. He's just not acting like a guy that's hiding something. He even agreed to take a polygraph." Alex shrugged. "I could be wrong but I just don't think he's involved in her disappearance. That being said, there is a list of guys a mile long that she was sleeping with, including the principal at the high school and the math teacher — the short guy."

"She got around," Dylan agreed. "I'm not getting a violent vibe off of any of those guys. The principal's a prick but I don't see him being dangerous. The math teacher's a wimp. Not only that, she's bigger than he is. She could probably have beaten his ass by herself."

Alex grinned halfway. "I noticed that too. So what about this Sutter woman? It sounds like we're back to her."

"It looks that way." Dylan thought about Baylie Sutter again. There was something about her that had gotten his attention. The day before, in the hallway of the school when the McClain kid had been hassling her, his protective instincts had come out. She was a tiny thing, barely over five feet tall. Her blonde hair hung in curly swirls, just past her shoulders. There was something endearing about those eyes of hers. They were round and blue and full of mistrust. Mistrust and fear.

"So you think we should keep her covered?"

Dylan was thoughtful. "Probably for the time being. After reading her file, it looks like what's happening here right now is just about identical to what happened back in Chapman. Her co-workers started disappearing first. It's like history repeating itself." He frowned.

"What?" Alex asked.

"I don't know where to start looking for Kevin Bledsoe," he finally admitted, leaning back in his chair. "He wanted her to know he's out there. So where is he?"

"Somewhere close."

Seattle had a huge population. The guy was probably blending right in with the rest of the crazies. That was the problem with big cities. Dylan stared at the computer screen again. "Where is he getting money? If he's been on the run all this time, he's managed to get some kind of gainful employment or he'd be living on the streets."

Alex nodded in agreement. Then he sat up straight. "What better place for a crazy to blend in? Maybe that's exactly where he's hiding out. In plain sight."

Dylan had to admit the idea had merit. He grabbed the snapshot of Kevin Bledsoe and stood up. "Maybe we need to take a little walk through some shelters and see what we come up with."

Alex didn't look excited. "Don't you think that's like looking for a needle in a haystack?"

"Maybe. It's better than doing nothing though."

By the next morning, Baylie's nerves were completely frazzled. She managed to shower and make a pot of coffee. Part of her wanted to pull the covers over her head and stay in bed for the day, or maybe even for the week. But that would be like sealing her own fate again and she couldn't let herself do that.

Pouring herself a steaming cup of brew, she grabbed her bags. Upon exiting her house, she noticed the officer in the marked Crown Victoria gave her a wave and waited as she backed up out of her driveway. He then pulled in behind her and followed her all the way to the high school. She was glad when he pulled in front of her and took a turn to circle the building, leaving her alone to get out of her car. At least he didn't look like he was stuck to her like glue. She didn't know if that was a good thing or a bad thing. She knew Kevin was out there watching her. Had he watched Giselle the same way? She shoved the notion aside. Detective Stone was right. It wasn't going to do her any good to keep reliving that phone message. Whoever had been on the line was out of her reach.

Taking a deep breath, Baylie opened her car door and climbed out of her car. She made her way to the front doors of the high school quickly. She didn't breathe comfortably until she was inside, safe and sound. Or so she thought.

"Well, well, if it isn't Ms. Sutter," a snarly voice said, nearly scaring her out of her wits. She knew it was Jeepers McClain before the boy even stepped out of the shadows. This time he was alone. Apparently his friends didn't get up this early, or had better things to do than lurk in the shadows of a school building in the early hours of the morning.

"What are you doing in here? It's before seven."

"I have detention, thanks to you."

She hadn't given him detention. In fact, she hadn't even reported the incident from the day before. She knew how things with Jeepers worked and it just wasn't worth the effort it took to get him reprimanded.

"Apparently your boyfriend had words with the principal and my dear old dad. I didn't figure you for someone who would fuck a pig."

Stone. She narrowed her eyes as Jeepers stepped toward her. It was sad that he was so angry at the world because he really was a nice looking boy. She reminded herself that Ted Bundy had been nice looking too. He had also been a teenage boy once.

"Don't look so scared, Baylie," he said, drawing out her first name with a smile. "I like that name a lot. It's cute. It fits you."

"If you're in detention, I suggest you go back there. You shouldn't be out here in the hall."

Jeepers continued to smile. "I'm on a bathroom pass. Don't worry. No one will miss me." He reached out a hand and this time, no long arm intercepted his fingers. They drifted down her cheek and then came together to clamp against her chin. "I don't like being messed with, Ms. Sutter. Not by you and not by some pig."

Baylie tried to back up, for the first time actually a little scared of the kid. She'd never really thought he'd do her harm until that moment. "Don't do anything you're going to regret, Hobart." The words were lame, considering they were alone in the hallway, but she said them anyway.

His smile died but he didn't step away. Instead, he leaned his head toward her and blew a breath in her ear. "I would never regret us, Ms. Sutter. Not in a million years. You're the golden ticket, don't you know? I'd do just about anything to get into your panties."

"McClain, what the hell are you doing?"

Baylie felt relief flow over her at the sound of Principal Harris's voice. She jerked her chin lose from Jeepers McClain's grasp and stepped back quickly. Jeepers grinned at her widely then turned to the principal, who was frowning intently.

"Nothing, Sir. Just saying good morning to Ms. Sutter. I offered to carry her books but she said she didn't need any help. I was just heading back to detention like a good little boy."

Baylie watched as Principal Harris glared at the boy. "Move faster," he suggested.

"Sure thing, Sir." Jeepers winked at Baylie for good measure, then sauntered off down the hallway.

"Ms. Sutter, I'd like to see you in my office."

Baylie felt her relief evaporate like water on a hot burner. She had no choice but to follow the principal down the hall and into the front office. When they were seated in his office, he frowned at her. "You apparently have made quite an impression on Hobart McClain."

She wasn't sure what he meant by impression, so she shrugged her shoulders. "He's somewhat of a problem around here. I've had several run-ins with him now and he makes me uncomfortable."

"Is that so? Just what kind of *run-ins* required you to involve the police department?"

Frowning, she straightened. "I didn't involve the police department, Principal Harris. They involved themselves. Detective Stone was in the hallway yesterday when Hobart McClain accosted me. He intervened."

Harris's face paled. He clearly didn't like the sound of this news. "Well, the boy has been reprimanded for his behavior. We don't tolerate such insubordination among our students around here. His parents were notified. He has been removed from your class and is subject to a week's detention. Now I'm asking you to stay away from him."

As if she went looking for Jeepers on her own. "I merely came to work, Mr. Harris. Jeepers confronted me again."

Harris folded his arms in front of him and stared at Baylie stiffly. "Phillip McClain is a very prominent member of this community, Ms. Sutter. I don't think I need to tell you that any problems with his son can bring about some very bad media. None of us want that, if you get my drift."

Just as she had figured, Principal Harris was in Phillip McClain's pocket. At this point she figured she had bigger problems so she only nodded her head.

"You won't have any further issues with the boy then?"

Was he really blaming this on her? She raised a brow when he continued staring at her. Clearly, he was. Visions of Chapman came back to haunt her and she shoved them away. Standing up, she gathered her things. "If that's all, I need to get to my classroom. I have a test to prepare for my students."

"One more thing—just so you know. I'm aware of your background. I would be very cautious of what I was doing around here, Ms. Sutter. We are all about second chances here in the great city of Seattle. But we have our limitations. We don't want trouble. It appears to me that you might possibly have brought some of that with you when you moved here. If the safety of my students becomes in jeopardy, I won't hesitate to act. Do I make myself clear?"

Knowing she had no choice, Baylie nodded. She didn't know if the police had talked to Harris already, or if he'd obtained her information on his own. She supposed it didn't really matter. The school district had known about her past when they had hired her. It was public knowledge.

Once she was back in her classroom, she sat down at her desk and rested her head in her hands. She had to pull herself together. Jeepers had managed to put her on Principal Harris's radar and now she would likely stay there until he found an actual reason to fire her.

"I tried calling you. Where the hell have you been?" Rob asked, stepping into the classroom and letting her door shut with a slam.

"I was in the office," she answered, not really in the mood for one of Rob's woe is me tales.

"Have you talked to Susan yet this morning?"

"I just got here, Rob. I haven't talked to anyone but Principal Harris and Jeepers McClain."

Rob grimaced. "I heard you finally managed to get the little shit some detention. Nice going."

How had word traveled that fast? She hadn't even known herself that she'd gotten Jeepers in trouble. Shaking her head, she forced herself to sit up straight and reach for the bottle of aspirin she kept in her right hand drawer.

"Is she really angry with me?"

"Who?" Baylie asked absently, popping two pills into her mouth and downing a few slugs of lukewarm coffee.

"Susan!" Rob exclaimed, clearly at his wits end at this point. "After we went to the police station last night, we got into a big fight. I dropped her off at home so she could cool off." He leaned against Baylie's desk, his brow furrowed. "She's got a lot of nerve being so angry with me. She was seeing other people too."

"I think we've already determined that she's angry with you for *sleeping* with other people, not *seeing* them." Baylie went to work pulling out the morning's reading assignment. First period was only a few minutes away and she was behind in her preparation. She wished Rob and Susan would leave her out of their newly public relationship troubles. She had more than enough problems of her own.

"I get that fact," Rob muttered. "I thought for sure she'd end up at your place last night. I've never seen her so angry."

"I didn't see her," she answered. She neglected to mention to him that she hadn't seen anyone but the police the night before. Better to keep that on the lowdown until she couldn't deny it anymore.

"You don't think she called in, do you?"

"Maybe she did. Maybe she's sick or tired. It was late when you guys were at my place. If you were up half the night, it's logical that she would need some extra rest this morning. Or maybe she just doesn't want to see you right now." She ignored the spark of irritation that flashed in his eyes.

"You think she'd call in to school to avoid me?" He looked generally perplexed.

Actually, Baylie didn't think that. Susan was one of those take the bull by the horns type of women. And Rob Barnes wasn't that good of a catch. It didn't seem likely that Susan would be that angry with someone she'd only been casually sleeping with. But what did Baylie know? Hell, she wasn't an expert on women and men, that was for sure. "Listen, Rob, school's about to start. I really need to get this stuff sorted out. Maybe you should just go call her."

"And have her rip me a new you know what again? I don't think so." He turned away from her. "If you talk to her, put in a good word for me, would you?"

"Why should I?" Baylie asked, before she could stop herself.

Rob glared at her. "We weren't exclusive."

"Maybe she thought you were when it came to sex."

He didn't dignify that with an answer. Instead, he turned abruptly and walked out of the room.

Clearly, he was angry with her too. Oh well, stand in line, she thought to herself.

Hours later, when the final bell had rung, Baylie gathered her things and headed for her car. She wanted nothing more than to take a hot bath and soak her troubles away for the time being. The bad thing was, she wasn't sure going home was the best idea for her. Kevin was still out there and he still knew where she lived. The thought made her skin crawl.

As it turned out, fate had other ideas for her evening anyway. The minute she reached her vehicle, she was accosted by Detective Dylan Stone. He was leaning against her SUV, dressed in his usual attire of black slacks and a white button up shirt. She figured he must have the same outfit clean and ready for each of the five business days of the week. Either that or he hadn't been home and changed in two days.

"Detective," she said, clicking her key pad to unlock her door. "This is a surprise. Are you here to escort me home?"

His somber expression caused her to frown. "What's wrong?"

"I have some bad news for you, Ms. Sutter. I'm going to need you to come with me."

Baylie stared at him dumbly. "God, you found her didn't you? You found Giselle."

He reached for her hand and took her key pad from her, zapping the locks back into place. "We did find a body. I need you to come downtown now. You can ride with me."

"I don't want to. I want to drive my own car," she snapped, knowing she was being irrational, but unable to help herself. She knew what he was going to say. They had found Giselle Lindsay, and she was dead. So why wouldn't he just say the words, damn it!

"We need to talk, Baylie. If you want, you can follow me downtown, but I think it would be better if you just ride with me. I'll bring you back for your car later."

"If she's dead, just tell me. Stop trying to sugarcoat things."

He met her gaze. "I don't know whether Giselle Lindsay is dead or alive. The body we found wasn't hers."

She narrowed her eyes. "What do you mean?"

He sighed and lowered his voice. "It was a man, Baylie. And if my hunch is right, I'm pretty sure it belonged to Kevin Bledsoe. He was murdered."

FIVE

Dylan Stone had seen more than one dead body in his time. He'd been a marine. He'd fought in wars where men and women were literally blown to shreds in front of his face. Still, the sight of Kevin Bledsoe's badly beaten body, lying broken in a drainage ditch, only a mile from the last homeless shelter that he and Alex had scoured that morning, had been a lot to stomach. The man had been beaten to a pulp, his lifeless blue eyes staring up into thin air as though mesmerized by something. A jogger had found him. It seemed like joggers always managed to be the first to stumble upon human destruction. Typically that meant more than one problem. Usually their puke managed to contaminate the crime scene. Their DNA was always everywhere. It created somewhat of a pain for forensics. But nothing they didn't always manage to muddle through.

The ride to the police station had been a silent one. Baylie Sutter sat in his unmarked cruiser, her eyes staring emotionless and straight-ahead. He didn't know if he should be concerned about that or not. In a way, she had to be feeling relief. A man who had tormented her was likely finally dead. Of course, they wouldn't have absolute proof of this fact until DNA or a positive ID was done. That's where Baylie came in.

"We need you to ID him," he said, breaking the news he knew she wasn't going to want to hear.

She blanched, snapping out of her trance. "Me? Why?"

"Because you're the closest thing to next of kin we have. We called his mother in Helena. She wasn't interested. Apparently, she's already tried and convicted him. She's too far away anyway. You'll be quicker."

"I haven't seen him in two years."

"Chances are you'll recognize him."

She didn't reply to that, she just stared out the window at the passing scenery.

"I wouldn't ask you to do this if it weren't necessary."

"Wouldn't you?" she asked, not even glancing at him. "I'm just a person on your case. A stranger you distrust."

The words cut him more than he wanted them to. The truth was, she'd gotten under his skin the night before. He'd read her file and he knew she had not another soul in the world that she could call family. She'd been a kid lost in the system from the time

70

she was too small to know any different. After going out on her own she'd hit more bad circumstances. She'd hooked up with Kevin Bledsoe and he'd brought her to her knees again. It didn't seem fair. She needed someone to be her ally. "I'm not out to get you, Baylie."

"Aren't you, *Dylan*?" She said his name a little crassly and he frowned.

"I've tried to help you."

She remained silent. He figured there wasn't much more he could say at this point. She had a blatant distrust of law enforcement and that had stemmed from her past. There wasn't anything he could do about that for the moment.

Once they reached the medical examiner's office, Dylan led her into the building and down a long staircase into the basement. It took only a moment for them to be ushered into the chamber that held the remains they'd found earlier that morning. Dylan watched Baylie's reaction carefully as the M.E. pulled the white sheet back, exposing the dead man's face to her view. She surprised him by just staring at it. No gasp, not even a blink. For a minute, he thought his hunch had been wrong. Maybe this wasn't Kevin Bledsoe after all. But then she spoke, her voice low and even.

"It's him." She turned on her heel and left the room without comment, leaving him staring behind her with narrow-eyed interest.

When Baylie reached the hallway, she lifted a hand up and braced it against the wall for support. She could still see Kevin's lifeless blue eyes staring up at her from that table. His lips had been blue and thin, his skin a pasty gray color. Bruises and cuts had covered his face. The last time she'd seen him he'd been tan and full of life. He'd been handsome. Taking a deep breath, she straightened. The door to the chamber opened and Stone stepped out, his gaze landing on hers immediately.

"Are you okay?"

"I'm fine. Can I go now?"

He frowned at her, his hands in his pockets again. "Not just yet. We need to have a talk, don't you think?"

She didn't want to talk to him. Or anyone else. She wanted to go home and be alone. Kevin was dead now and she had no one to fear anymore. At least she kept trying to tell herself that.

"Kevin Bledsoe is dead, Baylie. Don't you think that warrants a little discussion?"

"So we're on a permanent first name basis now?" She glared up at him, her stomach still somewhat unsettled from the sight of Kevin's dead body.

He snorted. "Okay, I can keep this completely formal if you want me to. I'm trying to make this easier for you."

"Well you're not. Now what do you want to know? I didn't kill him if that's what you're wondering."

"I didn't think you had," he said, taking a step toward the staircase.

She knew she had no choice but to follow. She wasn't about to hang out down here with dead bodies.

"Given his injuries, it took a person of considerable size to inflict them."

His words gave her pause. "Meaning what?"

"Meaning that a man probably did it." They reached the top of the staircase and he turned to her. "You may have been right about the final caller last night being different from the first. It appears you have more than one psycho on your tail."

She forced her expression to remain neutral. She didn't want to panic. At the same time, the idea that she had gotten rid of one crazy man in her life, only to replace him with another, did not thrill her.

"You're in danger, Baylie. I don't know how this is all leading back to you, but I have a bad feeling that it is. I think it started before you met Bledsoe."

"That's ridiculous. My life was fine until I met that jerk." She glared up at him. "Just because you read a case file on me, doesn't make you an expert on my life."

"I know you were a kid in the system. Let's start by talking about that."

73

"I don't want to talk about it." She stormed past him and out into the cool night air. Naturally, she didn't get far. He followed immediately. She wished she had her own car to hop into but she didn't. Instead, she was forced to ride with him again.

"I'll take you to your car eventually. But if I were you, I'd consider the facts here. People around you have been disappearing for years, and turning up dead. That's a bit concerning, isn't it?"

"The police tied the murders to Kevin," she said, though even to her, the words sounded lame. "He knew one of the victims." She avoided his gaze and went to work pulling her seatbelt over her. It was stuck and she had to yank several times. Still it didn't move. Once he'd slid into the driver's seat, he reached over her, in far too close proximity, and gave the belt a yank. Immediately it freed and he was able to clasp it easily. She looked up at him just as he looked down at her. Their eyes locked for several seconds and she was surprised to feel her heart hammer loudly inside her chest. Not only that, her stomach did something suspiciously similar to a somersault. Immediately she stiffened. He did the same and backed away from her. Neither spoke for a moment. Finally, he broke the silence when he started up the car. The police scanner came to life with a screech, making her jump.

"There are a lot of reasons that the police could have tied Kevin Bledsoe to those murders. For one thing, he was tied to you and so were all those women. Even if he did date one of them at one time, that doesn't mean much. Chapman is a smaller city. It's more than likely that everyone crossed paths with everyone else at one time or another, don't you think?"

He pulled out into traffic, clearly avoiding her gaze. She didn't like what he was insinuating. Naturally, he had everything tossed back into her lap again. "Who would be doing this to me? Do you have any theories about that?"

"Do you?" he countered.

"I already told you I don't." She found herself thinking about Kevin's lifeless eyes again and her stomach rolled in a very bad way. The idea that he had been murdered was disturbing, even if she had hated his guts in the end.

"I think you need to stop limiting yourself to one theory — that being Kevin." He pulled the car to a quick stop in front of the police station.

"You said you would take me back to my car."

"If you cooperate with us, I will. First we have some questions for you."

Of course he had lied to get her to do what he wanted. She should have known better than to trust him, not that she'd had any choice. "I don't have anything further to add, Detective. Don't you think I would have already said something if I did?"

"To be honest with you, I don't know what to think." He undid his seatbelt. "The fact that you barely blanched at the sight of a dead body has me intrigued."

Surprised, she met his gaze. He had an intent look on his face that reminded her of a Pitbull going after a bone. "What are you talking about?"

"I'm talking about the fact that you didn't even blink. Most civilians would lose it when seeing something that terrible for the first time."

"You see things like that every day. Do you pass out every time?"

"Not only am I a cop, but I was a marine in combat. I've seen more than my share of dead bodies in my time. My point is that as a teacher, you have not." He continued staring her down and she was determined not to blink first. Finally, he caved in and spoke. "Or have you?"

His words made her angry and she scowled. "Of course I haven't   I've never seen a dead person before."

He grimaced as his cell phone vibrated. He checked the ID, then reached over and unclasped her seatbelt for her. "I have more questions for you. You're going to need to come inside with me."

"And if I refuse?"

"Then I can get a warrant and haul you in as a person of interest. Either way, I'll get my questions answered."

She didn't like the sounds of that. Irritated and emotionally spent, she climbed out of the cruiser and followed him up the walk to the large brick building. She followed him through a series of cubicles and into an office, where a man she recognized as his partner was seated behind a large desk. When Alex Sinclair saw her behind Dylan, his face broke into an interested smile.

"Nice to see you again, Ms. Sutter."

"Detective Sinclair." Baylie had only spoken with Sinclair sporadically over the last couple of days and she wasn't in the mood for his smug attitude now. It rankled on her nerves more than Stone's did.

"We've got an ID. It's Bledsoe," Stone said.

Sinclair let out a whistle. "No surprise there. We've got another issue. Can I see you in the hallway?"

Baylie didn't miss the look that passed between the two detectives. Clearly this was something they couldn't talk about in front of her. She glowered at them, but flopped down in an empty chair. "Don't mind me. I'll just hang out here and file my nails."

Sinclair raised a brow as he stood up. The two men disappeared from the room. A moment later, they were back. Stone's face looked grim. Far more grim than it had earlier, if that were possible. She waited for him to speak. Instead, he set a Styrofoam cup full of coffee down in front of her and then took the spot Sinclair had been in moments earlier, behind the desk. Sinclair stood in a corner of the room, obviously giving his partner the floor.

Startled, Baylie sat up straight. "What's going on?"

"When was the last time you saw Susan Hanover?"

The words seeped into her head and she felt bile climb into her throat. "Last night, why?"

"Because someone just found a vehicle registered to her abandoned near I90. Is there any reason you can think of why she would abandon her car that way?"

"Only if it was disabled," she said quickly. She knew there was no way Susan would leave her car on the side of the freeway for no reason. What rational person would?

"It wasn't disabled. The door was wide open and her purse was inside. It's on its way to Impound right now. It was tagged the first time around three this morning."

Baylie instantly felt sick to her stomach. Nothing could have happened to Susan. She'd just seen her. Not twelve hours ago, she'd been sitting with her in her living room.

"Get her some water," Stone's voice said.

"I don't need any water." She looked up at him. "Did you talk to Rob?"

"Barnes? Yes, last night. And apparently tonight again after her car was found." Stone sat back and stared at her. "They didn't come right out and admit to anything but it was pretty clear they had a thing going. Are you suggesting he may have something to do with her disappearing?"

Was she? Hell, she didn't know Rob well enough to vouch for him either way. Truth be told, she didn't know Susan well enough to vouch for her either. "I don't know," she finally said. "I know they had a fight last night. He told me that this morning. She didn't show up to work."

Stone looked up at his partner. "Bring Barnes in again."

Sinclair nodded and disappeared. When the door had shut behind him, Baylie leaned forward, her head in her hands, determined not to look into the skeptical eyes of Dylan Stone.

"Your acquaintances seem to be disappearing at a rather alarming rate, don't you think?" he said quietly.

She didn't argue with him. She was thinking the same thing. This was the way things had happened before, back in Chapman. Only now, Kevin was dead — one of the victims.

"We need to look into your past, Baylie."

"Which part?" she asked, finally lifting her head. "I lived in numerous foster homes over the years."

He didn't answer right away. "We start with what you remember and work our way back."

"Okay," she relented, less than enthusiastic. She'd done her best to rid herself of the painful memories from her childhood.

"In the meantime, I don't need to tell you how careful you need to be."

"Because I'm being watched," she figured aloud, her stomach pitching again.

"I'd love to say I don't think so but I'd be lying. I have no bodies here. That's making this hard for me. With no bodies, I can't prove any crime has been committed against these women."

"Only Kevin."

"At this point, yes." He leaned back in his chair. "It will take a while to rule that officially. We need the autopsy report back to determine cause of death."

"What are you trying to tell me, Detective?" She had a bad feeling she knew.

"I'm trying to tell you that I can't put a uniform on your house tonight, officially."

Officially. What did that mean? "Are you trying to tell me that I'm a sitting duck again?"

He grimaced. "You have a way with words."

"That's what it is, isn't it? You told me last night that if I cooperated, you would make sure I was safe. Now you're telling me you can't. I've heard this all before." She stood up.

"Running will only put you in more danger."

"How would you know?" She shook her head at him. "I'm very good at disappearing, Detective. I've done it more than once."

"If he has Susan, and you run, he'll kill her."

"If that's the case, and he has Giselle too, where is she? He hasn't killed her yet. What makes you think he will?"

He leaned against his desk, his expression drawn. "The fact that she hasn't come home."

She wanted to kick him even though she knew he was right. Instead, she spun on her heel and stormed out of the office.

SIX

Dylan watched her storm off. He considered going after her but Alex walked through the door she'd vacated, a whistle sliding from between his teeth.

"Boy, you've charmed the crap out of her. What's your secret?"

Dylan ignored him.

"Seriously, Stone. Why does she hate you so much? Or is it the opposite?"

Dylan didn't dignify that with a comment. He did, however, think about the moment they'd shared in his car when he'd helped her with her seatbelt. He was a cop, but he was also a man. He hadn't missed the current of electricity that had passed between them in those few short seconds when they'd stared into each other's eyes. He was used to having reactions to attractive women. He was a warm-blooded male, after all. But he wasn't used to having a reaction to someone so close to a case he was working. Yet again, he also reminded himself that she was not his type. He liked leggy brunettes with curves, not tiny blondes with curly hair.

"Yo, Dylan. What gives? You're thinking something here."

Dylan met Alex's gaze. "The only thing I know for sure is that she's in danger."

Alex was quiet a moment. "Chief said no more protection. Not until we have something more concrete. M.E. won't have a report until tomorrow at least."

"I know that." Dylan shoveled some papers together. He included Baylie's case files in the pile.

"Where are you going with those?"

"My house." Dylan didn't have to look at Alex to know he was frowning. He and Alex were too close for Alex not to read between the lines and know where Dylan was going with this. Dylan didn't give a crap enough to deny it. He'd promised to keep Baylie Sutter safe, and that was exactly what he was going to do.

"You're going to fuck this up, aren't you?"

"She's in danger."

"You can't take her home with you. I know that look. Don't think with your dick."

He ignored the remark. He knew Alex was right, he shouldn't take Baylie home. But he would, if it was the only way to keep her safe. "I'll handle her.

Just question Barnes and see what you can find out about Susan Hanover. I'll keep my phone on."

Alex swore. "If Chief gets a hold of this he'll have our asses."

Dylan headed for the door. That was a chance he was just going to have to take.

Baylie wanted to run. She'd gotten halfway down the block and then she'd stopped. It was nearly nine o'clock at night and it was pitch dark out, even near the police station. Sure, there were people milling around, but they were all strangers to her. It had taken her thirty seconds to turn around and head back to Stone's unmarked cruiser. When he walked outside, she was leaning against it impatiently. He didn't look surprised that she was still there. The bastard.

"Come on."

She straightened as he headed down the block toward a parking lot. "Where are we going?"

"I don't take official vehicles home. I'm parked over here." He led her through the lot to a black Dodge 4x4 truck.

She waited as he unlocked the door. "Before I get in, I want to know if you're taking me to my car."

He let out a sound of exasperation. "Is that what you want? To go home to your empty house and sit there alone for the rest of the night?"

"What choice do I have?"

He reached around her and tossed a pile of paperwork into the cab of his truck. "I'm off duty right now. What I do on my own personal time is my choice."

She wasn't sure what he was trying to say. "Okay."

"I'm telling you that if you want my protection, you've got it. *Unofficially.*"

Her eyes widened. Now this was something she hadn't expected.

"Are you going to get in, or not?"

Without a word, she climbed into the cab of the truck. He slammed the door shut behind her. When he climbed in next to her, she looked over at him. "Why are you doing this?"

He started the engine then ripped his seatbelt across his front. "Because I made you a promise and I don't make promises that I don't keep."

She mulled that over as he pulled out of the parking lot.

"Do I have to fasten your seatbelt again?"

The words startled her. She quickly reached for the seatbelt and yanked it over her. "You're going to get in trouble for this, aren't you?"

He didn't answer right away. "Maybe," he finally said, taking a sharp right turn that nearly sent her flying into his lap. "If anyone besides Alex finds out."

She grabbed hold of the door handle and clasped it tightly. She couldn't think of a thing to say to that so she stayed quiet. No one had ever cared enough about her to step in and put their own ass on the line. Dylan Stone was doing just that. She didn't know how to react to him suddenly. She'd grown used to sparring with him. Now she would have to be nice.

"This doesn't change what I need from you," he said, breaking the silence. "We're going to spend a lot of time pouring over your past. Day and night, until we figure this mess out."

She grimaced at that. "And if I don't have any light to shed on that?"

"You will." He whipped his truck down her street and screeched to a halt in her driveway. He cut the engine and looked over at her. "Get a couple of days' worth of clothes and whatever toiletries you'll need. We need to make this quick." He climbed out of the truck before she could protest.

"Wait a minute!" she snapped, jumping down out of the truck. "Where are you taking me? And what about my car?"

He strode up to the porch and waited for her to follow and unlock the door.

Begrudgingly, she followed him. "You can't force me to go somewhere else, Dylan."

He surprised her by grinning down at her. "Good, you're finally past the detective crap." He pushed past her once she'd unlocked the door. She watched him take a good look around. Then he ushered her inside. "Go to it. I'll wait here. And as for your car, it will be fine for the night. I'll drop you at school in the morning on my way to work."

"Where are you taking me?" she repeated, refusing to move.

"I'm taking you to my place, where I can keep an eye on you."

She took the words in and digested them. His place. As in, *his house.*

"Don't overanalyze this. I told you before, I made you a promise and I intend to keep it. The only way I can do that is by keeping you with me for the time being." He gave her a gentle shove toward her bedroom. "Check your answering machine and let me know if you have any messages."

Annoyed, she glared at him over her shoulder. "This doesn't seem like a very good idea."

"Do you have a better one? Like maybe you staying here by yourself?"

No, she didn't want to do that. "Why can't you sit in your truck outside?"

His eyes narrowed. "You mean all night, in the cold?"

Okay, so that was asking a lot. "It's not that cold. That patrolman did it last night."

"He was being paid. I'm not on duty." He checked his vibrating phone absently, then scowled at her again. "Just don't argue for a change and get going. I need to get home."

For a moment, she pondered the idea that he might have a wife at home. Or maybe he had kids. He was probably in his early thirties, definitely old enough to have a family of his own. But he didn't wear a ring. She'd noticed that right off.

"I'm waiting," his voice said impatiently from the living room.

She forced herself to head for her bedroom. None of his personal life really mattered right then because he was all she had. She would have to learn to trust him, whether she wanted to or not.

By the time she checked her answering machine and determined there were no new messages, packed up a few different outfits and gathered some necessities, he was chomping at the bit. Clearly, this man was not big on patience. He all but herded her out of her own house, making double sure that she locked the door behind them. On the way to his house, he whipped them through a McDonalds drive thru, to her chagrin. She hated McDonalds. She hated all fast food. Judging by the number of items he ordered from the menu, he didn't share her distaste for deep fried grease. By the time they drove into his upper scale neighborhood it was after ten and she was tired and cranky.

He lived in a newer development near Queen Ann. His house was decent sized and two stories. He drove into the garage and pulled the truck to a stop, quick to push the garage button and lower the door behind him.

Baylie climbed out of the truck while he grabbed her bags and their food, along with his huge stack of papers. He led her through an entry door and into a large kitchen. When he flipped on the lights, it took her a moment to adjust to the now well-lit room. But when she did, her jaw dropped. The kitchen was probably the most state of the art kitchen she'd ever been in. It was tastefully decorated in yellows and blues. Sparkling white tile covered the floor, along with what looked like brand new stainless steel appliances. It was hardly what she would have expected from a bachelor. Again, she had a niggling fear that there was a Mrs. Stone lurking around somewhere. Either that or maybe he was gay.

She looked up at him. He was scanning a pile of mail that was left on the counter. She wasn't buying the gay thing. He was far too masculine to be gay. Wasn't he? Not only that, she'd seen the blatant interest in his eyes in the car earlier. Or maybe she had imagined it.

"What are you looking at?"

His question startled her. "Nothing," she answered quickly.

"My sister is an interior designer," he said, setting the bag of food down on the counter. "I had her do the house when I bought it."

"Your sister."

He frowned at her. "Yes, I have a sister. A twin, actually. She lives in Bellevue."

She tried to picture what his twin sister would look like. It was a hard stretch to make from his masculine features, to similar feminine ones.

"I'm going to go change. I can show you the guest room on the way if you want." He was already yanking his tie off as he spoke. Then he was walking down a hallway, leaving her no choice but to follow. "Bathroom downstairs is on the left of the kitchen. Upstairs it's the second door on the right."

She followed him up the stairs and down another hallway. He opened up a door and set her duffel bag inside the room. Then he flipped on the light. Like the kitchen, the room was very tastefully decorated, this time in a nice beige color. There were pictures of nature scenes on the walls. She stared at them, and then looked back at him. He was watching her curiously. Slowly, he backed up into the hallway.

"I'll meet you downstairs in ten minutes. I need a shower. You can start eating without me if you want." He disappeared before she could respond. A moment later she heard a shower turn on. He was a hard one to figure out. She guessed that came in handy, given his line of work.

Digging into her duffel, she pulled out a pair of sweats and a t-shirt. She was happy to kick off her heels and get into some comfortable slippers instead. Once she was changed, she turned off the light and headed down the hallway. She was curious how his bedroom was decorated. She just couldn't imagine him looking at pictures of nature every night. But then she didn't know him. Maybe he was a nature freak.

Once she was back downstairs, she took in the rest of the first floor. There were some double doors off the stairs that probably opened to an office, though she didn't feel comfortable snooping at that point. Next to that was the bathroom he'd told her about. And finally, there was a large great room, just off the kitchen. Now this room looked like what she pictured a man-cave to look like, large screen television and all.

She walked back into the kitchen and in spite of her hatred of good old Mickey D's, she opened up the bag and pulled out a carton of fries. She stared at them for a moment, still unable to completely vanquish the image of Kevin's death filled eyes and pasty skin from her head. She took a bite of one and grimaced. It tasted like cardboard.

"You want something to drink?" His voice startled her. He walked into the kitchen and she almost didn't recognize him. He was dressed casually now, in jeans and a Seattle PD t-shirt. His feet were bare and his hair was still damp. He hadn't shaved. His cheeks were spattered with five o'clock shadow. Damn it, he was appealing. He was more than appealing. He was hot.

He looked over at her, a bottle of water in his hand as if in offering. She forced herself to nod and he slid it down the counter to her, before grabbing a can of Coke for himself. Then he settled across from her as though it were the most natural thing in the world, and went to work pawing through the food bags. She just watched, in awe, as he polished off not only one double quarter pounder, but two. A container of fries followed.

He finally noticed her watching him and frowned in mid-chew. "What?"

"You have the worst eating habits of anyone I've ever seen."

After a moment, he grinned. "Really? Coming from you, that's probably a compliment."

She frowned. "It's not."

He didn't seem fazed. Instead, he crumpled up the garbage left over from his meal and emptied it into a trash can under the sink. Then he sat down across from her again.

"With a kitchen as nice as this, I can't believe you eat that way instead of cooking." She spoke her observation aloud, even though she knew it was rude and presumptuous. So what. He was rude and presumptuous too.

He shrugged his shoulders. "In case it's escaped your attention, I work a lot. Gourmet meals don't fit into my schedule very often."

"I take it a wife doesn't either?" Once the words were out, she wanted them back, but of course it was too late.

He took a long swallow of Coke as he met her gaze. "Are you fishing to find out if I'm married or not?"

She narrowed her eyes. "Of course not. Clearly you aren't."

He raised a brow. "What makes you think so? Maybe she's away visiting relatives."

"Your sister wouldn't be decorating your house if you had a wife," she reasoned, taking a sip of water. "Besides, you don't wear a ring."

"I guess you have a point. A lot of the time, cops and wives don't mix."

"Why is that?" She didn't know why she was encouraging this topic, but she found she was interested. That should have worried her but she forced herself not to think so hard.

"Because cops work around the clock and wives don't like to be alone that much. Anything else you want to know?"

"You said you have a twin sister," she said, wanting to keep the conversation carefully away from herself and her past. "Does she look like you?"

He leaned back in his chair. "I guess so. Enough anyway. This isn't going to work, you know. We're still going to talk about you."

"We've been talking about me for days. I need a reprieve."

He appeared to think that over. "Okay. For a few minutes anyway. What do you want to know?"

She hadn't expected him to readily agree. "Do you have any other brothers or sisters?" she asked, for lack of anything better. "And where are your parents? Still living around here? Is this where you grew up?"

He stared at her for several seconds then snorted. "You cut right to the chase, don't you?"

"You said I could ask."

"I guess I did." He crumpled up his Coke can, then tossed it across the kitchen and into a blue recycling bin. "I have an older brother and an older sister, besides my twin. She's ten minutes younger, by the way. I grew up in Spokane. My parents still live there."

So he came from a big family. She'd always wondered what that would be like. She'd had a myriad of foster siblings but none had left a lasting impression on her life. Neither had any of her foster parents.

"So how did you end up in the system?"

94

She'd known the question was coming. She was surprised it had taken him this long to ask. "My parents died in a fire when I was little." She avoided looking at him. She didn't want to see the pity in his eyes that she knew would be there.

"That's tough. Do you remember them at all?"

She thought that over. The truth was, she didn't. There were times when she saw visions of people she imagined were her parents, but she had no pictures and no concrete proof that she was right. "I don't. So what's your sister's name? Your twin, I mean."

"Danica. I call her Danni. She's married and has a kid. A little terror she named Cody. He's a handful and a half but I love him to pieces."

She smiled, enjoying the topic of conversation. She tried to picture a dark haired little boy that looked a little bit like Dylan. It was hard to imagine him as a child. "What does he look like?"

"Little blond tow-head. He pretty much looks like I did as a kid. Mirror image."

"You were blond?"

"Bleached blond. Didn't turn dark until I was five or six." He folded his arms over his chest and studied her warily. "Can you walk me through the names of your foster families?"

She had expected this question also. "I don't remember some of them. Only the last few. I lived with a family named Silcox from the time I was fourteen until I was sixteen and moved out on my own. Before that, I lived with the Claxtons for a year or two. They moved to Tampa and didn't have room for me." She didn't look up to see the pity she knew would be in his eyes. She'd seen pity enough times in her life. "Prior to that, I was with a family named Jones. They weren't interested in adopting, or anything long term, with a child my age. They wanted a baby. Anything before that is fuzzy for me."

He appeared to think that over. "Sixteen is young to be on your own. How old were you when your parents were killed?"

"They told me I was six. I don't remember. Like I said, they died in a fire." She got up and walked across the kitchen to the great room. There were a few family pictures over the gas fireplace and she took a minute to admire them.

"I'm sorry you've had it rough."

The soft tone to his voice startled her and she turned around. He was right behind her, his eyes full of that all familiar pity. "I didn't have such a rough time until later on in life. I was used to being shoved from home to home before that. It's all I knew."

"That doesn't make it right."

"Maybe not. But there's nothing I can do to change the past. I came through it."

"And put yourself through college. That's impressive."

Impressive? Maybe. But probably worthless, considering the mess her professional life was in. She was on the verge of losing yet another teaching job. It seemed to be par for her course.

"You've had a string of bad luck. If we can get to the bottom of this maybe we can stop it."

"I don't know. I seem to have been dealt a bad hand from the get go. One bad thing replaces another." She knew she sounded self-pitying and she hated herself for it. She needed to be tough, the way she had her entire life. That was going to get her through things. It always had before.

"From what I've heard, you're a good teacher, Baylie. You're well respected among your peers."

She snorted at that. "Not according to Principal Harris. According to him my career has one foot in the grave." She looked up at him. "Just what did you say to Phillip McClain anyway?"

He frowned. "Why do you ask?"

"Because I had a run-in with Jeepers again this morning and found out he got detention. He's never had detention before. No teacher has managed to make punishment stick on that kid."

"You mean he retaliated on you this morning?" His eyes narrowed. "That little bastard!"

"He's a kid with an anger problem. The school system is filled with them. He just happens to have a father with power. That power is likely going to get me fired."

97

"They can't fire you for reporting his inappropriate behavior."

"Maybe not, but they can look for other reasons to fire me." He obviously didn't realize how this all worked. She knew first hand. When a place of employment wanted to get rid of you, they managed to find a way.

"The kid pissed me off." He frowned again. "Harris shouldn't be letting him run roughshod through that school."

"Apparently his father doesn't agree with that opinion." She leaned against the back of a large cushioned couch, folding her arms over her chest. "Jeepers and his friends do whatever they please. When they get caught, his father gets them out of it. It was nice of you to stick up for me though."

"For all the good it did. Did the little bastard hurt you?"

"He just did a little talking dirty to me. Nothing that left any bruises." Not really, she silently added. She was in no hurry to run into Jeepers again though. "They took him out of my class and asked me to stay away from him."

He swore vehemently. "Harris is a prick. A *cheating* prick. I know he was screwing Giselle Lindsay. He all but admitted it. He's worried about his career. He doesn't want a scandal."

"Is he a suspect?"

"Everyone's a suspect until we figure this out. We still don't have any confirmation that the person who took Giselle—if she was even taken at all—is the same person who killed Kevin Bledsoe. And we don't have proof that the woman on your answering machine screaming is Giselle. We're going on a lot of *what if's* here."

She watched him walk over and sit down on the couch. The pile of papers he'd brought in earlier was tossed on the coffee table. She knew she had to face the inevitable. She had to go back to her past.

Walking over, she sat down next to him, careful to keep a comfortable space between them.

"I have the names of your foster families. Would hearing them help?"

She doubted it, but she shrugged.

"You were right about Jones, Silcox and Claxton. The families before that were Rycroft, Eisenberg and Lomax—not necessarily in that order."

The names didn't ring a bell to her. She shook her head, causing his frown to deepen.

"Maybe one of them had a daughter named Nikki."

She supposed that was possible but she didn't remember one. "I don't think so."

"I'll have Alex look into it. Maybe he can dig deeper—find locations on some of these people and see what they're up to."

"Dylan, what if that doesn't lead us anywhere? What if this person means nothing to me? He could be a random stalker."

99

He shook his head. "He has something personal against you, Baylie. No one does something like this without a damned good reason. You've unfortunately led a complicated life so this may take us awhile to figure out. But we will."

She wished she was as sure as he was.

"I think for tonight, we need to get some sleep. I'm going on forty-eight straight hours of working and I doubt you slept last night much either. We need to do some re-charging here."

"And then what?" She stood up when he did and watched as he reached over and turned out the lamp next to the couch. When he straightened, their eyes locked. A very familiar shiver of awareness passed through her again and she wanted to kick herself. He was a cop, damn it! Why wasn't her body remembering that fact?

He didn't answer right away. Instead he continued to stare at her. Eventually he sighed. "Don't."

"Don't what?"

"You know what."

She didn't. She wasn't good with men and she had no idea what he was talking about.

He cursed. "I shouldn't have brought you here. It was a bad idea."

"I told you so."

"Stop looking at me like that."

"Like what?" she asked quietly, her eyes never leaving his. She didn't know why she wasn't turning tail and running—she just knew she couldn't. Not when the only time she felt safe was when he was with her.

He cursed again, making no move to step toward her. "What happened in the car was just a fluke thing."

"I don't know what you're talking about," she lied.

"You do too. I know you felt it too. But it's not going anywhere. This...thing. It's got to stop now."

She didn't know what to say to that so she didn't say anything.

This time he did take a step toward her. "You're part of my case. I could lose my job just for letting you stay here."

"I get it, Detective. I'm not asking you for anything but protection."

He took another step toward her. It was almost as if he were warning her to step back. She didn't. She waited until he was directly in front of her and his bare toes were touching the tops of her pink slippers. She could smell the scent of shampoo and soap on his skin. Involuntarily she leaned forward and inhaled.

He swore again and she felt his head bend toward her. He inhaled too. They just stood there like that for a while. She didn't know for exactly how long.

"You're going to have to walk away from me." His voice caused her eyes to open and she stared into the muscular plains of his t-shirt covered chest.

"Okay."

"Okay."

Neither of them moved.

He swore again, and this time he stepped around her, quickly putting distance between them. He was on the stairs before she could protest. "I'm in the room at the end of the hall. If you have a problem, holler."

She turned, still a little dazed, and watched him stand at the foot of the staircase. She knew now that he felt the same awareness as she did. But he was obviously going to fight it. She knew she needed to fight it too. Her life was mess enough without adding an affair to things. Especially an affair with the only person in the world who could help her at this point.

"I'll be fine," she forced herself to say. She hurried past him and up the stairs, determined to keep herself in check. This was a heat of the moment thing. It would pass. They were strangers after all. When this was all over they would be strangers again.

Once she was in the sanctity of the guest room she shut the door and leaned back against it. Only then did she let a tear fall from her eyelid and drift down her cheek.

SEVEN

Smoke filled Baylie's lungs and she couldn't breathe. Turning her head, she tried to run, but her feet were stuck to the floor like they were glued there. Terror rolled over her with anguish. She could hear screaming. It was coming from all around her. She put her hands over her ears, wanting to block it out. She had to escape. The heat was coming closer and closer. She looked around for a way to get out but there didn't seem to be any. That's when she saw her. There was a child trapped in a torrent of blazing flames. Her hair was blonde and her face was black with soot. She was crying, her arms reaching out for help...

Baylie sat up abruptly, struggling for breath. She almost felt like she could taste soot in her mouth. At first, she thought the room she was in was on fire. When her vision cleared, she realized that it wasn't. She was in the guest room of Dylan Stone's house, and besides the shadows made from the trees dancing in the moonlight outside the window, there was no movement at all. No flames, no soot. No little girl.

Wiping at the sweat on her brow, she whipped the covers off her, desperate to get rid of the heat that had threatened to eat her alive. It had been a dream. A very *vivid* dream. Taking several deep breaths, she shuddered. She'd had nightmares before. Every now and then, they came at her out of nowhere. They were filled with people she didn't know. This was the first time she'd dreamed about a fire. The dream had been so vivid she was still almost convinced the house was on fire. But it wasn't. There was no smoke and no heat.

Knowing she wasn't going to be able to go back to sleep right away, she climbed out of bed and headed for the bathroom. A little water over her face might cool her down. She reached the restroom and turned on the tap water. For several seconds she splashed the tepid water over her face. Reaching for a towel, she carefully blotted the moisture away and then stared into the mirror. The last few days had taken a toll on her. Her eyes were rimmed with dark circles and her skin looked paler. No wonder Stone had walked away from her the night before. She looked awful.

Hearing a noise in the distance, she straightened. She tossed the towel down on the sink and crept out of the bathroom. From the upstairs hallway, it was easy enough to see into the downstairs. There was nothing there, but the sound of breaking glass caused her to jump. She was about to head downstairs when an arm snaked around her and a hand covered her mouth.

"Sh. It's me," Dylan's voice whispered in her ear. Her terror abated somewhat.

She moaned against his hand, trying to speak.

"Can you be quiet?" he asked, his voice low.

When she nodded, he loosened his hand from her mouth.

"There's someone downstairs. I want you to go into my bedroom and lock the door. Don't let anyone in until you hear my voice. If you don't hear my voice in five minutes, use my cell to call 911. It's on the bedside table."

She started to protest until she saw his gun in his other hand. She hated guns. Backing up, she did as he told her. When she was safely behind his bedroom door, she locked it and waited. Several minutes went by. She walked over to the bedside table and reached for his cell phone. Clasping it in her hands, she went back to the door and leaned against it, listening carefully. She nearly jumped out of her skin when she heard his voice.

"It's me. Open the door."

Quickly, she unlocked the door.

He stepped into the room, his gun tucked into the back of his jeans. "There was no one there. I found this though." He lifted the piece of paper so she could see it. "Apparently someone knows I brought you here besides Alex. This came through the kitchen window, attached to a rock."

Baylie felt her heart skip a beat. Written on the white paper in red ink were the words COME OUT, COME OUT, WHEREVER YOU ARE.

Immediately she felt as though all the air in the room evaporated. She knew she was starting to sway and was thankful when his hands reached out and steadied her.

"Baylie, look at me."

Her eyes wouldn't focus for several seconds. When they finally did, his face came into view, his eyes staring down at her concerned.

"Whoever threw it is long gone. I already looked around outside. Just sit down for a minute while I call this in." He pried his phone from between her fingers and dialed.

Baylie moved until the backs of her knees hit the bed. Then she sat and waited as he made a quick call to Alex. When he was through talking, he walked over and crouched down in front of her.

"Are you okay?"

She couldn't make herself answer.

"Shit." He reached forward and squeezed her knees. "Whoever did this is gone now. You're safe."

"He was out there. He's watching me."

"No one's going to hurt you. You have to trust me, Baylie."

She lifted her head and met his gaze. "I had a dream about a fire tonight. There was a little girl in the flames burning."

He winced at that. "What little girl?"

She could only stare at him dumbly. "I think it was me."

"Okay, listen, you're upset right now. And you're tired. Maybe you'll be thinking more clearly in the morning."

"I can't go back to sleep."

He was quiet for a moment, then he squeezed her knees again and stood up. "Okay, wait here. I'm going to go talk to Alex and then I'll be back."

"What if *he* comes back?"

"He's not going to, Baylie. He knows we're looking for him now. He wouldn't be that stupid."

She wanted to protest but instead she let him leave the room. Over and over again, she kept hearing the words COME OUT, COME OUT, WHEREVER YOU ARE. The scary thing was that she could hear a male voice chanting those words.

Dylan swept up the glass while Alex took another look around outside. There were two patrolmen with him also making some rounds. When Alex walked back into the kitchen, he was alone.

"Chief's pissed. You should know that. He doesn't like that you brought her here without running it by him first."

"I didn't think he'd be happy," was all Dylan said.

"He thinks it's a good idea now though. And he's calling it his." Alex grinned. "So in other words, you got lucky. He wants us to stick to Sutter like glue. I take it you've got that covered?"

Dylan read the undertone in Alex's voice and ignored it. "I've got it covered. I don't know about staying here after tonight, but I'll cross that bridge tomorrow."

"UNSUB's got to be watching pretty closely or he wouldn't have known you brought her here. How'd you miss that?"

Dylan had been wondering the same thing himself. "I don't know. I didn't see any obvious signs of a tail."

"So what now?" Alex wanted to know.

"We find a safer place for her tomorrow. In the meantime, I need you to do me a favor and find out what's happened to the families who fostered her as a kid. I think she and I are going to have to take a little trip down memory lane."

"You think this guy is someone who fostered her at one point?"

"I'm not sure. I've got a hunch he's connected to some part of her past. It's the only explanation."

"I'll look into it," Alex promised. He looked at Dylan closely. "When you first met her you said you thought she was hiding something. Are you sure she's on the up and up with you now?"

Was he? Not entirely. Baylie Sutter was a complicated woman, there was no two ways about it. But she was also terrified and that was definitely not an act. "I think so. Let me see if I can get more out of her."

When Alex left, Dylan covered the broken window with cardboard and locked up the rest of the house again. By the time he had the lights off and made his way back upstairs it was nearly four in the morning. So much for getting a good night's sleep. He found Baylie sitting in the same position she had been in when he'd left her earlier. Her face was pale and her hands were still shaking slightly. She looked up at him as he entered the bedroom. Immediately he felt sorry for her. She was having one hell of a couple of days. He crossed the room and sat down next to her on the bed.

"I've got good news and bad news. Which do you want first?"

"I've had enough bad news for a while," was all she said.

"The Chief gave his okay for us to keep you in protective custody — for now anyway. The bad news is that we won't be able to stay here.

109

Obviously we're being watched. Until we figure this out we need to lay low."

Startled, she met his gaze. "What about my job?"

That was another piece of bad news. "Until we figure this out, we need to lay low," he repeated.

She looked panicked at that.

"Baylie, I can't order you not to go to work. But I'm suggesting you call in—at least for a couple of days, until we do a little digging. It's the smart thing to do."

He knew she wanted to protest, but she didn't. Instead, she let out a hopeless sigh. "It's all happening again. The same way it did the last time."

"If the police had followed the proper protocol last time, they would have figured out that Kevin Bledsoe wasn't the person doing these things." He tried to say the words gently but they came out harsh anyway.

"I thought it was him," she said quietly. "The gifts and the phone calls—all of it. And then when the girls disappeared, I thought—"

"You couldn't have known. And some of it probably was him. The bottom line is that Kevin's dead so we know he's not the one doing this. What we need to do now is find out who is."

"Do you think Giselle and Susan are dead?"

He wanted to say something that would give her some positive hope, but he couldn't. "Every day they stay missing makes it look more that way. But until we have a body, there's still hope."

She paled considerably. "They had nothing to do with this. Why did he take them?"

"I don't know. That's what we need to figure out. Alex is doing some digging for me."

"I'm scared, Dylan."

When she used his first name that way it made things far more personal. He felt his demeanor softening. "I know you are. You have to learn to trust me."

"I'm trying."

And that said a lot, considering what the town of Chapman, including its police force, had put her through two years earlier.

"I don't know about you, but I'm too keyed up to sleep right now. What do you say we make some coffee and do a little legwork?"

She shrugged and nodded, standing up when he did. They both headed downstairs and he put a pot of coffee on before grabbing his laptop and booting it up. He sat down at the table and she sat down next to him. "Do you know where you were born?"

"I think Montana. But I was in a lot of places. I already told you I don't remember much about when I was little."

"Okay," he relented, doing some tapping on the computer keyboard. They knew that she was part of Montana's foster care system. That told him that she had likely started out there, or at the very least, lived there when her parents had died. Unfortunately, all but two of her foster parents were either dead or nowhere to be found. This was definitely discouraging. He zeroed in on the two he could find.

The first was Mabel Lomax. Though Samuel—her husband—had died years earlier, Mrs. Lomax was still living and had a small farm in Melville, Montana. It looked as though Baylie had spent about a year with the couple, before moving on.

"Do you think you would remember her if you saw her again? You apparently spent almost a year there. It looks like you were seven." He sat back and stared at her intently. He could tell by the look on her face that she didn't believe she would. She'd been young and traumatized at that point so it was likely she was right.

He turned back to his computer screen. "The only other foster parent you had that we can find in the state of Montana is George Rycroft. He was married to a woman named Harriet, though she passed away five years ago. George lives in Virginia City. Apparently, you spent six months with them. Looks like you were about eight or so."

She thought that over. "I don't know," she admitted honestly.

"Well, I suppose we start with them. They were the easiest to find. Alex will work on the others."

"They may not even remember me," she said, turning away from the computer and standing up. He could tell she was uncomfortable about the whole thing and he couldn't blame her.

"They may not. It's been a long time. It's worth a shot though. Right now it's all we have to go on."

Apparently, she realized he was right because she didn't argue. She walked over and stared at the broken kitchen window that he'd covered with cardboard earlier. "If he wants me, why hasn't he taken me?"

That was something Dylan had been thinking about himself. Clearly, the man had ample opportunity to take Baylie. Instead, he went for her friends, her acquaintances. "Most likely he's trying to send you a message of some kind. Obviously, he's angry. He's trying to get to you through the people you know."

"But why? I don't get why."

"I don't know, Baylie. The fact that you can't remember a whole lot about your childhood raises red flags for me." He shut down his computer and walked over to stand across from her. "Maybe your parents weren't the only ones who were in the fire. Maybe you were too. Did you think about that?"

"The little girl in the fire in my dreams was being engulfed by flames. She was burning. I have no burns on my body."

He couldn't argue with that. "That doesn't mean anything. Your mind could be playing tricks on you. It was a long time ago and you were young. Maybe you were outside looking in. Maybe now your mind is putting you in the middle of the flames."

She reached up and rubbed at her temples. "How could I forget something like that?"

"I don't know," he said honestly. "If your parents died in the fire, it probably traumatized the hell out of you. Maybe you blocked it out for that reason."

"And it's starting to come back to me now, only mixed up."

He shrugged and nodded. "I think we should definitely take a trip to Montana. The sooner you're ready to leave, the better. Virginia City is about six hundred miles from here. That's a good day's drive. We'll start there."

"I can leave whenever you're ready."

EIGHT

Baylie found herself dozing on and off over the next nine hours. They had left Dylan's house around six that morning. They'd made a quick stop at police headquarters, where Dylan had gotten authorization to make the trip to Virginia City and then Melville, Montana. His superior hadn't been especially supportive of the idea, but in the end Dylan had managed to make his point that the person who was stalking Baylie was likely the same person who was responsible for Kevin Bledsoe's death — and quite possibly the disappearances of Giselle Lindsay and Susan Hanover. So now here they were, driving down the interstate in his truck, on what the Chief of Police had called a wild goose chase.

Wild goose chase or not, Dylan had her convinced this was the only way. When they drove into the city limits of Virginia City, she expected to remember something about the place. According to her file, she had spent six months here when she was eight years old. Six months wasn't a life time but it was long enough to leave a memory. Unfortunately, nothing popped out at her. The place was almost like a ghost town. It was small and picturesque with older scale buildings lining its streets. It was a gold mining town and proud of it, judging from the multiple signs lining its town square. The weather was a little rough this time of year and the streets were lined with well-shoveled snow. At least the day was rather sunny. Crisp and cold, but bright.

"Anything look familiar to you?"

"Nothing." Disappointed, she sighed. "I don't have a good feeling about this."

"Baylie you're going to have to give this a real chance. Just because you don't recognize anything right off the bat, doesn't mean you won't remember George Rycroft, or he won't remember you. Maybe we should eat something before we head out toward his place." He gestured to a diner on the corner of Main Street.

"I'm not all that hungry. I'd just as soon get this over with."

He looked at his watch and then shrugged. "It's almost six. We'll probably interrupt his dinner."

She supposed he was right but she knew she wouldn't be able to eat a thing until she talked to the man. "I'm willing to take that chance."

He finally relented and took a look at the GPS system. After entering Rycroft's address, he

116

followed the navigation system until they reached a turn off that led to an un-kept dirt road. At the end of it sat a small blue house with a chain link fence. Baylie stared at it for several seconds. The grass was overgrown and there was a broken down station wagon in front of the house. Clearly, no one had been keeping the place up. Nothing about it looked familiar.

"Nothing?" Dylan asked, as though he was reading her mind.

She shook her head. All the same, she reached for the door handle and climbed out of the truck.

"Let me do the talking at first," he instructed when she had come around to his side and stood next to him. She was more than happy to let him take the lead. In fact, part of her wanted to climb into the truck and head back to Seattle.

"I've got your back, okay?" He surprised her by reaching down and squeezing her hand. Somehow, the gesture helped. The sound of the screen door slamming caused them both to look up. An old man with white hair and a full beard stepped out onto the rickety porch, his eyes wary as he clutched a shotgun in his hands.

Baylie didn't know how Dylan reacted so fast, but he had his own gun in his hands in seconds.

The old man on the porch looked startled. "Who the hell are you?"

"Detective Dylan Stone with the Seattle Police Department. You want to put that gun down please, Sir? And then I can show you some ID."

The man looked impertinent. He continued to frown, though the shotgun was lowered slightly. "What do I care about your city boy ID? I'm going to give the sheriff a call and see what he has to say."

Baylie could tell Dylan didn't like the sound of that. His back stiffened and he let out a weary sigh. "That really isn't necessary. You are Mr. George Rycroft, is that right?"

The old man's eyes narrowed even further. "That depends on what you're here for. I ain't been out of the state of Montana for fifteen years. Ain't ever been to Seattle."

"I think I lived here when I was a child." Baylie spoke the words meekly and both men turned their heads to look at her. The old man squinted against the late afternoon sunshine. He stared at her for so long that Baylie began to feel uncomfortable. Then suddenly he lowered his shotgun and scratched his chin.

"What makes you think so?"

The question surprised her. "Because I was a foster child. I spent six months here when I was eight years old. At least that's what my file says."

Rycroft frowned. "Well come over here and let me get a better look at you."

118

Dylan lowered his own gun and Baylie stepped around him so that the old man could see her better. "My name is Baylie Sutter."

"I know who you are," Rycroft said after a moment, surprising her. "I just can't figure out why you're here."

So he remembered her. This was something. "Mr. Rycroft, I just have some questions for you. I don't remember a lot about my childhood. I'm hoping that you can fill in some of the blanks."

"Don't know of any blanks to fill in," he said after a long pause. Then he set his shotgun against the screen door and took a few steps closer to the front walk. His eyes roamed over her several times from head to toe. Then he frowned again. "You've come to the wrong place. It's been nearly twenty years. We fostered several kids. What makes you think you stuck out?"

The words hurt and she forced herself not to react to them. Dylan, however, wasn't as good at hiding his irritation. "Ms. Sutter is involved in a police investigation at this time. We're going to need your cooperation, Mr. Rycroft."

"What kind of investigation?" Rycroft asked skeptically. "Cause I already told you I ain't done nothing. And I didn't do nothing to that kid when she was here either. She was catatonic when she got here. All we tried to do was get her to open up and

119

come out of her shell. She wouldn't interact with the other kids at all. And then she ran away."

This was interesting news. "What do you mean *catatonic*?" She asked the question, though she wasn't sure she was ready to hear the answer. "And I didn't run away."

"You sure as hell did," he said matter-of-factly. "We had two other children with us at the time. You wouldn't speak to them at all. You just sat in your room and drew pictures. Nearly broke my Harriet's heart." Rycroft looked at Baylie closely. "She couldn't have kids, you know. That's why we kept taking in strays. I didn't like it but I couldn't tell her no."

Baylie involuntarily winced. She was used to being called a stray but still the label hurt. "I didn't run away," she said firmly. "I would remember running away."

"I'm afraid you're mistaken, little girl. Either that or maybe you got the wrong place. The child we fostered ran away one night. The state worker came by a couple of days later and said she was in a new home."

She knew Dylan was looking at her questioningly but she didn't meet his gaze. She was as confused as he had to be. Could she have run away and not remembered? And why hadn't it said so in her file?

"Look, I don't know what kind of information you were hoping to find here but I ain't got anything for you. If you want to check out my claims, call the local police department. We filed a missing person's report on the girl. There will be a record." With that, he turned and walked back up to the house and disappeared inside, the door slamming behind him.

Baylie felt her hopes dash in a split second.

"It's okay. Don't look so defeated. He's only one person." Dylan re-holstered his gun and reached for her hand. He led her to his truck and got her seated before he climbed into his side. He started up the truck. "We could head to Melville tonight but it's a little over a two hour drive and I'm starving."

She wasn't the least bit hungry but she'd already learned in a very short amount of time that Dylan liked three meals a day. "We can stop and eat."

He headed for town and pulled the truck into the parking lot of the diner. As they walked inside, the smell of greasy, fried food filled her nostrils. This would likely be Dylan's heaven.

They were seated in a small booth in the corner by a short, plump woman with curly, red hair. She took their orders quickly and Baylie didn't miss the fact that she took a little extra time to bat her eyes at Dylan. He was too absorbed in the menu to notice. When the waitress was gone, he set his elbows on the table and looked at Baylie.

"I'm sorry he was such a crabby, old bastard."

121

"Me too," she agreed. "I'm surprised I don't remember someone that nasty."

"Maybe he wasn't nasty back then," he said, smiling as the waitress set a cup of coffee down in front of him and a water down in front of Baylie.

Baylie took a long sip of water then rubbed her hands over her face wearily. "Why doesn't this town look familiar to me, Dylan? Why don't I remember this?"

"I don't know." His voice was quiet and she could tell he was a little surprised about that fact himself.

She stared around the restaurant and out its large picture windows. "It's something out of the old west. How could someone forget living in a place like this?"

"You were only here for six months."

"I've been here for less than thirty minutes this time and I'm pretty sure I'll never forget it."

He leaned back in the booth, his blue eyes narrowed in concern. "I know this is disheartening. Maybe you're trying too hard to remember."

"I can't help it. I feel like I'm under the gun here. He's going to strike again."

He didn't deny her hunch. He took a long sip of coffee, his expression unreadable. "You're not going to be able to save the world overnight, Baylie. But you're trying and that's all anyone can ask."

The waitress brought their food and no words were said while Dylan dug into his. He was definitely one of those red meat and mashed potato guys. She, on the other hand, had ordered a turkey sandwich. As good as it looked, she could barely get down half.

"You haven't eaten much in a couple of days," he noticed as he took a look at the check and dug through his wallet for some cash. After setting several bills on the table, he looked at her. "You're going to crash if you're not careful. That will slow us down a lot."

"I ate half. I need to use the restroom. I'll be right back."

He nodded and headed to the cash register to pay the bill. She went the opposite direction toward the back of the restaurant. She pushed a green metal door open and was glad to notice the bathroom was empty. She entered a stall and locked it behind her, then sat down and did her business. Just as she was starting to get up, something on the metal wall caught her attention. She stared at the strange sign, her heart beginning to thunder inside of her chest. It was an odd Native American looking sign that resembled a snake in a way, with squiggly lines coming out of it. It was carved into the metal so deeply that even painting over it hadn't hidden its presence.

Baylie's head began to pound and she blinked several times. Suddenly the word *HELP* appeared next to the sign. Below it was something else — the name *Nikki* scrawled in red pen. Baylie felt dizziness assail her and she grabbed the doors for support. She shut her eyes tightly, willing the images in her head away. Forcing herself to breathe, she turned around and vomited everything she'd eaten earlier into the toilet. When she was finished, she took several deep breaths and turned back to the wall. The spot she'd been looking at earlier was empty except for the strange snake looking sign.

Dylan chewed a toothpick impatiently and waited for Baylie to come out of the bathroom. She'd been in there so long he was considering going in after her. Lucky for him, the door opened and she reappeared just before he made good on the consideration. One look at her face had him straightening from the spot he'd been leaning against the wall. Her face was ashen and her eyes were wide as saucers.

"What's wrong?" he asked, reaching her quickly.

"We have to go." She pushed past him and hurried into the parking lot as though a bat out of hell was chasing her. He tossed his toothpick into the trash and followed her.

"What's wrong?" he repeated, when he reached his truck. She was leaning against it, her eyes closed.

"We need to leave here now, Dylan. Please don't ask questions. We need to go."

"Something happened in there. We're not going anywhere until you tell me what. Did someone bother you?" He looked back over his shoulder at the diner, prepared to draw his weapon if necessary. Everything looked peaceful, although the red headed waitress was staring at them through the window with interest.

"I feel sick," she finally said, and took several deep breaths.

He reached over and put his hand on her neck, forcing her head down between her knees. "Just breathe for a minute. It will pass." He squeezed her tense muscles for several moments, while she tried to gather her wits. Finally, she straightened up again. Her color was better but she still looked distraught as hell. He wanted to question her further but instead he clicked the locks on the truck. "We're going to get a room and get some sleep. No arguing. I'm too tired to drive anymore."

She didn't protest, as he thought she would. She let him help her into the truck. He found the nearest motel—which was about a block down the road—and pulled into the parking lot.

"Do you want your own room or do you want to get a double?" He glanced at her uncertainly. He didn't really want to leave her alone for the night, but if that's what she wanted, he would go along with it and get them adjoining rooms.

She didn't hesitate. "Double is fine." Clearly, she didn't want to be alone either.

It took him only a few minutes to get them a room and unload their bags. In the meantime, she disappeared into the bathroom to take a quick shower.

"Take your time," he called after her. When the door was securely shut behind her, he dialed Alex.

"We've got trouble here," were the first words out of his partner's mouth. "I was about to call you. Giselle Lindsay was found in a dumpster this afternoon."

Dylan cursed, even though he had expected to hear the words eventually.

"Tell me you've got something on your end."

"Not yet," Dylan was sorry to say. "Any good evidence?"

"Nothing obvious. She was fully clothed." Alex paused. "There were ligature marks on the neck. Looks like she was strangled."

Suddenly Dylan's stomach wasn't settling any better than Baylie's had. "What about Susan?"

"Nothing. I'm still questioning the math teacher but he's not helpful. I honestly don't think he has anything to do with her disappearing." Alex paused. "I hate to be the bearer of too much bad news but I should probably tell you that someone trashed the hell out of your girl's car last night.

Tires slashed. A few nice words were spray painted on it. It's in Impound now."

From bad to worse, Dylan thought, letting out a sigh. "Do you think it's him?"

"The killer? I don't know. I'm more interested in looking at the McClain kid for the vandalism. I have a couple of witnesses who have him and his friends in the area of the school last night. We'll see what we can come up with. You said he has a beef with her, right?"

"He does. Let me know what you find out about Lindsay, once you get the M.E.'s report."

"Will do. Did she really come up completely empty in Virginia City?"

"I'm not sure, to be honest with you. Rycroft was no help but she's been acting strangely since we've been here. She says she doesn't remember anything but I'm not so sure at this point. I'll have to get back to you."

"I'll let Chief know."

Dylan disconnected the call just as Baylie exited the bathroom. She looked a little better now. She had changed into a pair of pajama pants and a tank top and her face was washed. Her hair hung in wet curls around her shoulders. He didn't want to find her attractive, but he did. She looked small and defenseless and unfortunately small, defenseless women were now one of his weaknesses. Or rather this small, defenseless woman was.

127

"Better?" he asked, knowing he was going to have to destroy her again with Alex's news.

"The shower helped. Were you on the phone with someone?"

He thought about lying to her, just so she would be able to sleep through the night, but part of him doubted she would be able to sleep anyway. He pocketed his phone and nodded at her.

"Alex. Unfortunately, there was an incident with your car last night. Some vandalism."

She paled again. "How bad?"

"Not good," he said, taking a couple of steps toward her. "Before you completely panic, this may be unrelated to what we're dealing with here. Alex is looking at the McClain kid. Apparently witnesses can put him and his friends in the area last night."

"Great. Now my car is trashed." She rubbed her face wearily. "This just gets better and better."

"Baylie, there's something else," he began, his voice softening. She looked up at him and he knew she knew what he was going to say. Her eyes narrowed and filled with moisture and she slowly shook her head.

"Oh God…"

"They found Giselle today. She's dead."

She didn't completely come apart. She just shut her eyes and let the tears tumble over her lids. They drifted down her cheeks and onto the floor. His heart cracked down the middle and he reached for her.

"I know this is bad. I'm sorry."

"It's my fault, Dylan. I caused this."

"It's not your fault. This is a sick person that's doing this, not you." He gripped her chin with his hand and tilted her head so she looked at him. "It's not your fault."

Her eyes were still filled with pain but she forced herself to nod sadly. He knew he should let her go and step away but they were too close and he was too attracted to her. He leaned over and his nose bumped against hers.

"I should walk away again, shouldn't I?"

He heard her words and he stopped moving toward her. His eyes roamed over her face. He could smell the sweet scent of soap on her skin. It clouded all of his senses and he just plain didn't give a damn if kissing her was a bad idea. He lowered his mouth and brushed it against hers, lightly at first. When she parted her lips, all rational thought fled his mind and he kissed her again, this time without caution. His tongue licked at her lips and darted between them. She met him halfway, and her arms wrapped around his neck. The kiss went on for so long he almost forgot to breathe. Moving his mouth from hers, he inhaled the scent of her skin again, his hands moving around to her back and the hem of her tank top.

"There are a lot of reasons why this isn't a great idea." He said the words against her neck.

"I know," she agreed quietly, her fingers tangling themselves in his hair.

He lifted her up and against him, his mouth covering hers again. He felt her legs wrap around his waist and he knew he was done for. She felt so good against him, and in all the right places. He turned and lowered her onto the bed, coming down on top of her seconds later.

She ran her hands over his back and stiffened. His gun. It was still tucked into the back of his pants. He lifted himself up enough to reach around and remove it, setting it on the night table. Then he lifted her tank up and lowered his mouth to the smooth skin of her stomach. He wanted to kiss every inch of her, but he didn't figure things were going to last that long. At least not the first time.

He slid his knee between her legs as he slowly moved up her body. When their eyes met, the electricity between them was palpable. She reached for him and he stopped her with his hand. "This is probably a really bad idea."

"You already said that." She reached down to her tank top and lifted its hem, pulling the shirt over her head and tossing it away. "I need you, Dylan. Please."

He didn't need any further encouragement. He lowered his mouth to her breasts, teasing one, then the other. When she was writhing beneath him, he lowered his head to her stomach again, while his hands pulled the drawstring on her pajamas loose.

130

She was doing her best to get his belt undone at the same time. Finally, he stopped what he was doing and helped her, yanking at the buckle and undoing it quickly. She jerked on the buttons of his jeans, quickly pulling them open. When her hand wrapped around him he nearly lost it.

"Baby, slow down."

"Do you have protection?" she asked, her hand stilling momentarily as she looked up at him.

His brain was so muddled, he hadn't thought about that. He reached into the back pocket of his jeans for his wallet. Thank God, he kept a condom in there at all times. He pulled the foil packet out and handed it to her before he tossed his wallet onto the bedside table and went for her pajama pants again. This time he easily slid them, and the panties beneath them, down her legs. When she had kicked them away and helped him get rid of his own clothes, he settled himself between her legs, gently pushing just inside her. The sensation was so intense he couldn't stop himself from pushing the rest of the way in. She gasped, her legs tightening around him.

"I knew you were going to feel like this. God, the minute I saw you, I wanted you." He said the words against her neck, his teeth scraping against her skin at the same time his tongue soothed it. They moved together, slowly at first. He gave into temptation and increased the rhythm, his hands braced firmly on either side of her head. A moment later he felt her body tighten around him, and that was all it took to send him spiraling over the edge. Several minutes passed before he was able to come back to reality after the climax had hit him. When he lifted his head and looked down at her she had her eyes closed, but she was smiling.

He braced his weight on his forearms and rubbed his nose against hers softly, causing her eyes to finally open. "You okay?"

"I think I'm better than okay, Detective."

"God, don't start that detective crap again. We're definitely past that."

She chuckled at that, her fingers reaching up and brushing a lock of sweaty hair from his brow. "Okay. Dylan."

"Better," he said, slowly disengaging himself and rolling off of her. He kept his eyes on her, waiting to see if regret would show up on her face. It didn't. She actually looked pretty relaxed. "Baylie?"

She turned onto her side and met his gaze. "Don't say my name that way."

"What way?"

"The way that says you're going to get all heavy on me. We don't have to over analyze this, do we?"

He wasn't sure what to say to that. In his experience, most women wanted men to get heavy on them after phenomenal sex. In fact, most women expected it.

132

HIDE AND SEEK

"Can we just be here together tonight — without all the baggage?" she asked, shocking him even more.

He thought that over and finally decided she was right. What else could they do? Clearly, there was attraction between them — sizzling attraction. What was wrong with going with it for the time being? Somewhere inside his head, alarm bells went off but he forced himself to ignore them. Instead, he turned toward her and pulled her against him, already up for round two. "We can. I'm afraid I have one more piece of bad news though."

"What?" she asked, those crystal blue eyes of hers narrowing.

"We only have one condom."

NINE

She stared at the flames, petrified. They were licking at her skin, threatening to engulf her. Over and over again, their orange tips swarmed across the floor, the ceiling. Everywhere. She wanted to scream but she couldn't find her voice. Turning her head, she saw the girl, her eyes wide as the flames moved up her body.

"Help me!" her small voice said. "Help me!"

"Come out, come out, wherever you are..." The words echoed inside her head.

Baylie sat up in bed, her heart pounding a mile a minute. The terror that washed over her was so real that again, she felt as though her skin was burning. Slowly, her vision cleared and the motel room in Virginia City came back into view. When she looked over at the spot next to her in bed, she found it empty. Dylan was gone.

The door to the bathroom was closed, so she assumed he was in there. She could hear the shower running. When she looked at the bedside

134

clock, she saw that it was after eight in the morning. Sighing, she shoved the covers aside and set her bare feet on the carpeted floor. Sometime during the night she had pulled on Dylan's t-shirt but that was all she wore. She could smell him on the material and for a moment, her world righted itself again.

She got up and crossed the floor to the bathroom. The door was unlocked so she went inside and just watched him through the curtain for a moment. She glanced at the counter and saw his gun and his cell phone sitting there. Clearly he never went anywhere without either one of them. The reality of her situation tried to rear its ugly head but she tamped down on it. Instead of letting fear eat at her, she reached for the hem of the t-shirt and pulled it over her head. Dropping it to the floor, she reached for the curtain and moved it aside enough so she could step into the enclosure behind him.

"Hey, I didn't know you were up," he said, swiping at some water that was running down his face. He had shaved and she had the sudden urge to run her fingers over his smooth skin. Instead, she stepped under the warm water and reached for him. His hands tangled in her hair as their eyes seemed to silently communicate. "Baby, I'm out of condoms."

"I just want to be near you. Just for a while before we have to go back out into the world." She ran her hands over his chest, her fingers meshing with the light coat of dark hair there. She felt his response against her stomach and she stepped closer. His head lowered until his mouth was on her neck. His tongue moved in delicious swirls against her skin. God she loved the way he felt against her. It was like he stood between her and the world. When he lifted her up slightly and backed her against the shower wall, she didn't protest. She felt him, hard and ready, at her entrance. All she had to do was move and he would be inside her.

"I don't know how effective the Amtrak method really is," he said, his teeth scraping against her chin. "But I'm willing to try it if you are."

She moved slightly and he was in. Both of them let out a breath. Somehow skin to skin was so much better than a barrier between them.

"God, you're so beautiful." He held her tightly against him, keeping her from moving.

"Dylan, I want you to move."

"If I move, I'm going to lose it."

"If you don't, I'm going to." Pressure had built up inside her that was so intense, she nearly couldn't stand it. When he withdrew, she thought he was backing away from her, but he didn't. He held her up and pushed into her again. Her body immediately began to unravel. Shards of ecstasy poured over her again and again. And then he was gone. This time he did back away slightly, though he still managed to brace her weight against him. After a moment, he lowered her to the floor and leaned against the wall. "God, I almost didn't make it. We have got to buy some condoms today."

She grinned at that. "I kind of liked the Amtrak method."

"I'm not all that convinced that it works. I'd just as soon not tempt fate again." He handed her a bar of soap and helped her suds up, then did the same thing to himself. When they were both clean, they got out of the shower and dressed. By then it was nearly nine-thirty. After loading up their bags, he went to settle the motel bill. She waited by the truck, her eyes scanning one side of Main Street and then the other. Virginia City really was quite a quaint little town. She still didn't understand why it didn't seem more familiar to her.

Hearing the sound of packed ice and snow crackle, she turned her head. A beat up pick-up truck rolled into the parking lot. It came to a screeching halt about a foot away from her, causing her to jump. She was surprised when George Rycroft climbed out of the cab and sauntered toward her. He didn't look much better today than he had the day before—same dirty, white hair and the same un-kept beard. His overalls were fresh though and his shirt was clean. He thrust his hand out to her, startling her a second time.

"Here, this is yours."

137

She looked at the notebook he held in his well weathered fingers.   It had a black cover on it that was dog eared on the corners. "What is this?"

He thrust it toward her again and this time she had no choice but to take it or have it land on the ground in the dirty snow. By this time, Dylan was coming up the sidewalk. He looked as surprised as Baylie had been, to see Mr. Rycroft standing there.

"It's her notebook. I told you she drew — for hours." He didn't smile at Dylan and he backed away from Baylie as though wary. "You don't want it, throw it away yourself. I got enough garbage of my own without other people's."

"Where did you find this?" Dylan asked, glancing curiously at the notebook.

"Does it matter?"

Baylie stared at the scarred, black sketchbook, feeling as though she should have some kind of connection to it. She didn't. She didn't recognize it at all. "Are you sure this was mine?"

Rycroft stared at her for a long time before he removed his hat and scratched his head. Then he shrugged his shoulders. "It was yours as far as we knew. You had it when you came to us. When you ran off, you left it behind. Was up to me, I would have thrown it in the trash but Harriet insisted on putting it away with her things — lucky for you. I ain't had the heart to get rid of them boxes of hers yet. Been fixing too but I just haven't gotten around to it."

Baylie didn't feel lucky, though she didn't know exactly why. If this was her notebook, it could shed some light on her childhood.

"You're welcome," Rycroft snapped, clearly insulted that she wasn't showing more appreciation for his offering.

"Thank you," she forced herself to say.

"I take it you're leaving." The words were not a question.

"What's it to you?" Dylan asked, frowning. Apparently his patience was thinning with George Rycroft's rudeness.

"I'd just as soon not dig up something from twenty years ago, that's all. I like my peace and quiet and I like my solitude. You get me?"

Baylie watched Dylan's frown grow more pronounced. "Yeah, we get you alright. Thanks for your hospitality."

"You young city boys," Rycroft mumbled, turning and walking back to his truck. "You're all smart asses, aren't you?" He didn't wait around for Dylan to answer—just climbed into his truck and peeled out of the parking lot the way he'd come.

"Are you going to open that?" Dylan asked, when Baylie made no move to open the notebook.

"I don't know."

"Can I open it?"

She held it against her chest tightly. "Not yet. Can we get out of here first?"

He shrugged his shoulders. "Whatever you say. We'll grab some coffee on the way out of town. Maybe you'll feel better after you've had some caffeine."

She climbed into the cab of the truck, the notebook still clutched to her chest. She wanted to remember the black sketchbook. She racked her brain again and again, but still it didn't look familiar to her. Finally, while Dylan gassed up the truck and retrieved some coffee for them, she opened it up and looked at the pages. The first few were pictures of stick people, drawn much the way a child would draw them. The faces were happy and smiling. There was a dog in them. Baylie stared at it for the longest time, a strange sense of déjà vu coming over her. She could hear barking, as though the dog on the page seemed to suddenly come to life. It was wagging its dark brown tail and jumping at her happily. She ran her fingers over it and it turned back into the stick drawn dog that it was.

Dylan returned to the truck and offered her some coffee. "What did you find?"

She took the coffee and then turned the pages of the notebook, shaking her head. "Just some drawings. Nothing much." As the pages went on, the drawings got better and better. The people weren't drawn with sticks and the detail got a little more in depth.

"Not bad. You must have loved art."

Had she? She didn't remember loving art. In fact, she didn't remember drawing at all. "I don't know. Maybe."

"It's got to be yours. Or at least you had it at one time. You must have liked to draw." He steered the truck onto the freeway, only casually glancing at her.

"I don't like art that much." She continued flipping through the pages, eventually growing frustrated. She had no recollection of the notebook. The only thing that had jarred her memory at all was the stick figure of a dog. A dog she didn't recognize. Slamming the book shut, she tossed it into the extended cab. "It's not mine."

"Rycroft seemed pretty positive it was."

"He's a crazy, mean old man. He's mistaken."

Dylan raised a brow. "Baby, calm down. It's okay."

"It's not okay. I don't remember him and I don't remember that notebook. I don't even remember this town!"

"Baylie, we've been over this. It's been twenty years. You were traumatized at the time. It's not all going to come back to you at once."

"Something's not right here, Dylan. I don't understand it."

"Maybe Melville will shine some light on things," he said hopefully.

"Maybe." She could only hope so.

141

Fortunately, the drive to Melville was only a couple of hours this time. They entered Sweet Grass County at just before noon. The weather had changed significantly from the forties and dry to what looked like near blizzard conditions. Typical for January in Montana. Baylie noted that this town was even smaller than Virginia City. There was a church, a convenience store and a post office on the main street. That was it.

"Not much here," Dylan mused. "And it's a damn good thing this is a 4x4."

Baylie didn't argue. Again, not much looked familiar. By the time they drove up and parked in front of a rather spacious looking farmhouse, she was ready to turn around and head back to Seattle.

"We've driven all this way. We're going to see what this woman has to say. If we hit a dead end, we hit a dead end. It's not your fault and you have to stop torturing yourself."

She knew he was right but she didn't understand what had happened to her childhood. Why had it been completely erased from her mind?

Reluctantly, she climbed out of the truck and looked around. The bitter cold air hit her square in the face and she shuddered, burrowing deeper into her coat. The farm wasn't operable, that was obvious. There were no signs of horses or cows, or even chickens. Of course it was the dead of winter. Maybe they were in the large barn that stood beside the house.

Anxious to get away from the blowing snow, they made their way to the large front porch. Baylie stopped and stared to the left of the front door. A swing hung there, swaying lonely in the breeze. Instantly, she knew she'd been here before. She looked up at Dylan, finally feeling a sense of hope. "I think I remember this — the swing."

Before he could respond, the front door opened and a small woman with white hair stood in the doorway.

"Goodness me, come in out of this horrible weather. Are you stranded here? Did your car break down?"

Not expecting such a warm welcome, Baylie stared at the woman, stunned. She sure was the opposite of George Rycroft.

"No Ma'am," Dylan said, taking the lead. He didn't step into the house though. Instead, he pulled out his ID and showed it to her. "I'm looking for Mabel Lomax."

"Goodness, I don't have my glasses on. That looks like some kind of a badge. Is there a problem?" The old woman looked from Baylie to Dylan and then back again. "Please come in. It's just frigid out there today."

This time Dylan did step through the front door. Baylie had no choice but to follow. The minute they entered the foyer the smell of something sweet and delicious filled the air. Baylie shut her eyes and let the sweet scent take over. She had been in this house before too. She knew it on instinct. Finally, somewhere she was certain she'd been.

"Young woman, are you alright?"

Baylie's eyes snapped open and locked with a pair of narrowed brown ones.

Mabel Lomax looked to be in her mid-seventies. She was attractive and in good physical shape. Her eyes were kind looking. Somehow Baylie knew this woman had been good to her.

"Mrs. Lomax, we're here because of a child you fostered some years ago," Dylan began.

Mrs. Lomax looked startled. "Well, my goodness, I haven't fostered any children in years. Not since my Samuel passed on."

"If you don't mind, we'd like to ask you a couple of questions. It won't take long." Dylan pocketed his ID again since Mrs. Lomax apparently wasn't too concerned about looking at it.

"My memory isn't so good. I'm not sure I'll be able to answer your questions." She gestured to a large sitting room, to the left of the foyer. "Please make yourselves comfortable and warm up. I'll go and get some coffee for us."

Baylie watched the woman walk off toward the kitchen.

"Are you okay?"

Dylan's question caught her off guard. She slowly nodded her head and peered around the corner, into the sitting room. It was nice and cozy, with a large fireplace. There was a well-stoked fire going and Baylie walked over and stood in front of it, reaching her hands down to warm them.

"I've brought some cream and sugar," Mrs. Lomax said, as she entered the room again, this time with a tray full of coffee and mugs. There was a small plate of cookies next to the coffee. Baylie knew what those cookies were going to taste like. They were gingersnaps — homemade gingersnaps.

"Gingersnaps," she said the word quietly, making her way across the room so that she was right in front of the table.

Mrs. Lomax smiled. "Why yes. Do you like gingersnaps? They're my favorite. My Samuel's too. I don't have much cause to bake so many now that he's gone."

"I love them," Baylie heard her own voice say. For some reason it almost sounded foreign to her. "I used to eat them when I was a child."

"How nice. Did your mother make them for you?" Mrs. Lomax filled three cups with coffee and then handed one to both Dylan and Baylie.

"No," Baylie said softly, her eyes locking with Mrs. Lomax's. "I think *you* did."

Mabel Lomax's smile faded somewhat. "Excuse me?"

"I lived here as a child. I used to play in front of that fireplace and swing on the porch swing on your front porch. And you used to make me gingersnaps and we would-"

"Sit at the kitchen table and count them out. One cookie, two cookie, three cookie four…" the older woman's voice finished for her and then broke off. Her face paled as she stared at Baylie. "I don't believe it."

Baylie wasn't sure what to say now.

"Maybe you should sit down," Dylan suggested, looking from one woman to the other.

"Oh, yes, certainly. Please sit." Mabel's eyes never left Baylie's as she took a chair near the couch Baylie and Dylan sat down on. "I'm so touched that you remember all of that. You were so small when you were here."

"I think I was seven or eight."

Mabel looked thoughtful. "So you must have been. I just remember a sweet, young girl with big, blue eyes and pretty, blonde curls."

Baylie smiled at that.

"Where have you been living? Do you have children of your own now?"

"I live in Seattle. I'm a teacher. And no, I don't have any children."

Mabel shook her head in awe as she took a sip of coffee. "You'll have to forgive my rudeness. I'm surprised to see you again. None of the other children have ever come back to see me."

"I have questions about my childhood that I'm hoping you might shed some light on."

146

"Oh," the woman said, frowning a little. "Well if I can, I certainly will. But you should know they didn't tell us a whole lot back then. They called when there was a child that needed a place to stay and we brought the child home until other arrangements were made. Usually the children didn't stay more than a few months."

"But Baylie was here for a year," Dylan prodded. "According to her records."

Mabel thought that over. "As I remember she was here for six months the first time and the second time she was here for six more months. So yes, I guess that equals a year."

"The second time?" Baylie asked, confused.

"Yes, you ran away twice."

Surprised, Baylie shook her head. "I ran away from here? Why?"

Mabel's eyes turned sad. "That's just it, I don't know. The first time it was a cold, winter night. We went up to check in on you and you were gone. Samuel took a horse out and searched for you well into the night, but you had vanished."

Baylie didn't understand that. Why would she have run away from a place as perfect as this?

"You said she came back," Dylan prodded.

"Yes. Five days later we got a call again. They said you had wandered off by accident. They sent you back to us." Her expression turned worried and she set her coffee cup down. "You just weren't

147

the same after that. It was like…" Her voice trailed off.

"Like what?" Baylie asked.

"I don't know exactly." Her lips thinned into a frown. "You just weren't the same little girl. You became timid and despondent."

"Did she ever talk about what happened to her during the five days she was missing?" Dylan asked.

"Not a word. In fact, she didn't say a word the rest of the time she was with us." Mabel looked over at Baylie. "You just withdrew inside yourself. Most of the time you sat in your room and drew pictures."

Baylie felt her chest tighten. *The sketchbook.* "Did I have a black notebook?"

Mabel nodded without hesitation. "Yes, you did. Samuel bought it for you after you came back the second time. You had been drawing on scrap paper and anything else you could find before he got you that notebook. He got you a nice set of crayons too."

"What was she like before she disappeared the first time?" Dylan asked, surprising both women.

Mabel looked thoughtful again. "Well, she was a sweet child. She had a soft, little voice and was a bit on the timid side with people she didn't know. It took us awhile to get her to open up to us." Mabel looked over at Baylie. "I'm sorry, I'm talking about you as though you aren't sitting right here. You were such a sweet little girl and you and I got along quite well. I had a doll that was mine as a child and you liked to play with her. You used to sit in front of the fire and brush her hair."

Baylie didn't remember that specifically but the idea of the memory made her smile.

"You also played with your imaginary friend. What was his name?" Mabel was quiet for a minute. "Marcus. That was it. I remember because I have a nephew named Marcus and the name stuck out to me."

"What do you mean, *imaginary* friend?" Baylie asked, her skin prickling.

Mabel shrugged her shoulders. "You talked to him. I heard you at night in your room. Sometimes you talked to him while you played in the porch swing. He sat next to you at the dinner table too."

Baylie shook her head. "I don't remember."

"I'm not surprised. When you came back the second time, you never talked again. And you didn't leave room at the table for Marcus anymore." Mabel smiled wistfully. "It's funny, now that you're here this is all coming back to me. I hadn't thought about you in years. It was just so long ago."

"I know. I'm sorry if I caused you trouble."

"On the contrary. We enjoyed you so much. We even considered petitioning for permanent custody."

149

"Why didn't you?" Dylan asked.

"Because she ran away again. And this time she didn't come back."

Dylan swore. "Did you report her missing?"

"We contacted the authorities. They looked for her but nothing ever came of it."

"Did you know who my parents were? The ones I was with before you?"

"Well, no. Not really. We were told sketchy details, as I said." Mabel looked thoughtful again. "But it seems to me they abandoned you."

Baylie narrowed her eyes. "My parents died in a fire before I came here to live with you. I was in the fire with them. I remember being in the fire."

Mabel looked startled. "I don't know of any fire. We were told your parents abandoned you."

Baylie felt that all familiar panic sliding over her again. If Dylan's strong fingers hadn't clasped her own suddenly, she probably would have lost her last shred of control.

"Goodness, I'm sorry. I could be wrong. I didn't mean to upset you." Mabel stood suddenly. "If you have a moment, I have something for you."

When Mabel Lomax had left the room, Baylie looked up at Dylan, confused. "She has to be wrong. My parents died in a fire. I was in the fire, Dylan. They didn't abandon me."

"Baby, calm down. You're white as a sheet." Dylan forced her to look into his eyes. "She may not have known the real story about your parents.

150

She told you herself that the state was sketchy about details back then."

"She has to be wrong," Baylie heard herself say again, just as Mabel Lomax returned to the room. She held something in her hand that she reached over and offered to Baylie. When Baylie held her hand out, a heart shaped locket slid into her palm. She stared at the trinket, her mind trying to process exactly what it was.

"This was yours. You wore it every day and night, even when you bathed. But that last night you were here, we found it on the floor next to your bed. You were gone."

Baylie looked closer at the locket. It was gold, with a scalloped border. Over the years it had tarnished somewhat. Using her fingers, she pried the heart open. Inside was a picture of a little girl with big, blue eyes and blonde curls. The same little girl in her nightmares. She knew instinctively, the picture was of her.

"Come out, come out, wherever you are..." The words echoed inside of her head, coming out of nowhere, repeatedly and over again. A moment later, everything went black.

TEN

Dylan looked over at the bed where Baylie was sleeping. They were in a motel, not far from Big Timber, Montana. After Baylie had passed out at Mabel Lomax's farm, he had decided that they needed a break for the time being. Besides, he wasn't sure where their next destination was going to be. He had Alex working on that one. Until his partner called, they were staying put. The town of Melville and Mabel Lomax was the first lead they'd gotten into Baylie's childhood. Clearly, they needed to follow her footsteps all those years ago, from here.

He took a sip of lukewarm coffee that he'd snagged from the vending machine, in the front office of the cheap motel. It was bitter and stale, but at least it had caffeine. At this point, he needed the charge.

Looking down at Baylie's sketchbook, he frowned. She was right; most of the pictures were just drawings out of a young child's mind. Stick people and rainbows. Even though the drawings got better as the pages went by, there still wasn't anything in them that seemed off.

"I'm sorry."

Hearing her voice, he looked over at the bed. She was awake now, rubbing her eyes wearily.

He set the notebook down and walked over to the bed, sitting down beside her. "Sorry for what, baby?"

"For freaking out like that. I don't know why I got so upset."

"Because you're running on empty, that's why. And you're trying to digest too many things at once." He reached a finger over and ran it down her cheek. "You're a brave girl, Baylie Sutter. Don't let anyone tell you differently."

She smiled halfway at that. "I don't suppose you have more coffee."

"There's a coffee maker by the bathroom. I'll make some. The crap I was drinking is from the office and it's like tar."

He got up and went over to the small bar, quickly putting a pot of coffee together. "We should consider getting something to eat soon. It would do your stomach good to get something substantial in it."

"Okay," she swung her jean-clad legs over the side of the bed. "Have you heard anything from Alex?"

153

"Not yet.   I was looking at your sketchbook." He leaned back against the wall and folded his arms over his chest. "You should take a look at it again, Bay. Something might jump out at you."

"I already looked at it." She gazed up at him. "The weird thing is, I don't feel connected to it. I mean I know it's mine. Samuel Lomax is the one who gave it to me, so Mabel would know. It just feels foreign to me."

"Maybe you stopped drawing after that."

"Maybe. But why? If I loved drawing that much then why would I stop?"

He didn't know the answer to that.   "Maybe because you got tired of it. Kids do that stuff. They're in to something one day and on to something else the next."

"I wish I could remember things better." She looked up at him. "Do you remember stuff like that from when you were a kid?"

He thought that over carefully. The truth was, he did. He remembered just about everything important from his childhood. But he didn't want to make things worse for her. "A lot of stuff," he finally said. "The important stuff."

"If I ran away from these places, how come I don't remember why?"

He didn't have an answer for that either. The truth was, he could understand her running away from George Rycroft. If his personality had been as crotchety and insidious as it was now, back then, it

154

was no wonder the child had run off. But Mabel Lomax seemed like the perfect, sweet grandmotherly type. It was hard to imagine her causing a child to run away. Of course, he didn't know her husband and never would. Perhaps a problem had come from him. The bottom line was that unless Baylie remembered, they would likely never know. "Things are coming back to you slowly, Bay. Just take things one day at a time."

"What about Susan? I know he has her. He's going to kill her."

The fact that Susan was likely already dead didn't warrant saying. Instead, he walked over and crouched down in front of her. "We're doing everything we can to figure this out. What we need to do now is find out where you went after you ran away from the Lomaxes. You stayed in the system. There is a paper trail."

"It won't tell me about the fire my parents died in, Dylan."

"Maybe there wasn't a fire."

"Then why am I dreaming about a fire? And why did someone tell me my parents died in a fire? I got the idea somewhere."

"Maybe because you're confused," he said, for lack of anything better.

She was quiet a moment. "It feels real. Every time I have the dream, it feels *very* real."

155

"I know it does, baby. Sometimes dreams do that. I've had some real weird nightmares before. The subconscious is like that. It can twist things around on you."

She didn't answer.

"Listen, why don't you get yourself cleaned up and we'll go eat." He squeezed her leg and stood up. "We need to make a quick stop at the drug store too." He winked at her suggestively, and she grinned back halfway.

"Okay, okay. I'll be out in ten minutes." She disappeared into the bathroom and he dug his cell phone from his pocket. He waited for the phone to connect to Alex.

"I was about to call you."

"Tell me you don't have bad news about Susan Hanover." He didn't want Baylie to be forced to take another hit.

"Not yet. I did bring in Jeepers McClain this morning. He and his friends trashed the car. They all but admitted it."

"Little bastards," Dylan said irritably.

"At least we know that it was them and not someone else. Anyways, I also found out a few other things. I've sent you some emails. You've got your laptop, right?"

"In the truck. What gives?"

"After the Lomax farm and George and Harriet Rycroft's, Baylie went to a family named Eisenberg. It took me a long time to find them—or *him* rather.

Carl Eisenberg has moved six times in the last fifteen years. At one point he was in Missoula, and that's where he was when Baylie lived with his family."

"Where is he now?"

"Harlowton. Lucky for you it's a lot closer to where you are now than Missoula. Twenty-eight minutes away if *MapQuest* is accurate. Just hop on 191." Alex rattled off Eisenberg's address and Dylan jotted it down.

"So, I remembered you mentioning a fire. It turns out there was one at the Eisenberg's house in 1995. It was bad. Two people survived. One died."

Dylan felt his heart jump. "I don't believe it."

"Yep. Your girl was one of the survivors. Carl Eisenberg was the other."

"That explains her nightmares," Dylan responded, unable to hide his surprise.

"It does," Alex agreed. "The article about the fire is in your email."

"I'll get the laptop." Dylan disconnected a moment later and went straight out to his truck to obtain his computer. When he came back in the room, Baylie was sitting on the bed pulling her shoes on.

He sat down at the table and booted the computer up. "I talked to Alex. You went to a family called Eisenberg after the Lomax farm. Carl

Eisenberg has moved so many times he's been hard for us to track. Alex found him in Harlowton. It's about a half an hour from here."

Her face remained impassive. "Anything about Susan?"

"No, I'm sorry," he said, frowning. He wished he could give her good news on that front. "However, I think I might have some insight on the fire you're dreaming about. Apparently there was a fire at the Eisenberg house while you were living there."

Confused, she crossed the room and looked over his shoulder as he tapped into his email. "I don't understand."

"That's got to be the fire you're dreaming about, Bay. It would make sense. Alex said you and Eisenberg were the only survivors of the fire." Just then his email opened up. The first one had an address for Carl Eisenberg. The second one was a copy of a newspaper article:

FIRE CLAIMS LIFE OF ONE AS TWO OTHERS ESCAPE. The headline was big and bold. Underneath it was a large picture of what appeared to be a burning house.

"Late last night, fire ripped through a home just outside of Missoula. The home belonged to Mr. and Mrs. Carl Eisenberg. In the home at the time of the fire were Carl and Maxine Eisenberg, as well as one foster child the Eisenberg's had custody of. Firefighters fought the blaze as quickly as they could but were unable to rescue

Maxine Eisenberg, who was trapped in an upstairs bedroom and quickly overcome with smoke. Mr. Eisenberg and the child escaped with minor cuts and burns."

Dylan finished reading and looked up at her. "This has to be what you're dreaming about. You must have been told about the fire later and whoever told you misunderstood that your birth parents were killed in it."

She leaned against the wall, clearly trying to absorb this latest news. "So I was abandoned."

He'd forgotten about that. He could tell the idea cut her deep and he couldn't blame her for feeling that way. He couldn't imagine how hurt he would be if his parents had abandoned him as a child. "You don't know that for sure, Baylie. Mrs. Lomax could have been wrong."

"You have my file. Why doesn't it go back that far?"

That was something he didn't know. He'd scoured her file numerous times and found nothing about her birth parents in it. That did seem rather odd, considering how many years she'd been in the system. "Papers get lost," he finally said, for lack of anything better. "Computers were just starting to come around back in the late eighties and early nineties so everything was paper at that time."

She shrugged her shoulders. "I take it you want to go to Harlowton?"

159

"Don't you? I would imagine you definitely have questions for this guy."

She didn't look enthusiastic but she slowly nodded her head. "We may as well go. I won't sleep until we do."

The town of Harlowton, Montana was even smaller than Melville. On the last census, their population had been 1,062. From the looks of things, the population hadn't grown significantly since then. Of course there was still a blizzard going on and most people were likely at home, doing their best to stay warm and safe.

Baylie was glad she didn't have to worry about recognizing this town. It was nice to know this wasn't on the list of places she had once lived.

After taking several wrong turns, they finally pulled up a newly paved road and into the driveway of a nicely painted red house. It wasn't large, but it was an attractive little bungalow. The grass was covered with snow and so were the flower beds so it was hard to tell what things looked like underneath.

Baylie climbed out of the truck and followed Dylan up to the front porch. Before they could knock, the door opened and an older, gray haired man with a receding hairline greeted them with a confused frown.

160

"You must be crazy to venture out in this storm, even with that truck."

Dylan reached into his pocket and pulled out his ID. "Dylan Stone with the Seattle Police Department. I'm looking for Carl Eisenberg."

"You've found him." The man glanced at Dylan's ID for several seconds. "What's this about?"

"Seventeen years ago, you had custody of a foster child named Baylie Sutter. Is that correct?" Dylan pocketed his ID again.

Eisenberg's expression altered considerably. He did not look happy. "Why would you ask about that after all this time?"

"Because my friend here is Baylie Sutter, and she has some questions for you if you're willing to answer them."

Eisenberg's eyes grew wide and they slid to look over Baylie. She felt her skin grow hot as she met his gaze. He didn't look familiar to her in any way. Not only that, he didn't look happy to see her.

"What do you want?" he asked, his expression turning even colder. He made no move to invite them in.

"I'm having trouble remembering a lot about my childhood. I know I lived with you and your wife for a short time and I know there was a fire. I have nightmares and I can't make heads or tails of them. I need your help to get past this, Mr. Eisenberg."

Eisenberg was quiet for a long time. Finally he stepped aside and invited them into the house, surprising both Dylan and Baylie. They walked inside and he led them into a living room, where a fire was burning nicely. The television was on and he walked over and muted the volume.

"I've got my dinner on the stove so this can't take long." He gestured for them to sit down on a black leather couch. He took a chair across the room. Then he leaned over and rested his elbows on his knees. He stared at Baylie again, a strange look in his eyes, almost as though he were seeing a ghost. "I have to admit I'm surprised to see you. When I carried you out of that house, I didn't expect to see you again. The state assured me that I wouldn't."

Baylie forced herself not to react to the cruel words. "Please tell me about that night. As much as you remember."

He was thoughtful for a moment. "My wife died that night. Did you know that?"

"I'm sorry for your loss," she said lamely. She didn't know what else she could say. The man was giving her a very strange vibe—something similar to resentment—and she wasn't sure exactly why. She hadn't asked him to bring her into his home all those years ago. He'd voluntarily taken her.

"I came home to see flames shooting from the interior of my house," Eisenberg began. "I worked late a lot back then and I think it was about nine or so when I got home. The entire house was literally

162

engulfed in flames." He shook his head. "I couldn't get in the front door. It was scorching hot. I went around to the back and looked through the window. I saw you standing in the kitchen." He looked over at Baylie. "You were just standing there, staring into the dining room. There were flames nearly an inch from your face and still you didn't move. I yelled for you to come out but you were frozen."

Baylie closed her eyes, the image of what he described, playing itself very clearly in her head.

"So what did you do?" Dylan asked, breaking an uncomfortable silence.

"I went in through the back door. I ran over and grabbed her. I screamed for my wife but there was no sign of her. All I could hear was cinder burning and posts collapsing. The entire place was going up. I turned and ran outside with the kid. By then the fire department was there. They were doing their best to get the blaze under control, but it was too late. I stood there on my front lawn and watched my wife burn to death."

"I didn't know she was in there," Baylie said, looking up at him sadly. "I didn't know."

"How could you not have known? You were home with her every night. You had been for four months. Night in and night out, you were there." Eisenberg shook his head. "I don't know what kind of game you're playing but I'm not playing too."

"I don't understand what you mean." He looked so angry he almost scared her.

"There's a reason I didn't want to see you anymore, Ms. Sutter. After that fire, I told the hospital staff to notify the state that I was turning you back over to them."

"She was a child. Why would you do that? You don't think she was traumatized enough?" Clearly Dylan didn't like what he was hearing.

"I'm sure she was. But you weren't there, Detective. And your wife isn't the one who died. Maxine was all I had."

"I didn't know she was in there," Baylie said again. She didn't know why she kept saying those words. They sounded lame, even to her.

"You did know she was in there, damn it!" Eisenberg stood up and so did Dylan. He stepped in front of her before the man could make contact with her.

"Sit down," Dylan said. His voice was quiet, but it held an air of warning.

"She set the fire, damn it!"

The words slapped Baylie in the face. She shook her head, shocked. It couldn't be true. There was no way she had set that fire. No way.

"I had seen her playing with matches only days before," he went on. "Outside in the backyard. She nearly set the woods on fire."

"That hardly proves she set your house on fire," Dylan snapped angrily. "You're way off base here."

164

"Am I? Read the fire report. Arson. That's what they thought."

Baylie stood up abruptly. "I didn't set the fire. I wouldn't have done anything like that."

"I hate to be the one to tell you this, Ms. Sutter, but you were an extremely troubled child. You didn't speak. The entire time you were here, you sat around and drew pictures. Pictures I didn't understand. Weird signs and people. Frankly, you scared the hell out of me."

Baylie turned and ran from the room. She couldn't listen to this anymore. She couldn't be the child he was describing. It just didn't feel right. None of this felt right.

Dylan followed her, though he didn't catch up to her until they reached his truck. He grabbed her by the arm. "Stop running, damn it!"

"I can't be that little girl. I can't."

"Baylie, what he said may not be true. All kids play with matches at one time or another. Most of them don't become arsonists. We need to look at the fire report."

"Oh God." She leaned over, her hands on her knees. "God, Dylan. What if I did set that fire? What if I was crazy the way he described? What else have I done that I don't remember?"

He ran a hand through his hair, and then looked at her closely. "You were only a little girl, Baylie."

165

"Some children are evil. Maybe I was. Maybe I meant to hurt his wife." She felt the beginnings of hysteria grabbing at her with a vengeance.

"Get in the truck."

"No!" Panic ate at her and she struggled for breath.

"Get in the damned truck!" He grabbed her arm and she struck out at him, catching him in the shoulder.

"Don't you see? I'm not what you think. I'm bad, Dylan! Bad, bad, bad!"

The words echoed inside her head, only someone else was saying them—a man's voice. She tried to block them out but she couldn't.

"Come out, come out, wherever you are."

She looked around at the now darkened yard. The snow was still falling and visibility was nearly non-existent. But the words—she could hear them coming from somewhere in the distance.

"Come out, come out, wherever you are."

She shut her eyes again and covered her ears with her hands, desperate for silence.

"I'm calling the cops if you don't leave right now!" Eisenberg's frantic threat traveled across the yard.

"What the hell do you think I'm trying to do?" Dylan's irate voice said. "Baby, come on. Get in the truck." He reached over and his fingers pried her hands from her ears. "We have to go. Come on."

"He's out here. I can hear him."

166

Dylan narrowed his eyes. "Baylie, no one is here but us."

"I heard him." She stared around herself again. "I swear it. I heard him."

Dylan followed her gaze around the yard. Everything was still and quiet. "We have to go. Eisenberg's going to call the cops if we don't leave."

Fear clawed at her and she struggled to tamp down on it. Her skin began to crawl. She felt Dylan tug her toward the truck and basically shove her into the passenger seat. A moment later, they backed out of the driveway. She turned her head and watched as the red house grew smaller and smaller and then eventually disappeared altogether.

ELEVEN

Dylan looked over at Baylie. She was sleeping soundly in the passenger seat of the car. She hadn't spoken a word since they'd left Carl Eisenberg's home. He'd hopped onto the freeway and headed as far away from Harlowton as they could get in the weather they were facing. The freeway wasn't too bad at this point. The plows had been out doing their jobs. He needed to get them back to Seattle where he could have full access to his resources. This trip had done nothing but turn up bad things for Baylie. They still had no idea who had killed Kevin or Giselle—or who quite possibly had Susan.

His phone vibrated and he answered quickly, knowing it was Alex returning the call he'd made earlier upon leaving Carl Eisenberg's home.

"There was talk of arson," Alex's voice said quietly. "But it was never officially ruled that. There was nothing left to analyze. Just rubble."

Dylan swore. He'd hoped to have something more concrete to give Baylie. Something that would take the weight off of her shoulders.

"She okay?"

"Not really. We're on 191. She's asleep for the moment. I'm going to head back in."

"I take it you think the final three families she stayed with won't help anything."

"She was older by the time she got to them. She remembers pretty much everything about them. So chances are, no."

"I've been tossing around everything you've told me. None of it makes much sense. I don't get it. Why wouldn't she remember something as terrible as that fire, especially if she started it? And really, how wouldn't she have known Maxine Eisenberg was in the house if she'd been living there all that time?"

Dylan didn't get that either. But Baylie had said twice that she hadn't known Mrs. Eisenberg was in the house. She seemed so certain. "Maybe Maxine Eisenberg went outside to get something and that's where Baylie thought she was."

"Maybe Maxine Eisenberg set the fire."

Dylan had thought of that. But it really didn't make much sense for her to start the fire either—especially when she had ended up trapped on the second floor.

"Maybe she didn't realize the kid was still in the house until it was too late and then went back in after her."

"I suppose it's possible." Dylan turned up his wipers as the snow came down harder. This weather was getting more difficult to navigate in by the minute, even with his truck.

"I'll mull things over a bit more. If I come up with anything I'll call you back."

Dylan agreed and disconnected the call.

"He thinks I did it, doesn't he?"

He looked over at Baylie. Clearly, she'd heard the entire conversation. "He got the fire report. It wasn't ruled an arson."

"But they *suspected* arson."

He couldn't lie to her so he shrugged his shoulders and nodded. "They suspected it. That doesn't prove Eisenberg's theory that you set the fire. Maxine Eisenberg was in the house that night too. Like Alex said, how do we know she didn't set it?"

"That's a stretch, don't you think?"

"Listen, Baylie, you may be finding out things about your childhood that you don't remember but none of this information is getting us any closer to knowing who killed Kevin or Giselle—who might have Susan. That was the whole point of this trip."

"I told you it might not help."

"So we should go back to Seattle. I'm a good cop. I'll catch this guy my own way."

170

"Are you forgetting that this was your way?" she asked pointedly. "I need to know the truth, Dylan. I know that's not why you brought me here but now that I've gotten this far, I have to know. I understand if you need to bail on me and head back to Seattle."

This surprised him. In the beginning, she hadn't wanted to even come to Montana. She hadn't wanted to meet these people. Now that she'd found out terrible things, she wanted to know more. Go figure. "You want me to leave you here alone to figure this out?"

"I don't *want* you to. But I can see that you're frustrated and you have a job to do." She shrugged as she looked away from him and out the window. "I can't just go home and pretend I didn't find all of this stuff out. I have to know if I set that fire. And if I did, I need to know why. Not only that, I need to know why I ran away from the Rycroft's home, and also the Lomax's. You met Mabel Lomax. Why would I have wanted to leave her? I have to know the truth, Dylan. There's more here than meets the eye."

He thought about what she said for a moment, then sighed. "Meaning you think maybe the guy we're looking for had something to do with all this."

"I don't know. Maybe."

He wasn't sure whether he agreed with her or not. It did seem suspicious that she had run away from so many places for no reason. Not only that, the idea that as a child she would have deliberately set fire to her own home sure as hell didn't make any sense.

"Carl Eisenberg thinks I'm evil."

He wanted to argue with her but he knew she wouldn't believe him. She'd seen the look in the man's eyes. His thoughts had been clear as day. "He's a grief stricken, old man. He doesn't know who to blame. If he really thought you were evil, he never would have let us into his house."

She didn't answer.

"Look, Baylie, I don't want to leave you here to do this alone. The thing is, you're right; I have a job to do. I'm on the payroll right now and the minute the chief pulls the plug on this, I have to head back."

"And he's pulled the plug," she said, but it didn't come out as a question.

"Not yet. But he's going to unless we come up with something concrete in the next several hours. The taxpayers of Washington State are paying for this excursion right now and if it's coming up empty the chief will end it."

"I already told you that I understand that. If you have to go, you have to go. I'm not going with you."

He didn't like the sound of that. He understood why she needed answers but he didn't feel good about leaving her on her own. He didn't feel good about it at all.

He heard his phone vibrate and cursed before answering.

"You need to turn around and go back," Alex said, his voice firm.

"What the hell are you talking about?"

"Harlowton. Now. I just got a call from the sheriff over there. Eisenberg is dead."

Dylan's blood ran cold. "What happened?"

"I don't know, but the sheriff's pissed as all get out. He says Eisenberg called him and told him some cop from Seattle was on his front lawn with his crazy girlfriend, refusing to leave. When the sheriff got there, he found Eisenberg dead on the front porch. His throat was cut."

Dylan swore. "I'm on my way back. Let him know."

"Play this carefully, dude. He's calling you both persons of interest."

"That's fucking crazy," Dylan said, whipping the truck off the freeway and backtracking to the on ramp going the other way.

"Crazy or not, you'd better start thinking like a cop here. Something tells me your judgment is getting muddled."

"Neither one of us murdered anyone, Alex. Fuck, you know me better than that."

"Yeah, but I don't know her."

"She was with me the whole time."

"Dude, your dick's in this. I could tell that this morning when we were talking. Hell, I saw it days ago. That complicates this."

"Are you saying you think I would cover something like this up?"

Alex was quiet a moment. "No," he said eventually. "No. That's not what I'm saying. This is a real mess, Dylan. Just get back there and straighten it out."

Dylan disconnected his phone and tossed it down angrily.

"What happened?" she asked, her voice soft.

He didn't even try to sugarcoat things. "Eisenberg's dead on his front porch. Someone slit his throat."

Baylie let out a moan, her head dropping back against the seat behind her. "Oh God."

"Calm down. We'll sort this out."

"They think I did it, don't they?"

"They don't think anything. All they know is that Eisenberg called them and told them we were there and were refusing to leave. By the time the sheriff got there, Eisenberg was dead and we were gone."

"No, no, no. This is not happening."

"Yes, it's happening."

Dylan's phone rang again. This time it wasn't Alex, it was Chief Runyon. And *pissed* didn't begin to cover his mood.

"Just what in the fuck are you doing, Stone!"

"I'm on my way back to Harlowton, Sir."

"You bet your ass you are. And then you're to get back here ASAP! I mean drive all night if you have to. You have royally fucked up this whole thing! You'll be lucky if you have a job by the time you get back here! What the hell were you thinking?"

"Sir, we just talked to the man. No one laid a hand on him."

"Well someone sure as hell did because he's dead!" Dylan grimaced, as the chief's voice grew louder. "I mean it, Stone. You fucked it up, now fix it!" The phone went dead and Dylan swore and tossed it down again.

"Did he fire you?"

"Not yet," was all he said. They weren't far from Harlowton, but in this kind of weather the drive took a while. By the time they pulled up in front of Eisenberg's house it was nearly midnight. The place was swarming with cops.

"Stay here." He opened his door and hopped out of the truck. Immediately he was accosted by several armed officers. One of them eyed the license plate on his truck and then hollered over his shoulder.

175

"Sheriff! The cop's here!"

A tall man in uniform with a brown hat on walked over and dismissed the other two officers. "Dylan Stone?"

"That's me," Dylan said, eyeing the crime scene with his cop's eye.

"Can I see some ID?"

Dylan dug into his pocket and pulled out his badge, handing it over. After perusing it carefully, the sheriff handed it back.

"Sheriff Tom Foley. I'm going to need a statement from both you and Ms. Sutter. Just what in the hell happened here?"

"He was alive when we left him," Dylan said, looking the man in the eye. "He was angry, but he was alive."

"We got a complaint called in by him shortly before he died. He said you were both refusing to leave."

"We had words, Sheriff. He said some things that weren't particularly easy for Ms. Sutter to take. She was upset and I had to calm her down before I could get her back in the truck. Once I did, we left. *Peacefully.*"

Foley looked in the window of the truck. "I need her to get out of the vehicle. I'm going to have to hear her side of it."

Dylan motioned Baylie out of the truck. She climbed out and stood next to him. Her eyes were glued to the front porch. Eisenberg's body had been

176

removed from the scene, but the white snow on the porch was tinted crimson red with his blood. The sight was disconcerting, to say the least.

"Ms. Sutter, I'm Sheriff Tom Foley. I'm going to need you to talk to one of my deputies while I speak to Detective Stone. If it would be more comfortable, he can take you inside the garage. It's freezing out here."

"I don't want to go in there," she said, her voice shaking.

Sheriff Foley indicated that one of his officers take her to a nearby cruiser. When they were gone, he looked at Dylan again. "Just what in the hell are you doing here all the way from Seattle?"

Dylan filled him in on all the information they had so far. When he was finished, the sheriff looked perplexed, to say the least.

"That's quite a story."

"It's been quite a trip. Unfortunately we're still no closer to figuring this out than we were when we started."

"This is a quiet town, Detective. We're still numbered under two thousand people. A stranger doesn't usually go unnoticed."

"Clearly one does," Dylan said evenly. "From one lawman to another, I know you know I didn't do this."

"I've been a policeman for twenty-five years. I've seen some cops do some pretty crazy shit in my time."

Dylan couldn't really argue with that. "She said she heard someone. While we were standing in the front yard, she said someone else was here. I thought she was just caught up in the moment so I didn't pay much attention to her. I was obviously wrong not to listen. There was someone else here, Sheriff."

The sheriff raised a brow, but remained silent.

"She had more reason to keep Eisenberg alive than she did to kill him. Even if he was being obstinate, he was the only survivor of that fire besides her. She just wanted some answers from him."

Foley made a few notes, then let out a sigh. "The last homicide we had here was back in 1991 — and that was a domestic dispute."

Dylan sympathized with the man. His quiet, small town life had just gotten a lot more complicated.

"I'm going to need you two to stick around for a day or so."

Dylan sighed, but he knew the drill. Baylie was on her way back over and he indicated for her to get into the truck.

"The motel's about a mile up the road, to the left. I'll be in touch in the morning after we've gone over this crime scene," Sheriff Foley said and turned away.

Dylan climbed into his truck and started the engine.

"They didn't let you look at the crime scene, did they?"

Annoyed, he glanced at her. "No, Baylie, they did not. This isn't my jurisdiction here. I'm lucky my ass isn't getting thrown in the county jail." He backed up the truck and then turned and threw it into gear.

"You're mad at me, aren't you?"

"If you had gotten into the fucking truck like I told you, none of this would have happened. We would have left and Eisenberg never would have called the sheriff."

She was quiet a moment. "He still would have been murdered."

Dylan supposed she was right about that, but he didn't tell her so. "Well I wouldn't be a suspect and neither would you!"

"The sheriff doesn't really think we did it, does he?"

"I don't know what he fucking thinks," he snapped, losing his patience. "All I know is that my boss is pissed as hell and I can't leave this fucking town until the sheriff of Podunk County tells me I can."

179

Obviously she got his point because she didn't answer. He cursed again, knowing things really weren't her fault. After all, the things that Eisenberg had said to her would have upset anyone.

"He's following us, Dylan. You know that, don't you?"

"It's beginning to look that way." This was another fact that was eating at him. He considered himself a good cop with good instincts, yet obviously this man had tailed them all the way to Harlowton. And for whatever reason, he had considered Carl Eisenberg a threat. Or maybe this was just another sick part of his game. None of the victims until now had a direct link to Baylie's childhood.

"So what are we going to do now?" she asked almost meekly, making him feel like an ass. Again, he reminded himself that this really wasn't her fault. He was a trained lawman and he should have known better than to go to Eisenberg without letting local law enforcement know first, especially in a town this small. Everyone knowing everyone was an understatement.

"We're going to do as Foley said and get a room for the night. He'll cut us loose tomorrow. I think he's smart enough to know that we didn't kill Carl Eisenberg."

"Then why are you so angry?"

He looked at her, sighing. "Because, Baylie, Alex is right; I've got my dick in this and it's screwing things up."

She was quiet for a moment. "He said that?"

"Yeah, he said that." He pulled the truck to a stop in front of what appeared to be the only motel in town. It was small and resembled the last motel they had stayed in—twenty or so rooms, all with outside entrances, on two floors. First-rate accommodations were not a possibility here. "Come in with me. You no longer have the privilege of being alone. Not until we find this guy."

She immediately followed him out of the truck. Apparently, Sheriff Foley had called ahead because there was a key ready for them. All Dylan had to do was give the night clerk his credit card and sign the sales slip. A few minutes later they were unloaded and inside their room. He booted up his laptop and checked his email. Alex had sent a copy of the fire report on the Eisenberg home. It said exactly what he'd already told Dylan. There were suspicions of arson but no concrete proof to back the suspicions up.

"Are you going to be mad at me all night?"

He turned and looked over at her. She had changed into some pajamas and was sitting on the bed watching him carefully. "I'm not mad. I'm frustrated."

"He shouldn't have died," she said quietly.

Sighing again, he ran a hand through his hair. "No, he shouldn't have. His wife shouldn't have died either. And for that matter, you shouldn't have been in that house in the first place. The bottom line is that these things happened and now we've opened up a real can of worms. There's no stopping now, Baylie. You're right, we have to see this through."

"What about your boss?"

"He's pissed, but he'll listen to me. I'll get my ass reprimanded later."

"He could be around here right now, Dylan. This is a small town. The weather's horrible. He couldn't have gone far."

The fear in her eyes softened him a little. "Trust me, baby. He's long gone. He made his point and split. He wouldn't take the chance on being noticed in a place like this."

Apparently, she decided he was right because she lay back on the bed and rested her head against the pillows. "Are you going to come to bed?"

He stared at her for a moment. He would have liked nothing better than to climb into bed and lose himself with her. Unfortunately, they had a problem. "We didn't get any condoms. I'm not risking the Amtrak method a second time."

"We could just lie here together. We don't have to do anything."

He wasn't so sure about that, but the sadness in her eyes was his undoing. He turned off his computer and shut down the lights. After checking the door, he shucked his jeans and shirt and climbed into the bed in his boxers. She snuggled up against him and for a moment everything was all right again.

TWELVE

The room was dark and she could barely see. She rubbed at the stain on her pants. She hated when her clothes got dirty. She smelled bad enough. There was no tub around and no shower. The small room had only a bucket for her to go potty in. It stank of mildew and urine, among other things. This place was a hole. A dirty, disgusting hole.

Tears ran down her face and she rubbed at them, tired of crying. But she couldn't help it. She was so tired and so scared. And she was lonely. She hated this place, and she hated him. Shutting her eyes, she prayed. She prayed for God to help her find a way out of here. She prayed for Him to help her find her way home again. Sometimes she found herself praying for death. It seemed like anything would be better than this hell she was living in. She didn't know how long she'd been praying but so far those prayers had gone unanswered. Still, she wouldn't give up. God would hear her eventually. She wanted so much to be free of this hell.

She felt herself starting to shake and she moaned into her fist. Panic ate at every limb of her body. She wrapped her arms around her knees and rocked back and forth desperately.

"I can see out."

Startled, she lifted her head and looked across the room. A small boy walked out of a dark corner. His hair was brown – his eyes blue like the sky. He was dressed in ratty, old jeans and a dirty t-shirt. He was smiling as he crossed to her.

"You cannot," she said, rocking herself back and forth again.

"I can too. And you know what I see? I see mountains and sunshine and beaches."

"Stop lying, Marcus."

"I'm not lying. I can see it. Come and look."

She glared at him. She didn't want to pretend. She was tired of pretending.

"We could have a tea party," he suggested. "With pretend cups like we did yesterday."

"There's no water left," she pointed out. That scared her. Maybe the man wasn't coming back this time. And if he didn't, there would be no food and no water. It would be only a matter of time before...

"I'm glad we're together," she heard Marcus say. "Aren't you? We'll always have each other." We'll always have each other...we'll always have each other...

Baylie came awake with a start. She sat up quickly, her eyes scanning the room around her. Suddenly she felt very claustrophobic. She started to shake before she could stop herself.

185

"Hey, it's okay," Dylan's voice said, bringing her back to reality. "You were dreaming."

She looked down at him, terrified. "I think he held me in a hole, Dylan—when I was little. And I think I created Marcus to keep from going crazy."

Dylan's face paled and he sat up abruptly, cursing. "What are you talking about, Baylie?"

"I don't know. God, I don't know." The shaking grew worse and she did her best to calm herself but she couldn't. Not this time.

"Okay, breathe." He shoved her head down between her knees again. "I want you to concentrate on my voice. Okay, baby? I'm right here and you're safe."

She did as he told her, desperate to find her way out of the nightmare that had clenched her so firmly only moments earlier. Gradually, the shaking stopped. She kept taking deep breaths until she felt like she could lift her head again. When she finally looked up, she saw two very concerned blue eyes staring at her.

"Do you want to talk about it again? Tell me what you saw in your dream."

She didn't. She wanted to pretend she'd never had the dream. It had been the worst one she'd had yet. She could still see the little boy with brown hair. His blue eyes had been so full of kindness. She wrapped her arms around her knees. "I was alone. I know there were no windows—but Marcus kept telling me he could see out. He kept telling me that he could see beaches and mountains. God, Dylan, I was down there alone in a hole with no toilet and no food and no water!" She rocked back and forth for a moment and then stopped when she realized that was exactly what she'd been doing in her dream.

Dylan cursed again, then stared directly into her eyes. "It was a dream, baby. It's over now."

"Maybe that's why I didn't talk. Maybe that's why all these people keep saying I was so disturbed. He was hiding me in a hole."

"*Who*, Baylie? Who was hiding you?"

She wished she knew. "I didn't see anyone in the dream but Marcus." She felt herself beginning to shake again and she started rocking. Surprisingly enough, the rocking seemed to help. Dylan's arms came around her again and this time he forced her against his chest. She felt the tears seeping from her eyelids and she couldn't do anything to stop them. She could hear Dylan's voice talking to her softly and it only made her cry harder. She cried for Giselle and for Susan. She cried for Carl Eisenberg and for Kevin. And she cried for each and every other victim that had been dragged into this nightmare. Lastly, she cried for the little girl that she had once been—the little girl she could no longer remember.

Dylan waited for Tom Foley to pick up the line. It was only six AM, but he really didn't care what the sheriff was doing. After all, Foley was the one who had made them stick around all night.

Somehow, during the night Dylan had managed to calm Baylie down. She had cried so hard it had scared the hell out of him at first. His heart broke for her. He knew she was going through some serious psychological terror and he couldn't really help her. He guessed all he could do was try to be there for her. The idea that she had been tossed in a hole like a piece of garbage made him sick. She'd been nothing but a child — an innocent, little girl. And some monster had taken her childhood away.

Once he'd gotten her calmed down and back to sleep, he'd stared at the ceiling and thought things over. He went over each and every detail they had learned in the last twenty-four hours. In the end, he came up with one conclusion. He had a bad hunch that Baylie had been kidnapped as a child. He didn't know if her parents were still alive, but it seemed highly unlikely now that they had died in a fire. At least not her *birth* parents. So where were they? Had they really abandoned her — or had she been *taken* from them?

"Foley," the voice said over the phone line.

"This is Dylan Stone."

"I was getting ready to call you. We brought the dogs out last night and combed the woods behind Eisenberg's house. We found tracks leading through

188

his backyard. Lost the scent about a mile and a half from the house. Clearly there was someone there besides you."

Dylan felt slight relief. "No other evidence?"

"Not unless there's some DNA under the fingernails. Apparently, Carl put up a fight. We won't know anything about that until the M.E.'s report comes in. You know the drill. In any case, you two are free to go. I know where you're from if I need you for anything."

"I appreciate that. The thing is, I need your help with something. Can you get me Montana state info on missing kids from back in the eighties and early nineties?"

"Can I ask why?" Foley asked, after a pause.

"I'll explain when I get there. I'm a Washington cop and it's harder for me to get at your state databases, especially when I'm on the road. You'd save me a lot of time."

"I'm at my office. If you want, bring lots of coffee and come on in. I'll see what I can dig up."

Dylan disconnected and went to wake up Baylie. By the time he had her up and moving it was six-thirty. They had to stop for coffee, which given the fact that there were no drive thru coffee stops, took another thirty minutes. Finally they walked into the sheriff's department, coffee and donuts in hand.

"Ah, donuts too. I like the way you think." Foley reached for the donut box and indicated his chair. "I've brought up what I can. Files like that, after all these years aren't complete."

Dylan slid into the chair, indicating Baylie sit down next to him.

"What are you looking for?" Foley asked, taking a large bite of a chocolate donut. "Maybe I can help."

"Her," Dylan said, gesturing to Baylie.

Foley looked confused. Then he swore. "You're shitting me."

"I wish I was." He filled Foley in on what Baylie had told him about her dream.

"Sonofabitch," Foley said, sitting down on the edge of his desk.

"Yeah," Dylan agreed, and started pouring through the files.

Baylie stared at the faces that flew by on the computer screen—child after child. Some had been missing for over twenty-five years. Most had vanished on their way home from school or a friend's house. A few had vanished from a mall or from their front yards. But it seemed they had all evaporated into thin air, as though they had never been alive. Had they been taken by monsters? Were there that many monsters in the world?

Nausea ate at her stomach and she swallowed. An hour went by and still there was no sign of her in the database.

190

"She may not have been taken, you know. I mean if her parents did abandon her." Foley spoke the words and she stiffened. She didn't want to believe that her parents had abandoned her, but she supposed it was possible.

She looked at Dylan. He was still scanning the computer carefully. Suddenly something caught her eye. A photo that flew by so quickly, she almost didn't see it. "Wait!"

Dylan stopped, his fingers still on the *Enter* button. "What?"

"Go back."

He went back one and Baylie felt the air leave her lungs. She jumped up, her eyes focused on the screen. She got closer and looked at the little boy, her eyes filling with tears. "Oh God."

"What? What is it?" Dylan demanded, clearly confused.

"Read the name, Dylan. The name!" she demanded, pointing.

"Marcus Hennings." The words came out of his mouth slowly. Then apparently he made the connection. He looked up at her, his eyes narrowed. "Baylie—"

"That little boy was in my dream last night," she said, her voice coming out in a croak as she continued to stare at the boy's face. Those blue eyes seemed to eat into her soul. She backed up and sat down as a vision filled her head. She was there in

191

the dark room and the little boy was with her. He was holding her hand and she was crying. Then he was hugging her. She blinked several times and Dylan's worried gaze met hers.

"Calm down, Baylie—" he began.

"I didn't make him up, Dylan. He was real. Oh my God, he was real."

Dylan swore. "I know it seems like maybe he was real, but a lot of little boys look the same, Baylie."

She shook her head. "It's him," she insisted. "He's right there. You're looking at him. I swear to you that is the little boy that was down in that hole with me."

Now Foley swore.

Dylan looked at the picture again. He read the information under it aloud: "Marcus Hennings. Disappeared October 19, 1993 from Missoula, Montana. He was seven years old."

Her head instantly began to pound and she tried to make her mind produce more images. Nothing happened. "It's him, Dylan. I know you don't believe me, but somehow I know it's him. I may have had an imaginary friend at Mabel Lomax's farm, but at one time Marcus was real."

Dylan leaned back in the chair, clearly frustrated. "For the sake of argument, let's say that he was. So what happened to him?"

Baylie wished she knew the answer to that question. The idea that Marcus was indeed real was so shocking to her that she wasn't sure what to think.

"We can sure try to find out. I'm going to run the name in our database and see what it brings up." Foley did some tapping on his computer. A moment later, he hit pay dirt. "I'll be damned," he said, shaking his head.

"What?" Baylie asked, crowding over his shoulder.

"Marcus Hennings was one of the lucky ones. He was found May 10, 1997."

"How?" Dylan asked, still sounding doubtful.

Foley did more tapping. "If you can believe this, he was arrested for stealing food from a Safeway. When the cops showed up to take him in he claimed he had been a runaway and just wanted to go home. He never mentioned a kidnapper." Foley looked at Baylie. "This could be coincidence, Ms. Sutter. You've been through a lot. It's possible this isn't the same boy you saw in your dream. In fact, it's probable."

She was tired of them telling her she was wrong. Frustrated, she glared at him. "I know it's him. If you spent days on end in a hole with someone, you wouldn't forget their face either."

That shut him up. He exchanged glances with Dylan.

"Where is he now?" Dylan asked on a sigh, stepping up behind Foley and reading over his shoulder.

"Let's see if we can find out." Foley did some more typing. Again, he got a hit. Unfortunately, it wasn't a good one. Foley shook his head. "He's in Powell County. Apparently he hasn't been a very good boy since he went home to his family."

Baylie looked at the two men dumbly.

"He's in prison, Baylie. Powell County is where the state prison is," Dylan said, straightening. "Are you sure you have the right Marcus Hennings?"

"I'm sure. Marcus Mathew Hennings. Birthdate matches up. He's apparently not a very nice guy."

"What'd he do?" Dylan asked.

"Murder Two. Two counts."

The words echoed inside of Baylie's head. She was having a hard time connecting the current Marcus Hennings with the little boy in her dreams. Could he possibly have turned into a murderer?

"How long has he been there?" she forced herself to ask.

Foley searched a little more. "Since 2004. Apparently he stabbed a woman and strangled a man with his bare hands."

Baylie stiffened. This was definitely unsettling news. "I don't believe it."

Dylan looked at her with skepticism. "If you knew him at all, you knew the boy, Baylie—not the man."

194

"What do you mean, *if* I knew him? Do you think I would randomly pick him out of all those children if I didn't?" She could tell by the look on his face that was exactly what he thought. She wasn't sure she could blame him for that. He was a cop and she'd learned over the past days that cops needed concrete evidence—not hunches and certainly not muddled memories taken from nightmares. His silence was her undoing. "I'm not crazy, Dylan."

"I never said you are. I'm just a little concerned about you, that's all. This is happening really fast and I don't want you unraveling before my eyes."

She glared at him. "I'm not unraveling. We came here for answers. That was our goal. I will admit this is more complicated than I thought it would be, but I'm not giving up until I know who I am."

He stared at her intently. "You're Baylie Sutter."

She shook her head. For some reason she knew now that she wasn't Baylie Sutter. She was someone else. She had to know who. She couldn't go home until she did. "I want to see him."

"Who?" Foley and Dylan asked at the same time.

"Marcus Hennings. That's where we're going next; Powell County."

Dylan's eyes grew wide and she turned away from them. She knew what he was going to say.

"The hell you are."

"You can't stop me. I have to talk to him."

"Baylie, this is crazy! The guy stabbed a woman to death and killed a man with his bare hands. Clearly he's fucked up."

"So am I, Dylan. Supposedly I set a man's house on fire."

He inwardly groaned. "You weren't convicted of anything! He was! He's in a maximum security prison! You are not going there."

"Yes, I am." She looked at Foley. "I may need a car. In this weather, how hard will it be to get there?"

"You won't be getting there at all without a 4x4," Foley said, not sounding any more thrilled about the idea than Dylan. "The prison's in Deer Lodge. It's about a three-hour drive from here on a good day. On a day like today? Who knows?"

She looked over at Dylan. "You can either come with me, or I'll go alone. Either way, I want to see him."

Dylan scowled at her. "Just what in the hell makes you think he'll even see you? He doesn't have to, you know."

She had to admit he had a point there. It was more than possible that Marcus Hennings wouldn't agree to see her. It wasn't like he knew who she was. "He'll see me," she finally said. "He has to."

"No, Baylie, he doesn't. He's been locked up for seven years now. Do you understand that? *Seven years*. Prison isn't a kind place and he's clearly not a kind person. He's not going to have sympathy for your plight."

Her plight. That's what he was calling it now. "How do you know that?" she finally asked. "Just maybe he will have sympathy for my *plight*, as you call it. Just maybe he will remember me—know who I am. I'm going and you can't stop me."

Dylan swore.

"If she's right, this could blow everything wide open," Foley surprised her by saying to Dylan. "I mean I see your side of things too—and it's a long shot—but you're tracking a killer. If it were me, I wouldn't leave any stone unturned. If this ends up being a dead end, at least she'll know he really wasn't real. That's something, right?"

She wasn't sure she liked the way Foley was doubting her either, but at least he was on her side. She could tell Dylan was softening too. He shook his head, clearly knowing he was defeated. "For the record, I think this is a really bad idea."

She didn't bother to dignify that with a response. The possibility that he was right was doing its best to rear its ugly head in the back of her mind. But she couldn't leave any stone unturned—just as Foley had said. If Marcus Hennings was the Marcus from her dreams then he was real. If he was real then he had lived through the same nightmare she had. And maybe, just maybe, he remembered it.

THIRTEEN

The Montana State Prison sat on 68 acres of land, just outside of Deer Lodge. It was a large and intimidating stone building, with chain link around it as far as the eye could see. The drive took them just over four hours. Baylie hadn't been happy when Dylan had suggested they stop for food, but he had eventually insisted. He had shoveled in some kind of greasy hamburger and she had merely picked at the food he'd ordered for her. Finally, he'd told her he wouldn't take her any farther unless she ate something, so she'd forced down half of a Turkey on Rye that was now sitting in the pit of her stomach like a rock.

As he pulled the truck up and parked, she began to get more nervous. She knew she had to confront Marcus Hennings, but at the same time she was terrified. There was a small part of her that reminded her of what Dylan had said. Maybe this was the wrong Marcus. Maybe he wouldn't remember her even if he was the right one. And he was a convicted killer.

"We don't have to do this," Dylan said quietly, from beside her.

"I do. I have to talk to him."

"You don't, Baylie. We have no proof that this man is actually connected to you. I know you think your Marcus is real, but considering the circumstances of your childhood, it would make sense if you *had* created an imaginary friend. Marcus Hennings was an average looking little boy. Maybe he just reminds you of your imaginary friend. Maybe it was the name that caught your eye. The possibilities are endless."

She wanted to argue his point but she knew she couldn't. He was right. All the same, something had caused her to find this man and she couldn't turn away until she was sure who he was—or rather, who he *wasn't*.

"Chief Runyon called ahead. We should be able to go right in once we're checked through security. That is if he's agreed to see us."

She knew Dylan's boss was mad as hell but he had softened a little overnight—especially after he had talked to Sheriff Foley, who backed up their story about Marcus. Chief Runyon had given them the okay to look into the situation. But he had also put Dylan on what he called a very short leash. He was to report in every few hours. Runyon wanted progress and he wanted it now.

Reaching for the door handle, she opened it and climbed out of the truck. It had finally stopped snowing. There was already a foot of powder on the ground and that was just from the storm that had hit overnight. There were piles of the stuff pushed to the side of the road by traffic. She had almost forgotten how cold and snowy the weather was in Montana during the winter months.

"I want you to do something for me, okay?" Dylan had rounded the vehicle and was standing in front of her.

"What?"

"I want you to be very careful in there. Keep in mind that this man is a convicted killer."

Shivers shot up her spine. She just couldn't picture her Marcus killing anyone.

"Baylie, did you hear me?"

"I heard you."

Reluctantly, he took her hand and led her into the prison. He had to check his weapon first and then they were ushered down a long, white hallway and into a dark, gray room with no windows. There was a guard standing in one corner of the room. He didn't even acknowledge them when they walked in.

"Mr. Hennings has agreed to see you. You are to have no physical contact with the inmate — understood?" the female officer who had ushered them in said, looking from Baylie to Dylan. "If physical contact ensues in any way, the visit will be terminated."

Baylie nodded and so did Dylan. When the woman had left the room, Dylan pulled a chair out for Baylie and gestured for her to sit. Then he took the seat next to her. Several minutes went by before the door opened and two guards walked in, a man in an orange jumpsuit and shackles in between them. Baylie was almost afraid to look at his face. When she did, she was very surprised. He was not what she had expected at all.

His face was long and lean, his nose slightly crooked. He had a coat of stubble on his cheeks and a thick head of dark hair. As he sat down, he looked at Dylan first, then her. His blue eyes narrowed with interest. He smiled halfway and a nice row of even, white teeth came into view.

"You got any cigarettes?" When he spoke the words, she nearly jumped out of her skin. She could only shake her head. Dylan had been right about one thing—this man was a stranger to her. She saw nothing in his face that reminded her of the little boy she'd seen in her nightmares.

"So what gives? Who are you and why are you here?" He clanked his shackled wrists against the metal table in front of them, and again, she jumped. He just smiled as he watched her, but the smile on his lips never quite reached his eyes. Her nerves unraveled just like that and she couldn't speak.

Apparently Dylan realized she couldn't talk and he spoke for her. "Are you the same Marcus Hennings that was kidnapped as a child?"

Hennings's smile died slowly. "What the fuck are you talking about?"

Baylie winced but Dylan wasn't fazed. "It's a simple question."

Hennings narrowed his eyes and his face turned ugly. "I don't know what the hell you're talking about."

"Let me rephrase the question then," Dylan said, a little impatient. "Are you the same Marcus Hennings that *ran away* as a child?"

Baylie could tell Hennings was getting angry. His lips had thinned into a frown. He looked at Baylie momentarily and then back at Dylan. "Just who in the hell are you?"

Dylan didn't seem to care that he'd hit a nerve. He sat up straight, looking the man in the eye. "Dylan Stone. This is a friend of mine. Her name is Baylie."

Hennings shrugged his shoulders. "Neither one of you mean shit to me. Whether I ran away as a kid or not is none of your fucking business."

"I think I know you," Baylie finally got the nerve to say. When Hennings looked at her again, she had the sudden urge to look away. Instead, she held his stare, determined not to be intimidated by him.

This time he smiled again. "Is that so?" He looked her over critically. "I suppose it's possible that we crossed paths at one time or another—hot little thing like you." He hissed out a whistle. "You're not here to tell me you have a kid by me, now are you? Cause I hate to break it to you, sweetheart, but I'm in no financial shape to help you out."

Baylie narrowed her eyes. She started to doubt herself again and her skin grew clammy. Her nerves were so on edge that she couldn't make herself speak. The kind, little boy she knew couldn't have turned into the jerk in front of her...could he?

Dylan swore from next to her. "She thinks she knew you when you were kids. Do you want to hear her out, or should we just go?"

Hennings glanced at Dylan absently and then back toward Baylie. He looked relatively amused by the whole situation. And she figured he probably was, given that normally he spent his days staring at cell walls.

"How would I have known you as a kid?"

She was surprised when he asked the question. He still looked amused, but clearly he was willing to play the game. She decided it was time to cut to

203

the chase.   "Because we were held in a hole together."

The words hung in the air like a bad smell. The smile on Hennings's face died so quickly that Baylie had a hard time believing it had ever been there. He narrowed his eyes, though he didn't speak.

She went on, suddenly finding her nerve. "We were maybe five or six. I don't know for sure. The hole was small and dirty. It was dark and smelled of rot—"

"Stop!" Hennings spoke loudly and she jumped. "I don't know what kind of shit you're pulling but I'm out of here." He started to stand up and she reached for his shackled hands. Both Dylan and the guard in the corner of the room stepped toward her to stop her.

"We're done here," Hennings told the guard.

Baylie dropped her hands, but she gave things one last-ditch effort. If he was truly her Marcus, these words would make a difference. "You held my hands when I cried and you told me stories about sunshine and beaches. We even had tea parties together when there was water for us."

Hennings stilled, but he didn't acknowledge her. She heard a hiss of breath leave his lungs. She thought he was going to turn around, but instead he signaled to the guard. "We're finished here."

Baylie felt her heart crack down the middle as he walked out of the room. Just like that, she was back where she'd started. She heard Dylan talking to the guard outside the door and she felt him take her hand. Only when they were outside in the cold, crisp air, did she breathe again. She looked up at him. "Did you see his face?"

Dylan avoided her gaze for a moment, before finally looking down at her. "I saw it."

"It's him. I know it is. It doesn't look like him — like the little boy I knew. But it is. He's real, Dylan."

Dylan didn't speak for a moment. "Baby, I think you're going to have to let this one go."

"But you saw his face!" Desperation tinged her voice and she struggled to get a hold of herself.

"What I saw, was a man who is angrier than hell at the entire world. If that little boy was ever inside him somewhere, he's long gone now. We have to look elsewhere."

She wanted to argue with him but she didn't. Instead, she let him lead her across the parking lot to his truck. After they were both inside and the vehicle was started, he looked over at her. "For the record, I believe you. I think it's him."

The words brought her a small sense of peace. At least he believed her and that was something.

"We need to regroup now and figure out what to do next."

"We need to find out if I was kidnapped or not, Dylan. If I'm not in the database, then how can we find out?"

205

He pulled the truck out onto the highway. "I don't know. Without a name or something, it's going to be next to impossible to dig back that far. We don't even know for sure where you came from, where you were born."

She thought that over. He was right. She had no name but Baylie Sutter. They drove for several minutes, neither speaking. "Where are we going?" she finally asked.

"We're going to re-fuel and head back to Washington. There's no reason for us to stick around here."

Disappointed, she sighed. Something told her the answers wouldn't be found in Washington. She'd spent the majority of her life in the state of Montana. Somehow, the answers had to be here. They just had to. "Can't you buy us more time?"

"Not really. At this point I have to follow orders." He reached over and squeezed her hand. "We'll figure this out, baby. I promise."

Baylie appreciated his positive attitude but she couldn't get past the fact that Marcus Hennings had turned his back on her. Suddenly a thought occurred to her. "He has family."

"Who?" Dylan asked absently as he pulled onto the interstate.

"Marcus Hennings. He was returned to his family so they must be around somewhere."

Dylan frowned. "I'm not following you."

206

"I want to talk to them—his mother and father or brother or sister—anyone who would have known him after he came back."

Dylan was quiet for a moment. "Why, Baylie? They weren't there with you, even if he was. They can't help you."

"I need to try. Can you get Alex to find them?"

Dylan swore. After a moment of hesitation, he picked up his cell phone.

It took Alex only a few minutes to locate the parents of Marcus Hennings. They still lived in the same house he'd grown up in, in Missoula, only an hour away from Deer Lodge.

Yet again, Dylan and Baylie were headed down the freeway to a new destination. Baylie didn't know how many miles they had driven in the last several days but it had to be a lot. Snow was beginning to fall again and she was more than thankful for the 4-wheel drive.

"What exactly are you going to say to them?" Dylan wanted to know.

The truth was, she wasn't sure. The Hennings family had obviously suffered the loss of their son not only once, but a second time when he was sent to prison. She had no idea if they were close to Marcus or not. She didn't even know if they were speaking to him anymore. He had been convicted of two very heinous crimes and families tended to back away from their loved ones with circumstances like his. "I don't know. I'll know when I get there."

The rest of the ride went by in silence. They drove up in front of a comfortable looking two-story home, in a nice suburb of Missoula, a little over an hour later. The street was covered in snow but the neighborhood still looked neat and tidy.

Baylie climbed out of the truck and took a quick look around before following Dylan up the walk way. There was a man outside shoveling snow from the driveway. He turned when he heard their approach, an easy smile on his face.

"Can I help you?"

Baylie studied the man critically. He looked to be in his late sixties. He had a cap over his head and a large, heavy coat on. But his eyes were familiar to her. This was definitely Marcus's father.

"Mr. Hennings?" Dylan asked.

"That's right." The man propped his arms up on the snow shovel as he eyed them curiously. "How can I help you?"

"My name is Dylan Stone. This is Baylie Sutter. I'm a police detective with the Seattle Police Department. We were hoping we could have a moment of your time to talk to you about your son."

Immediately Mr. Hennings didn't look so friendly anymore. He looked wary. "What about him?"

Baylie knew she needed to take the floor from here. "I believe I knew your son when he was a child."

Mr. Hennings looked skeptical, but his expression softened. "Really. And how would you have known Marcus? Did you go to school with him?"

"Not exactly," Baylie said. "Would it be possible for me to talk to you and your wife together?"

"I'm not sure I understand why you're here. I should tell you that he doesn't live here and hasn't for quite some time." Mr. Hennings was frowning now.

"I know that he's in Deer Lodge," she finally admitted, and watched as his frown grew more pronounced.

"If you know that, then what are you doing here?"

"I'm here because I think your son and I were kidnapped and held together as children."

The man's face completely drained of color. Baylie took a step forward. "I'm sorry. I know this is a shock to you."

"Marcus ran away," Hennings said, clearly taken aback.

"He was seven years old. That's a little young to be a runaway, don't you think?"

Hennings let the snow shovel fall and folded his arms over his chest. "Look, I'm not sure what you want, but I only know what Marcus shared with us about that time. And he told us he ran away. He claimed he got lost and couldn't find his way back home."

Baylie could literally feel the man's pain in her heart. Over the years, he had obviously battled his doubts regarding his son's disappearance.

"I don't know how he ended up with me, Mr. Hennings. But somehow, he did. And we were held together in a hole. A dark, dirty hole. I don't know how long we were there. I only know that until the other day, I thought your son was my imaginary friend. Then I saw his picture on the missing children website and realized he was real."

Hennings began to shake his head but Baylie's next words stopped him.

"The little boy that was with me in that hole wasn't a runaway. He wanted to go home." With her memories as vague as they were, she wasn't sure how she knew that—only that she did.

This time Hennings appeared to lose it. His eyes watered and he looked away from them for a moment. Then he let out an oath. "Come inside," he said finally. "It's freezing out here." He looked at Baylie closely, still emotional. "I'm not saying I'm buying all this. And if it upsets my wife, you'll leave immediately."

Baylie looked up at Dylan. He shrugged his shoulders and nodded at her. He was leaving this one to her. They both followed Hennings into the

210

house. The heat of the indoors was a welcome feeling. It had been awhile since Baylie had been able to warm up.

They were seated in a large living area and a moment later Marcus Hennings's mother carried a tray of coffee into the room and set it before them on a small table.

Lydia Hennings was a slim, sixty-something blonde woman, with a nice figure and a well-kept up appearance. She was stylishly dressed in a nice pantsuit with bright colors on it. She almost reminded Baylie of June Cleaver, with her open smile and friendly voice. When she heard what Baylie had told her husband, her smile turned sad. The weird thing about her was that she didn't look surprised.

"I knew something wasn't right with him when he came back," she said wistfully, stirring her coffee. "Marcus had been a very precocious and outgoing little boy. He loved sports and playing with other children. And he loved airplanes. He was going to be a pilot when he grew up." She gave Baylie a sad smile. "When he came back he didn't talk about any of those things anymore and he didn't like playing with other children."

"He was nearly twelve at the time," Mr. Hennings reminded his wife. "That's a little old to be playing like a little boy would, Lydia."

211

"He wasn't a happy child anymore," Mrs. Hennings said, ignoring her husband's remark. "We got him into counseling, terrified for what he'd been through. But they got nowhere with him either. He just kept saying he'd run away and couldn't find his way back. When he was asked about what happened to him during the time he was gone, he remained very closemouthed. He claimed he spent a lot of time on the streets."

"Do you really think he was a runaway?" Dylan asked, from where he sat next to Baylie.

Mrs. Hennings shook her head after a moment. "No. I don't. He had no reason to run away. Our family wasn't perfect by any means but we were happy. We did all the normal things that families do. And we loved him with everything we had." She breathed deeply, her eyes full of anguish. "I always had a hunch that he'd been taken but he just kept denying it. I asked him a hundred times about the years he was gone and he finally got angry and threatened to run away again if I kept bringing the subject up."

"I was told my parents abandoned me," Baylie said quietly.

"And you don't believe they did?" Mr. Hennings asked this.

"I don't know. Until a few days ago, I didn't know about any of my childhood. I spent a lot of time in the system. Now things are slowly coming back to me but there are a lot of holes. I still don't know who I am. That's why I tried to contact your son. I know we were together for some time. I was hoping he would remember me."

"You saw Marcus?" Mrs. Hennings looked surprised. "At the prison? He agreed to see you?"

"He agreed to see us but when I confronted him about the past—about what happened to us—he ended the visit."

"How can you be certain that the boy you were with all those years ago was my son?" Mr. Hennings stared at her intently. "A lot of little boys look alike, and you were a traumatized child. Maybe he *was* imaginary."

Baylie shook her head vehemently. "I saw the look on your son's face today when I told him who I was. I know he knew me. I could see it in his eyes. I have to talk to him again. I need to know what he remembers."

Mr. Hennings remained silent, his expression full of disbelief and a little distrust.

Mrs. Hennings just looked at Baylie sadly. "I wish I could help you but I can't. Marcus has had a tough life. He was a good boy and bad circumstances just seemed to keep eating him up, until he ended up where he is now. I'm sorry."

Baylie hated to admit defeat but she knew she had to. She stood up, prepared to leave, and that was when she noticed him—the small boy who stood in a corner of the room, peering around the back of a large chair. Both Mr. and Mrs. Hennings followed her gaze when she gasped.

"Nicky! I didn't even know you were there. You know eavesdropping is impolite," Lydia Hennings said, standing up and walking over to the boy. She was smiling, in spite of her lecturing tone.

Baylie knew before the child spoke, who he was. She knew because he was the spitting image of what his father had been at that age—the same light brown hair and the same round blue eyes. He was looking at Baylie, smiling shyly, and her heart started to melt.

"You know my daddy?"

The words surprised her. "I did at one time," she managed to say. "You look just like him."

"I see him once a month—on Friday. We play Chess and read stories."

Tears filled Baylie's eyes and she blinked them back. The poor little boy obviously loved his father to pieces. The image she had seen of Marcus Hennings today didn't fit what the child was describing.

"I think you should leave now. We just aren't able to help you," Mr. Hennings said, shoeing Nicky out of the room. "And I don't want my grandson hearing any more of this. He's been through enough, what with losing both of his parents the way he did. He's finally a happy little boy and I want to keep it that way."

Baylie saw the pain in his eyes and she relented from saying anything more. She and Dylan left, and for several moments after they climbed into the truck, they just sat there in silence.

"Can you call Alex?" she asked suddenly.

Dylan looked at her strangely. "What for? We've hit another dead end."

"I want to know who he killed, Dylan."

Dylan frowned. "What difference does it make at this point?"

"I don't know. I just have a feeling that it matters."

Dylan shrugged and reached for his phone.

FOURTEEN

Late afternoon approached before they finally heard back from Alex. Dylan wasn't surprised when he heard who Marcus Hennings had been convicted of killing—his wife and her lover. Apparently he'd caught them together and gone ballistic. At least that was what the police report said.

Dylan could tell the wheels in Baylie's brain were turning but she wasn't saying what she was thinking. They were in another tiny motel room, trying to figure out what to do next. He didn't like how quiet she had become. The information she'd learned over the past several days had taken its toll and she wasn't eating or sleeping anymore. She was close to a breaking point.

"Mr. and Mrs. Hennings looked sad," she remarked, leaning back against the pillows of the bed.

"I'm sure they've been through a lot," was all he said back. He tapped his fingers against the table and waited for her to say more. When she didn't, he found the silence nearly unbearable and sighed. "Baby, I'm sorry. I know how hard this is for you. If I could make it easier, I would. The bottom line is that you can't fix things for anyone else. If Marcus was the boy in that hole with you, he and his family will have to heal his wounds. You have to worry about your own."

A tear drifted down her face and he couldn't take it anymore. He got up and walked over to the bed, lying down next to her. He reached for her and she came willingly. "I promise you and I will get to the bottom of this. No matter what it takes. Do you trust me?"

She slowly nodded her head. He leaned over and nuzzled her nose with his. "Good. I care about you, Baylie. I do. I will keep you safe, above all else."

Her chin lifted and their mouths met. He didn't waste any time on preliminaries. His tongue moved between her teeth quickly. She curved herself intimately against his body and he pulled back, breathing deeply. He reached around her and into the duffel bag he'd tossed on the floor next to the bed. After digging for a moment, he pulled out a couple of foil wrapped packets. "I found them in the office. They were fifty cents apiece."

She grinned and pulled him toward her. "I like the way you think."

Dylan awoke to the sound of his phone vibrating. He looked over at the bedside clock. It read six PM. He and Baylie had fallen asleep and had two blissful hours of uninterrupted slumber. Clearly it had come to an end. He reached over her still sleeping form and grabbed the irritating device. It was Alex calling.

"What's up?"

"I just got an interesting phone call from the warden over at Deer Lodge," Alex said, without preamble. "Marcus Hennings wants her to come back. Apparently he's changed his mind about talking."

Dylan sat up. "You're shitting me."

"Nope. Warden said if you can get there within an hour, you're in. I'd get a move on. This guy impresses me as the type who changes his mind a lot."

Dylan disconnected the phone. He quickly woke Baylie and within ten minutes they were on the road again. The ride to the prison didn't take quite an hour. When they were ushered into the same gray room as before, they found Hennings was already there, shackles and all. He had a pack of cigarettes in his hand. When he saw Baylie, he shocked everyone by jumping up and advancing on her.

"What the hell are you trying to do? He's my fucking son! *My son!*"

Dylan moved in front of her quickly. Hennings was immediately apprehended by the guard, but he fought it. "Why did you come here? God, what are you trying to do to me? I told you I can't help you!" He was screaming at her, his eyes filled with a mixture of anger and sadness. Dylan watched as Baylie shrank away from him, her eyes wide as saucers. When the guards started to haul Hennings back toward the door, he fought them worse. "Damn it, just let me go!"

"I didn't know what else to do," Baylie said softly — so softly that she could barely be heard.

Hennings suddenly stopped struggling, his eyes full of moisture. "Don't you get it?" he asked, his eyes locking with Baylie's. *"He's going to go after my family."*

Suddenly Dylan understood. He looked at the guard. "Just let him go."

The guard started to protest.

"The warden is the one who called us here. You can report this if you have to, but let us talk for a minute. We came a long way."

The guard hesitated and then finally let the man go. Hennings yanked his shackled arms free with a clank. He glared at Dylan and then Baylie. His eyes softened when he saw the tears rolling down her cheeks. "Shit, don't cry. I'm sorry, Nikki."

The room grew quiet — deathly quiet. Baylie lifted her head, shocked. "What did you call me?"

219

Marcus stared at her for a long time, his eyes haunted. Finally he spoke. "I called you Nikki. That's your name."

Dylan pulled out a chair and shoved it under her before she fell to the ground. She sat in it without argument, her eyes dazed. "Oh God, it was you. You were there." She looked up at Marcus sadly. "All those days, you were there."

Marcus looked like he wanted to protest, but this time he didn't. Instead, he sat down across from her. He reached for the pack of cigarettes and quickly lit one up. "I was there," was all he finally said.

Baylie just stared at him, her eyes still wide and filled with moisture.

"Why did you lie to us before? If you'd told the truth we wouldn't have had to find your parents." Dylan spoke, breaking the silence.

Hennings looked away from Baylie's grief stricken face. "I lied because I don't ever want to go back to those days again. Not ever."

Dylan couldn't blame the guy. Unfortunately that fact didn't matter. "Neither did she, but she has no choice now. We need to get answers. The truth. Whatever you know."

Hennings took a long drag off of his cigarette. "I can't give you as much information as you think."

"Just tell us what you know," Dylan repeated, taking a seat next to Baylie.

"I want my family protected. I won't say anything else until I know that's taken care of."

Dylan narrowed his eyes. "Who do they need protecting from?"

Hennings just kept puffing on his cigarette, his eyes staring into Dylan's intently. Obviously he wasn't going to talk until he knew his family was safe.

"If you tell me what you know, I'll have grounds to get them taken into protective custody."

"I don't trust cops," Hennings said evenly. "You're a cop."

"You don't really have a choice now, do you? Your family is in danger even if you don't talk. If you talk, I'll make sure they're protected."

Hennings thought that over for several seconds. Finally, he looked at Baylie. "I don't know a lot about you. I only know your first name was Nikki. He took you from a park somewhere and brought you home."

"How do you know this?" Dylan demanded.

"Because he told me," Hennings said, taking a drag off his cigarette. He looked up at Dylan. "She wasn't his first offense. He'd been forcing me into his house for a while — since I was four or five. He played his games with me and then he would let me go."

Dylan instantly felt sick to his stomach. He knew now that things were about to get very bad. "Maybe you and I should talk alone."

"I was there, Dylan. I need to know," Baylie said, her voice somber.

"Baylie—"

"She's going to remember eventually. Lucky for her she's blocked it out this long. I go to sleep with it under my pillow every night, and have since I was four years old."

Dylan swore. "Who? Who is this bastard?"

Hennings tapped out his cigarette. "He was a neighbor that lived a few houses down. He was a nice guy at first. He liked to hang with the neighborhood kids. He played ball and that sort of stuff. Everyone loved him."

"Name. I need a name."

"I only know his first name is Fred. He had us all call him Freddy." Hennings looked at Baylie. "I saw you in his window by accident. You were in his basement. I was scared because he had threatened me before so I didn't tell anyone. But I kept coming back—sometimes when he wasn't home. I would talk to you through the basement window. Eventually, I tried to help you. That's when he kept me too. He knew I was finally going to tell. He took us both and tossed us down into that hole. We were there for weeks together. Maybe longer."

Baylie rubbed her hands over her face as she started to shake and Dylan knelt down before her, his hands reaching for hers. "Look at me."

She shook her head vehemently.

"Look at me, Baylie. I want you to look into my eyes."

After a moment, she finally lowered her hands and met his gaze.

"Nothing we find out is going to change anything between us, okay? We're a team and we can deal with this together."

She just stared at him, shaking her head.

"Yes, we can. I care about you, Baylie. More than I should. Do you hear me?" He was a little surprised that the words came out, but he realized he meant them. He meant them more than anything he'd ever said in his life. "When this is over we're going to see where this thing with us is going. Nothing that happens is going to change my mind about that. No matter what."

"There's more," Hennings said, quietly interrupting.

Dylan wasn't sure he wanted to hear more, but he took Baylie's cold hands in his and sat back down next to her. She looked small and defenseless and he felt rage begin to burn inside of him. When he looked at Marcus Hennings, he saw the same rage in his blue eyes. Immediately he found himself respecting the guy, in spite of the crimes he had committed. He obviously had cared for Baylie a great deal at one time. "What?" he finally asked. "What could be worse than what you've already told us?"

"He brought other kids home too. He didn't keep them around a long time. Just used them and threw them away. She was one of the lucky ones. So was I. That was what he used to tell us."

Dylan's blood began to boil even hotter. In all his years in law enforcement, he'd never heard of anything this bad. At that moment, as he looked from Marcus Hennings to Baylie, he vowed that he would get this guy—even if it was the last thing he did. "I need a description—any information you can give me on this guy."

Hennings let out a deep breath. "I haven't seen him in seven years. I don't know what he looks like now. He used to be tall, dark haired and light skinned. He had a tattoo on his arm."

"What did it look like?" Dylan asked, already writing this information down.

Hennings looked him dead in the eye. "It was a badge with numbers on it."

Dylan felt his blood suddenly run cold. He narrowed his eyes. "Are you telling me this guy is a cop?"

Hennings just kept his eyes locked with Dylan's. His silence spoke a thousand words.

"Sonofabitch," Dylan said, slamming his hand into the table.

"Why do you think children trusted him?" was all Hennings said, his voice flat.

Dylan cursed again. Then he straightened. "When did you see him last?"

"Seven years ago—the night he killed my wife."

Another bomb dropped with a thud onto the middle of the table.

"He also killed her lover, which I wouldn't really have minded, except for the fact that I'm now up shit creek for the rest of my life." Hennings didn't even blink when Dylan stared into his eyes. God, he was telling the truth. And it fit. Suddenly the pieces all fit together. This man had been terrorizing Baylie for years. Apparently, he'd been doing the same thing to Marcus Hennings.

"Why haven't you said anything until now? Once you were older, what did you have to lose?" Dylan asked the obvious questions.

"Because my son was in the house when I found the bodies of my wife and her lover. I called the cops and suddenly Freddy was there. He told me he'd kill my boy and my parents if I didn't keep my mouth shut. He told me if I behaved like a good little boy, he'd leave Nicky alone. So I did. It was the only way to finally get him out of my life."

Dylan muttered another oath.

"How did we get away from him?" Baylie asked, finally breaking her silence.

"Clearly we didn't," Hennings said.

225

"You got out of that hole," Dylan reminded him. "How?"

"Because he took us out. Now and then he would do that." Marcus lit up another cigarette as he looked at Baylie. "Don't you remember any of this?"

She shook her head.

"You were a feisty little thing at first. You wanted to go home so badly. You got away, though he never told me how. That was before he'd taken me. I don't know what happened to land you in the system, or why they didn't realize you'd been kidnapped. He filled your head with a lot of lies. It's a possibility that you just didn't know where you belonged by then."

"Brain washing," Dylan said quietly. He knew that pedophiles were notorious for behavior like that.

Hennings nodded. "He was an expert at that. I tried to help her but he started keeping us apart after a while—for long periods, at times. Finally, when I was eleven I managed to get away from him. I hadn't seen her in months by then," he said, indicating Baylie. "I honestly thought he had finally killed her. I somehow got out of his car while he was gassing up and I took off."

The story was so unbelievable it was hard to fathom. Dylan looked from Marcus to Baylie. "I hate to tell you this but you're going to have to rehash everything you just told me to local law enforcement. He'll be wanted in Washington, but also in Montana. They'll need to be familiar with the case. Kidnapping is a federal crime so we're probably talking about the FBI too."

"What about my family?" Marcus reminded him. "You said you'd protect them."

"You have my word." He looked at Baylie and crouched down in front of her. "We have a name to go on, baby. It should help us crack this open."

"So I'll know who I am," she figured out aloud.

"Yes, so you'll know who you are."

Marcus swore under his breath. "She was a tiny little kid. The shit he did to her..." His voice broke off and he suddenly reached up and wiped at his eyes. "I tried to help her. I really did. She cried all the time. Sometimes she was completely catatonic. I wanted to kill him."

Dylan wanted to kill him too. "I may do that for you. I have to get to a phone. We need the warden in here. If we can get this guy, you may be looking at getting out of here soon."

Marcus looked surprised. "Nobody's going to believe me. Not after all this time. If I've learned anything over the years, it's that cops only hear what they want to hear."

Dylan looked him right in the eye. "I'm a cop, and I believe you."

FIFTEEN

Dylan tried to mask his frustrations but it was getting harder and harder. Several hours had passed. They were now in a conference room in the prison. Baylie sat in a chair at a long, metal table. Marcus Hennings sat across from her, without shackles. He was still an inmate and would be until this whole mess could be figured out. But everyone involved had agreed that the shackles weren't necessary at this point.

Also present was the warden, George Fawcett, a portly man with a dark ring of hair around the outside of his head.

Now that the case was clearly a kidnapping case, the FBI had been called in. Agents Warner and Bartolatz had shown up and neither were making any points with Dylan. They were both pompous and bossy. This was the problem with trying to work with the feds. They didn't want to help out with an investigation—they wanted to take it over.

The case was now under their jurisdiction, which pissed Dylan off.

Also in the room was Marcus Hennings's attorney, Roland Ledbetter. He was an older man with gray hair and a rather upper class air about him. He was here to be sure his client was well represented in such a touchy situation. Dylan couldn't say he blamed Marcus for wanting his legal representation around. Clearly over the years he had been given a raw deal. The thing was, Marcus was answering all of their questions without preamble. He had described "Freddy" as best he could. He had told them everything he knew about the location in which they had been held — which unfortunately wasn't much, other than that it had been in a darkened area where there were a lot of trees. The woods? Probably. It was unlikely that a man would walk around in broad daylight, in the middle of a busy suburb, and toss two children into a hole.

Unfortunately, no one but Dylan was satisfied with Marcus's answers. No matter what he told them, it still wasn't enough and they wanted more. They were treating him as though he were the criminal, rather than the victim. Dylan began to understand why he had said the cops wouldn't believe him. He'd been right. Even when the reality of the situation was looking them directly in the face, they still wanted to argue that it wasn't possible.

"You said her name was Nikki. Why?"

Marcus frowned at Bartolatz. "Because that's what he called her."

"How do you know he didn't just make that up? Did he show you proof?"

"No, he didn't show me proof," Marcus snapped irritably. "I was a seven-year-old kid. I just know that's what he called her and that's what she called herself—at least back then she did. Her name is Nikki."

"You sound very sure of that," Warner said, stepping up and leaning against the table as he stared down at Marcus. "How do you know he didn't change her name?"

"I don't know that," Marcus answered crossly. "But he never changed my name."

"He has a point," Dylan said, frowning. "We need to follow up on what he's saying. Arguing with him is wasting precious time."

"This is not your case, Detective," Warner said, obviously anxious to start a pissing contest with Dylan. "We are in charge here."

Dylan glared at the guy. "I have no intention of backing off here. I've followed this so far and I'm sticking with it until the end. In case you have forgotten, I still have two unsolved murders and a missing person back in Seattle."

"This isn't Seattle. Here you're not involved in an official capacity," Bartolatz said snidely. "Now you're a gofer."

Warner snickered.

Dylan took a threatening step forward and Warden Fawcett stepped in.

"I think you boys are out of line here. Working together will catch this person faster than fighting amongst yourselves."

Bartolatz grunted a response and then turned to Baylie. "I would hope that you begin remembering things now, Ms. Sutter. Is any of this ringing a bell with you?"

Dylan watched Baylie's eyes lower and he knew before she spoke, pretty much what she was going to say.

"I don't remember much of anything about my childhood. I already told you that."

"I find it hard to believe that you could be held in a hole as a six-year-old and repeatedly abused and not remember it." This came from Warner.

Dylan snapped so fast he didn't see it coming himself. He had Warner by the collar and shoved up against the wall before anyone could even speak. He heard Baylie shout his name and still he couldn't stop himself from yanking harder. "I don't care who you are, or who you work for, you will talk to her with some respect. She is the victim here, not the criminal." The fact that Dylan had nearly a head on Warner made it easier for him to stare down into the creep's agitated gray eyes.

"Let him go," Warden Fawcett said, though his voice didn't hold much conviction.

Dylan glared at Warner another few seconds and then roughly dropped his hands.

"You're finished, Stone. I'll have your badge before the end of the day," Warner said breathlessly, doing his best to straighten his tie.

"I'm shaking," Dylan snapped, turning away from the guy before he hauled off and slugged him. Feeling his cell phone vibrate from his pocket, he reached for it, answering it quickly. He assumed it would be Alex and it was.

"David Frederick Melvin," Alex said evenly. "He lived at 109 Ridge Valley Road in Missoula back in 1993. That's two houses down from our friends, the Hennings'. And guess what? He just happened to be a sergeant for the Missoula PD."

Bingo, Dylan thought to himself. "Last known address?"

"4531 Madison Street. Missoula. I've got local law enforcement on it as we speak. He's no longer a cop. He retired a few years ago."

"The sonofabitch," Dylan snapped.

"One more thing," Alex said, before hanging up. "We got a call a few minutes ago from a guy who says he has some information on the case. He wouldn't talk to anyone but you so I gave him your cell number."

Dylan disconnected the call and repeated the name aloud. "He's still living in Missoula. The cops are on their way there."

Both FBI agents frowned, but neither spoke.

"So what now?" Marcus asked.

"Now we wait."

Dylan's cell phone rang again and he answered it curtly.

"Hello, Detective," the voice said quietly. "Have I called at a bad time?"

Dylan's eyes narrowed. "Who is this?"

"Just consider me a friend. A very *good* friend. You've been a very bad boy. I'm afraid you have something that belongs to me. I want it back..." The voice trailed off into a rather sinister sounding laugh. "Otherwise I may have to replace her again."

Suddenly Dylan knew exactly who he was talking to. His skin began to crawl and he forced himself to remain calm. "When I find you, I'm going to cut your heart out and feed it to you for dinner. Do you hear me, *Freddy*?" The minute he said Freddy, he wanted the word back. But it was too late. Dead silence ensued. And then, the line went dead.

"Who the hell was that?" Warner demanded. "Tell me that wasn't him and you didn't just let him know we're onto him."

Dylan knew he'd just made a very big mistake. He slammed his phone down on the table and leaned over, shutting his eyes. Things had gotten way too personal for him at this point and now he'd screwed up royally. If Melvin had been at his house, there was no way he'd be there for long. That meant that local law enforcement would likely miss him — because Dylan had all but told him they were on their way.

"Nice going," Bartolatz said, picking up his own phone and dialing.

"So what does this mean?" Baylie asked, her voice raising a notch. "Is he going to get away now?"

"He's going to try," Bartolatz said, glaring at Dylan.

Dylan straightened and finally looked down at Baylie. "It means I fucked up."

The ride back to their motel room was in silence. Baylie knew Dylan was tied up in knots over the way things had gone down back at the prison. After Bartolatz and Warner had called in to their superiors, Dylan had been taken off the case officially by Chief Runyon. He'd also gotten one hell of an ass chewing. Baylie had heard the chief screaming from across the room. He'd ordered Dylan back to Seattle immediately.

234

"What are we going to do?" she finally got up the nerve to ask.

"I don't know," was his answer. He kept driving. Finally he pulled into the motel and silently climbed out of the truck. She followed. When they were safely inside their room again, he sat down at the foot of the bed and ran his hands through his hair. "I'm sorry, Baylie. I fucked up."

"You didn't do anything on purpose, Dylan." She walked over and sat down next to him. "You've done nothing but try to help me this whole time."

He sighed, rubbing at his face wearily. "That's the problem. If I had kept this professional, this wouldn't have happened. I would have been thinking like a cop when that bastard called me, not a boyfriend. This is bad. Really bad."

"Will you lose your job?" she asked quietly.

"I don't know," he answered honestly. "Maybe."

"I'm sorry." Guilt ate at her. This was her fault and she knew it. She had let things get personal too. He had been right, back at his house, when he'd warned her to walk away from him.

"When I heard him talking about you the way he was I just snapped. I kept picturing you as a little girl. I couldn't stand thinking of you suffering through the things he did to you." He leaned over and rested his elbows on his knees dejectedly. "It made me sick, Baylie. I want to kill him. That's all I can think about now. I want to kill him with my bare hands. And even that doesn't feel like it will be enough."

"You're the only person who's ever believed in me, Dylan. I'm sorry you got mixed up in all this, but I'm not sorry I met you." She couldn't lie to him, even though she wanted to in a way. She wished she could tell him to go back to Washington and leave her behind—that she would be okay on her own—that she didn't need him. But she couldn't.

He looked over at her, his eyes filled with angst. "I'm not sorry I met you either. But I'm sure as hell sorry for how this has turned out."

"When you get back there things will be okay. You'll just get a slap on the wrist, right?"

He was quiet for a long time. "I'm not going back. At least not now."

She raised a brow when he spoke the words. "What do you mean?"

"I'm not leaving you here alone, Baylie. And I'm not letting Marcus down. We're going to do what we set out to do here. I'm going to see this through. I'm on everyone's shit list anyway right now, so what have I got to lose?"

"You could lose your job, Dylan. I don't want to be responsible for that." As much as she didn't want him to go, she couldn't deal with the fact that she quite possibly could be costing him his career.

236

Dylan was a good cop. She knew that firsthand. She couldn't let him throw all that away.

"What's done is done." He stood up and walked over to the table, where he'd left his laptop earlier. "In the meantime, maybe we should try to figure out who you are."

"We already tried that."

"We looked through the state database for Montana. Maybe you're not from Montana." He sat down and booted up the computer. "Wyoming, Idaho and unfortunately Canada, all border the state of Montana. Washington's not far from here either."

"Canada? That's an entire country!"

He nodded in agreement. "Let's go with the assumption that you came from somewhere in the US first."

Baylie sat down and waited as he pulled up a missing children database. While she was waiting, she picked up the black sketchbook that George Rycroft had given her. She turned page after page, looking each drawing over and still having a strange feeling of detachment to the pictures. On one page was a picture of two girls playing in a grassy green colored area. There was what looked to be water behind them. Had she been to a place like this? Was that why she'd drawn it in the sketchbook?

She turned the page and continued to look the drawings over again and again. On the last page, something caught her eye. She blinked several times, almost convinced she was seeing things. But the image was still there. The same insignia she'd seen carved into the bathroom stall in Virginia City was staring up at her from the pages of her own sketchbook.

"Oh my God." The words came out so fast they nearly startled her.

"What?" Dylan asked, looking at her with interest.

She stared at the picture a moment longer. Then she set the book down on the table next to his computer and pointed. "I've seen this before, Dylan."

He looked at the picture, confused. "Seen what?"

"The snake with the coils and squiggly lines. I saw it back in Virginia City."

He looked at the drawing again, still confused. "I don't understand. You mean you saw it on a building or something?"

Suddenly she remembered something else. "I saw it carved into a stall in the bathroom of that diner we ate in. I remember when I saw it, it startled me for a while and I kept staring at it. And then I had this weird vision that at one time the sign wasn't the only thing that was carved in there. The words *Help* and *Nikki* were underneath it in red pen." *Nikki*...The name played itself over and over inside of her head.

He swore. "Are you sure?"

"I can't be sure of anything. I just know what my mind showed me." She waited for him to say something. He didn't. He just looked at the drawing critically.

"Do you think that's when I got away? Do you think I ran into that bathroom and wrote on the wall?"

"I don't know," he finally said, meeting her gaze sadly. "It's a possibility. But without you remembering more, it's not a lot to go on."

Hearing his cell phone vibrate against the table, she waited while he answered it. She could tell immediately, by the look on his face, that whatever was being said was not good news. He spoke only a few words and then hung up.

"What's happened?"

"The Hennings family home just burned to the ground."

She let out a gasp, her heart stopping. "God were they — ?"

"They're safe. They left town earlier this afternoon." Dylan leaned back in his chair, his face a mask of disappointment. "But if they had been..."

"But they weren't," she said firmly. "Because you kept your promise to Marcus. You kept them safe. The cops didn't get *Freddy*, did they?"

"No. But they're in his house. They'll go through his things. It's possible that something in there will give them more insight as to where he hides out. There's no way that this guy is bringing child after child into a residential neighborhood and hiding them in his basement. No fucking way. He has to be hiding them somewhere else."

"In that hole," she said, without thinking.

"Probably. We need to know where that hole is."

Baylie felt a sense of guilt again for the fact that she couldn't remember. "I'm sorry, Dylan. I know this is all my fault. I want to remember. I just can't."

He met her gaze, his eyes full of sympathy. "It's not your fault. You were a little girl."

"Marcus remembers."

"Not everything. He doesn't know where that hole is either."

That was true, she supposed. "What do you think this sign is?" she asked, turning back to the picture in the sketchbook.

"The question isn't what I think, it's what you think. Maybe we need to go back to Virginia City and take a look in that bathroom. Maybe something else will come to you."

"Or maybe nothing will come to me."

"You may never remember, Baylie." He said the words gently. "It's more than possible that after all this time your mind just erased that part of your life. You can't tear yourself up about it."

"People are dying," she reminded him, anguish squeezing her heart. "And he's probably taken more children. What about them? Maybe he has someone alive right now — someone besides Susan. Someone's little girl or little boy. Someone I can save if I remember."

He didn't answer, but his silence spoke a thousand words. He agreed with her.

"I have to try. If another trip to Virginia City may help, we need to go back."

SIXTEEN

Dylan pulled into Virginia City just before ten PM. The snow had lessened the farther south they had gone, and now at least they were only dealing with remnants of a previous storm. All the same, the streets of the small town were deserted. Dylan pulled the truck into the diner they had eaten at the last time they had been in Virginia City. Fortunately, it was open until midnight. This time when they walked in, he noticed that Baylie was looking at things much more closely. Her eyes were carefully perusing each nook and cranny.

"Show me where you saw the sign," he said quietly.

"It's in the women's restroom," she answered, looking up at him unsurely.

Dylan looked around them. The place was pretty much deserted besides a waitress behind the counter and someone in the kitchen who was obviously required to stay in case of a customer.

Dylan indicated Baylie lead the way. If he had to flash his badge, he would. But for now, no one was paying them any mind and since technically he was no longer on the job officially, he didn't want the Seattle PD dragged any further into this.

Baylie led him to the back of the diner and into the ladies restroom. The first stall on the left stood open and she walked inside and knelt down. He followed suit. Sure enough, just below the toilet paper holder, the strange sign they'd seen in Baylie's sketchbook was carved into the metal. It was faint, obviously having been painted over throughout the years, but it was there. Dylan ran his fingers over it, then reached for his phone. He took several pictures of it, before looking at Baylie. "Anything else coming to you?"

She shook her head, her eyes sad.

He stood up, pulling her up with him. They both went back out into the restaurant and looked around. Dylan noticed that the waitress was now looking at them curiously. He knew Baylie wasn't hungry but he figured they needed some kind of sustenance to get them through the night. He ushered her up to the counter and indicated she take a stool. Then he sat down next to her.

"What can I get you?" the waitress asked, chewing on a piece of gum loudly. Her expression was full of annoyance. Clearly, she hadn't counted on having any late night patrons to take care of.

"Two burgers, fries and Cokes."

The waitress called the order over her shoulder, then went to work filling up two glasses with Coke.

"Do you know how long this place has been here?" Dylan asked curiously.

The waitress looked surprised. He noted that her nametag read *Connie*.

"Gosh, forever. Why? You been here before?"

"Maybe. Anyone still working here that would have been here back in the nineties?" It was a long shot but Dylan figured the question was worth asking.

Connie frowned. "Jeeze, Mister, I don't know. I'm only twenty-one. I was just a kid back then." She slid their plates over to them, her expression curious. "Why do you ask?"

"Because my friend was here years ago and thinks she carved something into your bathroom wall."

Connie looked interested. "Like a phone number or something? Don't let Johnny hear you say that. He gets ticked as all get out when graffiti ends up on the wall in there. Costs a fortune to paint over."

"She was a little girl when it happened," Dylan said carefully. "And I think she may have been asking for help. I'm trying to find out if anyone remembers anything about her being here back then."

Connie chewed her gum avidly. "Wow, really? That's a neat story. But I don't know anyone who

244

was here back then. Most of us move on and get the hell out of here one way or another."

This news wasn't surprising. After all, it had been almost twenty years.

Dylan and Baylie finished their meals and headed for the local motel again. By the time they were checked in and safely in their room, it was after midnight. While she showered, Dylan made a quick call to Alex.

"Any news on Melvin?"

"Nope. Apparently, they've taken boxes and boxes of shit from his house though. It will take a while to go through it all," Alex answered. "I'm on route to Missoula as we speak."

The words hung in the air between them. Dylan had been removed from the case but clearly Alex hadn't. Dylan reminded himself that this was a good thing. At least Alex would keep him up to date on things. "I'm sending you a picture. Baylie noticed this carved into a bathroom wall in Virginia City. It's also in a drawing she made in her sketchbook as a kid. I don't know what it means. Maybe you can get something out of it."

"You're in Virginia City again?" Alex asked, clearly skeptical. "I thought you were heading back to Seattle."

Dylan knew Alex wasn't going to like his answer, but he said it anyway. "I'm seeing this one through, man. We're close."

"Dylan, Chief is pissed as hell. He thinks you're on your way back."

"I am. I have a few stops to make first," was all he said.

Alex was quiet a moment. "You don't know her, dude. Why would you risk your career for her?"

"I admit that I've let my personal feelings cloud my judgment some, but justice is what I'm after, Alex. You weren't there. You didn't hear the things Marcus Hennings said about what happened to them as kids. It was bad. Someone like that has to be brought to justice."

"So let us do it."

"Last I heard I was one of *us*."

Alex sighed. "You let things get to you, Dylan. Whenever that happens, it fucks things up."

"I'm seeing this through," Dylan finally said, unwilling to argue anymore. He knew Alex was right but he couldn't walk away from Baylie. Not now. "Keep me in the loop." He disconnected the call before Alex could comment.

"What did he say?"

Dylan looked up at the sound of Baylie's voice. She was walking out of the bathroom, a large towel wrapped around her securely. Her blonde hair was damp and hung in wet swirls around her shoulders. For a minute, his breath caught in his throat. In a very short amount of time, he'd let her get under his skin. Alex was right. "He's on his way to

Missoula," he finally said, then walked toward her. Her eyes followed his.

"So you're still off the case."

"I am. Officially anyway. Alex will keep me in the loop and you and I are going to see this through. I told you that before." When he was right in front of her, he leaned over and breathed in her scent. It was a clean smell—motel soap and some kind of shampoo. It was sweet and musky at the same time. "I sent him a picture of the bathroom stall. We'll see if he can make heads or tails out of it." He let his hands cup her hips and pull her toward him. She rested her head against his chest and they stayed like that for a few moments.

"No one has ever gone out on a limb like this for me, Dylan." She lifted her head and looked up at him solemnly. "Thank you."

He sighed, not sure what to say to that. She'd obviously had a terrible childhood and a rather unconventional adulthood. Clearly, their relationship was one of the only positive ones in her life. And it consisted of seven days. "You're welcome," he finally said, for lack of anything better. Their noses bumped and then their mouths. He tangled the fingers of one hand in her hair, his other hand pulling her lower body tightly against his. A fire seemed to ignite immediately. It was crazy, the response he had to her. He moved his mouth down her jaw and then slid his tongue along the side of her neck. She let out a deep breath, her head lolling back, allowing him better access. He raised his head and looked at her as he lifted her up against him, wrapping her legs around his waist. The towel she wore seemed to evaporate between them as he backed her up against the wall. All at once, her hands shoved at his jacket, pushing it quickly off of his shoulders and letting it fall to the floor in a heap. Her fingers moved under the hem of his t-shirt and he inhaled once she encountered the bare skin of his abs. He kissed her again, this time deeply, his tongue quickly moving between her teeth and mating with hers in an erotic dance.

"Dylan," she said on a moan, her hands fumbling with his belt and then yanking at it. He reached between them and helped her, quickly pulling the belt buckle apart and yanking at the buttons on his jeans. When he was free, he slid between her legs and inside her in one long thrust, bracing them both against the wall firmly as he slammed into her. Her legs tightened around him and she met him halfway in another earth-shattering kiss. Without disengaging, he turned them and lowered them toward the bed. Once she was flat on her back, he began moving again, this time gentler. His mouth slid over her neck, her breasts and then back up to her ear.

"You make it hard for me to breathe." He said the words on a whisper, then cursed when she tightened around him.   He watched as her eyes shut and she came apart in his arms. It was the most intensely erotic sight he'd ever seen. When his own climax grabbed him, it seemed to shake him from his head to his toes. He held himself inside her and let the waves pound through him violently. Then he collapsed on top of her, feeling as though his bones had all turned to rubber.

"You make it hard for me to breathe too."

The words were soft, but he heard them and lifted his head. He let his nose bump against hers softly and then he grinned. "I don't know if that's good or bad, but I'm willing to go with it if you are."

She didn't answer. Instead, she wrapped her legs around his waist again and pulled his body more tightly into her. That was all the encouragement he needed. He heard his cell phone beep from the spot he'd laid it on the bed earlier, but he was too far lost in her to reach for it.

An hour later, after showering and returning to the bed, he finally noticed the red light blinking on the device. Just as he was about to check his voicemail, the phone vibrated in his hand. Alex.

"Hey," he answered, quickly.

"Where the hell have you been? I've been calling for an hour."

"I was in the shower," he said, for lack of anything better.

"Next time take your phone with you. We got the sonofabitch. Took him into custody an hour ago."

Dylan's heart nearly stopped. "You're kidding. How? Where?"

"You're not going to believe this one. Missoula PD traced him to Seattle. Apparently, he has another residence here—an apartment he's been renting for a while now. After setting the Hennings house on fire in Missoula, he headed for his Seattle digs."

"You're shitting me." Dylan was already working on getting dressed.

"Nope. You'd better get back here as soon as you can."

Dylan disconnected and looked over at Baylie, who was now sitting up in bed, her eyes narrowed in question as she waited for him to say something.

"We got him."

She stared at him dumbly for several seconds, clearly at a loss for words.

"Did you hear me?" He walked over and crouched down at the side of the bed. "He's in custody in Seattle."

"Is Susan…?" Her voice trailed off.

He hadn't thought to ask about Susan and Alex hadn't volunteered any information. "I don't know anything about Susan at this point. But we've got him. We need to head back to Seattle, Baylie. Right now."

She looked as though she wanted to say more, but she didn't. Instead, she climbed out of bed and went to work getting dressed.

SEVENTEEN

The drive to Seattle took half the time it normally would have, given the fact that Dylan kept the pedal to the metal. He pulled up in front of the police station in just under five hours. Baylie had stayed awake the entire way, staring out the window at the passing scenery.

Shutting off the ignition, Dylan looked over at her. "I can take you to your house if you want. You can clean up and get a little rest."

"I won't sleep," was all she said.

He couldn't say he blamed her. Inside the building in front of them, was the monster who had robbed her of her childhood. The idea of facing that had to be terrifying.

"Chances of you identifying him as your attacker are slim to none, Bay. You didn't remember him before now and you probably won't after you see him."

"But you want me to try."

"They'll want you to take a look at him, yes. Probably through a two way mirror."

She turned away from the window and met his gaze. "He knows who I am, Dylan. And he knows where I came from. I need to talk to him."

"We need to question him first," he said firmly. Then he gentled his tone. "Susan is still missing, Baylie. Our priority is finding her alive."

"She may already be dead."

The likelihood was, that she was right. Susan Hanover was probably dead. But they didn't have a body and as long as they didn't have a body, she had a chance. "We need to get him to admit that he's got her—or that he at least had her. And we need to talk to him about Giselle Lindsay and Kevin Bledsoe. I know this is a chance for you to get to the bottom of who you are but you have to remember why we started this whole thing. It was for Giselle—for Susan. And it was to find out who killed Kevin. That's what the police are investigating here."

She turned, her eyes narrowed in irritation. "So the fact that I got caught in this shuffle doesn't matter anymore? And what about Marcus? What about his wife and her murder? Is that on the back burner too?"

He winced at that. The truth was, he didn't know how long it would take to get the situation with Marcus Hennings straightened out. Now that

David Melvin was in custody, the ball would be rolling but there was a lot of bureaucratic red tape to go through. Things in the legal system rarely happened over night. Instead of telling her so, he tapped his fingers against the steering wheel and shook his head. "It's not on the back burner. Once Melvin confesses to the murders, a judge will set Marcus free."

"What makes you think he's going to confess?"

"That's why we're questioning him, Baylie. And you have to cooperate with us. You're part of this investigation and for now you have to do what we tell you to do."

She scowled at him, her fists clenched. "What happened to us being in this together?"

"We are in this together. But I do have a job to do. I meant what I said about us getting to the bottom of this but we need to do things my way. Now that we have him in custody, everything we do is critical. Can you understand that? There are no do-overs, if you get my drift. I've seen people walk when they were damned straight guilty. That can't happen here."

Her face seemed to soften a little. She sighed, rubbing her hands over her face wearily. He could tell that she knew he was right.

"Listen, I'll do what I can to get you in there — eventually. But it won't be right away and you have to play it cool. Runyon's calling the shots."

254

She clearly wanted to protest but eventually she nodded her head. "Okay, you win. We'll do it your way. But I can't stop looking for answers, Dylan. I need to know who I am."

"Fair enough," he agreed, figuring he'd be saying the same thing if he were in her shoes. He reached over and offered her his hand. She stared at it for a long time and then finally folded her fingers in his. He squeezed gently before reaching for the door handle.

An hour later, the room they walked into was about the size of a small bedroom. Baylie immediately noticed there were no windows. The walls were painted a drab gray color and there was a long glass partition that took up nearly the entire side of one wall. Several chairs were strewn about the room and various officers were seated in them, all carefully viewing what was taking place on the other side of that long opening.

"Ms. Sutter, it's nice to see you again." Chief Runyon stepped up and gave her a polite smile. He was a nice looking, middle aged man, with dark brown hair that was graying on the sides. He was tall, nearly as tall as Dylan, and in decent physical shape for a man his age. She pegged him to be around fifty or so. She nodded at him, not really knowing what to say. She'd caused him a lot of trouble over the past few days and she doubted very much if she was his favorite person. She knew he had already had words with Dylan, though she didn't know exactly what had been said between the two men.

"This is a two way mirror," Dylan said from behind her. He'd been so quiet she'd almost forgotten he was there. "You can see him, but he can't see you."

She knew he was giving her the go ahead to look at the scene on the other side of that glass. She just wasn't sure she was ready to.

"Why don't you sit down," Runyon suggested, pulling a chair over and sliding it behind her. "And take your time. I know this can't be easy for you."

That was an understatement. But she knew she needed to get it over with. If she was going to face this man, she had to at least be able to look at him first. Turning her head, she looked through the two-way mirror and into the room that adjoined this one. Alex was the only police officer in the room. He was sitting in a chair near a long, metal table, his legs stretched out in front of him and crossed at the ankles. He looked almost...relaxed, she thought to herself. Like he was sitting down to dinner with family or something. Only he was tapping impatiently against the metal table with his pencil and he was frowning.

Baylie forced her eyes to move to the other occupant of the room. She wasn't sure what she expected to see when she set her eyes on David Melvin for the first time, but it wasn't what she got. She had pictured a monster in her mind — someone ugly and frightening and obviously crazy. What she saw was a handsome man, who looked to be in his late forties. He had dark brown hair that though it appeared to be thinning a little on top, still covered his scalp. His face was long and angular, his dark colored eyes wide set. His lips were thinned into a rather insipid frown. Baylie felt her skin begin to crawl. She wasn't sure what triggered the reaction because she didn't recognize the man. Nothing about him was familiar. Disappointment ate at her and she breathed deeply.

"Sit down," Dylan warned, giving her a gentle shove into the chair Runyon had provided.

Baylie sat, her eyes never leaving David Melvin's face. She could hear Alex talking now.

"You've refused a lawyer. You know your rights. So talk."

David Melvin leaned back in the metal chair he sat in, his frown lifting a little. "I have nothing to say," was all he said.

"Is that right?" Alex sat up straight. "You're going to be charged with murder, Melvin. Two counts, maybe more. The Missoula PD already has piles of evidence against you there. You may as well come clean about Giselle Lindsay and Kevin

Bledsoe. And you may as well tell us where Susan Hanover is."

Melvin snickered at that. "I don't know any of those people. I have no idea what you're talking about."

"You're a liar," Alex said, clearly disgusted. "You were playing a game earlier. What do you hope to gain by continuing, now that we have you?"

"I don't know what you're talking about," Melvin repeated, and reached a hand up to bite at a fingernail. For some reason that caught Baylie's eye. She wasn't sure why. Somehow, she got the feeling that she had seen him do this before.

"What?" Dylan asked, crouching down beside her. "Do you recognize him?"

She couldn't lie to him, no matter how much she wanted to. "Marcus would."

He exchanged glances with Runyon.

"We're working on that one. Mr. Hennings is still in custody in Montana." Runyon crouched beside her too. "Anything you can give us may help, Ms. Sutter."

"I don't remember him," Baylie responded. "His face doesn't ring a bell with me."

"What about his voice?"

"It doesn't sound like the one on the answering machine. That one was deeper," she said thoughtfully.

"It was voice disguised. We had one of our techs go over it." Runyon straightened. "Listen awhile longer. Maybe something will come to you." He looked at another officer in the room. "I need someone to expedite the Hennings case. I need Marcus Hennings to ID this bastard."

A couple of detectives left the room. Baylie looked back at David Melvin again. He was scratching his head, his expression impassive. It was almost as though he hadn't a care in the world. It was unreal. Could this man really have kidnapped and abused children his entire adult life?

"Don't let his looks fool you," Runyon said, obviously reading her mind. "We know for sure they found child pornography at his residence in Montana. At the very least, he is a very sick man."

"Why can't I remember him?" Frustrated, she stood up again and stepped closer to the window. Melvin was tapping his fingers against the table now, clearly growing bored with his situation.

"Did you have anything to do with the disappearance of Susan Hanover?" Alex was asking again.

"Susan Hanover. I don't know a Susan Hanover," Melvin said, tipping his head sideways, as though he didn't understand the question. "I think you might be barking up the wrong tree, Detective."

Alex stared at Melvin long and hard. Then he sat up straight and sighed. "Okay, David. I can see

259

you don't feel like talking here. The thing is, unless you come clean we can't help you."

Melvin's mouth quirked as though he found that statement amusing.

"Is something funny?" Alex asked, leaning back in his chair again.

"The fact that you say you want to help me is very amusing to me. You're trying to pin two murders on me, Detective. I would hardly call that trying to help me."

"What you're doing here are stall tactics, David. It's wasting my time and I value my time."

"Because you have a wife and kids at home? A *little girl*, maybe?"

Alex's eyes narrowed into slits and Baylie could see it was taking all of his strength not to punch David Melvin. "No one will pin anything on you that you didn't do," Alex finally said, his voice low and even. "If you talk, it's possible that the DA will work out a deal with you."

"I was a cop, Detective. I'm well aware of how your deals work."

"Where is Susan Hanover?" Alex asked again. "Is she dead, David? Did you kill her?"

"I'm a little hungry. Maybe I could think better if I had a quick bite. It's been awhile since I've eaten. Not since breakfast this morning." Melvin straightened and looked directly at the mirror where Baylie stood. "Did you hear that, Chief? I'm a little hungry. I'd really like a pizza and some soda. Pepperoni and I'm partial to Dr. Pepper."

Baylie heard Chief Runyon swear from behind her. But that was all she heard, because at that moment her eyes seemed to lock with David Melvin's. It was as if they were drawn together like magnets. She discovered his eyes weren't brown, they were green. And the longer she stared into them, the more they seemed to narrow into slits. Her skin began to pebble and she felt her heart rate speed up. Sweat beaded on her forehead as panic began ebbing its way to the surface. Instinctively, she reached for Dylan. He wasn't there. Suddenly everyone in the room faded away and it was just her and David Melvin. He was staring through that glass as if he could see right into her eyes. And then he smiled, a nice, even row of perfect, white teeth coming into view.

"Come out, come out, wherever you are..." She watched his lips move—heard the words. And it felt like her entire world crashed in on her. She could see that hole again. She could smell the dirt, the rot. She could feel the pain of ropes around her wrists. And she could hear that voice talking to her, whispering in her ear. A moment later, everything went black.

261

Dylan stared through the window at the monster who sat at the table eating the pizza that Washington State's taxpayers had just paid for. Anger was bubbling so close to the surface that it was all Dylan could do not to pounce through that window and kill the bastard with his bare hands.

After Melvin's little charade, Baylie had passed out cold. He'd tried to get to her—had seen her reach for him—but he'd gotten there too late. She'd crumpled into a heap on the floor. At that point, Dylan had known she'd had enough. He'd sent her to her house with a female officer to watch over her until he could get there himself.

"He couldn't have known she was there," Alex said, interrupting Dylan's thoughts.

"The fuck he didn't," Dylan said quietly. "Who else would he have been talking to but her? The words he said were something he said to her as a kid. He knew she was there."

"How could he have known?"

"I don't know!" Dylan snapped, frustrated. All he did know was that seeing Baylie crumble the way she had—and the fear on her face when she'd been escorted out of the police station earlier—had nearly been his undoing. She was literally going through hell and there was nothing he could do to stop it.

"She remembered something," Runyon said, sitting down in a chair across from Dylan's.

262

"She recognized him," Dylan agreed. Baylie hadn't admitted anything. She'd clearly been too distraught. But it had been more than obvious that David Melvin's words had struck a chord with her. "He's a sick bastard. I'd like to poison that fucking pizza he's eating."

"You and me both," Runyon agreed.

"So what now? We let him eat and play some more games? Because I'm telling you that if he says one more sick fuck word I'm going to shoot the bastard," Alex warned, running a hand through his already disheveled blond hair.

"I want to talk to him," Dylan said, his eyes still watching as Melvin ate his food.

"Not a good idea," Runyon said, shaking his head. "It's obvious you're in this far too personally."

"With all due respect, Sir, the guy is a child molester. I think that makes this personal for all of us. He's the worst kind of scum." Dylan straightened and looked his boss in the eye. "I can't lie to you and tell you I don't have feelings for her. Is that what you're fishing for?"

Runyon swore and rolled his eyes. "Of all the times for one of my best guys to start thinking with his dick, it had to be you and it had to be now. It just figures."

Dylan didn't dignify that with a response. "I'm good at what I do, Sir. I can get him to talk."

Runyon snorted. "I don't doubt that. It's your personal stake in this that has me concerned. There's a line here, Stone, and you've managed to cross it." Runyon folded his hands in front of him and thought things over for several seconds. "I have to admit that after meeting Baylie Sutter myself and seeing her in here today, she's gotten under my skin to a point too. It's hard not to let a case like hers get to you." He looked at Dylan seriously. "But that doesn't change the fact that he hasn't been charged with anything yet and he's good at playing the system. Until we have some hardcore evidence, one wrong move and we'll lose him. He was a cop, Stone. He knows how we work."

"Five minutes," Dylan said again, knowing he had to get into that room. "I know how psychos like him work. I can break him down."

After a moment, Runyon cursed. "Hell, five minutes. And I'm watching you like a hawk. You step out of line, you're done. In more ways than one." He looked at Alex. "Go with him. Keep him out of trouble."

Relieved, Dylan stood up. He followed Alex out the door and down the hall. An officer on guard outside the door where Melvin was being held unlocked it for them and ushered them inside.

David Melvin looked up from the slice of pizza he was eating. He looked content with his pepperoni pizza and six-pack of Dr. Pepper. It made Dylan's blood boil all over again. Instead of reacting to the sight, he folded his arms over his chest and stared at the disgusting excuse for a man.

"Hello, Detective Stone." Melvin smiled. "I must say, I was wondering what took you so long to show up. I would have thought you'd be here with bells on."

"How's your pizza?" Dylan forced himself to ask, careful to keep his voice neutral.

Melvin reached up and wiped his mouth with a napkin, his eyes never leaving Dylan's. "It's quite good. Thank you for asking. I'll have to remember Roberto's Pizza Palace when I go to dinner next time."

There wasn't going to be a next time, but Dylan refrained from taking Melvin's bait. Instead, he walked over and sat down at the table. "How do you know Baylie Sutter?"

Melvin chewed on a piece of pepperoni, his eyes expressionless. Then he swallowed. "I'm not familiar with anyone by that name."

"We both know you're lying. If you lie to me, I won't be able to help you."

"You aren't planning to help me anyway," Melvin said, folding his napkin neatly and laying it on his empty paper plate.

"Why did you kill Giselle Lindsay and Kevin Bledsoe?" Dylan prodded. "It's because they're tied to Baylie Sutter, isn't it?"

265

Melvin didn't respond. He just sat there, as if waiting for Dylan to say more.

Dylan forced himself to keep his temper in check. He reminded himself several times over, that this man was crazy. "I'm afraid we're out of time, David. You wanted food, we got it for you. We even gave you time to eat. Now we need to talk."

"I know you heard me before, Detective. You don't think I know this mirror is two sided? You don't think I know that there are police all over in the room next door, listening to our every word?"

Dylan decided to try another tactic. "Marcus Hennings is on his way here. Once he's here, he'll ID you and it's all over."

Now a flicker of emotion flashed in Melvin's eyes. Ah, so those were the magic words. Sitting up straight, Dylan was the one who now smiled. "They were little kids, Melvin. You're one sick fucker."

Melvin's face remained impassive but Dylan could tell he'd hit his mark.

"We've got a lot of pending charges against you, David. At the very least, you're looking at kidnapping and child rape. At the most, murder. Nothing is going to change that now. It's done."

"Marcus Hennings is a convicted murderer," Melvin surprised Dylan by saying. "No one will believe a word he says."

"Are you sure about that?" Dylan asked, his eyes narrowed.

Melvin looked slightly uncomfortable for a moment. Just as quickly, he seemed to relax. "It's his word against mine. Hearsay."

"It's not hearsay if he lived it. He has witnesses."

"You're full of shit, Detective. I know what you're trying to do and it isn't going to work. I don't know any Marcus Hennings. And I don't know a Baylie Sutter. I was a cop, for crying out loud. A highly decorated cop."

Alex snorted at that.

Dylan just shrugged. "I've seen some pretty highly decorated cops do some pretty shitty things. And prison unfortunately isn't a very good place for them to end up."

Looking far less comfortable now, Melvin remained silent, his eyes boring into Dylan's.

"You got yourself a double whammy, David," Dylan continued, enjoying the fact that he was finally breaking through that bullshit exterior of Melvin's. "After all, not only are you a highly decorated cop, but you're also a child rapist. Those are two things that guys in the pen just love to get their hands on. Way to go."

"You have nothing on me."

"I have all I need," Dylan assured him. "So tell me, how many children were there? Five, ten — twenty?"

"Fuck you," Melvin said, his voice low. His teeth were ground tightly together and he could barely get the words out.

"Who is she, David? Where did you take her from?"

"Fuck you," Melvin said again, this time quieter.

"I don't think so. I'm a little old for you, don't you think? A sick fuck like you would rather have a defenseless little boy or girl, isn't that right?"

"I don't have to take this!" Melvin said, clearly upset now. "I didn't do nothing to any little kids. They're both lying! You're lying. This is entrapment!"

"I think you know better than that, David. This is questioning. It's standard protocol. You should know that, being a highly decorated cop and all."

"I want to talk to my lawyer," Melvin said, after a moment. "I'm not saying another word to you until I do."

Dylan exchanged glances with Alex.

"Then let's just make that phone call for you," Alex said, straightening. Dylan stood and they both exited the room. Runyon met them in the hallway.

"I don't know whether you pissed him off into more silence or scared him into considering his options."

"He's considering his options, trust me," Dylan said, folding his arms over his chest. "He knows what happens to cops and child rapists behind bars. He's going to try to work the system again."

Runyon swore. "We still have nothing on Hanover."

"We will. Give him thirty minutes with his lawyer and he's going to start singing like a canary."

EIGHTEEN

Baylie stared at the television screen, not really watching the program playing. It was an old sitcom from the nineties that she had hoped might make her laugh or at the very least, concentrate on something besides the fact that her life appeared to be unraveling before her eyes. Unfortunately, it had accomplished neither.

Catherine Russo, the officer who had accompanied her back to her house, sat in a chair across the room surfing the internet on her cell phone. She was a nice enough, younger woman with dark, curling hair and brown eyes. Her heavyset form had sat in the chair for pretty much the entire time they'd been home.

Hours had gone by since she'd left Dylan at the police station. She'd heard nothing from him, not that she had expected to. She was a witness, not a police officer. Likely, she would be on a need to know basis again and that fact annoyed her. At least when she and Dylan had been traveling together, he'd had no choice but to let her know what information he found out. Now she wouldn't know what things he was leaving out. Certainly, he would leave all the important things out.

Hearing tapping on the front door, she jumped and sat up. Immediately Officer Russo was on it. She crossed the room quickly, her hand on her gun. A moment later, Dylan stepped into the foyer. Relief washed over Baylie and she watched as he exchanged a few words with Russo, before sending her on her way and shutting the door behind her.

Baylie took in his disheveled appearance and immediately felt guilty. He didn't look so hot. His dark hair was messy, as though he'd run his hands through it a few too many times. His jaw was covered with a good layer of five o'clock shadow and his eyes were red. Obviously he was exhausted. When she thought about it, she realized he really hadn't had any good sleep in the last several days. He'd been too busy watching out for her.

"Hey," he said quietly, his eyes scanning hers carefully. "You okay?"

She smiled halfway. "Apparently better than you. You're looking a little rough, Detective."

He snorted and walked over to flop down next to her on the couch. "Long day."

"So what happened?"

"He's requesting a lawyer," he finally said, meeting her gaze. "I think he's getting the clue that he's in real trouble now. Marcus is on his way here. Once he IDs the bastard, a whole new ball of wax is started."

"I'm sorry," she said, reading into his words and realizing that she had held things up by not being able to ID Melvin herself.

"It's not your fault, Baylie." She saw the understanding in his eyes, but something else was there as well. A little bit of scrutiny. It set her on edge and she avoided his gaze.

"You wanna tell me what you remembered about him tonight? Right before you fainted I could tell you remembered something."

She'd known the question was coming and she still didn't know quite how to answer him. "I remembered the words."

"What else?" he prodded, sitting up and resting his elbows on his knees. "Just tell me whatever it is because even if it doesn't make any sense to you, it might make sense to me."

"I don't know, Dylan. I see images but they don't make sense." She leaned back against the couch, determined not to let the visions she'd had earlier come back into her mind. She knew she needed to remember, but somehow she was afraid it would destroy her if she did.

"What images, Baylie?"

272

She looked down at the blanket she had covering her lap, her eyes concentrating on the stitching as she tried to figure out how to explain what she'd seen to him. "I *felt*, more than saw."

"What do you mean by felt?"

"I don't know." She sat up again, frustrated. "I think he had me tied up at one point because when he spoke through that mirror tonight, I remembered hearing that voice before and at the time there was pain in my wrists. Like I had ropes around them. I could hear his voice whispering in my ear." She swallowed hard, trying to tamp down on the revulsion she was feeling.

"Did you see his face?" he asked quietly.

"I didn't see his face. I heard his voice."

"Okay, that's good. That's something, right?" He reached over and took her hand, entwining his fingers with hers.

She met his gaze and her anxiety calmed down somewhat. He didn't look repulsed, as she was afraid he would. He just looked sorry. Leaning back, she let her head rest against his shoulder.
"I didn't think you were going to be coming back here tonight."

"I didn't either," he said, his breath fanning against her hair. "Right now Melvin's playing a game. He won't get his lawyer in there until morning. By then Marcus will be here and that's when we should have some kind of progress. Until then, we both need some sleep."

She still didn't think she'd be able to sleep but she got up and followed him toward her bedroom. While he showered, she lay there in the dark and stared up at the ceiling. Five minutes later he was lying beside her, snoring softly. She snuggled up against him, desperate for that feeling of safety she got only from being as close to him as possible. He appeared to understand her need, even in his sleep, because his arm snaked around her and gently pulled her back against his chest. A few minutes later, she felt herself drift off to sleep.

It didn't feel like she'd been asleep more than a few minutes, before a loud crashing noise jolted her from a sleepy haze. Before she could react, Dylan's hand was on her chest, pushing her back onto the bed. He sat up straight, his gun in his hand and his eyes instantly on alert.

"Stay here," his voice said sternly, as he slid out of bed. He reached for the jeans he'd tossed on the floor earlier and yanked them up over his hips. Then he disappeared from the room, leaving her staring terrified behind him. She heard the front door open, then close again. Sitting up, she reached for his cell phone, ready to dial 911 if the need arose. Fortunately it didn't. Dylan walked back into the bedroom suddenly, nearly scaring her half to death.

She climbed out from under the covers and crawled toward the foot of the bed. She could tell by the grim look on his face that something bad had happened. "What's going on?"

"Where's my phone?" was all he said.

"Dylan, what is going on?" she demanded, though she wasn't entirely sure she wanted to know.

"I need my phone, Baylie," he said impatiently. Clearly, he was in no hurry to explain himself. She handed him his phone and waited as he dialed someone.

"We have a problem here," he said into the cell phone. "Someone just threw a rock through Baylie Sutter's window." His voice lowered and he walked out into the hallway, obviously so she wouldn't hear him. Angry, she slid her bare feet to the floor and followed him. When she reached the living room, she grimaced. Her front window was in pieces all over the carpeted floor. Sure enough, there was a large rock in the midst of the mess. Baylie stared at it dumbly.

"Stay back. You'll get cut."

Dylan's voice startled her and she looked up at him. "Who would do this?"

"Hell, Baylie, I don't know. We know one person who *didn't* do it because he's in custody. Don't touch anything. Alex has a patrol officer on the way. We'll have him take some pictures and bag

275

any evidence." He crossed his arms over his bare chest as he looked at her closely. "Just how angry do you think Jeepers McClain is at you, anyway?"

Baylie shuddered. "I don't know. The fact that you said something to his father and got him detention probably really made him mad. Is your truck okay?"

"I looked at it. It's fine." He swore, shoving his gun into the back of his jeans. "If I find out McClain did this, his daddy won't be getting him out of any punishment this time. He's going to jail."

"I'm going to lose my job anyway, Dylan. I haven't been in for a week. Principal Harris isn't my biggest fan. Trust me, I probably won't ever see Jeepers McClain again."

He looked at her, his expression serious. "This is his second attempt to get your attention, Baylie. He's got some kind of weird fixation with you and I don't like it. He's not going to go away easily. Not unless he finally gets what he deserves."

She didn't get a chance to answer because a patrol officer knocked on the door. Obviously, Dylan knew the two men because he called them by name. They both looked more than interested in the fact that Dylan Stone was standing in the living room in nothing but a pair of jeans. Apparently, Dylan didn't give a rip because he gave them both stern looks and told them to get to work. Thirty minutes later, they had taken their pictures and bagged anything they felt was important. After they left, Dylan cleaned up the mess and managed to find a tarp in her garage to plaster over the front window. She would have to call a repairman in the morning.

The rest of the night was restless at best. Dylan managed to doze on her couch for another couple of hours. She lay in her bed, staring up at the ceiling. By the time light poked through the curtains and dawn was upon them, she was thankful. She got up and showered, then quickly dressed. She needed to find a repairman to fix her window and she didn't want Dylan sneaking off without her this morning, which it turned out, was exactly what he'd planned to do. When she walked into the kitchen he was already dressed in the jeans he'd worn the day before. He had a clean Seattle PD t-shirt on and his hair was damp from the shower he'd apparently managed to snag without her knowing, earlier in the morning.

"I've got Catherine Russo heading back over here. She'll stay with you until I come up with something better. Someone's bringing McClain in for questioning about your window. I need to be there."

"What about me?" she asked, irritated. She walked over to the coffee pot, which he had taken the liberty of starting. After pouring herself a cup, she glared at him. "I'm not going to be a prisoner here, Dylan. I want to see Marcus."

277

"He'll be in a holding cell, Baylie. He'll be there until we figure all this out."

"He's innocent. You know that."

He took a long drink of his own coffee. "I told you yesterday, this is going to take some time to figure out. It doesn't matter whether I believe him or not. A judge will have to overturn his sentence. Until that happens he's still an inmate at the Montana State Prison." He swallowed the last of his coffee and set the cup down, just as a knock sounded at the door. He walked over and opened it, allowing Catherine Russo to enter the room. Baylie scowled at him. Apparently he was unmoved by her expression because he just winked at her and walked out the front door. A moment later, his truck backed out of the driveway and sped off down the street.

By the time Dylan got into the station it was after eight. He'd had to go home, shave and change clothes into something more business appropriate. Then his caffeine fix had to be taken care of. One cup of coffee was never enough, especially after the night he'd had. As he walked through the doors, Alex accosted him.

"Runyon's looking for you. Hobart McClain and his father are here."

Dylan had planned on sucking down at least two cups of coffee before he dealt with Jeepers McClain.

Clearly, that was not to be. He grimaced. "What's the little bastard saying? I suppose he claims he didn't throw the rock through Baylie's window?"

"Did you really think he would admit to it?"

"He admitted it last time, didn't he? You said he confessed to trashing her car."

"Not in so many words," Alex said, shrugging his shoulders. "He pretty much said he might have and what was I going to do about it? About that point, his father smacked him on the back of the head and ordered him to quit fucking around. Within minutes, we had a deal worked out so that he stayed out of jail. That's the way Patrick McClain works. And trust me, he's pissed right now."

Dylan wasn't sure he was calm enough at this point to deal with Jeepers McClain. What he really wanted to do was plant his fist in the kid's face. Reaching for Runyon's door, he and Alex walked into the office. As expected, Patrick McClain was standing near the chief's desk, a look of utter disbelief on his face. Runyon looked bored to death. Clearly, he was already tired of dealing with the situation. When he saw Dylan, he motioned him over.

"You've met Patrick McClain, I assume?"

Dylan exchanged stares with Mr. McClain, though neither of them spoke. The guy was a pompous ass, even if he was on the road to political

Utopia. Pretty much the mirror image of his son with a few wrinkles, he had light brown hair and a dark complexion. His hair was neatly trimmed, his face clean-shaven. He was dressed to the hilt, in a suit that probably cost more than Dylan's entire wardrobe. Dylan supposed women probably found him attractive. Unfortunately, Dylan didn't share that opinion. He turned to Jeepers, his expression drawn. "Just what do you have against Baylie Sutter, Hobart?"

The kid snorted an expletive and looked up at his father. "I told you, Dad. The guy has it in for me. This whole department has it in for me."

"Shut up, Hobart." Patrick McClain stepped toward Dylan. "What evidence do you have that supports you hauling my son in here?"

"He already admitted to trashing her car," Dylan said evenly. "And he's been harassing her on a regular basis for a while now."

"He was reprimanded for his alleged bad behavior, Detective Stone. And he says he's left Ms. Sutter alone since then."

"Except when he trashed her car," Dylan pointed out a second time.

Patrick McClain's expression darkened considerably. "I think you've decided to pick on my boy. I'm curious as to why. He mentioned that you're personally involved with Ms. Sutter. Is that your motivation here? You've got it in for my boy?"

"That's a bunch of crap," Dylan said, stepping back and leaning against the wall. "And my personal relationship with Ms. Sutter is none of your damned business."

"I think it is," McClain went on. "Especially when you keep dragging my son in here and throwing accusations at him. He didn't throw any rock through that woman's window. I know that for a fact because he was home with us last night."

Dylan's brow furrowed. "Is that right? All night?"

"Yes," McClain snapped. "All night."

"Your wife was home too?" Runyon asked, finally intervening in the conversation.

"What the hell does that have to do with anything? Are you insinuating that I'm lying?"

"I'm trying to establish who your son was with last night, McClain." Runyon looked at Dylan. "Did you actually see the boy?"

Dylan wished he could say yes. "No. By the time I got outside, whoever threw the rock was gone. But he's trashed her car before and has threatened her on various occasions. I've witnessed his behavior with my own eyes."

"That doesn't mean he threw a rock through her window," McClain argued, checking his cell phone absently as it vibrated. He cursed and hit the ignore button. Then he looked at Runyon. "He admitted he didn't see the boy. You can't tell me you're going to charge Hobart after hearing that."

"I don't know what I'm going to do," Runyon said irritably. "But you sure as hell aren't going to dictate to me. Now sit down."

"For God's sake—" McClain began, but was cut off by Runyon.

"I'm tired of seeing your kid in here, McClain. I've turned the other cheek for months now. He's shoplifted, harassed, assaulted and God knows what else. And you don't do anything about it but throw your weight around as though you're the fucking president."

"I don't believe this!" McClain snapped, glaring at Runyon and then Dylan again. "I'll talk to the mayor! He'll see things my way."

"I don't give a shit if he does see things your way. I run this department." Runyon looked at Dylan. "In light of the lack of evidence, I'm going to have to cut Hobart loose."

"Sir—" Dylan began, but was cut off.

"There's not sufficient evidence to charge him. You didn't see him, nor did anyone else. And," Runyon looked over at Patrick McClain as though he were a serpent. "His father claims he was at home with him. He has an alibi."

"This is bullshit," Dylan snapped. "The kid is a deviant. He's been in more trouble than any other kid around here. It's about time he pays for it. A couple days in lock up should do the trick."

"Hell no!" Jeepers exclaimed, jumping out of his seat. "I ain't going to jail! I didn't do anything! I didn't touch that bitch!"

Dylan reined in his temper and ignored the kid. He looked at the elder McClain instead. "The fact that you keep ignoring your son's behavior and bailing him out of trouble is only making things worse. Don't you see that?"

"Who in the hell do you think you are?" Patrick roared and then turned to Chief Runyon. "Are you going to allow this kind of railroading, Mitch? You know damn well this is bullshit."

"Sit down, Patrick," Runyon said, sighing as he leaned back in his chair. "You too," he snapped at Jeepers, who continued to swear under his breath, but took his seat again. "Stone has a point. It's not the first time your son has been involved in bad news. Seems to me you should be a little more concerned with his discipline, rather than always getting him out of things without a consequence."

"I don't need you to tell me how to parent," McClain snapped angrily. "Now is he free to go?"

Runyon frowned, but shrugged his shoulders. "I already told you I won't hold him."

"Now that's more like it," McClain said, standing up and indicating Jeepers follow him.

"Sit down," Runyon said, his voice low and threatening. "I'm not quite finished here."

"I have a meeting in ten minutes, Runyon. I don't have time for this today," McClain complained.

"Make time."

McClain frowned but sat back down.

Runyon looked at Jeepers. "For the record, son, I think you did throw that rock through her window. Or at the very least, you were there when it happened and encouraged the incident. Regardless, I can't stick a charge on you so you're getting away this time. But this will be the *last* time. Do you understand me? I'm done with these shenanigans of yours. Finished. I'd better not see you back in here again. And if I hear one complaint from Ms. Sutter about you harassing her, I'll haul your ass in here and formally charge you. You got that?"

Jeepers didn't answer until his father smacked him in the back of the head. Then he merely nodded.

"Good. Now get out of here and go to school."

Jeepers and his father were gone moments later.

Dylan swore. "He had something to do with it."

"You're a detective, Stone. No evidence, no charge." Runyon leaned back in his chair again. "We have more important fish to fry. Melvin's been in with his attorney since seven-thirty this morning. We had a change in plans with Marcus Hennings. Pictures were faxed to him at Deer Lodge and he positively identified Melvin."

"So we've got him on kidnapping then?"

284

"It's definitely enough to keep him here for the time being. They'll want him in Montana eventually to face those charges."

"I thought he was coming here himself," Dylan said, referring to Marcus.

"He refused," Runyon said, eyeing Dylan curiously. "Apparently he's not the most cooperative person on earth. He wanted to talk to only you and when we told him that wasn't possible at the time, he shut up tight as a drum."

That didn't really surprise Dylan. Marcus distrusted law enforcement for obvious reasons. "He's had a rough time with the police. It shouldn't be a surprise to any of us that he's skeptical of our motives."

"If he wants to get out of Deer Lodge, he'd better learn to trust us. There's been no proof brought to my attention yet that he didn't kill his wife and her lover. He certainly had the motive."

"He didn't do it, Sir. And Kevin Bledsoe didn't kill any of those women in Chapman either. Melvin is responsible for all of this. I'd stake my badge on it."

"That's a mighty high bet to make, Stone. You'd better hope you're right. Now get out of here and let me get some work done. The attorney will let you know when Melvin is ready to talk — if he's ever ready to talk."

Dylan and Alex left the chief's office.

285

"Detective Stone?"

Dylan turned around to see a short, portly man, with thin, graying hair coming toward him. He carried a brief case and file folder in his hands. Dylan guessed him to be in his early fifties and his persona screamed lawyer. He knew this had to be Melvin's representation.

"I'm Lawrence Jacoby. Mr. Melvin has hired me as representation." The man shuffled his belongings and held out his hand. Dylan reached forward and shook it, frowning.

"Is your client ready to talk to us now?"

"Is it possible for you and I to talk for a moment?"

Dylan exchanged glances with Alex. Here it was. Melvin was obviously going to try and make a deal.

"We can talk in the conference room." Dylan and Alex led Jacoby down the hallway and into an empty room with a long table. When they were all seated around it, Dylan leaned back in his chair and met Jacoby's gaze. "So what does the bastard want?"

"First of all, let me start by saying that my client has not admitted any guilt to anything. In fact, quite the opposite."

"He's lying."

"You have no proof of this."

"I'll get proof, Mr. Jacoby. It's only a matter of time before this puzzle pieces itself together. There was DNA left behind on the body of Giselle Lindsay and also on Kevin Bledsoe and Carl Eisenberg. I've got a pretty good hunch whose DNA it is. Not only that, there were four murders in Chapman, Montana that are being looked at more closely. Originally, Kevin Bledsoe was charged with those crimes. The cases have since been re-opened." Dylan gave Jacoby a knowing look. "And let's not forget Marcus Hennings. He has positively identified your client as his kidnapper. I assume you are aware that there is no statute of limitations on kidnapping a child under the age of eighteen. Not as long as the child is still alive."

"Don't forget the child rape charges," Alex added.

Jacoby had the decency to wince. "My client admits nothing. He has never heard of Marcus Hennings."

"What is it that he wants?" Dylan asked, growing bored with the conversation. It was clear that Melvin was going to pull out all the stops.

"As a matter of fact, he wants something rather simple." Jacoby opened up his notebook, which Dylan presumed had his notes from his conversation with Melvin in it. "He asked that you bring Nikki here. He wants to see her. And that's a quote." Jacoby met Dylan's gaze. "He said you would know who Nikki is. Do you?"

Dylan felt his blood run cold. He narrowed his eyes. "That bastard."

287

"Dylan-" Alex began.

"Tell him to fuck off," Dylan said firmly.

Jacoby raised a brow. "Do you want to explain to me what's going on here? I had a sixty-minute conversation with this man. He did not go into detail. He denied the charges against him and made a simple request."

"A simple request?" Dylan said, standing up and leaning over the table to glare down at Jacoby. "Nikki is a woman he kidnapped when she was six years old, held in a dirty hole and repeatedly raped."

Jacoby narrowed his eyes and then swore. "For God's sake, you're kidding me."

"It might help if you asked your client to be more specific with you when he asks for things," Alex said, frowning. "He's playing a game here. Don't you see that? He wouldn't ask to see her if he didn't know who she was."

"No charges pending against him have anything to do with a woman named Nikki," Jacoby argued, ripping through the papers he had in front of him.

"That's because she doesn't remember the first twelve years of her life," Dylan snapped, so angry he could barely see straight. "She didn't even remember that her first name is Nikki. Not until Marcus Hennings told her so."

Jacoby swore again. "Why would he want to see her then?"

"Because he's a sick fuck," Dylan said, slamming his fist into the table.

"He's playing a game," Alex said again, shooting Dylan a look that told him to pull himself together. "It's unlikely that Ms. Sutter will agree to see him."

"It's not unlikely, it's plain damn not happening," Dylan said, glaring from Alex to Jacoby. "He's going to hell, with or without talking to her."

"Perhaps I should speak with my client again," Jacoby said, standing up and gathering his papers together.

"Perhaps you should," Alex agreed snidely. When Jacoby had left the room, he turned to Dylan. "Get it together, dude. I can't say I blame you but you're letting your dick get in the way again. This may be the only way to get him to talk. He already said her name. That proves that Marcus was telling the truth. He's slipping up."

"I'm not forcing her in there with that sick fuck," Dylan said, leaning back against the table and sighing in frustration. "It took balls for him to ask for her."

"Clearly his attorney had no idea what he's gotten himself into," Alex agreed. "If he's smart, he'll tell his client to cooperate now."

Dylan didn't believe for a minute that David Melvin was going to cooperate. His apparent goal in life was to torment the hell out of Marcus

Hennings and Baylie, for whatever reason. And now that he was caught and most likely knew he was going down, he had nothing to lose anymore.

"Detectives?" a desk sergeant said, stepping into the room. "Mr. Jacoby asked me to come and get you. Apparently Mr. Melvin wants to speak with you both."

NINETEEN

Dylan wasn't sure he'd be able to control himself now. As he walked into the meeting room, his anger bubbled into nearly uncontrollable rage.

David Melvin sat at the table again, and this time there were waffles in front of him. Waffles! Like he was a freaking prince or something.

"Ah, Detectives. It's nice to see you both again. The waffles are great this morning. Have you had some?" Melvin swallowed and wiped his mouth. "I must say I'm being treated first rate here."

"I can see that," Alex said blandly. "Now cut the crap. What do you want?"

"Please sit down. It makes me uncomfortable when you're all standing around the room staring down at me."

Dylan opened his mouth to tell the guy to fuck off, but Alex's elbow in his ribs stopped him. Alex sat down, but Dylan refused. "I'm not playing this game anymore. Talk, or quit wasting our time. We don't need a confession out of you anyway. We've already got live witnesses. You can tell your story to a jury and deal with them."

"My client is aware of this," Jacoby said quietly.

"Shut up, Lawrence," Melvin said thinly, his eyes never leaving Dylan's. "I've decided your services are no longer needed."

Jacoby looked stunned as he faced his client. "But—"

"Leave," Melvin said simply, as though he were a parent talking to a disobedient child.

Jacoby's face reddened. He stood quickly. "You're making a huge mistake, Mr. Melvin. If I were you I would re-think what you're doing here."

"Leave," Melvin repeated.

Jacoby swore, but gathered his things and left the room.

Dylan raised a brow, crossing his arms over his chest. This guy was either really, really stupid or really, really smart. The trouble was, Dylan couldn't tell which.

"Now," Melvin said, pushing his breakfast plate aside. "I've come to the conclusion that you've got a fairly good case coming along or I wouldn't still be here. Therefore I'm not going drag the inevitable out any further."

The words surprised the hell out of Dylan and he frowned. "And?"

"And, I'd like to talk with you both. But first, I need something from you."

Dylan's blood began to boil. "No."

Melvin was quiet a moment, then he smiled. "So you've grown attached to her. I can see how you would. She's a pretty little thing, isn't she?"

Alex stepped between them before Dylan could get his hands around Melvin's neck.

"I'm only stating a fact, Detective. Clearly you agree with me." Melvin continued to smile as Alex shoved Dylan back toward the door.

"You are a sick fucker," Alex said, taking the words right out of Dylan's mouth. His fingers were clenched in Dylan's shirt, holding him back firmly.

"I want to talk to her. It's as simple as that. You can cooperate, or she dies."

Dylan shoved at Alex's hands and finally succeeded in getting free of them. "You'll never hurt her again, you sick fuck! I'll tear your heart out with my bare hands first!"

"Detective, Detective, you're awfully simple minded, aren't you? I expected better from you."

Dylan wanted to choke the man to death. At that moment, he wanted nothing more than to literally see the life leave this man's eyes. Instead, he glared down at him, his teeth clenched together. "I'm going to take you down, Melvin. Personally. And that's a promise."

"I'm sure you'll do your best to," Melvin said, his eyes emotionless. "But I would suggest you listen to me good if you want them to live."

293

"Them," Alex repeated, before Dylan had the chance. "Who are you talking about?"

"I'm talking about Susie," Melvin said simply, his smile widening. "After all, I've been in here almost two days now. And before that I was on the run for three. That's five days she's been without food — and five days since I've refilled her water."

The words hung in the room like a bad odor.

Alex swore. "Where is she?"

"Bring Nikki here. I want to talk to her first."

Dylan shook his head. "No."

"Then Susie will slowly die. Starvation and dehydration are rough. What a rather painful way to go."

"You said *them*," Alex prodded, shaking his head at Dylan to keep quiet. "Who else are we talking about here?"

Melvin appeared to think his answer over carefully. "Well I couldn't very well leave Susie in there alone, now could I?"

The room was deathly quiet for several seconds before Alex finally swore, then spoke. "If they die, you're looking at two more counts of murder."

"Two, five, ten...what's the difference? One life sentence is ten life sentences." Melvin sat back and folded his hands in front of him. "I suggest you do as I ask, Detectives. Now I'd like to go back to my nice, comfy holding cell. All this talking and that filling breakfast have made me a little sleepy."

Before Dylan could react, Alex shoved him toward the now open door and into the hallway.

Runyon was waiting for them. He frowned at Dylan but didn't speak directly to him. "I heard what he said. Do you think he's bluffing?"

Alex answered first. "I don't know, Sir."

"He's not bluffing," Dylan said through his teeth. "I wish to hell he was. They're in that hole somewhere. The same hole he held Baylie and Marcus in when they were children."

"Hole. What the hell kind of *hole* could they be in? It's not easy to dig a fucking hole big enough to hold people," Runyon said, his voice raised. "Get your girl back in here. I want to talk to her."

"Sir—" Dylan began.

"Don't fuck with me here, Stone. I get that you're in this dick deep. I don't give a shit. She's the key and I want her in here."

"She doesn't remember anything," Dylan argued. "We've already tried this. She couldn't even positively identify him."

"I'm going to get Hennings on the phone. You get Baylie Sutter in here within the hour or you're fired." Runyon turned and stormed down the hallway, clearly in no mood to argue further.

Dylan slammed his fist against the wall and swore.

295

"He's right. There are lives hanging in the balance here, Dylan. Just bring her in. She wanted to talk to him anyway. You told me that."

"That's before he scared the hell out of her," Dylan said, sighing as he straightened. "I'm not sure she can face him."

"She needs to. It may be what finally makes her remember."

That was exactly what Dylan was afraid of.

Baylie knew things were bad the minute she walked into the police station. Dylan had phoned and ordered Catherine Russo to bring her in. And apparently, he'd told Catherine to hurry because Baylie wasn't even allowed to stay around and make sure her window got finished properly. An officer was assigned to stay at the house until the job was done.

She was ushered down a hallway and into a room where Alex and Dylan were seated, both with rather grim looks on their faces. When Dylan saw her, he stood and walked over to her.

"What's going on?" she asked, before he could speak.

Dylan shoved his hands into the pockets of his black trousers and stared at her for a long moment. "He admitted that he has Susie. She's still alive."

Relief washed over Baylie and for the first time in days, she felt hope. "That's good news." She looked over at Alex when Dylan didn't confirm this. "It is good news, right?"

Alex was frowning too. She shook her head at both of them. "Why isn't this good news?"

"Because, Baylie. He's holding her in that hole — wherever it is — and he hasn't been there to give her water or food for five days." Dylan's words came out quietly, but firmly. Immediately she felt despair again. Five days in a hole. Susan was living the same nightmare Baylie had lived through.

"Oh God."

Dylan reached for her, obviously afraid she was going to faint. She slapped his hands away. "He told you he has her. He must have told you where she is."

Dylan slowly began shaking his head and Baylie felt her world rotate again. "But why? Why won't he tell you?"

Dylan leaned back against the table, his arms crossed over his broad chest. "Because, Baylie, he wants to talk to you first. He asked for Nikki."

Nikki...The name played itself over inside her head. Immediately she felt a pounding in her temples. Nikki was her name. A name she still didn't fully remember.

"Have her sit down," Runyon said, stepping into the room and shutting the door behind him.

"I don't want to sit down," she said, hearing her own voice shake. Her hands were trembling too

297

and she clenched them together in the hopes of stopping the reaction.

"Ms. Sutter, I realize this is a lot for you to handle."

"I'm not sure you do," she said, setting her purse down and finally giving in to the urge to sit down. She breathed deeply, desperate to slow her heart rate and gain control of her panic.

"You don't have to talk to him," Dylan said, crouching down in front of her. "It's your decision to make. Marcus positively identified him. We've got enough to keep him here for kidnapping and child rape."

Baylie winced and rubbed at her temples. The words were so ugly she didn't want to attach them to herself—yet she had to. She had been a victim of this man too.

"If you don't talk to him, he won't tell us where Susan Hanover is," Runyon said, cutting to the chase. "And as of right now, Marcus Hennings has no idea where the hole is that you and he were held in as children. So that means—"

"That Susan will die of starvation or dehydration, whichever comes first," she figured out aloud, the idea making her stomach roll. Suddenly she could feel Susan's fear. She could feel the anguish of being locked up in a dark, miserable hole with no windows and no contact with the outside world.

"I'll see him." She heard herself say the words, before she'd fully decided to do so. But she didn't try to take them back. If Susan died because of her—that was just one more person's face she would see in her nightmares every night. That was something she couldn't live with. She looked up at Dylan. "Will you be there with me?"

"Damn right," he said, reaching over and squeezing her hands. "Every step of the way."

TWENTY

Baylie wasn't sure what to expect when she walked into the small conference room a few minutes later, Dylan in front of her.

The man sitting at the table in the middle of the room was smaller than he had seemed the day before, through the two-way mirror. His skin was pale and lined with age and his hair was dark with salt and pepper streaks in it. He immediately looked up at her when she entered the room. She felt his gaze on her and it made her skin crawl.

Dylan's eyes roamed over her face and eventually locked with hers. He spoke to her without words, his hand indicating the empty chair on the other side of the table. She knew that if she gave him the word, he would usher her out of the room without question. The concern was there on his face. But she couldn't run away. Not anymore.

Reluctantly, she sat down, her eyes avoiding David Melvin's. He was too real to her now. They

300

were breathing the same air. She could smell his sweat. And likely, he could smell her fear.

"You wanted to see her. Say your piece and keep up your end of the bargain," Dylan said shortly, as he stood only a foot or so away from Baylie. He clearly had her back. For once she was thankful for the gun he always kept clipped to his side.

"I'd like to talk to her alone," Melvin said evenly.

"No," Dylan answered, leaning against the wall and crossing his arms over his chest. "You've got as long as she's willing to sit here and not a minute more."

Baylie felt Melvin's eyes on her again. He let out a deep sigh that seemed to penetrate her skin all the way to her bones.

"I've missed you, Nikki."

Baylie forced herself to meet his gaze. Revulsion washed over her. "Where is Susan? You said if I came here, you would tell them where you're holding her."

Melvin continued to stare at her until she felt like squirming. "You know you were such a pretty little girl. Blonde curls and big, blue eyes. I'm having a hard time tying you to the picture I have in my head anymore."

"Where is Susan?" she said again, this time with more conviction.

"She's safe and sound at home. Don't worry. We have time for a good, long chat."

301

"I don't want to chat with you."

"I took care of you, Nikki. You should appreciate that."

"Appreciate what? That you hurt me over and over and over again?" The words came out of their own volition.

"You were my special baby girl, Nikki. Don't you know that? I never hurt you. I loved you."

Baylie felt her stomach roll. "Please just tell them where Susan is. This was never about her. You've hurt enough people."

"I suppose that in a way you're right," he agreed, frowning. "But I had to get your attention someway."

"Why? I'm not your daughter!" she finally said, her voice rising. "I don't know you!"

"You did," he said, his expression darkening. "And you were my daughter. I fed and clothed you. I took care of you."

Baylie shook her head, the sound of his voice finally getting to her. It was that gravelly, monotone. It was digging into her subconscious in a way she didn't want it to.

Come out, come out, wherever you are...

The words echoed over and over inside of her head and she rubbed at her temples, determined to block the memory trying to surface out of her mind. The face of a terrified little girl filled her head and no matter how hard she tried, she couldn't block it out.

"You know, when you were little you climbed into my lap and cried yourself to sleep. I rubbed your back and told you stories to make you feel better."

Melvin's words interrupted her thoughts and her mind drew a quick blank. She stared at him, a deep sated anger eating at her. She wanted to kill this man, she realized. She hated him. Even though she couldn't remember him—remember what he'd done to her— she instinctively knew she hated him.

"You're not my father," she said emphatically. "I don't know who you are, but I know that much. And I don't remember my name being Nikki. I think you're lying. I think you just called me that. So who am I really?"

Melvin seemed surprised at the question. "You really don't remember?"

"I remember enough to know you are evil to your core." Baylie spat the words out quietly.

Melvin's eyes flashed with something akin to anger. "You always were ungrateful. That's why I let you go. You only caused problems when you were around. She never would behave and you always got in the way."

Baylie found her eyes narrowing. "Tell me where Susan is," she tried for a third time, knowing her stomach was going to give way soon. It was churning back and forth with a vengeance. It was all she could do not to run out of the room.

303

"You're really that concerned about your friend?"

"She has nothing to do with this," Baylie forced herself to say again. "And neither did anyone else you've hurt. Kevin, Giselle, Carl Eisenberg—those young girls back in Chapman." Baylie shook her head sadly. "You didn't hurt me, you hurt them. Why?"

"Kevin was not the man for you," Melvin said matter-of-factly. "He was overzealous and he would have hurt you eventually. I saved you from him."

Baylie shook her head, not wanting to hear this. "You didn't do anything for me. It was all for you and your sick, delusional mind."

"I'm sorry you feel that way," Melvin said, shrugging his shoulders. "Those women in Chapman—none of them were real friends to you. They talked about you behind your back. Each and every one of them. And Giselle? She was as big of a bitch as they come. She made your life miserable with her department protocol. I heard you say so yourself. I heard you say you could kill her. And that's a quote."

"My God, it was a job!" Baylie interrupted him, shaking her head again sadly. This man had obviously been tracking her for years. He'd heard things she'd said, watched every move she had made. The thought was enough to make her feel faint again. "I didn't really mean that I could kill anyone and I didn't want you to kill anyone!"

"You're ungrateful!" Melvin said, suddenly raising his voice. "This is why I let you go!"

He'd said the words earlier and this time she thought them over carefully. "I got away and you didn't come after me until now. Why?"

"Because I didn't need you. Not until now." The words were simple. Too simple.

"Why would you need me now?" She was almost too afraid to hear his answer.

Melvin was quiet for several seconds. Then he shrugged his shoulders. "It broke my heart when he took you from me. It was time to get you back."

Frustrated, Baylie shook her head. "Who took me? You're not making any sense. I just want the truth! Who am I?"

"I already told you. You're Nikki. You're my little girl and Carl Eisenberg took you. Don't you remember the fire?"

The fire. Instantly she felt her skin grow hot, almost as though she were in those torrent flames again. Almost as if she could smell the smoke and the burning wood. "Carl Eisenberg didn't *take* me. He was my foster father."

Melvin slowly smiled as he shook his head. "No. I'm afraid you're confused, Nikki. You were my little girl and he took you that night. We went there together. *You* and *me*."

Baylie felt the blood rush from her head. This couldn't be true. It didn't make sense. "I lived with him. For six months."

Melvin shook his head. "No."

"You're lying," Dylan said, taking the words right out of her mouth. She watched as he stepped forward and leaned over the table, his hands braced tightly against the metal. He glared at David Melvin, those intent blue eyes of his full of disgust. "Don't fuck with her, Melvin. She's not a helpless little girl anymore and she's not alone in the world. If you have something to say, say it. And it had better be the truth. Because if it's not, I'm going to rip your heart out myself."

Melvin didn't even blink. He just smiled. "I have no reason to lie anymore, Detective. But in order for the truth to be told, you have to expand your simple mind and really listen. Nikki was not Carl Eisenberg's foster child. Before that night, he'd never even seen her before."

"Then why would I have been there?" Baylie interjected.

"For God's sake, Melvin, we have the paperwork. We talked to Eisenberg. He recognized her."

"Did he now?" Melvin leaned back in his chair. "And what do you remember about him?" He looked at Baylie. "And how about some of the other families you lived with? What do you remember about any of them?"

Baylie narrowed her eyes. As he sat there staring at her, she could almost feel the evil radiating from his pale skin. "I have things — things that were given to me by my foster families. Things that were mine that prove I was with them at one time or another."

"You never lived with George Rycroft either," Melvin said matter-of-factly. "In fact, you had never even met him until the other day when you showed up at his house."

"He recognized her," Dylan pointed out irritably. "Now stop bullshitting us."

"Did he?" Melvin folded his hands in front of him and looked at Baylie carefully. "Don't you find it odd that you don't recognize any of them?"

"Not considering what you put her through before she got to them," Dylan said, his expression tight. "And obviously after she left them."

"I remember Mabel Lomax," Baylie said, finally finding her voice. "I remember her house. And I remember Marcus."

Melvin's smile faded a bit. "I'm not sure that what you remember is really what happened. Marcus seems to have a bit of a selective memory as well."

"You kidnapped him and you kidnapped her. Now why don't you just come clean and tell us the truth instead of trying to weave a web of lies here? It would save us a whole lot of aggravation." This came from Dylan. Obviously he was tiring of David Melvin's riddles. "The only way you're going to get any kind of deal here, is if you come clean. If Susan Hanover dies, forget a deal."

"I'm not concerned about a deal," Melvin said, his eyes never leaving Baylie's. "Do you think I don't realize what's going to happen here? I was a cop, remember?"

"What do you want from me?" Baylie stammered, still trying to make heads or tails of what Melvin was saying.

Melvin stared at her for a long time. Then almost suddenly, his eyes turned sad. "I fell in love with you, you know. You were so pretty and sweet—so innocent. I never wanted to hurt you."

"That sounds sick," she replied, her skin beginning to crawl. "I was a child."

He thought that over. "So you were." He leaned back in his chair, his eyes never leaving hers. "I don't need to tell you where Susan is, Nikki. You will remember in your own time.   And I want you to remember."

"You are a sick—" Dylan began, but Baylie interrupted him.

"I can't remember. Susan will die. Why do you want her to die?"

Melvin smiled sadly. "Don't you get it? It's not Susan I want to die."

The words echoed inside Baylie's head and again the vision of herself as a child, terrified and alone, played inside her head.

Dylan swore from behind her but Baylie held up her hand to stop him from intervening. "Tell me where she is," she said softly, her eyes imploring him to give in and end the torment she was feeling inside. "Please."

Melvin was quiet a minute. Then he sat up straight and looked her in the eye. "No, I'm afraid I can't do that. But I will tell you something. Maybe it will help you remember." The look he gave her was so haunting that she honestly didn't believe she would ever forget it. At that moment, before he spoke his next words, she could have sworn she literally saw the face of the devil staring back at her.

"Your name was Nikki Anissa Tate."

Before Baylie could even reply, Melvin lifted his hand. No one saw the fork clutched in his fingers until it was already embedded in his jugular, a mere seconds later.

TWENTY-ONE

Dylan looked over Alex's shoulder to the bench near the closed door of Chief Runyon's office, where Baylie sat staring straight ahead, her eyes void of any emotion. She was wrapped tightly up in his jacket, looking small and defenseless. If David Melvin hadn't already been pronounced dead, Dylan would have killed him.

But no, the coward had taken the easy way out. And he'd died quickly, right before Baylie's eyes. Dylan had been unable to do more than try to pull her away from the mess, but he'd been far too late to shield her. The sound of her screaming wasn't likely to leave his head any time soon.

Now, tucked back in the chief's office away from the circus going on outside its doors, the computer was booted and searching for anything on Nikki Anissa Tate.

"There's nothing here," Alex said, interrupting Dylan's thoughts.

Looking over his partner's shoulder, he grimaced. "There has to be."

"What makes you think he was telling the truth? He was a fucking liar."

This was a good point. Melvin had done nothing but lie from the get-go. But something told Dylan that at one time Baylie had been Nikki Tate. And he intended to find out just where the bastard had stolen her from. "He dropped that last bomb for a reason. He wanted her to remember and he thought that would be enough to do the trick."

"Well there's no Nikki Anissa Tate reported missing in the state of Montana and that's where all of his other victims were taken from."

"Maybe. Maybe not," Dylan said, looking at Baylie again. He wanted to do something to help her—to bring her out of her state of shock—but he wasn't sure what to do for her. She had literally refused to allow him to take her home until he ran the name Melvin had given them through the system.

"She's fucked up, Dylan. You need to get her out of here."

"She won't go until she has an answer. Keep looking. Go to Washington, Oregon, Idaho—whatever it takes. Check Sutter out too. Maybe the names are mixed up somehow."

Alex shrugged his shoulders and kept typing. In the meantime, Dylan walked over and crouched down in front of Baylie. Her eyes looked into his but she didn't speak.

"There's nothing in Montana for the name Nikki Anissa Tate," he said quietly. "This could take hours, baby. You should go home."

"I think I had a dog, Dylan. And I think her name was Baylie."

The words were so unexpected that Dylan found himself frowning. "What are you talking about?"

"She was a little brown spaniel, with white spots on her ears. She could sit and stay and roll over. And she knew how to play dead."

Dylan cringed at the way her posture changed. Her eyes looked so haunted he could almost feel her pain. "Did this all just come to you now?"

She nodded slowly.

The idea that maybe Melvin had opened up the locked away memories of her mind became somewhat encouraging. "What else do you remember?"

She was quiet a moment, and then she shrugged, taking a deep breath. "I don't know. Nothing, I guess. I just remember the dog. She was in the sketchbook. The one that Rycroft gave me." She shivered again and he had the urge to sit down and pull her into his lap. He wished like hell that he could take all of her pain away but he knew he couldn't. The only way her pain was going to go away was if she remembered what had happened to her. And the thing that scared him most was the idea that she wouldn't be able to handle the truth.

"Did you hear me?" she asked impatiently. "The dog was in the book, Dylan. He was lying. I was with George Rycroft at one time. That sketchbook is mine."

Dylan wasn't sure how to respond to that. "This isn't adding up, Baylie," was all he finally said.

She didn't argue. "How did I take on the name of a dog?" She asked the obvious question and he wasn't sure how to answer her.

"I don't know, baby. At one time, someone must have asked you your name and that's what you told them. It's the name listed on your file so it obviously came from somewhere."

"What about Sutter? Why was that listed as my last name? I don't know anyone by that name."

"You mean you don't *remember* anyone by that name," Dylan corrected gently.

"Maybe my name was Nikki Sutter."

"We're checking that too. Believe me we want answers just as much as you do. But it's like looking for a needle in a haystack. Back at the time you were likely taken, provided it was in the late eighties or early nineties, records were just becoming completely computerized. A lot of documentation was still on paper. And not only that, Melvin had access to things. He was a cop.

There's no telling what he's done over the years to cover his tracks."

Baylie's face fell and again Dylan felt his heart break for her. "I wish I could give you more hope, baby."

"Susan is going to die," she said quietly, her voice shaking. "God, I don't think I can live with that on my conscience, Dylan. And all the others…all because of me…"

He sighed, wanting to kill David Melvin all over again. "It's all on him, Baylie. Not you. You were a victim just like Giselle and Kevin and Susan. And just like Marcus and all of the others."

"He's right," Alex said, stepping up behind them and speaking to Baylie quietly. When Dylan looked up and into Alex's face, he knew something was up. Alex had his cop face on, but there was a look of concern mixed in with it. Immediately Dylan stiffened and stood up. Clearly Alex wanted Dylan to look at whatever he'd found before Baylie caught on.

"I heard you tell Dylan about this dog. I want you to tell me about her again," Alex said, giving Dylan the open door to check out what he'd found. Still too distraught to catch on, Baylie only shrugged and began telling Alex about the dog. Dylan took his chance and walked behind Runyon's desk to stare at the computer.

What he saw made his breath catch. The picture of a little girl stared back at him. Her hair was blonde and curly. Her face was round and so were her eyes. But it was their deep blue color that got to him. They were almost the color of the sky on a bright sunny day. The smile on her face ate into his very soul and he found himself plopping down into the chief's chair and staring numbly.

Anissa Nikole Tate, the name under the child's face read. *Missing: July 4, 1992 - Lincoln City, Oregon.* Not *Nikki Anissa* Tate, but *Anissa Nikole* Tate. Melvin had transposed the name.

Just like that, they knew who Baylie was, and where she'd come from. *Oregon.* She'd been taken from Oregon, which explained why they hadn't been able to find her in Montana. There was very little information on the kidnapping, only the girl's height and weight. It listed the clothes she'd been wearing at the time of her disappearance as blue jean shorts, a purple t-shirt and tennis shoes — all average things that any child would have been wearing back in those days. Dylan looked at the child's face again, and he couldn't stop himself from swearing. She had been six years old at the time of the picture, yet still he could see Baylie's adult features in her face.

He hit the print button and waited for the flier to print out. It took only a moment. When it was in his hands, he stood and carried it over to Baylie, who had finished talking with Alex by then and was watching him cautiously. He held out the flier to her. When she saw what he was holding, she stared at it silently for several moments before reaching out and taking it from him.

Baylie stared at the little girl in the picture that adorned the flier. It was the same little girl from her dreams—the same little girl from the locket Mabel Lomax had given her. Those deep blue eyes and shiny blonde curls belonged to her. That wide smile and tiny upturned nose were also hers. Instinctively she knew it, and yet she didn't recognize her own face. Panic swarmed and threatened to surface but she tamped down on it. *Anissa Nikole Tate.* She read the name several times, waiting for the recognition to course through her. A shiver washed over her and she clenched her fingers together to keep from losing her control. *Lincoln City, Oregon.* She repeated the name of the town inside her head several times. Why wasn't it jogging her memory?

"Bay?" Dylan's voice said quietly.

She kept staring at the picture, hating the fact that the smiling child before her seemed like a complete stranger. How could she be a stranger to herself?

"Is she okay?" she heard Alex ask.

"Oregon," she said in response, and finally looked up to meet Dylan's gaze. "He took me from Oregon."

316

"It looks like it," Dylan agreed, crouching down before her again. "Lincoln City. It's a couple of hours outside of Portland."

Baylie thought that over. She looked at the flier again, carefully taking in every detail of the photo from the unruly, curly blonde hair, to the slightly chipped front tooth, exposed between the smiling, red lips on the little girl's face. Then she looked back at Dylan again. "Why don't I recognize my own face?"

Dylan frowned, obviously somewhat startled by the admission. "You've had a lot to deal with today. You can't expect all this to fall into place instantly."

"He's right," Alex agreed, leaning back against the chief's desk and folding his arms over his chest. "Give this time to sink in."

"It's you, Baylie. I see it in the eyes," Dylan said, causing her to look closer at the picture again. He was right. Her own piercing blue eyes were staring back at her.

She felt the ache in her chest grow wider and she wanted to lie down and cry. She was so tired of nothing making any sense to her, that it was nearly driving her mad. "What else can you find out, now that you know who I am?"

Dylan shrugged his shoulders. "There will be a police file. I'll have to obtain it from Oregon. It's a cold case so it could take a while. And it may not be complete anymore. That's the problem with evidence after years like this. Stuff gets lost."

"She's going to die if I don't remember, Dylan. I have to remember."

Dylan straightened and exchanged glances with Alex.

"I'll make some calls," Alex said, disappearing around the chief's desk.

Dylan met her gaze somberly. "We are going through his house in Montana and his apartment here, Baylie. Chances are we will find something that leads us to that hole, even if you don't remember. It's just going to take a little time."

"Susan doesn't have time," Baylie reminded him, looking away from the flier and into his eyes. "She could be nearly dead right now." She could tell by the look in his eyes that Dylan was thinking the same thing. He didn't say so. Instead, he stood up.

"You need to get some rest. You may be having trouble remembering because you're on overload right now. Give your body a chance to rejuvenate. I know that's hard to do, given the trauma you've been through today, but I think it's our only chance of helping Susan."

The idea of sleep seemed ludicrous to her. "Every time I shut my eyes I see his face, covered in blood. I hear his voice." She shivered again and took a deep, painful breath.

Dylan winced and he swore. "Yeah, I know. Me too. But we can't think about him anymore. We have to think about Susan."

"I'll do some digging around and call you when I find out anything," Alex promised, giving her a sympathetic look. "There's no point in you sitting here all night. You may need to do some traveling tomorrow, depending on what I can get my hands on." The chief's phone rang and he turned away from Dylan and Baylie to answer it.

Baylie let Dylan lead her outside and into the cool night air. She breathed in a deep gulp of it, her hand still clenching the flier with her childhood face on it. Only when she was safely strapped into the passenger seat of his truck, did she let herself glance at the picture again. The more she looked at it, the more she began to grow uneasy. There was something off—something that just wasn't right. Suddenly, she heard the sound of a voice inside her head and realized it belonged to that of a child. It was sweet and even, and almost chiding.

"*Come out, come out, wherever you are...*" The voice echoed over and over again. Baylie clenched at the paper, crumpling it in her hand unintentionally. She could see her own face now. She could hear herself laughing. Her curls were bouncing as she ran around with a small dog on her heels. *Baylie*, she knew. This dog was Baylie.

"Come out, come out, wherever you are..." the voice said again. *"Ready or not, here I come."*

Giggles sounded. Screams followed. She saw her face...the tears streaming down it...the dirt smudged across it. And then she saw another face...

Dylan stared at Baylie as she seemed to drift away before his eyes. Her skin had paled and she was no longer staring at the flier she clenched in her hands. Before he could say anything to her, his cell phone began to buzz. Cursing, he grabbed it.

"Get back in here," Alex's voice said emphatically.

"What? Why?" Dylan asked, still concerned about the look on Baylie's face. She was close to finally coming apart and he was worried as hell about her.

"Because I just figured out why she doesn't recognize the face in that picture," Alex said quickly. "It's not her. *The picture's not of her.*"

Dylan felt the breath leave his lungs. "What are you talking about? It's her. I know those eyes."

"You aren't listening to me. Her name wasn't Anissa Nikole Tate. It was *Nikole Anissa Tate,* just like Melvin said." Alex spoke impatiently. "She had a *twin,* Dylan."

TWENTY-TWO

A twin. The word played itself repeatedly inside Dylan's head. It wasn't a foreign word to him. After all, he had a twin himself. "Are you sure?" he finally found his voice to ask.

"There was a CC: at the bottom of the page on Anissa Tate. When I clicked on it, it brought up the other girl—our Baylie, if my eyes are seeing right. They're pretty much identical from what I can tell. The same age, birthdate and location of abduction—Lincoln City, Oregon."

Dylan swore and slowly disconnected the phone. When he looked over at Baylie she was staring at him strangely. Then she reached out and handed him the crumpled piece of paper that she'd been clutching tightly in her hand.

"This isn't me."

Her words surprised him at first. He took the paper and stared down at it a moment, before looking at her again.

321

"It's not me, Dylan." She said the words with a certainty that would haunt him for a long time to come. Clearly she had remembered something about her sister on her own.

"I know it's not," he finally said, and her brows rose in surprise.

"You believe me?"

He may not have five minutes earlier, but he did now. "You had a sister, Baylie—a twin. And that's her picture, not yours."

Baylie stared at the two fliers set out on the table in front of her. Back inside the police station, they were sitting at the chief's desk again. Alex had blown up the pictures on the fliers of Nikole and Anissa Tate, although she hadn't needed him to. For some reason, she could now see her sister's face clear as day in her head. She couldn't understand how she hadn't remembered Anissa until now.

"She had a mole next to her right eye," she said quietly, and leaned back in the chair. "And she had a chipped front tooth."

Dylan leaned on the desk, his arms crossed over his chest. Alex stood across the room, Chief Runyon now here and standing next to him, just as interested. Clearly, they all felt this was the break they'd been waiting for.

"Do you remember anything about her specifically?" Dylan asked. "Besides what you're seeing in the picture."

Pain radiated through her body as she thought of Anissa. She shut her eyes and rubbed at her temples, trying to get the ache pounding there to subside. Anissa's face filled her head and this time she didn't try to stop the memory from making its way to the surface. She could see the flames surrounding her sister. She could hear the crackling of the burning wood around her. Nissa was crying, begging for help. And she couldn't help her. She was just standing there watching as her sister — her twin — burned in the raging inferno.

Heat threatened to engulf her as smoke scorched the roof of her mouth and all the way down her throat. She couldn't breathe. Her eyes were burning. God, she was going to die. And then she heard him. A voice. She turned her head and that's when she saw him. Through the back door of the burning house, she could see a man. He was screaming for her to come to him, reaching out to her.

"Where is she?" he kept screaming.

Confused, Baylie looked toward Anissa again. She was batting at the flames that threatened to climb up her legs. The sound of her crying was so painful Baylie almost couldn't stand it. Just as she began to reach through the inferno toward her sister, two strong arms closed around her from behind and she was yanked roughly from her feet.

323

"Baylie!"

The voice startled her and her eyes snapped open. Dylan was staring down at her, a concerned look on his face. Both Alex and Chief Runyon were close behind him.

"She needs sleep," Dylan said, crouching down in front of her. "Can you hear me, Bay?"

She blinked several times before she met his gaze. "She was there the night of that fire, Dylan. It wasn't me I was seeing burning in those flames, it was Anissa. I think that's where she died."

His expression softened and he let out a sigh as he studied her face carefully. "It's late and you've processed a lot today. You may be mixing your facts up."

"I saw her. I didn't help her. I was there, Melvin was right. I was in that house and I was watching her burn. And then someone grabbed me and carried me outside." She could see the man's face clearly in her head now. "It was Carl Eisenberg. He pulled me out of that fire. He saved my life."

"Baylie—" Dylan began.

"I had never seen him before that night. I was standing in that kitchen and when I heard his voice calling for me, I didn't know who he was."

Chief Runyon let out an oath.

"Then why in the hell were you there at all?" Alex asked the obvious question.

She didn't know how she knew, but she knew. "Because *Freddy* wanted Anissa back and we went there to get her." Once the words were out, several pieces of the puzzle seemed to slip together.

Suddenly Dylan let out a curse. Apparently he was catching on himself. "Sonofabitch."

"Are you trying to tell me that that sick bastard was trying to kidnap your sister back again, after she'd been placed in foster care?" Alex asked incredulously.

Baylie shut her eyes again, willing her mind to relinquish more information. God, she wanted to remember so badly. Tension gripped every limb of her body and her mind remained blank. She opened her eyes finally, and looked up at Alex. "I don't know. But I know we were both in that house together that night." She dropped her gaze to meet Dylan's. "And I know that's the last time I ever saw my sister." Moisture pooled beneath her eyelids and she couldn't stop it. "I let her die that night. She burned because of me."

Dylan reached out a hand and cupped her cheek. "You didn't let her do anything, Baylie. You were a little girl."

His words were only mildly comforting. She wiped at her eyes and turned away from the men, determined to get herself together.

"I'm sorry, baby. For what you've gone through—for what you're going through now."

Dylan's gentle voice was her undoing. Letting the tears slide down her face, she shook her head sadly. "How could I have forgotten my own twin sister? Could you ever forget Danica?" Through her tears, she watched Dylan's eyes. They were narrowed and she knew the answer before he said it. Of course he didn't think he could forget his twin.

"I didn't go through what you've been through, Baylie. Trauma can do that to a kid. I've seen some pretty bad stuff in my career."

"He's right," Alex said quietly. "It's a wonder you've functioned in society at all."

Taking a deep breath, she quickly swiped at her tears. "I still don't know where he has Susan."

"You're remembering more and more as we go on. It's a matter of time," Dylan answered, his voice laced with sympathy. "I think you should consider getting some rest and maybe that will help you clear your head. Right now you're running on empty."

"I can't sleep, Dylan. I need to be doing something to try and help her. Maybe going back would help. Seeing the fliers helped me remember. Going home might too." She could tell he was skeptical, but he shrugged his shoulders and looked up at Chief Runyon.

"I suppose it couldn't hurt," the chief finally said thoughtfully. "Although you haven't remembered much about any of the other places you've re-visited."

Baylie couldn't argue, but she suddenly realized there was likely a very good reason for that. "That's because I don't think I was ever in any of those places. I think *Anissa* was."

"You mean you think Anissa was the foster child that George Rycroft and his wife had?" Dylan figured out aloud.

"That would explain why I don't remember them. And it would also explain why I don't remember running away from any of them. I don't think I ever did run away. I think I was with Melvin most of the time until somehow I ended up with the Lomaxes. I know for sure that Anissa and I were never held in that hole together. The only person I remember ever being down there with is Marcus."

Alex swore. "He was playing the system— switching you out over and over again. I'm guessing that the places you don't remember being were actually Anissa's foster families."

"The question is, how the hell did they ever get into the system to begin with?" This came from Dylan, who had now straightened and stood up. "Why would he kidnap both of them and then give one of them up?"

"I don't think he gave one of us up willingly," Baylie said, not sure how she knew that fact—only that she did. "I think one of us ran away."

"And ended up with the police," Alex said, nodding. "That makes sense."

327

"That should have tipped the authorities off right away," Dylan said thoughtfully. "There is protocol for stuff like this. It wasn't much different back then. It's not easy but we always do our best to locate a child's parents. The media would have been involved. Why didn't anyone come forward?"

The question hung in the air and Baylie knew what the likelihood was. Maybe no one in her family was left to claim her. Maybe they had all been gone by that time.

Dylan swore again, his eyes locked on hers. "We don't know anything for sure, Baylie. Any number of things could have gone on back then that kept your parents from reuniting with you. The fact that you were basically catatonic half the time could have caused a lot of confusion. You couldn't tell anyone your real name or where you came from. Everyone only knew you as Baylie and we both know that wasn't your name."

She knew he was right but she couldn't shake the fear that maybe her parents were dead. Maybe she had no family left at all. No twin sister. No mom and dad. Anguish ate at her soul and she avoided Dylan's gaze.

"There's no point in playing a guessing game. We'll know soon enough what happened to her parents," Runyon said swiftly. "I think you should head for Lincoln City as soon as possible. In the meantime, we'll keep on top of the investigation and the search of Melvin's properties. One way or another we're going to find that hole."

"What if we're not in time?" Baylie asked the question that apparently no one else wanted to voice aloud.

"That's not an option," Runyon said and grimaced as his cell phone rang. He took the call and stepped out of the office momentarily.

Dylan took up where Runyon had left off. "He's right. You can't think about that part of this right now, Baylie. You've come a long way in a week. Think about that. You actually know who you are now. You're remembering more and more every day, with every step we take. So we keep taking steps. Together."

The weight on her heart lightened somewhat. Even after everything he'd heard, Dylan was still sticking by her. Part of her couldn't believe that fact. Another part of her thanked God, regardless of her disbelief. Without him by her side, she didn't think she could face any of this.

Chief Runyon stepped back into the room, a grim look on his face. "That was the Missoula PD. They found some rather interesting information in Melvin's house. Apparently he has a son."

Both Dylan and Alex looked surprised.

"What makes them think so?" Dylan asked.

"There's a bedroom set up in the home. Boys stuff. Xbox, the whole bit. It's been used recently enough. The funny thing is, Melvin has never fathered a child that we know of."

The meaning of those words cut into Baylie's soul and she flinched.

Dylan swore. "Do they know where the boy is? *Who* he is?"

"Not at this point. We're checking on next of kin. It may take awhile."

"He stole another child. That's the only explanation," Baylie said her thoughts aloud.

"It's possible," was all Runyon said.

"It's more than possible. It's more than likely," Dylan corrected.

"So where is he?" Baylie asked quietly. She didn't want to believe there was a little boy down in that hole with Susan. But the likelihood was that that's exactly where the child was.

"There's no point in speculating that, okay?" Dylan crouched before her again. "He told us that Susan wasn't in there alone, baby. It's likely that the boy is in that hole with her." He reached for her hands and squeezed them softly. "But it's also possible that he's not. Maybe he ran away. We won't know anything until we find that hole. You have to concentrate on that, Bay. I know it's hard as hell and I wish I could make it easier on you but I can't."

She could see in his eyes that he was being honest. His cop face had completely vanished. She knew at that moment that she'd fallen for him—

hook, line and sinker. She wasn't sure if that was a good or a bad thing. The only thing she knew for sure was that he was the only thing that stood between her and the rest of the world, and right then she needed his shield.

TWENTY-THREE

The ride to Lincoln City took around five and half hours. The original plan had been for them to fly. Unfortunately, due to inclement weather, there were no available flights until morning. Rather than wait, they hopped in Dylan's truck and headed out. They pulled into the Motel 6 on the outskirts of town around two in the morning. Dylan got them a room and even though Baylie insisted she didn't want to sleep, he all but forced her to shower and climb under the covers next to him. They both needed rest badly. Surprisingly, she was exhausted once she hit the sheets. She listened to Dylan snore lightly for only a few minutes before she fell into a restless sleep herself. Faces drifted in and out of her dreams like a kaleidoscope of colors. Voices, some quiet, some loud, echoed inside of her head. The only face she recognized was her sister's.

"We can play for a little longer. It's not dark yet." Nikki nodded for her sister to follow her.

Nissa looked up at her stubbornly, her eyes narrowed as she clutched her ratty doll to her chest tightly. "We're supposed to head back to the picnic. If we don't Mama will get mad."

"We have to find Baylie. We'll just tell her that. She won't get mad." Nikki bent to pick some flowers from behind a large barrel of water. This part of the park was relatively empty. Everyone was on the south side of the lake eating and enjoying the day's activities. Fourth of July was always exciting at the lake. Everyone looked forward to the late night firework show. Both girls hated the loud booms, yet they loved the glorified colors that lit up the night sky.

"Baylie isn't here, Nikki. We should go back," Nissa said again, now sounding a little scared. Nissa wasn't as adventurous as Nikki was. Even though they were best friends, Nikki found herself annoyed with the fact that her sister really never wanted to have any fun.

"She ran this way. We'll find her. I wanna pick Mama some flowers first."

Nissa's lower lip came out in a pout, but she continued to stand by her sister's side, just the way Nikki knew she would. Nissa was always eager to make her sister happy, even when she wasn't pleased with whatever plan Nikki had, that would likely get them into trouble.

Hearing barking, Nikki turned her head. Baylie. The dog had run off earlier and disappeared into a *thicket of trees. She was supposed to be on the leash but Nikki had unclipped the metal clasp the way she'd seen their father do a million times before when they were in the park. He always said Baylie needed to run free now and then. And Nikki liked to chase her. Only without Daddy there, Baylie hadn't been obedient. She'd scampered off in search of something unknown to the girls. Now they were stuck with the task of getting her back.*

"I wanna go back," Nissa whined again.

Nikki stood up straight, a nice, but small bouquet of dandelions and wildflowers clutched in her fingers. "You're being a baby. You're no fun. Let's play a quick game of Hide and Seek. There are lots of places to hide around here. I bet we'll find Baylie too. It will be fun."

Nissa looked skeptical, but Nikki knew Hide and Seek was her favorite game. They played it all the time at home.

"You can hide first. I'll count." Not waiting for her sister to agree, Nikki turned her head, closed her eyes and began to count.

"Ready or not, here I come!" She called the words loudly as she dropped her hands from her eyes a few seconds later. She looked around the immediate area, expecting to see the tip of Nissa's sneaker behind the barrel in front of her, or hear a giggle a ways off in the distance. Nissa was never very good at hiding. But apparently this time she'd found a better spot to shield herself because she was nowhere to be seen. Nikki took her time walking around behind a large elm tree, not far

from the barrel. She looked behind a broken old boathouse, near the dock that stretched into the lake. She even checked in the tall grass, just beyond the lake's shore. Nissa was nowhere to be found.

"Come out, come out, wherever you are," she said, using the signal she and Nissa always used when they were tired of looking and wanted the game to end. But Nissa didn't come out. Aside from the carnival noise off in the distance, things were deathly quiet. For some reason Nikki began to feel tense. Maybe her sister had run after Baylie and gotten lost in the woods. Her blue eyes scanned the large thicket of trees off in the distance. They looked very dark and ominous suddenly.

"Come out, come out, wherever you are!" she called, louder, her voice cracking slightly. Fear slowly began to wash over her when she received no answer. Still Nissa did not come out. Walking closer to the trees, Nikki squinted. There was an object not ten feet in front of her. It was a doll – Nissa's doll. It lay on the ground, as though tossed there carelessly, which was something she knew her sister would never do. She loved her dolly, ratty and nasty as it was. Stepping past the toy, Nikki peered into the darkness of the forest.

When Baylie opened her eyes, she was no longer standing in the park looking for her sister. She was in a dark room she didn't recognize. Panic seized her. She turned over, half expecting to find her face buried in dirt and grime. She had woken that way before, too many times to count. Suddenly she remembered those times. She remembered the fear and terror she felt at waking up and not being able to see anything but the dirty floor in front of her. No windows, no sun. No contact with the outside world.

Blinking her eyes several times, she forced herself back into reality. She was in a bed, not on the floor. After several moments of excruciating dread and confusion, she realized that Dylan was lying next to her, breathing softly. She knew his sounds and she knew his scent. The panic that had washed over her slowly ebbed and was replaced by irrepressible sadness. Turning over, she buried her face in her pillow, willing the anguish inside her to abate, but it didn't. It kept growing stronger and stronger until she felt like she was going to self-destruct. Forcing herself, she sat up straight and pushed air in and out of her lungs. The effort caused pain in both her chest and her lungs.

"Baylie?"

She heard his voice but she couldn't answer him. Her chest was heaving by that point and she didn't know how to make it stop.

"Hey, it's me. It's okay." Dylan sat up, reaching for her quickly. He ran his hands over her hair and then her face, cupping her chin and forcing her to look at him. "Look at me."

Her eyes met his and immediately filled with tears. She shook her head and tried to pull away but he stopped her easily. "Look at me, Baylie.

336

It's just you and me now. No one else is here. You were dreaming."

She knew he was right but she couldn't shake the images from her head — her sister, so alive and so young. How could she have lost these memories for so long? How was it possible that she had erased her entire childhood from her head?

"I know this has been bad for you and I'm sorry about that," he said softly, his eyes still locked with hers. "But we can get through this, baby. We're close. Really, really close. You want answers too, don't you?"

She did want answers — for Susan's sake. But for her own? She wasn't sure she could take the answers. With every memory that she regained, her heart felt more and more hollow.

"You're not in this alone. I'm here and not just as a cop." He looked at her intently. "I'm here for you on whatever level you need me. Does that help at all?"

Breathing became a little easier and she found herself nodding at him.

He gave her a small, sympathetic smile. "You and me, we're a team now, okay? Just remember that when things get overwhelming."

She wanted to. But there was a big part of her that worried about him being able to deal with the skeletons that were slowly coming out of her closet. Once his job was done, it would be easy enough for him to walk away. She wasn't sure she could take that. Somehow, it seemed a lot easier to be the one who walked away, rather than the one being walked away from.

"Stop."

His words startled her. "Stop what?" she said, when she was sure she could get the words out. She was finally able to breathe again.

"I'm not sure what you're thinking but I don't like the look in your eyes. I saw it when we first met and you were thinking about running. We've come too far for that, Baylie." His eyes narrowed and he dropped his hand from her chin.

Suddenly she felt bereft. Somehow, his hands on her gave her a sense of security. "I'm not running anywhere, Dylan." The words were quiet and he didn't respond right away.

Finally, he reached over and brushed his fingers down her cheek. "You're one hell of a woman, Baylie Sutter. When this is all over, you and I are going to take some time and figure out just where this thing with us is supposed to go."

The words warmed her and she leaned into his touch, thankful to have a physical connection to him again. They both leaned back and she snuggled up against him. Once his arms were around her and she was burrowed into the warmth of his chest, she was able to shut her eyes

338

and go back to sleep. And fortunately it was a dreamless sleep.

The next morning they were both up at seven-thirty. They showered quickly. After that, they'd dressed and headed for the nearest coffee shop — a small building shaped like a teapot, just outside of town.

Dylan had fielded several phone calls already that morning. One had been from Alex, who had told him they had no real new leads from anything they had found in David Melvin's homes. They still had no identity on the apparent boy that was living with him, either.

Another call had been from Lincoln City Police Department Detective Ryan Wilshire. He was waiting for them at the local precinct, though his voice had held more than a little skepticism when he'd spoken to Dylan earlier. This was a small town and just like all the other small towns they'd visited in the last couple of weeks, they would have to penetrate the small town veneer to gain any trust from law enforcement around here.

Baylie had been relatively silent all morning. She hadn't told him what she'd dreamed about the night before but he knew the nightmares had been bad. When he'd woken up to her panic attack, he'd acted quickly, but inside he'd been scared to death. She'd been pale as a ghost and almost unable to get air into her lungs. He was no doctor but he knew what sheer terror looked like when he saw it. Just as quickly as the terror had appeared, it had evaporated and the Baylie he knew and loved was back, sipping her coffee next to him as though nothing was wrong.

The Baylie he knew and loved. Where the *hell* had that come from?

Cursing, he pushed the thought from his mind.

"What?" she asked, taking a drink of her Mocha.

"Nothing," he muttered, steering the car down the highway. When they had pulled into the area the night before it had been pitch dark and they hadn't been able to see much. Now it was broad daylight and he was interested in seeing her reaction to her new surroundings. Only thus far, she hadn't had much of a reaction to anything.

"I'm sorry I kept you up last night. I know you were tired."

"I'm fine," he said, still irritated with his earlier thoughts. He did not love any woman. He wasn't the type to fall in love. It just wasn't in his make-up. They were involved in extenuating circumstances, that's all. It was muddling up his ability to think clearly. At the same time, he reminded himself of the words he'd said to her the night before and he inwardly cringed. He'd told her they were a team. He'd told her that they would see where things went when this was all over. Damn it to hell, he'd meant the words, he realized. The idea of her disappearing from his life bothered him more than he wanted to admit. He cursed again and avoided her gaze.

"Okay," she said, drawing the word out slowly.

Knowing the day was going to be hard enough on her, he relented a little. "Sorry. I didn't mean to snap at you. I know you had a bad night."

"It's not the first time." Her eyes slid away from his and peered out the window at the passing scenery. They were just on the outskirts of Lincoln City. There was a large lake to the right as they drove down the road. Devil's Lake, if he remembered from the map in the glove box. Her eyes seemed to narrow, but she didn't say anything so he kept going about a mile down the road and pulled to a stop in front of the small building that housed the police station. Shutting off the engine, he looked at the nice, tree-lined street. It was typical for a small town. It sat just on the edge of the Oregon coast, overlooking the great Pacific Ocean. There were the normal buildings that every town needed to survive — a city hall, a library, a couple of supermarkets — though on a rather small scale. There was also a post office and a hardware store mixed in among the restaurants and small businesses. All in all, the town was quaint — appealing. But nothing like the large city Dylan had grown up in.

341

"I can smell the ocean," was the first thing Baylie said when she stepped out of the car. The air was crisp and cool and she was right, he decided, as he got a whiff of salt water.

"Nothing like the smog I'm used to," he said, leading the way up the walk to the police station. She didn't reply. Her eyes were too busy adjusting to her surroundings. Again, no obvious recognition registered on her face, but the town had her interest. He just watched her, preparing himself for the worst when something finally did ring a bell. They made it up to the glass double doors of the building without so much as a blink from her. He frowned, realizing that she obviously didn't recognize anything about this town either. Her mind, it seemed, had been completely erased. He couldn't help but wonder what it was going to take to jog her memories this time.

Baylie allowed herself plenty of time to take in her surroundings. The little town was quaint. It was not what she had expected. Of course she couldn't remember what it had looked like when she'd lived here as a child, so she wasn't sure why she'd had any expectations at all.

Once they were inside the police station, they were asked to wait in a conference room that looked much the same as the ones they had back in Seattle—long table, several chairs and a two way mirror. It reminded Baylie a lot of the room they'd been in with David Melvin the day before, and she shivered involuntarily at the memory.

Five minutes after they arrived, a tall man entered the room, a pile of papers in his hands. He was a nice looking guy, whom Baylie figured was in his mid to late thirties. His hair was a dusty blond color and a little on the longer side. He was wearing slacks and a work shirt—no tie and his sleeves were rolled up to his elbows. The gun clipped to his belt and the badge at his side pretty much told her that this was likely Detective Ryan Wilshire. A moment later, the man confirmed Baylie's hunch when he introduced himself. His greeting was rather gruff. She hadn't expected the warmest reception in the world, but this guy was borderline cold. Immediately she felt a sense of unease.

"So why don't you explain to me again, why you're here?" Wilshire set down the papers he'd been carrying and leaned against the conference table, his arms crossed over his chest.

"I thought we made that pretty clear on the phone. You spoke with my partner earlier. And you spoke with me." Dylan returned the gruff tone and Baylie knew he had taken an instant dislike to Detective Wilshire's attitude.

Wilshire continued frowning, but his eyes shifted from Dylan's face to Baylie's. He stared at

343

her for a long time, nearly to the point where she wanted to squirm. Then he sighed and turned back to Dylan. "I don't want any of this leaked to the media. That needs to be understood right now. So if you're in this to get attention, turn the hell around and head back where you came from."

Dylan bristled, his eyes darkening. "I don't want any more media coverage of this than you do. The bottom line is that I have a woman being held somewhere with no food and no water and her days are numbered if we don't find her quickly."

Wilshire appeared to think that over. Then he turned and looked at Baylie again. "I have a hard time believing that you're Nikole Tate."

Baylie looked the detective dead in the eye. "So do I," was all she said.

Wilshire looked momentarily taken aback. "Then why are you here?"

"Because my friend is going to die if I don't find out where she is. And I can't do that unless I can remember how this all started. I was kidnapped as a child and the man who kidnapped me told me my name was once Nikki Tate right before he severed his own jugular in front of my face. Trust me, I'm not playing a game here."

Wilshire had the decency to blanch this time. Then he swore. After a tense moment, he motioned for both Baylie and Dylan to sit down at the table. Then he dug through some papers. "I

344

can have you read all this crap. There are pages and pages of it. But I can probably tell you more about the disappearance of the Tate Twins myself. I was close to the family back then. I was there the day they disappeared."

This caught Baylie's interest. Finally, someone who apparently knew her family first hand. Now it was her turn to look him over. Nothing about him seemed familiar. But then that was really no surprise. She hadn't even recognized her own twin at first.

"I'd like to see the files," Dylan interrupted.

Wilshire slid the files across the table and then returned his gaze to Baylie. "Tell me what you remember."

She knew he was fishing for something that proved she was Nikole Tate. Unfortunately, she didn't have much to give him. "There's not a lot. I only remembered my sister yesterday and that was because I saw her picture."

Wilshire's eyes darkened. "Nikki and Anissa were twins. They were very close. Don't you find it odd that you would forget your own twin?"

"Not when you consider the fact that they were separated almost immediately after they were kidnapped. She was held in a hole and repeatedly tortured for years. She's not on trial here, Detective," Dylan said, before she had the chance to answer him.

Again, Wilshire winced. He was obviously trying to keep from staring at her but he was having a hard time.

"We had a dog named Baylie. Somehow, at some point after I was taken, I ended up taking her name."

The arrow of her words seemed to hit their mark, because Wilshire's face paled. He cursed again and this time his expression mellowed. "I almost forgot about her. The dog."

"Look, Detective," Dylan began. "As a cop I can appreciate your determination to do your job. And as a friend of the Tate family at one time, I can respect the fact that you're concerned about their welfare. But right now, I don't have time to give a shit about that. I'm a cop too and up until two weeks ago, I didn't know Baylie Sutter from Adam. We have painstakingly, over the past fourteen days, tried to piece her childhood together. We have been over hundreds of miles and now we are here, not on a whim, but because of cold, hard evidence that lead us here. Rather than question her, just tell us the facts."

Wilshire folded his arms across his chest, relaxing his posture somewhat. Then he leaned back in his chair. "They disappeared on the 4th of July in 1992 from Devil's Lake. There's a festival there every year on the 4th. The whole town comes out for it." Wilshire reached for the file folder he'd given Dylan and pulled some papers

346

out. He set a newspaper article on to the table for them to look at.

Baylie saw the pictures from the fliers, printed largely on the front page of the Picayune. The word *MISSING* was typed in big, bold print. A throbbing slowly began in her temples again.

"It wasn't unusual for the kids to run off and play amongst themselves and apparently that's what Nikki and Anissa did that day. They were always together so no one was concerned when they didn't come back right away. It wasn't until the fireworks were about to start that people got a little worried. We all searched but we didn't find anything." He glanced at Baylie, his eyes looking a little haunted. "Nothing but their dog running leash-less on the east side of the lake, and Nissa's ratty doll. It was like they had vanished into thin air."

"You said the whole town was there. Nobody saw anything?" Dylan prodded.

"Not a thing. But like I said, people were milling about and busy. This isn't a large city but there are also tourists. A stranger can go unnoticed." Wilshire looked at Baylie. "It was suggested that the twins may have drowned. They were only six years old and the lake can be murky and deep in spots. No bodies were found though. It was combed several times." Wilshire paused as he observed Baylie quizzically again. "What do you remember about that dog?"

"She was brown and white with floppy ears," she answered instantly. "She could sit and stay and roll over." Feeling the moisture fill her eyes, she blinked it away. "And she could lie down and play dead."

Wilshire's face paled again and this time he let out a hiss of breath. "It can't be. There's just no way."

"I don't remember my mother or father. And I don't remember you," she said emphatically. "How did you know my family?"

After a moment, the man relaxed a little, his eyes still haunted. "I was best friends with Steven Tate. Anissa and Nikki were his sisters."

The words echoed inside her head. She had a brother — a brother named Steven.

"I moved here in the spring of '92," Wilshire continued. "Steve and I became quick buddies. We were together pretty much all the time that summer."

Steve. She took the name in and digested it. Something about it seemed familiar but she couldn't place a face with the name. "Do you know where he is? My..." Her voice broke off and she cleared her throat. "Brother," she finally managed.

"I know where he is. He's got a construction company just outside of Portland. He's got a couple of kids and a wife."

Baylie found herself longing to remember her brother. Her heart ached with the need to establish some kind of connection with someone who had been her family at one time.

"What about her parents?" Dylan asked, before she had the chance.

"They moved away years ago. When the girls disappeared it nearly destroyed their marriage. Far as I know, they're in California now. I'd have to ask Steve."

"Call him," she heard herself say. "Please."

Wilshire frowned again. "I'm not sure that's a good idea at this point, Ms. Sutter. Until we've ironed a few things out, I'd just as soon leave Steve and the Tate family alone."

"I can't prove to you anything more than what I've told you."

Wilshire looked less skeptical but he still frowned. "I assume you'll want to see the old house. It's occupied now by a nice, older couple with no kids. They moved in about five years ago. Before that Steve lived there for a few years until moving to the city." Wilshire cocked his head to one side and studied her again. "You mentioned that you remember your sister, but you haven't said where she is. If you talked to the man who kidnapped you, didn't you ask him what happened to her?"

"I didn't get the chance. Right after he told me who I was, he killed himself. I only remembered Anissa existed once the police pulled up the fliers with our pictures on them," Baylie continued. "There was a fire years ago. I'm fairly sure she died in it."

Wilshire swore, his eyes never leaving hers. "You've got to know how crazy and farfetched this all sounds."

"I knew about the dog, Detective," she reminded him evenly. "And I remember bits and pieces about the carnival we were at the day we disappeared. Maybe if we go to the lake, I'll be able to make heads or tails of what I remember."

"I can take you over there," Wilshire offered, shrugging his shoulders. "Things have changed over the years. You probably won't recognize anything."

"It may help her remember something," Dylan said, shoving the police file back toward Detective Wilshire. "What about the house? Can you get us access to that?"

"I'll have to call the Whitacres and get permission but I doubt it will be a problem. Let me see what I can do."

TWENTY-FOUR

The house that Baylie had spent the first six years of her life in was a plain, white clapboard home with a chain link fence separating the front yard from the sidewalk. It was newly painted and the grass was green and nicely manicured. As Baylie climbed out of Dylan's truck, she stared at the home, blinking several times. This was where she'd lived. The first six years of her life — presumably the only happy years of her life — had been spent here.

Rose and Frank Whitacre had left for the day to visit family upstate. They had given Detective Wilshire the keys and their permission to take a look around. He and Dylan stood silently behind her as she carefully looked over the front yard. Nothing jumped out at her particularly. The place was an average looking, middle class home. The wind whistled through the front yard and her head turned toward the sound. To the left of the porch there was a large elm tree. Baylie stared at it for a long time, not sure why it seemed to stick out in her memory.

"Did there used to be a swing there?" She looked over at Detective Wilshire, who narrowed his eyes.

"No." He stared at her for a long time. "But there's one in the backyard."

Baylie felt her heartbeat speed up. A swing. A *tire* swing. She remembered a tire swing. She and her sister had played on it for hours as kids.

She walked around to the back of the house and carefully lifted the latch on the back gate. When she rounded the corner, she saw that there was indeed a tire swing still hanging from another large tree. The tire was moving silently in the breeze and Baylie felt her skin chill, even through her heavy coat. She walked over and stood in front of it, her fingers reaching out to touch the slightly fraying rope that held the tire. The minute her fingers made contact, images filled her head.

She was giggling as someone pushed her back and forth through the air—a boy who looked to be a teenager. He was tall and gangly with blond hair and dark eyes. She could see Baylie too, running around the swing in a circle, barking madly.

"My turn, my turn," Anissa whined, coming up behind the boy and tugging on his t-shirt.

Baylie let go of the rope and the image vanished. She turned and looked up at Dylan sadly. "My brother pushed me on this swing. We played out here for hours. All of us." She looked at Ryan Wilshire. "Were you here too? Do you remember?"

The man remained silent for a moment, and then he shrugged his shoulders. "Maybe a time or two. When I was around, Steve didn't hang out with his little sisters. We mostly hung out at the lake with the other kids our age."

He looked haunted again. She turned away from him and walked toward the back garage. It was small and detached with a man-door to the side of it. "We played in here. Daddy never parked the car in here because it was too small. Instead he let us use it as a playhouse." She didn't know where the words came from but they flowed out of her freely. She reached down and turned the knob. The door creaked open with a moan of protest. The smell of gasoline and dirt filled her nostrils. Obviously, Mr. Whitacre used the garage for more practical purposes. There was a lawnmower sitting inside the door and a wall of built in work benches next to it. Baylie immediately felt disappointment at the sight. There was something she was missing and she couldn't put her finger on what. It was there, itching to make itself seen, but she just couldn't grasp it. For the longest time, she stared around the garage, willing her mind to open up and spill its contents. Behind her, Dylan flipped on a light. When the room became illuminated, Baylie's eyes focused on a corner of the floor near the tightly shut garage door. She walked over and stared at the big bag of potting soil that sat on the floor next to a shovel and a rake.

"We're going to get in trouble," Nissa said, scowling as Nikki kneeled down and stared at the nice new cement Daddy had poured. "Daddy told us not to touch it."

"He didn't say that. Not exactly," Nikki said, the urge to bury her hands in the wet liquid too much for her to turn away from. She let the muddy mess seep between her small fingers and held them there momentarily. When she pulled them away there were two, perfect handprints in the floor. "Daddy will like them. Like a decoration. He and Mama like decorations. It will be a surprise…surprise…surprise…."

"Baylie?" Dylan's voice interrupted her thoughts and she blinked, causing the image to disappear. Without speaking, she reached for the bag of soil. As she slid it out of the way and then moved the shovel and the rake, two sets of small handprints came into view. Next to them were the words, *Nikki and Nissa age 5*. Tears swarmed in Baylie's eyes as she forced the image of the man she now knew was her father, back into her mind. She hadn't thought of him—hadn't been able to in so long—that the memory of that day actually caused her heart to tighten.

"He'd just filled in a hole out here because animals were getting in." Baylie looked up at Dylan. "It was my idea to put our hands in here. Nissa didn't want to. I was always getting her into trouble." Her voice hitched and she reached her hand up and covered her mouth. "I got her into trouble all the time. I remember that now."

"I'll be damned," Wilshire said from behind her, his eyes growing wide. "It is you."

Dylan stepped forward and smiled down at her halfway. "One twin is always more trouble than the other. I don't need to tell you which twin I am."

She wanted to laugh at that, but she couldn't. "She's gone, Dylan. And I can't bring her back. I let her burn."

"No, Baylie. We've been over this. It wasn't your fault." He set his hands on her shoulders. "You were a victim just as much as she was. Do you remember anything else?"

She stared around the garage and shrugged her shoulders. The truth was, she did remember things. She remembered playing here with her siblings. And she remembered her father. An image of a woman with smiling, lavender colored eyes and the smell of jasmine attached to her also filled Baylie's head. Her mother, she decided.

"We can go in the house if you want," Wilshire said quietly.

"I don't need to go in the house. I know this is where I came from now. Nothing in there is going to lead me to Susan. We need to go to the lake," she said, reluctantly stepping out of the garage and back into the daylight. "I want to go now, before I change my mind."

Neither man argued with her. The ride to Devil's Lake took less than ten minutes. The lake itself was approximately three miles long. Half of it lay within the city limits of Lincoln City and half of it lay outside. The minute they climbed out of the truck, Baylie felt a sense of familiarity. The air was cold and crisp and the wind blew against her cheeks as she stared around the recreation area.

"It's too cold for too much activity around here right now," Wilshire said, stepping out of his police cruiser. "In the summer there's always something going on—kids swimming, birthday parties, barbecues. You name it."

"The carnival was here," Baylie said, gesturing to the area around her. She started walking, her mind taking the lead. There were trails around the park and as they walked, they went farther and farther away from the recreation area. Soon it was significantly off in the distance. Suddenly Baylie stopped. She was standing in the middle of some very tall grass. The smell of musty water filled her nostrils and its familiarity hit her full force. She closed her eyes and she could see things the way they had been all those years ago. She took several steps forward as her eyes blinked open. "There were barrels here. And wildflowers—lots of dandelions."

Wilshire followed her gaze and nodded halfway. "There used to be junk lying around here from miscellaneous activities. I remember the barrels."

"We let the dog off the leash that day," she said suddenly. The images from her nightmare flashed through her mind and she shivered as she looked around the area. Her eyes landed on some tall grass, just outside of a large thicket of trees that lead into the forest. Not too far to the left was a watershed. The dock she remembered being there was gone now, but the shed was the same as the one she'd seen in her nightmares.

She could hear her sister's voice telling her she wanted to go back — that they were going to be in trouble. She winced, her head shooting around, almost as though she expected Nissa to be standing beside her again. But her sister wasn't there. Dylan stood behind her, his blue eyes filled with what looked like a mixture of curiosity and concern.

"I let the dog off her leash," she went on, after a tense moment of silence. "Daddy did it all the time and I thought it would be okay, but it wasn't. Baylie ran away. She took off into the trees." She took several steps toward the dense thicket of trees. The whistling wind grew louder and Baylie almost felt as if she were six years old again, standing there waiting for her sister to come out of her hiding place.

"Come out, come out, wherever you are..."

Baylie battled the words, willing them to stop pounding through her head. She turned in all directions, wishing she could go back in time and that her sister would jump out of her hiding place and yell surprise. But nothing stirred, other than the leaves on the trees and the swaying strands of tall grass that whirled around her legs.

Suddenly she remembered. As long as the memories had been buried, they seemed to work their way out of her subconscious with sudden, brutal force.

"I picked flowers for Mama," she said, her voice quiet. "Nissa wanted to go back and I told her to quit being a baby. I told her to wait while I picked flowers. And then we heard Baylie barking from the trees." She looked at the trees again. "We never went in the woods alone—only with Stevie sometimes, or Daddy. I talked Nissa into playing a game of Hide and Seek while we waited for Baylie to come back." Her mind began to wander again and she forced herself to blink. Panic was beginning to take hold of her chest and she breathed deeply to will it away.

"Maybe we should take her out of here," Wilshire's voice said, clearly full of concern.

She turned and looked at Dylan. "When I was done counting, I opened my eyes and Nissa was gone. I looked everywhere and I couldn't find her. We had a signal, Dylan. When we were tired of playing the game we'd call come out, come out,

358

wherever you are..." Her voice broke off, the pain in her chest growing bigger. "I called to her and she didn't come out. I waited and waited and still she didn't come back," she finished, and rubbed at her now throbbing temples.

Dylan stepped toward her and she stopped him with her hand. Nissa's voice was in her head again, this time it was quiet and almost wary sounding.

"Come out, come out, wherever you are..." Over and over, Baylie heard the words until they just about drove her mad. She looked toward the trees. She could almost hear the dog barking again, just like she had so many years ago.

When she spoke, her voice lowered considerably. "I was about to go back and get Mama when I heard her call out to me and the dog started barking again. Her voice was coming from the trees, so I went in there after her. I saw her doll. It was lying on the ground, just outside these trees." She took a step toward the trees and stopped, her eyes watering — a little bit from the wind whipping against her face and little bit from the emotion taking over her body.

"What happened, baby?" Dylan asked quietly, stepping up beside her.

"When I stepped into the forest, he was there. He had Nissa in his lap and she was crying." She turned and met Dylan's gaze. "He told us he was a police officer and we didn't need to be scared. Then he told us that he would help us find Baylie."

The air seemed to turn even colder and Dylan heard Wilshire swear again. His own blood began to boil and he reached for Baylie but she pulled away. Her eyes were haunted and full of terror as she stared up at him, yet didn't really seem to see him.

"We got in his car. My mother told us time and time again to never ever go anywhere with a stranger, and I did. Nissa was scared and didn't want to, but she always did what I said. When I got into his car, she got into his car. And now she's dead."

He reached for her again and this time he ignored her attempts to ward him off. He pulled her against him tightly and did his best to quiet the sobs that were now racking her body.

"It's really just too fucking bad this guy is dead," Wilshire muttered under his breath as he picked up his now ringing phone and checked the caller ID. Then he pushed a button and silenced the call. "Because I'd love to have just five minutes with him."

"You and me both," Dylan said, leaning his head over Baylie's and trying to calm her down with soothing words. But how could someone sooth wounds as deep as the ones she was harboring?

"I need to make a call if you're okay with it," Wilshire said softly, looking at Baylie.

Her sobs quieted somewhat and she lifted her head from Dylan's chest as she looked up at the detective questioningly.

"I'd like to call your brother."

TWENTY-FIVE

An hour later, they were back at the police station deciding what their next move should be. Detective Wilshire had obviously cleared his mind of any doubts he had that Baylie had once been Nikki Tate. He made his phone call to Steven Tate, and although her brother had voiced some doubts similar to the ones Wilshire himself had initially had, he agreed to come to Lincoln City.

At this point, Baylie had decided that taking another look at her sketchbook was in order. She remembered more things about her past now and it was possible that something in the book might make more sense to her.

Dylan and Detective Wilshire both watched with interest as she turned the pages of the sketchbook avidly, taking in each picture in a new light, now that she remembered who she was. Something dawned on her suddenly. She closely observed the drawings, noticing the way the pictures seemed to be slanted sideways to the left. Just like that she figured it out.

"The reason I didn't recognize this book is because it isn't mine. It was Nissa's."

Dylan frowned. "Are you sure?"

"I'm sure. I didn't like to draw but she did. Whenever I drew anything it always was very simple minded, with very little imagination. Not only that, I tend to slant to the right. Nissa slanted to the left. Even her drawings. I'm a lefty, and she was a righty." She felt even more certain as she turned page after page. "I knew it, Dylan. I didn't run away from Mabel Lomax. He took me. And Nissa went back there in my place. That's why Mabel and her husband thought *I* liked to draw and he got *her* the sketchbook. It was Nissa, not me. She's the one who took it with her to George Rycroft's and she's the one who left it behind." She rubbed her hands over her face tiredly as she continued looking at the drawings. Sadly, the pictures lying before her were all she had left of her sister.

"Sick fuck," Wilshire said crassly, leaning against the wall. "You really think he moved you two back and forth again and again?"

She couldn't swear she was positive but it would certainly explain things. "Why else would I only remember Mabel Lomax and none of the others? Why would I not remember loving to draw and yet each of the foster parents we talked to insisted that I did? I remember Mabel Lomax and Marcus. I know I was there at the Lomax's farm at one time. The only explanation is that he switched us out, over and over."

"Why?" Wilshire asked the obvious question. "Why not leave well enough alone? Hell, he could have gotten caught at any given time."

"Maybe because he had a sick obsession with them," Dylan said, clearly disgusted. "Why else would he still be stalking Baylie after all these years?"

"If we look at these drawings closely something may pop out at us," she finally suggested, and continued perusing the pictures closely.

"She was a terrified child," Wilshire said skeptically. "I'm not sure how much you're going to get out of a traumatized mind."

"Maybe a lot," Baylie said, staring at the picture of the strange sign she'd seen carved into the door of the bathroom in Virginia City. "I wish I knew what this sign was."

Both Dylan and Wilshire looked at the picture silently. Then Wilshire spoke.

"It's a snake, right? I can't be sure, but it looks like something I've seen before."

Immediately Baylie met his gaze. "Where?"

"I'm not sure." He frowned. "But it looks awfully familiar. Tell me the places you're sure you or Nissa have been."

Baylie thought that over. "Virginia City and Melville. Missoula." Baylie looked up at Dylan. "I'm not sure where else."

"Her file's incomplete," Dylan explained.

"Figures." Thoughtful, Wilshire grimaced. "What we need to do, is figure out where you went from here. He took you from the lake. Did he take you back to Missoula?"

Baylie was drawing a blank after the lake. "I'm not sure. I don't think so. I have the weird feeling that Nissa never made it to Missoula. He told me she would never behave when I was around, so that tells me we were together for a while, but not for long. I don't know why but I feel like I was locked in his basement alone when Marcus found me. He never mentioned a thing about there being two of us and I'm sure he would have told me if he'd known."

"She's right," Dylan agreed.

"So maybe Nissa got away first. Somewhere between here and Missoula," Wilshire said, still thinking aloud. "She ended up in the system in Montana so we know that's where she was eventually picked up. It had to have been a significant amount of time after the kidnapping. The Tate Twins disappearing was pretty big news around here for a while. Someone would have recognized her if she'd turned up right away."

"Not necessarily," Dylan said thoughtfully. Then he looked at Wilshire intently. "Not if only one twin turned up. Now if two had, on the other hand..." His voice trailed off and he finally looked over at Baylie.

"You think that's why he kept us apart over the years? Because we attracted less attention that way?"

"I think it's one theory that makes a whole lot of sense. Maybe the fire at the Eisenberg's was what finally ended it for him. Nissa died and you were sent to foster care and at that point he would have had to kidnap you again—bringing too much attention to you—in order to get you back. He didn't have Nissa to replace you with anymore. You spent several uninterrupted years with your last three foster families and eventually went out on your own. He must have decided to find you around the time you finished college and started working in Chapman. The timeline is right."

In a very sick way, what Dylan said made sense. It made Baylie overwhelmingly sad to think of Nissa dying the way she had. Her twin had burned to death in a home she'd never belonged in, in the first place. She'd had no kind of life—no love. God, it broke Baylie's heart. Frustration ate at her and she wanted to scream.

"Who's the first known foster family?" Wilshire asked curiously. "And where?"

"The first listed foster home we have documentation on is Samuel and Mabel Lomax in Melville, Montana. That was in 1994. She spent a year there." Dylan looked thoughtful. "Or maybe I should assume they both spent six months there. Mabel told us that she ran away and then was sent back to them."

"And when I came back I was different," Baylie finished for him, her breath hitching. "Because it was Nissa who came back, not me. I think we can pretty much count on that now."

Dylan nodded in agreement. He then went on to fill Wilshire in on the time line of all the foster homes Baylie had supposedly been in.

"So where were you for the two years in between when you were kidnapped and when you ended up with Mabel and Samuel Lomax?"

Baylie didn't have an answer for that. "I don't know." Just as frustrated as they were, she sighed. "I don't really remember being in Melvin's basement for very long. And I didn't remember Marcus until Mabel Lomax reminded me of him. It's like these things are coming back to me, but only when something triggers the memory." She looked up at Dylan sadly. "How am I ever going to find that hole?"

His expression was somber and he didn't answer her. Wilshire, however, did.

"We're looking for a needle in a haystack. It could literally be anywhere. But my thoughts are that if we look at a map, we can route the trip from here to Missoula. He wouldn't have kept you hidden in a place where you weren't conveniently accessible to him. He would have had to feed and give you water frequently."

Baylie thought that over. She supposed Wilshire was right. "That still doesn't narrow the options down."

"No. But if we take a look at a map, we can finger some cities that are possibilities. Maybe then I'll remember where I've seen that snake insignia before."

She guessed it couldn't hurt. Wilshire disappeared to retrieve some maps. Baylie looked at Dylan. "It's been a long time, Dylan. Do you think Susan's even still alive?"

He stared at her for a moment, his lips thinning into a frown. "Maybe," he finally said, without much conviction. "I don't know when he put her in there and I don't know how much food or water she was given the last time he checked on her."

Wilshire returned with the maps of the states of Oregon, Idaho and Montana. They poured over them for the next hour.

"He obviously would have taken the 18 and headed northeast," Dylan reasoned, running his finger over the map. "That would have taken him through all these cities. There are too many to count."

Disappointment ate at Baylie as she looked over the map closely. None of the names of the cities stuck out to her in any way.

"It was a long shot," Wilshire said, stepping away from the map and sitting down in a chair dejectedly. "He could have turned off at any one of them."

"Maybe if we drove the route again I would remember something," she suggested lamely, looking over at Dylan.

He thought that over. "It's not a terrible idea." Straightening he looked at the map again. "We would be guessing which way he went though. We could guess wrong."

"Think about it. He had two kidnapped little girls in the car. Chances are he took the quickest way possible," Wilshire interjected, suddenly seeming more hopeful.

Dylan looked at Baylie. "Are you fairly sure that Nissa never made it to that basement in Missoula with you?"

For some reason she was positive of that. "I'm sure. I was in there alone. For days I was in there alone."

He nodded his head. "Okay then. That tells us that she either got away, or he dropped her off somewhere before you got there. Judging by the fact that she never made it back home to your parents, I don't think she escaped from him right away. She would have told someone who she was at that point and they would have been able to help her. People were looking for you both back then. I'm guessing that he got rid of her for the time being. Took her somewhere where no one would find her—where she wouldn't have a chance to have contact with anyone who could help her or find out what had really happened."

"In the hole," she figured out aloud.

"In the hole," he confirmed. "He wasn't stupid. He likely knew that showing up with two of you would have raised some serious red flags. And it was easier to keep one of you quiet at a time."

Baylie felt her stomach roil. She knew she hadn't been quiet back then. She'd screamed and screamed and screamed, and no one had come to help her. Not until Marcus.

"We should get started while we have some good daylight," Dylan said quietly, reaching for her hand. "I know Wilshire called your brother but—"

"We can go. We'll be back." As much as she wanted to be reunited with her brother, she knew Susan's life was hanging in the balance.

"Good luck," Wilshire said, cocking his head to the side and studying Baylie closely again. "For what it's worth, you're one hell of a tough cookie, Nikki Tate."

370

Hearing her given name addressed to her, she smiled halfway. "Thanks for your help. Tell my brother I'll be back."

"I'll tell him." Wilshire shook Dylan's hand. "I'll do my best to keep this quiet but I'm sure the town is buzzing with news by now. You should be prepared for some attention from the media. I don't know how big this will get but..." He shrugged his shoulders. "Just be prepared."

A few minutes later, they were in his truck and on their way. The drive across Oregon was tiresome. It took hours and Baylie found herself nodding off numerous times. Always she dreamed. Sometimes of Nissa and her family. Sometimes of being in that hole alone. Sometimes of Marcus. But none of the dreams made much sense to her, or led her any closer to the location where Susan was likely being held.

By the time late evening hit they had crossed through the Idaho/Montana state line.

Dylan stopped just off the highway, about an hour outside of Missoula, for gas and some sustenance. They hadn't stopped for lunch or anything else and she had to admit she was hungry. While he gassed up the truck, she went into the small convenience store attached to the gas station. She loaded a basket up with a bag of chips and a few candy bars. Then she grabbed a Coke for him and a bottle of water for herself. She was just

371

heading for the counter when a bin full of maps and brochures caught her eye.

Walking over to the bin, she set her basket down and reached for one of the brightly colored brochures. *Rattlesnake Junction Cabins*, the words read on the front of the folded paper. In the middle of the page was the insignia of a rattlesnake with fangs and a swirling body. It looked eerily similar to the drawing in Nissa's sketchbook and the strange sign carved into the bathroom wall in Virginia City. Baylie felt faint for a moment and she dropped her basket and grabbed hold of the metal bin to steady herself.

"You about ready?" Dylan asked, stepping up behind her. When he saw the look on her face, he reached for her. "What?"

She turned and offered the brochure to him silently.

"Sonofabitch," he muttered, looking the brochure over. Then he met her gaze cautiously. "Do you think this is the insignia in the sketchbook?"

She nodded her head, without hesitation.

"Can I help you find something?" a plump brunette behind the counter asked, eyeing both Dylan and Baylie curiously.

Dylan picked up the basket she'd dropped and set it on the counter. "I think we're good."

While she rang up the purchases, Dylan held the brochure out to her. "Do you know how far this place is from here?"

372

She glanced at the brochure and shrugged her beefy shoulders. "About thirty minutes. But it's closed up this time of year. You'd be crazy to camp in the cold up there. To book the cabins you have to call ahead of time. But I wouldn't want to be up in those woods by myself in the winter."

Dylan didn't respond to her comment. Instead, he paid for their purchases and led Baylie back to the truck. Once they were inside the cab, he reached for the map of Montana he had stowed in the glove box and began looking it over.

"She said it's closed up," she reminded him.

"I heard what she said." He continued looking the map over. After a moment, he shoved it back toward her and looked at the brochure again.

"It's dark, Dylan." Her voice sounded meek, even to her, and she inwardly cringed. She knew somehow that they were on the right track, and all of the sudden that fact scared the hell out of her. Before, it had been an unknown place that she didn't remember. It was starting to climb its way out of her subconscious now and she wasn't sure if she could face the place again.

He obviously heard the tremor in her voice because he set the brochure aside and observed her silently for a minute. When he spoke, his voice was low and gentle. "I know this is going to be hard for you, baby. I'm sorry about that. But you're not going in there alone this time. We're together and we're a team. Remember what I said about that?"

She nodded her head. Even though she knew he meant what he said, she was still terrified. Somehow, she knew the last time she'd left that hole behind, she had vowed never to come back to it. And now here she was.

"He's dead, Baylie. He can't hurt you anymore."

"He'll never be dead in my nightmares."

He was quiet a moment. Then he reached over and laced his fingers with hers. "No. I guess he won't. But here, now, he can't hurt you. No one can. Because I've got your back every step of the way."

"Susan might be dead," she said, her voice cracking. She felt the tears in her eyes and they burned mercilessly.

"She might be alive, too. We owe it to her to help her if we can."

She knew he was right. The whole reason she'd done all this, was to help Susan. Taking several deep breaths, she sat up straight and wiped at her eyes. "Okay. I know you're right. Just give me a minute here."

"Take all the time you need. I'm looking this brochure over."

Baylie stared out into the darkness, determined to get her wits about her. She could do this. She had to. She hadn't helped her sister all those years ago. She wouldn't do the same thing to Susan.

"It looks like the lady in the store was right. It says the resort is closed for the season between October and March. But it lists the names of each cabin and who owns them. There are phone numbers too. Apparently if you want to stay out of season you contact the owners directly and the places can still be rented."

"He couldn't possibly have rented one of those all year long, could he?"

Dylan thought that over as he started up his truck. "I doubt it. The owner names on the brochure don't look familiar to me either. Why don't you take a look?"

Baylie looked at the listed properties and the names of their owners.

Potluck was the first cabin. Max Walker was listed as the owner of that particular cabin. The next was *Whispering Horse*. Abigail Beecher was listed as that owner. *Nantucket* was the third cabin. Its owner was Michael Sanders. The last cabin was *Lakeside*. It was owned by Beatrice Channing. None of the names meant anything to Baylie. She shook her head solemnly.

"I didn't think so." Dylan put the truck in gear. "There are camping spots up there too. It's possible that the hole is near one of those. We just need to take a look around. I'm going to call the local authorities. I don't want another incident like the one that occurred at the Eisenberg's." He picked up his phone to dial then grimaced.

"What?"

"No service." He tossed the cell phone down and glanced at her. "We'll just do a quick drive thru and come back out. It'll be okay."

What he said sounded reasonable but she found herself objecting. "Maybe we should just go to the local sheriff."

"We will. After I do a quick drive thru. This place may mean nothing to you. It's a hunch, Baylie. I don't want to get a bunch more people involved on a hunch."

It wasn't a hunch. Not to her, but she remained silent. The farther up into the hills they went, the more uncomfortable she became. It was dark and she couldn't see much but somehow she knew she'd been here before. Her skin grew clammy and her heart started to pound faster. They had neared the top of the hill, where a huge sign held between two posts stretched over the road before them. When Dylan's truck lights shined on it, they saw the words *Rattlesnake Junction Cabins* written in big, white letters. Next to them was a carving of the rattlesnake insignia. For a moment, her mind blanked out. She was still in a vehicle, but it wasn't Dylan's vehicle. It was a car. And it was daytime.

The car was rattling down the dirt road, jostling Nikki from where she'd sat in the back seat sleeping. Nissa lay curled next to her, her tear stained cheeks still noticeable even though he'd forced her to wipe them with a tissue earlier.

Looking out the window, she watched the trees go by, wishing again and again that her mother would appear — or her daddy. Even Stevie. She just wanted to go home. She'd begged and pleaded with Freddy to take them back there but he'd told them they were home. He was their daddy now. She didn't want him to be their daddy. Their daddy was kind and gentle and funny. He liked to make them laugh. All Freddy wanted to do was make them cry. He'd forced them to do things that they both knew were wrong and bad. And when they'd cried and tried to get away, he'd spanked them both and locked them in the trunk of the car. They'd rode that way for hours, until the last time he'd pulled over to eat. He'd finally let them out, but not before making them promise to behave.

"I see you're awake. It's good that you got a nice nap."

She looked into the front seat where Freddy was seated, a baseball cap pulled low over his eyes as he drove. "I want to go home."

"You will be going home. Very soon, love. In the meantime, sit back and enjoy the view."

She stared out the window, wishing she could jump out of the moving car and scream for help. But she'd tried that already. He had the doors locked and there was no way to get them open from the back seat.

As they passed a small house, she watched the children play in the front yard, with longing. There was a picnic table set up outside and two adults were seated at its bench laughing as they watched the children. She put her hands up on the window, willing them to look her way. But they didn't. A moment later she saw nothing but trees again.

"Wake your sister up. We'll be there shortly."

The command was sharp and she knew better than to argue with him. She shook Nissa gently. Her sister came awake. When Nissa realized where they were, she started to cry again.

"Shut up! I told you about that crying! You're big girls now."

Nissa's crying grew louder, until he pulled over to the side of the deserted road and reached into the backseat. Before Nissa could move away, his fingers yanked her by the arm so hard that she flew against the back of the front seat. "Shut up! Do you hear me?"

Trying to help her sister, she grabbed at his arm, but he was too strong. He backhanded her quickly. She flew back against the door, her head smacking with a thud. Momentarily stunned, she lay still.

"I'm done being nice to you two! Now sit back and shut up!"

Cringing, she shut her eyes and started to count inside her head. She felt Nissa curl up beside her. They rode that way for what seemed like hours. And then suddenly they came to an abrupt stop. The front driver's side door opened and Freddy climbed out of the car. He reached for the back door and yanked it open. Before either girl could react, he yanked Nissa across the back seat and out of the *car. She kicked and she screamed but it took very little effort for him to overpower her.*

Nikki waited for him to grab her next. He didn't. Instead, he shocked her by looking at her, his evil eyes staring at her so intently that it caused her to wet her pants. "Stay here and shut up. If you don't, I'll kill you both." With that, he slammed the door and while she watched, carried her sister off down the road and into the trees.

"Baylie?"

She heard Dylan's voice, felt his hands on her shoulders, but she couldn't let go of the sight of her sister being carried off into the trees. She tried to hang onto the vision but it slowly faded away.

"Damn it, Baylie, talk to me!"

She batted against his hands, panic taking over inside of her. She hadn't realized she was crying until she heard her own terrified sobs.

"Baby, stop. It's okay. I've got you."

She heard his words but she didn't feel any comfort from them. Not this time. She yanked at the door handle, desperate to get away from the confinement of the truck cab that surrounded her. Her feet hit the dirt road hard and she fell to her knees, using her hands to keep from falling the rest of the way. There was snow on the ground and it was cold. It was icy and numbing. Chest heaving, she stood up and looked around the dark area. It was pitch black and nothing but forest surrounded her.

"Baylie, wait!" Dylan's voice called to her as he rounded the truck and caught her by the elbows. She shoved at him and he yanked her harder. "I know you're afraid but I'm not going to hurt you. Talk to me, damn it."

It hurt to breathe and for a moment she bent over and let her hands rest on her knees. As she stared at the snow-covered ground, she felt such despair that she didn't know what to do. How was she ever going to get past this?

"Baylie, talk to me." Dylan crouched down in front of her, his blue eyes looking up into hers with sympathy and concern.

She didn't even bother to swipe at the tears that were running down her face. Instead she sniffled a moment, then looked him in the eye. "He brought us here. He did bad things to us, Dylan."

Dylan's eyes narrowed and she saw the sadness in them. "God, I'm sorry, baby." He reached for her and she let him pull her toward him. The warmth of his arms was marginally comforting and she let herself be swallowed up in them for the moment.

"I didn't want you to have to remember this, Baylie. I swear I didn't. There was no other way."

She could hear the anguish in his voice and she knew he meant the words. She buried her head in his chest and held on, thankful for the connection she had to him that somehow always managed to keep her sane. When she felt as though she could

380

stand on her own again, she backed away from him and looked at the forest around them. "I was bad. I tried to get away. That's why he brought Nissa here. I didn't remember a lot about where this place is because we were in the trunk part of the time. He put us in there because we tried to get away."

He stared at her a moment, then shook his head solemnly. "It's a wonder you're still alive."

He was right, she realized. For a moment, she gave into the urge to bury her head against his chest again. She wanted nothing more than to stay there in his arms but she knew she couldn't. Susan needed her help. She backed up and met his worried gaze as she wiped her eyes. "If we keep driving straight, eventually we'll come to the last cabin. It's by a lake. I know the hole has got to be somewhere back there."

He looked as though he wanted to say something, but apparently thought the better of it, because he squeezed her hands and nodded. She climbed back up into the truck while he stood at the door and waited for her to buckle in. When she was secure, he leaned over her and looked into her eyes. "Just so you know, I love you."

The words were so unexpected that for a moment she just stared at him dumbly.

He leaned in and covered her mouth with his quickly. Then he was gone, the door shutting behind him.

Baylie, still in shock, lifted her fingers to touch her lips. She loved him too, she realized. She waited for him to climb in on the driver's side, but when the door opened, it wasn't Dylan who climbed into the other side of the truck. Before she could scream, a fist came down hard across her head and everything went black.

TWENTY-SIX

The pounding in her head was so extreme that Baylie felt nauseous as she opened her eyes. Darkness surrounded her, and for a moment, she felt as though she were dreaming again. She felt like a helpless six-year-old, tossed in a dirty hole and left to die. But when she moved her feet, she realized she wasn't lying on a dirt floor. She was lying on a bed, on top of a patchwork quilt. There was a dimly lit lantern on a table that sat next to the double bed.

Biting back the nausea, she tried to remember where she was and how she had gotten here. She looked around for Dylan but she didn't see him. She didn't see anyone. The door to what looked like a small bedroom was closed. Forcing herself, she sat up, grasping the quilt on both sides of her to keep the dizziness from knocking her onto her back again.

And then she remembered. Someone had hit her. Someone had climbed into Dylan's truck and cold cocked her. She blinked her eyes, trying to remember the person she'd see in the darkened truck cab. She hadn't gotten a good look at him before a fist had plowed into her face. All she remembered seeing was a red hood and a glimpse of dark hair underneath it.

Fear clawed at her from every direction. Where was Dylan?

Hearing a sound outside the door, she stiffened. She wanted to hide. Instinct had her climbing off the bed, ignoring the pain that shot threw her skull. She peered around the room, desperate for a place to hide. There was nowhere. She backed up and into the corner, wishing the room would swallow her up. The knob on the bedroom door was turning. Whoever had brought her here was back.

Without thinking about it, she dropped to her knees and slid her body underneath the bed. And then she waited. The door was opening. Two black sneakers came into view a moment later, along with the frayed edges of very well worn jeans. The figure stopped just inside the door. Dead silence ensued. And then he laughed. *"Come out, come out, wherever you are."*

Again, fear clawed at her. It wasn't possible. *Those words.* She wasn't hearing them. David Melvin was dead. She'd watched him die.

"You're under the bed, aren't you?" The voice spoke again. It was deep and male. It was eerily familiar, though she couldn't put her finger on

384

where she'd heard it before. Anxiety twisted her insides and she stayed still, even though she knew what the inevitable was.

"Not the best hiding place. I know, I've tried it too."

She felt her skin crawl at his words. His feet stopped when they were a foot or so from the edge of the bed.

"I'm afraid Detective Stone is a bloody mess. I didn't mean to hit him so hard." The voice sounded oddly concerned. Baylie felt her heart stop as she thought of Dylan hurt. God, she'd gotten him into this mess, just like she'd gotten Nissa into this mess so many years before.

"You know, I never would have hit you if you would have shut up. But I knew you wouldn't. After all, you aren't very cooperative." He surprised her by sitting down on the bed. He didn't reach for her—didn't make any move to touch her at all. He just sat down.

Confused and frozen with fear, she lay there silently, her eyes peering around the immediate area for a way of escape.

"This used to be my room, you know." His voice rambled on. "I spent summers here when I was really small. My mother loved it. She wanted to live here year round but he wouldn't let her. He wasn't much for sharing." He paused, apparently thinking his next words over carefully. "But he was all I had. And now he's dead."

Baylie shut her eyes tightly, willing him to stop talking. God, she knew who he was now. He had to be the boy who'd been living with David Melvin. Was it possible that Melvin hadn't kidnapped him? Was it possible that he was David's son?

"I know he wasn't much," he continued. "But since Mother died, he's all I had left. And you made him kill himself. Why?"

She watched his feet move slightly and she slithered back away from the edge of the bed as quietly as she could.

"Why?" His voice raised and he bent over. Suddenly their gazes locked. Surprised, she stared into the eyes of Jonah Kramer. Only his eyes didn't look anything like the eyes that she had seen at school. They now looked hurt and angry, and a little bit confused, if she was seeing right.

Jonah Kramer. He'd been the nice boy. The one who'd always tried to stop Jeepers McClain from harassing her.

As they stared at one another, he smiled halfway. "You can come out now. I'm not going to hurt you unless you give me reason to."

She backed away from him, but made no move to come out from under the bed. Even though he was a kid, and she knew that now for a fact, there was something in his eyes that scared her to her core.

"Suit yourself," he said. Instead of reaching in and grabbing her, he stood up and turned. He surprised her again by plopping down on the floor and sitting Indian style in front of her. "I don't blame you for being afraid. I've been afraid plenty too. I won't make you come out of there — at least not now." He gave her a quizzical look. "I knew when he made me go to the school where you were teaching that things were going to get bad. I would have warned you but you wouldn't have listened to me, would you?"

"I would have," she managed to croak out.

He snickered at that. "You were too busy playing games with Jeepers."

"He played games with me," she found herself defending. "Why are you here, Jonah? Are you telling me David Melvin was your father?"

"Hell no," the boy said emphatically. "He was my uncle. The bastard."

Baylie wasn't sure what to say to that. "What happened to your mother?" she finally asked.

"She died. Two years ago. After that, I was sent to live with dear old Uncle David." His expression darkened. "For years before that, he was messing with me. I hated the bastard. I begged and pleaded not to go with him but there was no one else to take me. Social workers tend not to care much what a fifteen-year-old boy wants. Especially when a caring relative like Uncle David is around to convince them how much he loves his nephew and how it was his dead sister's wish that he take care of her baby boy."

"I'm sorry," was all Baylie could think of to say. Suddenly the fact that she was still huddled under the bed seemed odd. She moved in the opposite direction and climbed out from under the mattresses. Her head pounded violently and for a moment she thought she was going to faint. Grabbing hold of the side of the bed, she managed to steady herself. When she looked up, Jonah was there staring at her again.

"Why did you hit me?"

"I told you before. Because you wouldn't have come with me quietly. I knew you would fight me. I wanted to talk to you."

His explanation was that simple.

"You assaulted a police officer," she reminded him, still unsure of him and backing away from the bed.

"The doors are locked. You can't get out without a key," Jonah said, and stood up suddenly. A shiny, gold key glittered in between his fingertips. "And I didn't plan to hurt Detective Stone but I had to get him out of the way. Like I said, I wanted to talk to you."

"About what?" she asked carefully.

"About Uncle David. I know he hurt you too. He told me."

"He told you. Why would he do that?"

"Because that's how he kept me in line. He told me that as long as I behaved myself and did what he said, he'd leave me alone. So I did it. I did what he told me to do. Only I didn't know he was going to hurt Ms. Lindsay or Ms. Hanover. I swear I didn't know. They trusted him because of me, and then he hurt them."

In spite of her own pain, Baylie found herself sympathizing with the boy. Their childhoods had unfortunately been eerily similar. "He was a bad man, Jonah. None of this was your fault." Dylan had said nearly the same words to her several times and until this moment she hadn't believed him. Now, while looking at the pathetic boy in front of her, she realized that things hadn't been her fault. She'd been a victim, just like Dylan had said.

"He was a bastard," Jonah agreed. "He made me trash your car, you know. And he made me throw that rock through Detective Stone's window. Jeepers hates you so he agreed to help me. He's the one who broke the window in your house."

The fact that Jeepers McClain hated her was the least of her worries. "I know you don't want to hurt anyone, Jonah. You're not like him."

"I already hurt Detective Stone." Jonah pulled an object from his pocket, gripping it carefully in his fingers. A gun, Baylie realized. The kid had a gun.

She looked toward the door but his warning stopped her. *The doors are locked.* She was trapped.

"I'll talk to him. I'll explain that you were scared — that you just wanted to talk to me. It will be okay if you just let me go now."

"I feel bad about this, Ms. Sutter. I really do. But Uncle told me that you made him kill my mother. He told me that he had no choice, because of you. She was all I had." Jonah's voice shook somewhat, as he lifted his hand and swiped at his eyes. "How could you make him kill her?"

"Jonah, I didn't make him do anything. He was a sick man who hurt a lot of people. I didn't even know your mother."

"You did. Her name was Bethany Kramer. He killed her because you were bad. He told me that."

Bethany Kramer. God, the woman she had worked with in Chapman at the high school. One of the women the police had thought Kevin had murdered. She had been this boy's mother. Guilt ate at Baylie. "I didn't want him to hurt anyone," she tried telling him again. His expression didn't soften.

"But he did hurt her."

"He hurt my sister. She's dead too. And he hurt me."

Jonah's hand shook fiercely and Baylie grew a little alarmed that the gun might go off accidentally.

"If *you* hadn't run away, he wouldn't have hurt me. He wouldn't have hurt my mother."

"He hurt people because he was sick, not because of me. I was a child when he took me and my sister. He kidnapped us."

Jonah shook his head in disbelief. "He told me you would say that."

"It's the truth. You already know he hurt us. He told you that. How do you think I knew how to get here? He brought us here when we were little. He locked us up in a hole."

Jonah narrowed his eyes. "He's a liar, you're a liar. I don't know who to believe."

"Why would I lie?"

"Because you want me to feel sorry for you and let you go. But I can't. My mother died because of you. She didn't deserve that."

"She died because of your uncle. I liked your mother. We worked together. You lived in Chapman, didn't you? She worked at the school I taught at."

He frowned. "It's not going to work. You're not going to turn the tables on me. I hated him but I don't believe you either."

Desperation had Baylie walking toward him. When he raised the gun, she stopped. "He did lie to you. He lied to me and to my sister and to a lot of other people too. He was a bad man."

Jonah began to shake again. He was clearly close to a breaking point. The sad thing was, that even while he was holding that gun she got the impression that he was nothing but a scared little boy.

"If you let me out of here, I can help you."

"I'll be in trouble for hitting Detective Stone. And for trashing your car."

"No one's going to blame you for anything, Jonah. Not if you let me go before anyone else gets hurt. This has gone far enough. He's dead. You and I are free."

"My mother will never be free."

He was right about that. Bethany Kramer had been a victim of her brother's circumstances. Nothing was going to be able to change that. "I'm sorry about that. If there was a way for me to bring her back, I would."

He wiped at his eyes again, the gun waving around haphazardly as he did so. "I don't believe you. I don't! He told me you would say all the things you're saying!"

"That's because he knew that I would tell you the truth!" Baylie took another cautious step toward Jonah. "Don't you see? That's why he killed himself. He knew that once the police got him, he was finished. He was going to go to prison. Cops and child molesters don't survive long in prison. He knew that. He took the easy way out."

Jonah let out a small sob, shaking his head at her. "I just want my mother back."

"There's nothing I can do that will bring her back, Jonah. I can't bring back my sister. There's nothing you can do that will bring them back either. I wish there was."

The gun was low and pointed toward the floor now and Baylie took the opportunity to charge at him. Her only chance was to get the gun away from him and force him to let her out of the cabin. To do that, she had to try and overpower him. Jonah wasn't a large kid, but Baylie was small and half his size. When she hit him, the impact was enough to knock him backward and jar the gun loose. It flew across the room and crashed into the wall. Baylie felt his hands grasp her shoulders and shove her roughly against the wall. He grasped her neck and squeezed, his eyes never leaving hers. Her fingers defensively came up to pry at his. She felt her feet leave the floor.

Suddenly, all hell broke loose. She heard a crash off in the distance and then the door to the bedroom slammed open.

"Freeze! Police!" The voice was loud and authoritative. Black spots began to pop in her eyes and she felt dangerously close to passing out. Still, she knew the voice was Dylan's and relief that he was okay washed over her.

"Let her go," Dylan warned, this time louder.

Baylie felt the fingers around her neck loosen quickly.

"I wasn't going to hurt her! I swear it. I was just trying to scare her!" Jonah said, his expression terrified now.

"Shut the fuck up, raise your hands above your head and step away from her."

Jonah's eyes never left hers as he backed up, now letting her go completely. He slowly raised his hands into the air. At the same time, a tear drifted down his cheek.

Weak from lack of oxygen, she felt herself crumple down to her knees. In the same instant, several police officers tackled Jonah Kramer and shoved him face down to the floor. It took her a moment to realize Dylan was one of them. He kept his foot in the boy's back until a sheriff's deputy took over and cuffed him. And then he was crouched down in front of her, his hands roaming over her hair.

"God, are you okay? Did he hurt you?"

It took her a moment but she finally managed to shake her head.

"I'm sorry, baby. He hit me from behind. I didn't see him coming."

She looked up at him, and for the first time, noticed he had a dribble of blood flowing down the side of his head. "You're hurt," she said quietly, reaching up and gently touching his head. He winced when her fingers made contact with a rather large bump behind his left ear.

"I'm okay." He pulled her shaking form against him and held her tightly for a few moments. "I thought he killed you. I woke up and you were gone."

"He was David Melvin's nephew," she said, slowly pulling her head back so she could look into his face. "Bethany Kramer was his mother."

"I know," Dylan said quietly. "Wilshire got a call from Missoula. They found the deed for this place in his house. It's still in his aunt's name, that's why we didn't recognize the owner on the brochure. Apparently, Wilshire remembered where he saw the snake insignia. His grandparents rented a cabin up here occasionally when he was a kid. Lucky for us he called local law enforcement when he couldn't get a hold of us. He sent them up to look for the hole. They showed up in the nick of time."

"Did they find her?" she asked hopefully.

"Not yet," he answered honestly, and her heart fell.

"You were our first worry. We weren't sure what we were dealing with here." He backed up as she attempted to brace herself against him and stand. "Easy." He clasped her fingers in his and helped her to her feet.

She turned to Jonah, who was now standing, his hands cuffed behind his back. "Where is the hole, Jonah?"

395

He looked at her blankly for several moments. Then he shook his head. "I don't know what you're talking about."

"You're lying." She stepped toward him. "Where is it? He has Susan Hanover in there. She's dying."

He continued to shake his head. "I really don't know what you're talking about."

"He's lying," she told Dylan. "He has to know. He spent time up here as a kid."

"So did you!" Jonah said accusingly.

"Do you expect me to believe that he never shoved you into that hole?" She glared at him, her eyes filling with tears again. "Because I spent day in and day out in there!"

"He didn't have to shove me into a hole. The state *gave* me to him! What did he have to hide?"

The reality of his words slapped her in the face. *God, he was right.* "Oh God, I don't know where it is, Dylan. *I don't know.*"

"But you know it's up here somewhere," he prodded, shaking her slightly. "Where, Baylie? Where is it?"

"I don't know!" She batted at his hands as hysteria finally took over her.

"You told me in the truck earlier that you knew it was up here. You know where it is. I know you do. Now calm down and give yourself a chance to think straight."

His words seeped their way into her brain and she breathed deeply, forcing herself to calm down. He was right. Hysteria wasn't going to help matters any. She did know the hole was up here somewhere. She knew how to get there. She'd been there before. She just had to clear her head and think.

"There's a cellar," Jonah said, breaking the silence suddenly. "It's a ways out from the cabin. Maybe that's what she's talking about."

"Where?" Dylan asked, dropping his hands from Baylie's shoulders.

"In the dark, it's hard to find. You'll need flashlights or a lantern."

"Let him go," Baylie said, grabbing Dylan's hand.

He looked down at her, his eyes narrowed. "He just tried to strangle you, Baylie."

"I wasn't trying to strangle her. Not intentionally. She knocked me down," Jonah said quietly.

Baylie could see the boy was regretting his behavior. Her heart softened somewhat. "He was a victim too, Dylan. He can lead us to that cellar. That's got to be where Melvin held us."

Dylan grimaced but looked over at the sheriff, who still had his hands wrapped around Jonah's forearms from behind.

"It's your call," the sheriff said, shrugging his shoulders. "It's not like the kid can get far with all of us around anyway."

Dylan nodded his head then turned back to Baylie. "I want you to wait here."

At one time, she would have been happier than hell to hear him say those words. But now? Now she knew she couldn't wait here. She had to face her childhood demons head on, in order to make them go away.

"I can't hide anymore, Dylan. Not from my mind, and not from my nightmares. I have to face them."

He looked like he wanted to argue, but he remained silent.

"We're wasting time," the sheriff said impatiently, as he unlocked Jonah's handcuffs.

Obviously realizing she wasn't going to change her mind, Dylan nodded. "Okay, if you're sure."

The sad thing was, she wasn't sure. The only thing she was sure of, was the fact that she couldn't walk away from here and not look back unless she finally faced the dungeon that had taken away all of her memories.

TWENTY-SEVEN

Jonah Kramer was right. The forest behind the Lakeside cabin was pitch black at night. The snowfall that had probably been off and on throughout the winter season had left a significant amount of powder on the ground. There were several inches, making it even harder to see what was underneath it. The farther they walked, the more Baylie was convinced it was impossible for anyone to survive somewhere underground in these conditions. It also became painfully clear why no one had heard her screams as a child. The place was literally deserted, besides the Lakeside cabin. Nothing but trees and a small lake to the left of the house. The last cabin Baylie had seen had been a couple of miles back. David Melvin had picked the perfect place for his torture chamber.

Several deputies were with them, as well as Jonah Kramer and Sheriff Bob Tucker. Everyone had either a lantern or a flashlight. Between each of their beams, the immediate area in front of them was lit up well enough to see any tracks or disturbances.

"It's freezing as hell out here," one deputy complained. "Are we even sure we're going the right way?"

"I'm sure," Jonah said steadfastly.

"I hope so, kid. Cause I'm about to freeze my —"

"Quit bitching," the sheriff interrupted before the deputy could finish his sentence.

"He told me it was for storage," Jonah said, his voice quiet. "He said it was dilapidated and dangerous down there so I never bothered to even check it out."

Dylan grunted at that.

"When I was up here, he kept a very close eye on me, Detective. I didn't get the chance to do much exploring. Now I know why."

"Well, that's a relief," Dylan snapped, clearly unsympathetic toward the teenager, not that Baylie blamed him. She was annoyed herself that he'd hit her in the head and scared the hell out of her. Overall, Jonah Kramer had managed to tick off a lot of people tonight, to say the least. Obviously, he realized this because his posture seemed to wither a little and he shrugged his shoulders dejectedly.

"In any case, it's not too far from the house. With all the snow it's hard to see." Jonah's eyes scanned the area carefully.

400

"That's my point," the deputy muttered under his breath.

"Wait a minute," Dylan said suddenly, and everyone stopped. They were around thirty yards from the Lakeside cabin. When he stomped his foot a hollow sound followed the movement.

Baylie's heart stopped for a moment. This was it. Somehow, she knew it. She was standing on top of the hole that had once been her prison. Instinctively, she backed away.

"I'll be damned," the complaining deputy said, stepping up next to Dylan and shining his lantern on the ground. To the naked eye, it looked like a white pile of snow—just another area of the forest floor. If Dylan hadn't stepped on it, they would have walked right past it.

Everyone else came forward and crowded around Dylan, who handed his lantern to Baylie and leaned over to brush the snowy ground with his gloved hands. "We need a shovel. It's the only way we're going to get in there."

This didn't sound good to Baylie at all. If Susan was in there, could she have survived?

"There are probably air holes, even with the snow," Dylan said, reading her mind. "Right now we just need to get in there." He continued pawing at the frozen ground, while a couple of the deputies went back to the cabin for a shovel. It didn't take them long to return with two. Immediately, Dylan and Jonah began to dig.

"Do you really think Ms. Hanover is down there?" Jonah asked suddenly, his eyes now looking very much like those of a scared little boy again.

"I know he kept me down there for weeks on end," Baylie answered.

Jonah swore, shaking his head. "I swear to God I had no idea. If I had known…" His voice broke off.

"Tell it to a judge," Dylan said irritably. "Now keep digging."

It took them the good part of fifteen minutes to dig away the snow well enough to make out the large wooden door that covered a three-foot span of ground. Dylan tossed down the shovel and grabbed the flashlight from Baylie. When he shined the light on the door, Baylie felt her hopes dash again. There was a very large padlock on it.

"Fuck," Dylan said, taking the words right out of her mouth. He looked over at Jonah. "I don't suppose you have the key."

Jonah only shook his head dejectedly.

"Can't anything be easy?" the sheriff asked irritably.

"Not that I've noticed," Dylan snapped. He picked up the shovel. "Stand back."

Everyone backed up and he lifted the shovel and then came down on the lock hard. It took him three tries but he finally snapped it open with a clank.

The moment of truth had arrived. Dylan looked down at her. "You should wait out here."

"No." She didn't hesitate. "She'll be afraid, Dylan. Terrified. If she's alive, I want her to see my face first. Not a stranger's."

He started to argue but Sheriff Tucker cut him off. "Just let her go first. At this point what difference does it make? There's no one dangerous down there."

"I wouldn't have thought there was anyone dangerous up here either," Dylan said, shooting a glare at Jonah, who had the decency to wince. All the same, he reached over and grasped the handle on the cellar door. Yanking, he pulled it up and open. Immediately a foul smell floated up and through the opening. It was nearly gagging.

One of the deputies swore and backed up.

"Holy hell," the sheriff agreed. He looked at Baylie. "Maybe you should let us go first after all."

She wanted to. God, she wanted to. But she knew she had to do this. Whatever was down there, she had to face it. "There is no plumbing down there. That's probably what you're smelling." At least she hoped it was.

Tucker swore but looked at Dylan, giving him the final say.

"Baylie, you've done what you set out to do. No one expects you to go down there and prove yourself. It won't bring her back if she's already dead. You don't need to see anything like that."

Instead of answering, she took a deep breath and shined her flashlight down into the darkness below. There was a rickety, wooden staircase that went down as far as the eye could see. There was no way of knowing what lay beyond those stairs. The unknown was terrifying. She took the first step very slowly. Then the second. As she moved down farther into the darkness, the foul smell of human waste grew more potent, along with something else — the smell of decay and death. She stopped, momentarily scared frozen.

"I'm right behind you, baby." Dylan's voice came from the step above her. She silently thanked God for him yet again, and then continued down the stairs. When she reached the bottom, her booted feet landed on a hard patch of what she knew was dirt. The smell of waste wasn't the only thing she remembered from this hole. The smell of mildew overcame her quickly and she instantly felt nauseous. She had to remind herself several times that she wasn't a scared, defenseless, six-year-old anymore. She was an adult and she was free to leave this hell any time she wanted to.

"Susan?" she forced her voice to call. The name came out in more of a croak and she cleared her throat and tried again. She received no answer in return.

Dylan shined his flashlight around the room from beside her. Dirty brown walls came into view. The room itself was probably around 24' X 24'. When she shined her light down one end of the room, she saw a bucket, most likely the source of the foul smell overcoming them. There were a couple of rolls of toilet paper next to it. A pile of dirty old towels lay in a mound, not far from the toilet paper.

As the sheriff stepped down onto the dirt, he shined his light directly across from them. Baylie saw the blanket covered lump lying crosswise on the floor and her heart stopped. The lump was completely still. She took several steps toward it, ignoring Dylan's warning voice from behind her. She knelt down, her heart breaking. She knew the lump was too still — not even the slight rise and fall of a sleeping person's chest. A tear ran down her face before she even touched the blanket.

Dylan crouched down beside her. "Don't."

"I have to," she said on a hiccup and reached for the blanket. She pulled it back quickly. The lifeless, partially decayed face that stared up at her was not Susan's. Baylie let out a shriek and dropped the blanket. She turned her face quickly around and buried it in Dylan's chest. "God, it's not her. Who is it?"

"I don't know," he said, standing up with her and pulling her back out of the way. Sheriff Tucker

405

took the lead and leaned over the dead woman's corpse, shining his light on her face. The deputy following behind him cursed.

"He said he had someone else in here with her," Dylan said quietly to Baylie. She heard the words but her mind didn't want to comprehend them.

"Who did he take, Dylan? Who?"

"It's definitely a woman," Tucker said. "I can tell by the hair and the shape of her body. Either that or it's a very small man." He grimaced, replacing the blanket. "She's been here awhile."

Suddenly Baylie felt very claustrophobic. The walls instantly seemed to close in on her. She clutched at Dylan's jacket, desperate for some light to break up the unbearable darkness threatening to surround her.

"I've got you. You're okay," he said softly against her hair. She breathed in his scent, determined to get the smell of death out of her nostrils.

"There's another one over here," a deputy called from across the room. Baylie lifted her head, her eyes following the sound of the deputy's voice.

"Holy shit, this one's alive!"

Relief slammed through Baylie so quickly she almost fell to her knees. She directed her light toward the sound of the deputy's voice and then made her way across the room quickly. He was kneeling down, not far from a rotten cot that sat lonely in one end of the room. Just in front of him lay Susan's unconscious, but still breathing body. Dropping to her knees next to him, Baylie yanked off her gloves and reached for Susan's hand. It was cold and clammy. As the light was shone on Susan's pale face, Baylie felt instant terror. Her friend almost looked like a stranger. Her eyes were closed. Her lips were raw and chapped. Her skin had taken a sickly look to it. If her chest hadn't been slowly moving up and down, Baylie would have thought she was dead too.

"Susan?" She called her friend's name but Susan didn't respond.

"We need an ambulance right away," Tucker said into his radio. He rattled off as much information as he could gather from a quick assessment of Susan's injuries, then turned to Dylan. "We're going to need you to get her out of here. This is a crime scene now."

"Baylie?" Dylan said, crouching down next to her. "Baby, we need to go."

"I can't leave her. She's scared and alone." Her voice came out softly.

"She's not alone anymore. We're going to get her out of here. This is a crime scene and the police need to do their jobs. You did what you came here to do."

A tear slid down her cheek and she reached up to wipe it away. Several more lanterns had been dragged down into the cellar and now the room was relatively well lit up with a somewhat eerie glow. As she stared around the surroundings, she felt the battered little girl buried inside her climb her way to the surface. Tears began to swarm in her eyes and dribble down her cheeks. This place was literal hell, and she had spent days and weeks here. This hell had been her home.

The shakes hit her before she could stop them. Every area of the room she looked at had a horrible memory attached to it. She remembered the pail in the corner and the stench attached to it. She remembered not being able to clean herself for days. She remembered wetting her pants every time that cellar door opened up and his heavy, booted feet clomped their way down those old, rickety stairs. And she remembered hiding in the darkness, praying he wouldn't find her and would just go away. But he always found her. No matter where she hid, he always found her.

"Come out, come out, wherever you are…" The words ate at her soul and she took a deep breath. He'd taken the game she'd played with her sister and turned it into a dirty, horrible nightmare. How had something so innocent turned into something so unbearably evil?

"Baylie?" Dylan's voice said from somewhere behind her.

"I used to hide under here," she said, her voice somber. "I'd hear him coming and I'd crawl under this cot and hide." Almost without conscious

408

thought, she bent her head and shined her flashlight underneath the rickety, old cot — and found herself staring straight into her own face.

Dylan nearly jumped thirty feet into the air when Baylie dropped her flashlight and began screaming at the top of her lungs. He had his gun out in seconds, as did every other deputy in the room, along with the sheriff. He grabbed her by the arm and yanked her back roughly, instantly putting himself between her and whatever danger was under that cot. Whatever it was that was under there moved quickly, climbing out from underneath the cot, and disappearing into a dark corner of the room. Dylan was so startled by the movement that he jumped again.

"What the fuck?" Sheriff Tucker said from behind him.

Dylan re-holstered his gun and shined the flashlight into the dark corner the figure had disappeared into. At that moment his heart cracked down the middle. Because even though Baylie was still screaming in front of him, someone who shared her face was cowering like a terrified animal in that corner across the room.

The sheriff let out an oath before Dylan had the chance.

Keeping the light on the terrified girl, Dylan crouched down to her level. She was staring up at him, her huge, round eyes full of fear and confusion. Barefoot and wearing a tattered white dress that was several sizes too big, she looked small and frail. He could tell her skin had a horrible gray pallor to it. She was definitely not well. But she was clearly Baylie's sister. And she was alive. She looked from Dylan, to Baylie's screaming form, and then back again.

"Baylie, stop it," he said quietly, reaching for her and dragging her toward him. "Stop it!" He shook her gently and she seemed to snap out of the trance she was in. She suddenly stopped wailing. When she looked up at him, her eyes were still tightly closed.

"Open your eyes and look at me."

She didn't obey right away. Instead, she reached up and grabbed two huge handfuls of his jacket. "I need to get out of here. *Now. Now. Now.*"

The hysteria in her voice made him wince. "Okay. We'll get you out of here. But you need to see something first."

"No. Please, no." She shook her head, her eyes still shut. "I can't breathe in here. I have to get out." She tried to stand up but he stopped her. He cupped her face with his hands and leaned in close.

"Open your eyes, Baylie. She's real."

410

TWENTY-EIGHT

Terror gripped every part of Baylie's body as she slowly turned her head and followed the beam of Dylan's flashlight. When at last she opened up her eyes, she found herself looking into her own face again. The breath whooshed from her lungs and had Dylan not reached forward and steadied her, she probably would have fallen.

The room suddenly grew deathly quiet. The girl in the corner reminded Baylie of an animal caught in a trap. Her eyes were wide with fear as they stared into the bright light pointed at her face.

Baylie's breath hitched as she looked at the woman. Her skin was gray and pasty; her lips almost tinted blue, obviously from lack of sunlight. She was so thin that her bones seemed to poke out of her too large dress. Her legs were tucked up in front of her chest in the fetal position and her eyes were wide with terror. Her blue eyes. *Blue eyes that were the same color as Baylie's own.*

411

Baylie took a cautious step forward and the woman made an abrupt move to crawl away. That was when Baylie saw them. Burns, puckered and prominent, all the way up one side of her left leg. A sob involuntarily left her throat. She had no doubt now that she was indeed looking into Nissa's face. Her sister was alive.

"Take it easy," Dylan warned softly, his voice in her ear.

She stopped moving and found herself crouching down to Nissa's eye level. Her sister stared at her as though she were a stranger.

"She doesn't know you, Baylie," Dylan said, as he crouched down next to her. "I seriously doubt if she knows her own face. I don't think she's seen a mirror in a while. Tell her who you are."

At first, the idea seemed ludicrous. Pale and gray or not, this woman's face was identical to Baylie's in every way. It was almost alarming. But unless she'd seen her own face recently, Nissa wouldn't know that. Baylie realized quickly that Dylan was probably right. There were no mirrors down in this hell.

She crawled slowly closer to her sister, trying to be careful not to scare her. When Nissa flinched again, Baylie stopped. She sat on her knees, only a couple of feet away and stared at her twin. The emotions going through her were overwhelming and she ignored the tears she knew were running down her cheeks.

412

"Nissa?" She said the word quietly, her voice more of a croak.

The woman's eyes narrowed a little, but she remained frozen otherwise. Baylie repeated her name again, and leaned a little closer still.

Nissa backed herself up as far into the corner as she could go. God, didn't she even remember her own name?

Baylie was suddenly reminded of the fact that she hadn't remembered her real name either. Not until the day before. Frustrated, she dropped her hand and narrowed her eyes in sadness.

"Tell her who you are," Dylan repeated, almost in a whisper.

"It's me," she tried a moment later. "It's Nikki."

This time she got a small reaction. Nissa's head slowly tilted to the side as she observed Baylie carefully.

"Do you remember me? I'm your sister. We're twins."

Nissa's head tipped again. She surprised Baylie by dropping her arms from around her knees. She slowly reached a hand forward and Baylie felt her cold, bony fingers make contact with the skin of her face. The contact was light, almost feathery. Abruptly the fingers dropped away.

At the loss of contact, Baylie blinked. Then she lifted one of her own hands out, as if in offering. It took a minute, but eventually Nissa's hand raised

413

again and met hers. Their fingers entwined. Nissa climbed up on her knees. She opened her mouth but no words came out. She licked at her lips several times and then said quietly, "I tried to help her. I gave her water. I didn't want her to die."

The words were a mere whisper, but Baylie heard them. Her heart squeezed painfully.

"I know you helped her. She's still alive, Nissa. You saved her." She forced a sad smile, trying to hold her tears back. "I've missed you."

Nissa reached down into the pocket of her tattered dress. She lifted her hand up, her fingers clenched around something tightly. When those fingers opened up, a small, gold, heart shaped locket was visible in her palm. Baylie recognized it right away. It was identical to the one that Mabel Lomax had returned to her days earlier. She remembered now, that she and her sister had both had the necklaces. They'd been a Christmas gift one year from their parents. They'd put each other's pictures in them. Nissa had kept hers close to her all this time.

Baylie felt a tear dribble down her cheek. She reached forward and for the first time in nearly twenty years, she pulled her sister into her arms and held her as tightly as she could.

Dylan propped his arm up on the side of the chair he sat in. The smell of hospitals always got to him and he grimaced, letting out a sigh. Then he let his arm drop again, and rested it over Baylie's sleeping form. She had her head in his lap, her small arms wrapped around his leg. Clearly, she was worried about him disappearing on her, which he'd already guaranteed her there wasn't a chance in hell of happening.

They had been at the hospital for several hours now. Both Nissa and Susan had been checked in. Both suffered from severe dehydration, among other things. Susan had several physical injuries, including a broken arm and collarbone. She had regained consciousness earlier and Baylie had spoken with her briefly. Dylan knew Baylie had needed to hear her friend's voice before she could rest herself.

As for Nissa, her injuries weren't physical, for the most part, but far more serious, as one could imagine. She hadn't spoken again since she'd talked to Baylie down in the cellar. When the EMTs had attempted to touch her, she had come unglued at the seams and it had taken Baylie to finally get her calmed down enough to get her into the ambulance. Eventually she'd been sedated, just so the doctors could give her an exam. She was going to need some serious psychiatric treatment. But she was alive. And she knew who she was, which was amazing all in itself. Dylan had a feeling that off and on, for most of her life, she had been shoved down inside that cellar. It was going to take a lot to bring her out of that hell.

As for Baylie, she had refused to leave the hospital, but she'd finally crashed in his lap. Adrenaline had finally run out. His was ebbing too. But he would stay awake for now. If she needed him, he'd be there.

He looked up as Detective Ryan Wilshire pushed through the double doors and entered the waiting room, his hands in his pockets as he glanced around the area. When he saw Dylan and Baylie, he walked over and gazed down at her sympathetically. "How's she doing?"

"She'll be okay. Adrenaline wore off. She needs some sleep."

Wilshire nodded, his face still filled with bewilder. "I gotta tell you, I'm having a hard time digesting all this."

"You and me both," Dylan said, grazing his hand over Baylie's hair as she moaned in her sleep. She instantly quieted.

"How are the others?"

"Dehydrated. Susan has some broken bones. He roughed her up good. She'll be a mess for a while but she'll recover."

"And Anissa?"

Thinking of Nissa, Dylan felt his eyes water. "That's a little more complicated."

416

Wilshire nodded his understanding. "I was afraid of that. She was really down there in that cellar for all that time?"

"We probably won't know that for a while. I'm guessing Melvin had her other places too. But from the color of her skin and the way she looks at people, it's pretty likely that she hasn't had much human contact besides him in years."

Wilshire's fists clenched and he swore. "Like I said before, I wish the guy wasn't dead already. I'd like to kill him myself."

"You and me both."

Wilshire took a seat next to Dylan and ran his hands over his face. Then he sighed. "Her family flew in earlier. They're on their way here. Steven wanted to wait for the parents. You might want to warn her so she doesn't freak out."

Dylan looked down at Baylie. Restless as her sleep was, he was hesitant to wake her just yet. "Give her a few minutes and I'll wake her up."

"I got a call from Missoula. They found some pretty interesting crap in the bastard's house, including a few pages that seemed to come from her missing file."

That didn't surprise Dylan in the least. He'd known her file was incomplete. "That's no surprise."

"She was with a family before the Lomaxes, Dylan. A man and a woman. They were young, early twenties. Just married. They were killed in a car accident in late 1993. She spent about a year with them and from the report the social worker made, they were considering adopting her."

Dylan didn't know that it mattered much anymore and he shrugged his shoulders.

"Their name was Sutter."

That, Dylan hadn't expected. So that was where she'd gotten her last name. He looked at the ceiling for a moment, exhaling a deep breath. He hated that Baylie had been put through so much misery in her life. Over the years, she'd lost person after person — pretty much anyone who gave a child any kind of sense of security. He couldn't help wondering if her life would have been different, had the Sutters not died in that car accident. Chances were, it wouldn't have. David Melvin never would have given up on his obsession.

"I know it sucks. It will be hard to tell which twin was with the Sutters at that time. But that explains where her name came from," Wilshire said, sitting back in the chair. He was quiet a moment. "This is one of those stories that's only in the movies — too horrible to think about being real."

Wilshire was right. The story of Nikki and Anissa Tate was almost too horrific to be believed. It was blatant proof that the world was indeed full of monsters. Monsters that even hard working cops like Dylan and Ryan couldn't slay. The fact that

Nikki and Nissa Tate had both survived such brutality was nothing short of a miracle.

Thinking of Baylie as Nikki was going to take some doing, he decided, tossing the name around inside his head. She had still been referring to herself as *Baylie* so until she told him to do otherwise, that's what he would do too.

"So what now?" Wilshire asked. "You going back to Seattle?"

He hadn't really thought that far. Seattle was his home. He'd made a life for himself there and so had Baylie. He had a feeling she would have her job back at the high school if she wanted it. The question was, did she? She now had her sister to consider, and the rest of her family. He knew she had missed out on too much time with them already.

"In a day or two," he eventually answered. "I'm not sure about her. She'll want to be with her family."

Wilshire considered that. "I guess so. I know she'll have their support. She won't be alone."

Dylan knew Wilshire was letting him know she'd be okay if he had to leave. But the thing was, he didn't want to leave her. He knew she had some serious demons to deal with, on top of the life changes that being with her family again would entail. But the idea of her not being part of his life was more disconcerting than he wanted to admit.

419

Not only that, he had told her he loved her and he'd meant it. For the first time in his life, he was head over heels in love with someone.

"I was married once. Love sucks," Wilshire agreed, as though reading Dylan's mind. "Of course my wife turned out to be a cheating, lying bitch, whose problems she brought on herself. A little different situation."

Dylan had to smile at that. He liked Wilshire. Under different circumstances, he was the type of guy Dylan probably would have been buddies with.

"So I heard she doesn't want to press charges against Jonah Kramer." Wilshire shook his head. "The kid cold cocked you, didn't he?"

Thinking of Jonah Kramer, Dylan scowled. "She thinks he needs help."

"He probably does. That's pretty upstanding of her. How'd you keep from beating the little shit to a pulp?"

After a moment of thought, Dylan snorted. "I got a good foot to his back. Little fucker nearly gave me a concussion."

Wilshire grinned halfway. "Good for you. For what it's worth, he's giving the police a lot of information. Your friend Marcus Hennings should be released soon. Kramer told the police that Melvin confessed to him about killing Marcus's wife and her lover. Apparently the murder weapon was somewhere in the Missoula house. The police have it."

This was good news. Dylan knew Baylie would be happy to hear about Marcus. But there was more bad news to come. "The woman in the cellar — the dead one. You heard anything on her?"

"It'll be awhile. But I have a hunch. Melvin had a cleaning lady in Missoula. She turned up missing about seven months ago. Cute, little Hispanic girl named Carmella Roberto. Her description fits what's left of the body you found in that cellar."

"Fuck," was all Dylan said.

"Yeah, this guy was the worst kind of sicko. And the terrible thing about it is that he hid behind his badge for all these years. People trusted him. *Kids* trusted him. According to the Missoula PD, he trolled areas. That's how he came upon Nikki and Nissa. He just happened to pull off the freeway on that 4th of July. He saw the Devil's Lake celebration and the rest is history. God only knows how many times he did the same thing elsewhere."

Dylan felt his stomach turn. They would probably never know the answer to that question. He turned and met Wilshire's gaze. "I should thank you. It's a damn good thing you remembered staying up at those cabins with your grandparents. If I hadn't had back up, things could have turned out a lot differently. I think the kid would have come to his senses before he actually killed her, but you never know."

421

"True enough. Sometimes things piece themselves together. I'm just glad it all worked out."

"Me too."

Seeing the double doors open up, Dylan straightened. A man walked into the waiting room, his eyes scanning the area intently. Dylan knew immediately that he was Baylie's brother.

Tall, with blond hair and dark eyes, he looked to be around the same age as Dylan's thirty-four years. When his gaze landed on them, it lowered immediately to Baylie's sleeping form. He ran a hand over his mouth, obviously at a loss.

"You made it," Wilshire said, standing up and walking over to clap his friend on the shoulder. Dylan would have stood too but he couldn't with Baylie's head in his lap. Instead, he sized the guy up, just the way the guy was sizing him up.

"Steven Tate, Dylan Stone." Wilshire said, making the introductions.

Steve Tate stepped forward after an awkward moment of silence. He held his hand out to Dylan, who reached up and gripped it in a firm shake. Steve turned to Wilshire. "This is her?"

"It is," Wilshire said, stepping back.

Steve Tate crouched down and looked at Baylie, his eyes brimming with moisture. Then he reached out a hand and let his fingers tug on one of her blonde curls.

422

Dylan felt her stir and lifted his arm so she could move easily. Her eyes slowly opened and she looked at her brother, momentarily disoriented.

"Hey, squirt. Long time, no see." Tears ran down the man's face, even though Dylan could tell that he was trying to blink them away.

Just like that, Baylie climbed from Dylan's lap and into her brother's arms. Dylan felt himself tearing up again. He'd been doing that a lot over the past few hours. He quickly realized this was only the beginning. The double doors opened again and this time a middle-aged couple stepped into the waiting room.

Baylie saw the couple step through the waiting room doors. The man was tall and trim, with graying dark hair and tanned skin. She was an attractive blonde, with curls just like Baylie's. When the woman's blue eyes locked with Baylie's, she let out a painful gasp.

"Mom..." Steve began, but his voice trailed off as he watched his sister and mother stare at each other for the first time in twenty years.

"Mama?" Baylie said, her voice cracking with emotion.

The woman seemed to crumble before her eyes. Baylie crossed the room and stepped into her open embrace. Immediately she was enveloped in jasmine — that so familiar scent that was her mother's. Security wrapped itself around her and she let herself be swept away by it until she heard a choked back sob from the man standing next to her mother. Slowly she pulled back and looked up into her father's face. He was staring at her as though she were a ghost.

"Daddy." She said the word quietly, taken aback by the emotion she saw in his face. Her father had never been one for crying.

He reached for her, quickly enfolding her against his strong chest. At that moment, she let go of her anguish and let herself cry.

Dylan watched the exchange, feeling a little like an intruder.

"You're the cop, right?" Steven Tate stepped up to Dylan, his eyes still moist with emotion. "The one that brought my sister home."

"She brought herself home. I just helped her find the way."

Steve reached forward and clapped Dylan on the shoulder. "Thank you. You have no idea what you've done for my family."

Dylan wanted to say he'd only been doing his job, but he knew that wouldn't be true. Instead, he nodded his acceptance of the gratitude.

Once Baylie and her parents had been reunited, they — along with their son — rushed off to check in on their other daughter's condition. Dylan watched as Baylie stared after them, clearly distraught at the idea of them leaving her sight for even a moment.

He shoved his hands into the pockets of his jeans and walked over to stand in front of her. When she looked up at him she was smiling sadly. He smiled back, then reached down and tweaked her nose affectionately. "Don't worry, baby. They'll be back. I have a feeling you're going to be seeing a lot of them from now on."

She walked closer, burying her head against his chest. He shut his eyes, feeling his heart crack down the middle again. Involuntarily, his arms wrapped around her and he rested his chin on top of her head.

"I love you too, Dylan."

The words were soft but he heard them. He backed up and looked down into her face. They just stared at each other for several seconds. Just like that, he knew he was done for. At that moment he would have done anything she asked, including quit his job and move to Timbuktu.

"Did you change your mind?" she asked, her voice almost a whisper.

He snorted at that. "No, baby, I didn't change my mind. I love you. Probably more now than I did the last time I said the words."

She smiled. "So what does this mean? I've never said I love you to a man before."

"I've never said the words to a woman either," he mused, leaning over and resting his forehead against hers. "I suppose I should probably court you for a while, huh? I mean do the whole flower and candy and dinner thing?"

"A movie might be nice, Detective," she said, rubbing her nose against his.

"A movie, huh? I don't suppose you like action flicks."

She shook her head. "I'm a *romcom* kind of girl."

He grimaced, but kept the smile on his face. "I was afraid you were going to say that."

EPILOGUE

One year later...

The wedding reception was in full swing. As Baylie looked up into the face of her new husband, she couldn't stop smiling. She wrapped her arms around his neck and gave him a firm kiss on the lips.

"I love you too, baby," he said, without hesitation. He pulled her closer into the cradle of his thighs as they danced to a nice, slow song.

True to his word, Dylan had spent the last year *courting* her, as he called it. Having him by her side had literally kept her sane. Not only had he helped her through her own nightmares, but he'd helped her repair her relationship with her sister.

Nissa had spent the first three months after getting out of the hospital in an inpatient mental care unit in Seattle. She had undergone extensive psychological counseling to try and help her deal with her own demons. She had made a lot of progress. She was now living with Daniel and Monica Tate, in a nice house on Queen Ann Hill, not far from where Dylan's house was.

Throughout her therapy, a lot had come to light. Over the past twenty years, Nissa's life had been similar to Baylie's. The first few years after the kidnapping, she'd been in and out of foster homes, just as her sister had. Melvin had switched the girls in and out of homes for years, without so much as attracting an ounce of attention from authorities. It was unreal. But the night of the fire at the Eisenberg's had been the turning point. He had gone to the house to get Nissa back and instead, nearly killed her by trapping her in the flames. The vision Baylie had seen in her nightmares had definitely been more like a memory. That night in the fire had been the first time the twins had seen each other in nearly three years. It would be the last time they saw each other for fifteen more.

David Melvin had started the fire. Baylie had been with him at the time — had seen him do it. According to Nissa's accounts, he'd shown up and pulled her from the flames just before the entire house was engulfed. He'd taken her home with him. Over the years she'd gone from the cabin to the cellar and back again. Her existence had been literal hell, as Baylie had imagined. Now, after months of working through things, she seemed to accept her past and was trying to move on.

428

She and Baylie spent time together constantly. They talked and laughed now. Nissa had gotten used to Dylan. At first he'd barely been able to coax a smile out of her. But the other day, she'd actually let him give her a piggyback ride. For Nissa, that was a huge step.

Steven Tate was still living down in Oregon with his wife and two children. Baylie had two nephews, Anthony and Cameron. They were adorable six and eight-year-olds with a penchant for mischief, which Baylie and Dylan had learned the first time they'd volunteered to babysit.

Having family had been a major change for Baylie to adapt to. Dylan was used to having people around him. He'd been that way his entire life. Baylie hadn't. So having his mother stop by, or her father, had been something to get used to at first. Now she found that she loved having people around. In fact, aside from the quiet nights at home alone with Dylan, she loved entertaining her family. And she actually had real friends.

Susan had made a full recovery. The first few weeks after her rescue had been hard on her, but surprisingly, Rob Barnes had stepped up to the plate and become a constant in her life. They had been dating exclusively for almost eight months. Baylie was happy for her friends. Now that they had gotten their priorities in order, they seemed to be making things work.

Both Susan and Baylie had quit their jobs at the high school. Susan wasn't sure when she would be ready to go back to work and Baylie was more concerned with helping her sister and starting her new life with Dylan. At some point, she knew she would go back to teaching. But maybe kindergarten this time. The *Jeepers McClains* of the world had soured her on high school kids for the time being.

Thinking of Jeepers made her think of Jonah Kramer. He was thankfully in college now, across the country. He'd managed to graduate with honors, in spite of the events that had taken place up at that cabin one year ago. He'd gone through counseling of his own and was now majoring in Political Science. Somehow she could see him being a politician.

"Can I cut in for just one minute?"

Baylie looked up to see Marcus Hennings — or rather Marc, as he was commonly known now — standing before her in a suit and tie. He'd cleaned up nicely since his days in Deer Lodge. His sandy hair was neatly trimmed and his face was clean-shaven. His blue eyes held a more carefree look now and Baylie found herself thinking he was quite handsome.

Dylan glared at him good-naturedly, but stepped back. "You've got five minutes. That's it."

Marc grinned, then looked down at Baylie as he pulled her into his arms. "This has been a great

430

day. Nice wedding. You remind me of a fairy princess."

The endearment made her smile. It was still hard for her to look into that face and not see the little boy she'd spent so many days with, so long ago. Even though he was a man now, he would always be that little boy to her.

Over the past several months, he'd managed to clean up his act. He had a job now, working with computers—something he'd studied a lot about in prison. He had custody of little Nicky. He and his son had moved to California, desperate for a fresh start. They'd successfully made one. Baylie couldn't be happier for her friend.

"I still can't believe there are two of you."

Baylie followed Marc's gaze over her shoulder. He was staring at Nissa, who was sitting with her parents, Steve and his family and Ryan Wilshire, at a table just off the dance floor. "Sometimes I still find it hard to believe too."

Marc looked down at her. "You know you helped me through those dark days just as much as I helped you. I want you to know that. I probably would have gone crazy if you hadn't been there, Nikki."

Baylie felt her chest tighten. She still wasn't used to people calling her Nikki, least of all Marcus. She was still Baylie to most everyone but her family. "I know. You named your little boy after me." She grinned at him and he grinned back.

"I always did like the name Nicholas. By the way, you've got yourself a great guy. He put in a good word for me at the place I'm working now. It pays to have a cop as one of your references— especially a cop that's a hero."

Her smile grew bigger. If there was one thing she was proud of, it was Dylan. She loved his family too. They had opened their arms to her, his twin sister, Danica, in particular. They were all very close now. "I picked a good guy," she agreed. "Maybe you should find yourself a good woman."

Marc shook his head, though his smile stayed in place. "Nope. Not for a while. I'm going to get my shit together and take care of my boy. If I meet someone along the way, that's cool, but I sure as heck don't plan on looking for it."

"That's when it usually happens," Baylie told him. "Just look at me. I'm living proof."

He shook his head as the song ended. "Yeah, I guess you are."

"You about done with my wife?" Dylan asked, as though on cue.

Marc stepped back, offering Dylan his hand. "Take good care of her. She deserves the best."

Dylan shook Marc's hand firmly. "I plan to. Don't be a stranger."

When Marc was gone, Baylie slid easily back into her husband's arms. "Do you think he'll be okay?"

Dylan looked over her head at Marc's retreating figure. "Yeah, baby, I do. He's a tough guy. He's been through a lot but he's got his priorities straight. Guys like him always land on their feet. It just takes them awhile sometimes."

She thought that over and decided he was right. Marc was a tough guy. He and Nicky would be okay now. They would always have her. No matter what, she would never forget Marcus Hennings or his role in her life again.

"Well would you look at that?"

Baylie turned her head and followed Dylan's gaze to where Ryan Wilshire had just stepped onto the dance floor. The surprising thing was that Nissa had followed him. Although she had him at an arm's length, she had her hands on his shoulders and they were dancing. Baylie found herself smiling halfway. "You say that with a strange tone, Detective Stone."

"Six months ago she wouldn't even let me help her out of the car. Now she's dancing with *Casanova* over there."

"Casanova?" Baylie couldn't hide her worry. "You don't think he's—"

"Into her?" Dylan interrupted, grinning. "Yeah, maybe. But he's a good guy so I wouldn't worry too much."

Baylie continued to frown as she watched her sister dance with the detective. "He lives in Lincoln City. She's not moving to Lincoln City."

"They're dancing at a wedding, Baylie. I don't think you need to get worried about anything like that just yet. I'm just happy to see her learning to trust people again. She deserves the best of everything."

She had to smile at that. He was right—Nissa did deserve the best of everything.

"Just like you," he added, pulling her tightly against him.

"I already have the best of everything," she said honestly, looking him in the eye. "But I have to tell you, my mother asked me just after the wedding when she can expect some grandkids."

Dylan's face paled significantly and he looked over at the table Steven sat at with his wife and children. The kids were running in circles around their parents, howling at the top of their lungs. Anthony chose that moment to trip over his mother's chair and take a flying leap straight into a passing waiter, whose tray of champagne came crashing down to the floor. Cameron's response was to laugh and then kick his brother in the backside. A moment later, both boys were hauled out of the room by their very angry father.

Dylan looked back down at Baylie. "I'm in no rush, are you?"

She had to admit that her nephews had shown her a new side of children. They were adorable, but precocious. "No. Not as long as we can still practice making them."

"I'm with you on that one," he said, grinning against her ear as he pulled her closer. "And just so you keep it in mind, the fact that both you and I have a twin doubles our odds on having a set of them ourselves."

She thought that over and decided she wouldn't mind having a little tow-headed set of twins to chase around.

"I don't mean to kill the honeymoon before it starts, but before you get that look on your face you may want to have a chat with my mother. On the off chance that we have boys, you should know that I was hell on wheels."

"We might have two little girls, like me and Nissa."

"Yeah, and I'll have to get a really large bat to beat the *Jeepers McClains* of the world off our doorstep." He shook his head. "Like I said, I'm in no rush." He dipped her backward and leaned over to kiss her. She wasn't either, she realized as she kissed him back. After all, they had all the time in the world.

KEEP READING FOR A SNEAK PEAK AT BOOK 2
IN THE
HIDE AND SEEK MYSTERY SERIES

UNBROKEN

AVAILABLE NOW

ABOUT THE AUTHOR

Jennifer Hayden lives in the Pacific Northwest with her husband and children. She is the author of several romantic suspense novels, including:

HIDE AND SEEK
(Book 1 Hide and Seek Mystery Series)
UNBROKEN
(Book 2 Hide and Seek Mystery Series)
COLLISION
(Book 3 Hide and Seek Mystery Series)
SWEET REVENGE
SAY MERCY
SOUNDS OF NIGHT
ROOT OF ALL EVIL
AFTER THE RAIN
(Book 1 – The Callahan Series)
IN THE EYE OF THE STORM
(Book 2 – The Callahan Series)
AFTERSHOCK
(Book 3 – The Callahan Series)
LESS THAN PERFECT
(Book 4 - The Callahan Series)
HOPE FOR CHRISTMAS
(Book 1 in Noel, Montana Series)
HEAD OVER HEELS FOR CHRISTMAS
(Book 2 in Noel, Montana Series)
SKELETONS IN THE MIST
BENEATH BURIED SECRETS
HIDDEN MEMORIES
SHAMELESS
ON THIN ICE
WWW.JENNIFERHAYDENBOOKS.COM

UNBROKEN
BOOK 2 HIDE AND SEEK MYSTERY SERIES
AVAILABLE NOW

PREFACE
Missoula, MT
Fifteen years earlier…

A noise interrupted her sleep. As she sat up groggily, she ignored the pain that gripped her insides and rolled over. It was dark in the room, much as it always was. There were no windows, no lights. It had been hours since he'd come back. Or had it been days? She wasn't sure. She only knew she was thirsty and she was scared. She reached up and wiped at the tears on her face. They were dry by now and itchy. Without water, she couldn't wash them off. She had no towels and no food either, not that she was hungry.

Why wasn't he coming back? Where was he? He'd promised he wouldn't leave her alone for long. He'd promised he would take care of her.

Feeling the beginnings of panic eat at her soul, she forced herself to take a deep breath. God, it was so dark. The quiet that surrounded her was nearly her undoing and she breathed in again.

That's when she heard it. A mewling sound. It was faint and sounded as though it were coming from across the room. She turned her head toward the sound. Her temples began to throb harder. The mewling grew louder and her panic worsened. Oh God, it was there and it was still alive...

ONE

Seattle, Washington
Present Day

Nissa Tate took a step back and studied the painting in front of her critically. She held the brush between her fingers tightly and bit her bottom lip. Something was off. She wasn't sure what she didn't like about the scene before her but there was definitely something missing. After a moment more of thought, she set her brush down and backed away from the canvas. Too much staring and studying wouldn't make a difference. Whatever was missing would come to her with time.

Six months ago, when Dr. Walsh had suggested she start painting as part of her therapy, she'd warmed to the idea immediately. She'd always loved art. She loved drawing, painting, sketching. Anything that had to do with taking something from deep inside her mind, and bringing it to life.

Of course thus far, all of her paintings had been rather cryptic. She knew her sister, Nikki, or Baylie as she was known to everyone but Nissa, didn't understand the paintings for the most part. Neither did Nikki's husband of a year, Dylan Stone. They were forced to look at the paintings day in and day out. After all, Nissa was living in their house. She had been for the better part of six months. Dylan had set her up a studio in the garage, where she spent hour after hour painting. While both Dylan and Nikki worked, Nissa painted. She'd started out creating stick figures, most of whom she couldn't even identify herself. Eventually she'd started painting actual people, places. The scenes were dark, which Dr. Walsh had told her over and over, was normal. This was the point of the painting. To get those dark thoughts and memories out.

As Nissa looked from painting to painting, her heart squeezed. The better part of her childhood was on display before her. The images were disturbing, even to her. But somehow getting them out of her head and onto the canvases in front of her did help. It was a cleansing so to speak. She only wished she could talk to someone about them. Someone who could understand the darkness that was still inside her.

Though Nikki and Nissa had been abducted as children together and both put through the same terror very early in their lives, Nikki had managed to escape. She'd lived a good portion of her life

440

free. She'd gone to school, college and then become a teacher. Although she too had been kept from her family until two years earlier, she had lived in foster homes with other families who were loving and caring for the most part. Nissa hadn't been so lucky. She'd spent the better part of twenty years locked between a dirty, dark cellar and a lonely old cabin by a rather deserted lake. Her contact with other human beings had been limited to no one but David Melvin—a sociopathic pedophile, and a handful of his other victims, some not lucky enough to have survived.

For Nissa, being pulled literally from the depths of hell two years earlier by her sister and a slew of police detectives had been more surreal to her than the fact that she'd spent most of her life in captivity. Adjusting to the outside world—to her family, and to people in general—was something she was working through every day. She'd gotten better and better at it. She no longer cringed at being alone, at silence. In fact, out here in the studio she craved the silence. It brought the memories back. It helped her to make the images in her head real. But she knew that no one would ever understand the torment that still ate at her insides. Even Nikki, though her sister tried.

Over the past two years, Nissa had made amazing strides. Time and time again, Dr. Walsh reiterated the fact that Nissa was a survivor. She had triumphed in a situation where most people would have given up. Sometimes, Nissa believed her. And other times? Other times, when she woke up at night in a cold sweat, battling the demons that still haunted her dreams, she felt like that helpless, dirty little girl, who had spent twenty years trying to claw her way out of the hellhole she'd called home.

The night before had been one of those times. She'd ended up in her sister's bed, shaking and clinging to what little shred of sanity she could find. As always, Nikki had been there for her. She'd stroked her hair and talked to her in that soft voice that always reminded Nissa she wasn't alone anymore. Somehow, Nikki made the demons go away.

That morning when Nissa had padded into the kitchen after Nikki had already gone to work, Dylan had been leaned against the counter sipping his morning cup of coffee. He'd smiled at her halfway over the rim of his cup, though his eyes had radiated an element of concern. He hadn't spoken. In a way, she appreciated that. Of course it was likely he knew she probably wouldn't answer him anyway. She'd been doing that a lot lately—hiding in her own solitude, not speaking. She knew it mystified her family. That was half the reason she'd moved to Nikki's and Dylan's. Her parents had begun to smother her with their need to make her "normal" again. Normal was something she knew

442

she would never be.

Turning back to her paintings, she thought of Dylan again. Dylan Stone had to be the most understanding husband on the face of the earth. Not only had he helped Nikki through her own nightmares, but he'd done his best to help Nissa too. He had opened his house up to her, and treated her with nothing but kindness. He'd helped her to curb her fear of men in general. There wasn't a mean bone in Dylan's body. At least not where his family was concerned. She'd seen him in action as a cop and he could be a force to be reckoned with when he had to be, but at home he was like a big teddy bear. She supposed the fact that he had a twin sister himself made it easier for him to understand Nissa and Nikki's bond. He somehow managed to never get between them, even when Nissa was cowering in the middle he and Nikki in their bed like a terrified child.

Again, embarrassment clawed through her. Last night hadn't been one of her finer moments. The nightmare she'd had had been terrifying and so real. There were times when she could actually smell the rot from that cellar. She could feel the dirty floor and swear the filth from it was climbing its way under her fingernails again, the way it had for so many years. The sounds from that dream were still in her head, even now, in broad daylight.

She sat down on a wooden stool and stared at

the floor momentarily. She had recently begun showing the paintings to Dr. Walsh. The one she'd just painted would bring more questions from both the doctor and her family. Questions she couldn't answer.

God, how she wished Ryan would come back.

The thought ate at her a moment and she frowned. She wasn't quite sure why she was thinking about Ryan Wilshire again. The man had walked out of her life six months ago, without a backward glance. To this day, she had no idea why. She supposed if she were being honest with herself, she had to admit that likely she was just too much for him to deal with.

Detective Ryan Wilshire had been a detective with the Lincoln City Police Department. He had been in on the investigation that had brought Nissa home after twenty years. He had seen her at her worst, the night she'd been brought kicking and screaming into the hospital in Missoula. And he'd kept coming back. Nearly every weekend, he'd slept in Nikki and Dylan's guest room. When they'd visited her during her stay for inpatient therapy, he'd visited with them. He'd been there the day they'd brought her home to her parents' house for the first time. Weekend after weekend, he'd shown up, slowly bringing her out of her shell. He'd listened to her talk and hadn't analyzed everything she'd said. He'd just let her vent. He had also taken her to her first movie, her first baseball game. Every Friday night, she'd waited in anticipation for him to arrive and take her on another adventure. For the first time, Nissa had felt secure in another person's presence. And then one Friday night, he hadn't shown. He hadn't shown up the next weekend either. Weeks turned into months. No phone calls. Nothing. He'd turned his back and disappeared.

The betrayal had stung. Nissa hadn't understood his sudden departure. She still didn't, to this day. She knew Dylan occasionally talked to Ryan by phone. At first she had questioned her brother-in-law about Ryan's reasons for no longer coming around. All Dylan had said was that Ryan had moved to Portland and gotten a new job with the Portland PD. He was busy. He had told Dylan to apologize for him for not making it up to see her in a while. He would be up sooner or later, once things weren't so hectic for him.

Nissa had quit asking about him after a few weeks. Gradually, the darkness seemed to surround her again. The nightmares took back over and her days were spent trying to bring them to life so she could face the demons that controlled them.

As much as she would have liked to talk to her sister about the dreams, she knew she couldn't. Nikki had started her life over. She had a husband, a career. A few weeks earlier, she and Dylan had announced that they were going to have a baby.

Nikki was pregnant. She was starting a family. Nissa was only going to be in the way.

With that thought eating at her, she breathed deeply. The scent of fresh air filled her lungs and she looked toward the open window. It was a sunny day in Seattle that day. June was looking to be good to a city where it seemed to rain so much of the year.

Nissa smiled halfway at the scene outside the window. Sunshine. Blue sky. The grass was green and the birds were singing. She could go outside and feel the warmth on her face if she wanted. She could breathe the fresh air.

A tightness enveloped her chest and she felt the slight stirrings of panic as her eyes landed on one of her paintings again. Darkness took a pull at her and suddenly the sunny scene outside her window evaporated.

Picking up her paint brush she stepped quickly toward the unfinished canvas. She dipped her brush into the red acrylic and rapidly began to paint.

Detective Ryan Wilshire shoved the last bite of his hotdog into his mouth and chewed quickly. He took a giant swig of Coke, before tossing what was left of the drink into a passing trash can.

He'd been living in Portland for five months now. The switch from Lincoln City had been an adjustment. Portland was a big city with a lot more law enforcement activity. Ryan had signed on with narcotics. For the better part of six months he'd worked undercover off and on. He and his partner Travis Lassiter had finished up a case that morning. Now, finally, they were looking at a few days off.

Travis Lassiter had been a big part of Ryan's decision to move to Portland. The pair had attended the police academy together years before, right out of the Air Force. Travis had gone on to Portland and joined the Portland PD and Ryan had gone back home to Lincoln City and gotten a job there. Six months earlier, Travis had called and offered Ryan the chance for a transfer.

Thinking back to that time, Ryan remembered the place he'd been at in his life. It was a place he'd struggled to leave behind since then. He'd jumped at the chance for a change and here he was.

Travis was not only his partner, but his best friend. They spent off time together, hunting, fishing, playing basketball. Travis's wife, Annie, was practically like a sister to Ryan. Since his own parents had moved out of town years before, Ryan considered Travis's family his family.

"A few days off. What will we do?" Travis asked, grinning widely as he wiped his mouth on a napkin, then tossed it into the trash.

"Go home to your wife before she starts cheating on you with the plumber or the next randy thing that comes by," Ryan joked, grimacing as his phone vibrated.

"If they're calling us back in—" Travis began, but Ryan stopped him as he read the caller ID.

"It's not the station." He noted Dylan Stone's name and number on the caller ID and felt that all familiar guilt creep up on him. "Shit."

"Trouble?" Travis asked curiously.

"I should take this," Ryan finally decided. He'd ignored the last few calls Dylan had placed to him—and the messages he'd left. He knew the calls would only be about one thing. Or rather, one person.

"I'll just catch you later," Travis said as his own phone vibrated.

Once his partner had walked off, Ryan lifted the phone to his ear.

"Dylan. What's up?"

"What the fuck is your problem?" Dylan's angry voice said. "I thought maybe you were dead, but clearly you're not. You're just being a dick."

Ryan wasn't surprised by Dylan's words. It had been more than a while since they'd last talked. "Are you finished?"

"That depends. Are you finished being a dick?"

"I've been busy," Ryan said lamely, running a hand through his overly long hair. He made a mental note to get a haircut soon—and a shave. His face was getting itchy.

"Is that right? Too busy to keep in touch with

your friends?"

"I've been undercover, not able to use my phone." It wasn't a total lie. But Dylan was a cop too. He knew the drill. Snowing him wouldn't be easy.

"Whatever, man. I never thought I'd have to call bullshit on you. Not where Nissa is concerned."

At the mention of her name, Ryan winced. There it was. His one weakness. The weakness that had driven him nearly mad six months earlier. The weakness that had caused him to grapple for the change that would right the wrongs in his life. *Nissa Tate.*

He sighed, forcing the image of her big blue eyes out of his head. He couldn't go back there. Not again. It had taken him months to get her out of his head. Months to move past the fact that he'd hurt her — that she likely hated him now. Or worse, the fact that maybe she didn't.

"Just what the hell is your problem?" Dylan asked again. "It's been six months, do you realize that?"

He did. The months hadn't gone by easily. "No. I didn't." Admitting the truth wouldn't help anything.

He heard Dylan sigh. "Tell me this, what made you run? Was it all too much? Is that it? Because she's been left behind too many times, dude. You know that as well as I do."

Ryan didn't want to hear this. He didn't want to hear this because Nissa became real to him again. She hadn't been real to him for the past several months. Shutting his eyes briefly, he thought his next words over carefully. "I can't do this right now, Dylan," he finally muttered.

Dylan was quiet for a moment. "She's in trouble, Ryan. You should know that."

The words echoed in Ryan's head and he stiffened. "What do you mean, she's in trouble?"

ALSO AVAILABLE – BOOK 3
HIDE AND SEEK MYSTERY SERIES

COLLISION

Made in the USA
Middletown, DE
12 November 2018